Flyleaf

Modern Shop Practice

THE PATTERN MAKER

Richard Snodgrass

A Novel

Calling Crow Press

Pittsburgh

Also by Richard Snodgrass

Fiction

There's Something in the Back Yard

The Books of Furnass

All That Will Remain

Across the River

Holding On

Book of Days

The Pattern Maker

Furrow and Slice

The Building

Some Rise

All Fall Down

Redding Up

Books of Photographs and Text

An Uncommon Field: The Flight 93
Temporary Memorial

Kitchen Things: An Album of Vintage Utensils
and Farm-Kitchen Recipes

Memoir

The House with Round Windows

Published by Calling Crow Press
Pittsburgh, Pennsylvania

Book design by Book Design Templates, LLC
Cover design by Jack Ritchie

Printed in the United States of America
ISBN 978-0-9997700-1-6
Library of Congress catalog control number: 2019904489

For Barbara Clark
and, of course, as with all things,
for Marty

In this world, there is one terrible thing,

and that is that everyone has his reasons.

—Jean Renoir

Prelude

She was tied to a tree. A small slender tree standing by itself, away from the grove of trees off to one side of the grassy slope, near some playground equipment, away from the headlights of cars passing along the drive, the cars turning in to park along the overlook. She was sitting slumped at the base of the tree, her arms tied around the trunk behind her, her legs splayed awkwardly in front of her. Her skirt had been pulled up to expose her crotch, her torn panties thrown into the grass and dead leaves nearby. There was nothing left of her face, it had been beaten to a semi-congealed mass; strands of her long red hair were stuck, embedded in the clotted blood and ooze.

The intensity of the portable work lights made the scene seem hyper-realistic, almost too real, or not real at all. As the police photographer finished taking his pictures, Lieutenant Nathan White looked away, looked up into the trees overhead, the undersides of the lower branches pale and overexposed in the glow of the lights, the darker branches beyond, stirring in the late spring breeze. It was the only tree that was different among the nearby grove—an oak? Elm? Thinking, I never did know my trees. I wonder if it's important, the report needs to be accurate. Then he shook his head at himself. No, it wasn't important. The kind of tree was the least important thing here.

When the photographer was done, White's partner, Sergeant MacCarron, snapped on a pair of latex gloves and bent over, fighting the bulge of his stomach—"Oof," he said to Stan, the coroner's assistant, who was starting to examine the body, "Getting too old for this kind of thing"—to pick up the purse that lay on the ground beside her. It was a brown leather purse, a cheap version of a classic Coach design, the kind of purse, White thought, that a young woman would buy if she was trying to look classy and didn't have much money to spend. It went along with the clothes she was wearing, the imitation silk blouse with its large ribbon collar tied in a bow, the material crumpled and worn, the blue cotton skirt not quite tailored enough. So much for trying to look classy. Look where it got her. Nothing classy about her now. Poor girl. MacCarron sorted through the contents of the purse, held up a set of keys on a ring for White to see, then stuck them in his sport-coat pocket. After removing the wallet, he handed the purse to a technician to bag.

"Says here," MacCarron said, looking at the driver's license, tilting his head and racking the wallet back and forth, trying to get a bead on it in the light, "her name is Sandra Love. Four Thirty-Five South Aiken. That's out near Friendship. Born 1951. What does that make her, twenty-six?"

"Twenty-four."

"Yeah, right. Twenty-four."

"Can you verify it's her from the picture?"

"Compared to that?" Mac said, nodding to the bloody, swollen mass that was once a face. He showed the picture to White, then studied it himself again. "If it's her, she must have been a really pretty girl, to look this good on a driver's license."

"What else is in the wallet?" White said, not wanting to get his partner started.

"Let's see. There's a student card from the University of Pittsburgh, says she's in graduate law. *Was* in graduate law. Photos of probably parents . . . kids with another woman, probably a sister . . . thirty-five dollars in bills. Nothing seems to be missing."

"So it wasn't a robbery."

"Does that look like a robbery to you?" MacCarron said, pulling his head back into his thick neck and making a face.

Lieutenant White exchanged looks with him and turned back to the girl. MacCarron wrote down the girl's address and handed the wallet to a technician. Then he bent over at the waist beside Stan, resting his elbows on his thighs to support his heavy frame, hunkered over like a downhill racer on a run.

"Weapon?" White said.

"Blunt instrument of some kind," Stan said into the side of MacCarron's face. Ignoring White across from him.

"Wood?" MacCarron said.

"Offhand I'd say metal."

"Like a pipe?"

"Maybe. Maybe even a gun barrel. Gun butt."

"Whoever did it, looks like he enjoyed it way too much. He really got into it." MacCarron, in his crouch, looked up at White. White was a tall, slender African-American in a close-fitting night-blue suit, ten years younger than his partner. He unknowingly touched the buttons of his suit coat, looked back at the girl again.

"She's still warm," Stan said, still addressing his comments to MacCarron. "Must have happened only a couple hours ago, three at most." He took a tongue depressor and carefully parted the young woman's thighs to examine her genitalia, shining a pocket flashlight up between her legs.

"Sexually assaulted?" White said.

Stan glanced at White, then said to MacCarron, "Nothing overt. We'll know for sure when we get her back to the lab."

"A rape gone wrong?" MacCarron said.

Or maybe somebody's idea of love, White thought. But thought better than to say it.

"A natural redhead," MacCarron said. "Orange as a Popsicle. And shaved in a heart. How about that?"

Stan looked at White again, to see if there was a reaction. Nathan looked off into the darkness, down the grassy slopes of Schenley Park to a line of dark trees. A mile or so away, beyond the park and Panther Hollow and the houses of the East End, the mill along Second Avenue, Eliza Furnace, flared above the bluffs along the river.

"It must have happened pretty quick," MacCarron said, standing up to face Nathan, ratcheting his baggy pants into position over the swell of the stomach. "He didn't bother to gag her. So she must not have expected what was coming. It's a wonder somebody didn't hear something up at the overlook. Though the couples in those cars were probably too busy with their own kind of lovemaking."

"Let's pick it up in the morning," Nathan said. "The other shift can do the legwork tonight. There's nothing much we can do anyway until we get the uniforms' reports and the prelims from the lab."

"Sandy Love," Mac said, shaking his head, looking at the girl. "Ironic, huh?"

Nathan turned away, out of the circle of the work lights, and started back across the grass, up the dark slope toward the overlook, the flashing lights of the police cars and ambulances. He started to comment to MacCarron but realized the sergeant wasn't with him—Mac was still back among the trees talking to Stan, the young man speaking confidentially to the sergeant about something. Nathan waited in the playground, leaning against the ladder of the slide, until Mac caught up to him.

"What was that about?" Nathan said.

Mac grinned, panting a bit at the slight grade. "Seems Stan is bothered about a black police lieutenant looking at the crotch of a white girl. Even a dead white girl. Doesn't think it's quite proper."

"Why did he tell you about it?"

"He wanted to know what I thought about it."

"And what did you say?

Mac grinned again, shook his head, puffed a little air up over his face and started past him toward their car. "Better make yourself all pretty, Nathan. TV trucks are here. They'll want a statement from their favorite flavor of the month."

White pushed off from the slide and fell in behind him, studying the back of his partner, the bulk of the guy, his brush-topped head, the fleshy rolls of his neck, thinking We've worked together a couple of years now and I don't know you at all, do I, Sergeant MacCarron, heading across the dark slope and into the parking area, into the wash of lights, ignoring the stares of the small crowd that had gathered to see what was going on, stepping into the circle of reporters and microphones aimed his direction, the calls of "Lieutenant! Hey Lieutenant!" "Can you tell us what happened?" "Hey, Lieutenant!" the red glowing eyes of the TV cameras—he instinctively touched the knot of his tie, wishing as he did so that he hadn't—thinking Flavor of the month? What the hell does that mean? Something you not telling me about your own concerns, Sergeant?

. . . and in the darkness of the park there are two pools of light, one toward the base of the slope where several technicians in their white lab coveralls bend over the crumpled form of the girl who was killed here, and the other at the top of the slope at the edge of the parking area and turnaround where the lights of several television cameras are trained on the middle-aged black police lieutenant who is trying his best to answer questions without divulging any pertinent information that could jeopardize the case and come back and bite him in the ass later on, while in the distance beyond the line of trees at the base of the slope are the lights of the Oakland District, the lights of the universities, the tower of the Cathedral of Learning, and the hospitals and medical buildings on what is locally referred to as Pill Hill, and beyond those, the lights of downtown Pittsburgh, the high-rise office buildings of the Golden Triangle, and overall, the glow of the steel mills along the rivers, the orange and red and yellow of the open hearths and Bessemer converters, the blast furnaces and basic oxygen furnaces, pulsing against the night sky over the city, flaring up and diminishing and then flaring up again, like living things, the low clouds preventing the smoke from the mills to rise

and so lowering the sky even farther, a shelf of gray over the city and the entire region, beyond the line of the hills surrounding the city more flare-ups, more pulsing orange and red against the sky like heartbeats from the mills up and down the rivers, down the Monongahela at Clairton and Homestead, in the opposite direction down the Ohio toward Aliquippa and Ambridge, Wyandotte and Furnass, the mills and little mill towns tucked into every available space between the rivers and the hills, Pittsburgh and the surrounding area thinking that it's in its heyday and that the steel industry will never die—it isn't; within a few years the mills will start to close, the steel industry will go away, hundreds of thousands here out of work, but that's another story—tonight the story is the murder of a young woman in a park in Western Pennsylvania, and how her death affects people she never knew in life, in ways she could never have imagined, not only the police who investigate her death but others who have their own relationship with violence, among them a Grade B movie director whose career is based on portraying the link between sexuality and violence, his wife who used her own sexuality to facilitate her husband's violent portrayals, a young man whose desire for fame leads him to confront his own capacity for violence, a young woman who is sadly unaware of the violence around her or the role her sexuality plays in provoking it, an aging dropout whose peaceful nature only goes as far as his own search for love, and a machinist, a specialist called a pattern maker, a workman in one of the mills in the region who among all our players is the most acquainted with violence, his ability to kill and then get up the next morning and go on with his life, and who, although he doesn't know it, is trying to find his capacity to love—but we're getting ahead of ourselves, gentle reader . . . these things have yet to unfold . . . come, let's take a look. . . .

Thursday, May 1, 1975

complete knowledge of the principles involved. To the extent, then, of being able, when necessary, to make a full-sized drawing of the article to be made, the pattern maker must be a draftsman.

In large establishments, where all the work comes to the pattern shop in the form of carefully executed drawings, the pattern maker is the means for putting the ideas of others into tangible shape. In smaller places, where no draftsman is employed, the pattern maker will be called upon to work out the designs for which he is to make his patterns, and he thus becomes the real designer.

Drawings are made for the machine shop to guide the machinist in cutting, turning, planing, and fitting the parts given, so as to produce in the castings the shapes, sizes, and general requirements of the articles to be constructed. Hence there is less liability for mistakes after the castings reach the machinist, as he has before him not only the drawing with its accurate dimensions to work from, but also the castings for the machine or its parts, from all of which the construction and uses of these several parts can easily be understood.

On the other hand, the pattern maker, with the aid of the same drawing, must imagine the casting before him, and must build something in wood which will produce that casting in metal. This pattern, in some cases, will be a duplicate of the required casting, but more often it has only a general resemblance to it, with core prints attached, and is external only, with nothing to show the internal openings, chambers, and winding passages that must be provided for by coring. The core boxes in which the cores are to be formed are not shown in the drawings furnished to the pattern maker, but must be provided by him in correct shapes and sizes, in addition to the pattern itself with its added core prints.

Finally, the pattern maker is seldom required to make two patterns that are identically the same. His work, therefore, is varied, and he must be prepared to apply to the solution of new problems that arise such principles as he may already have learned.

WORKING MEDIUM

As patterns are subjected to more or less rough usage and are alternately wet and dry, it follows that the ideal material is one whose hardness is such that it will withstand the wear and tear of

Pattern Making

Part I — Practical Requirements

Modern Shop Practice

"I don't want to start anything before lunch," Tronzo said, lean-ing against the doorway to Slater's work area, paging through the morning's *Post-Gazette*, the open paper covering his upper body and face, a newspaper with legs. "I'll just get interrupted."

Paul ignored him. Blanked him out of his thoughts. He was concentrating on the block of wood, the core block in his hand, comparing it to the drawing, the pattern for the mold to be used for a bronze bushing. For the third time he took his tri-square and checked the accuracy of the curve the length of the core. Thinking of the principle involved, the paradox of using a right angle to check a curve. He smiled to himself—though it barely showed, his face a study of angles and scrapings of its own—in his mind's eye he could see the drawing in his manual for pattern makers,

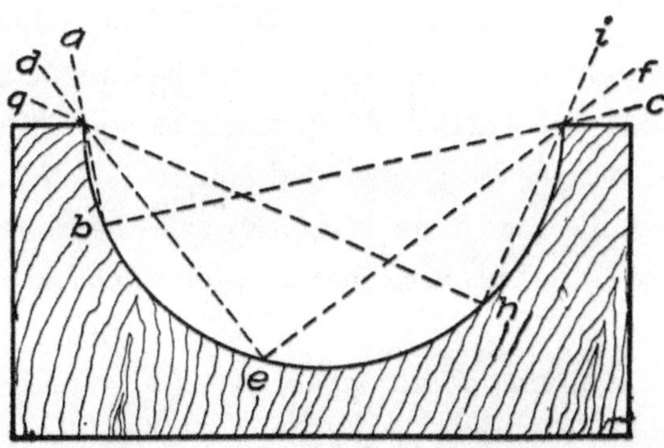

thought he could probably remember the principle involved, the entry in the manual, if he tried:

> *If the sides of a right angle lie upon the extremities of*
> *the diameter of a circle, the vertex of the right angle*
> *will lie upon the circumference of the circle . . .*

thinking What the hell got me thinking of that all of a sudden?

"Did you see this in the paper?" Tronzo said. He held the paper off to the side, peeking around it. On the front page was a picture of a helicopter perched on a rooftop in Saigon, a line of people like a trail of ants climbing up a ladder trying to get to it.

Paul glanced at it, looked away. Having seen it earlier at home before he left for work. The same photo that was on all the news broadcasts. "I hope they got everyone out. But I'll bet they didn't."

"What are you talking about?" Tronzo said, looking closer at the paper. Made a face. "I meant about the girl they found last night in the park."

Paul was ready to finish off the radius of the core. Some men in the shop liked to use a router, but Paul preferred the traditional core-box plane, he found it slower but truer, giving him more control. He returned the core box to the vise, tightening the jaws carefully so as not to damage the sides of the box, and, from the rows of tools above his workbench—jack plane and smooth plane, circular plane and rabbit plane, files and chisels of every length and configuration, saws and squares, each tool with its outline carefully drawn on the pegboard—he took the angle plane, adjusted the cutter so that it barely showed.

> *Cut out the remaining stock as shown to allow breaking out the stock left standing. Remove the remaining stock with the core-box plane, as described in the section on Hand Cutting Tools in Part I.*

"Her face beaten to a pulp," Tronzo said. "Dead, of course."

Those who didn't like the core-box plane said it wore down the corners of the semicircle as it was being worked. But whoever said that obviously didn't know what they were doing—or was too lazy to do it right. Paul thought he could probably remember what the manual said about that too, though the procedures by now were second nature to him:

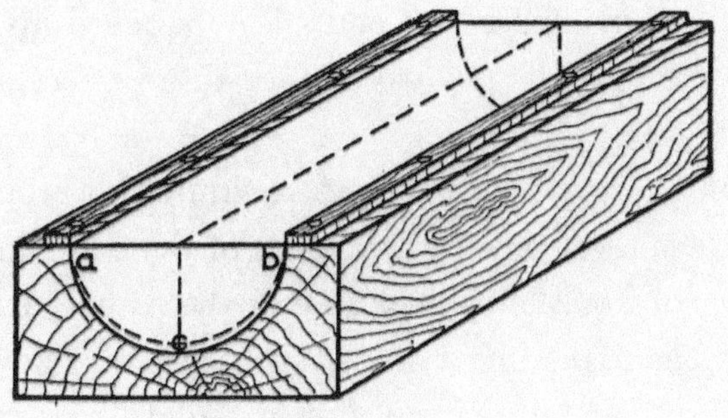

Tack two very thin strips of hardwood along the outside of the wood to be cut away, as shown at a and b in figure 65. These strips form rests for the sides of the plane while the heavier part of the work is being done. After the semicircle of the block has been worked out as far as the strips will allow as shown by the dotted arc acb, the strips are removed.

Common sense, if you think about it, he thought. Still, words to live by. People need the words. Something to live by. For.

"Who'd want to do a thing like that, to a pretty girl like that?" Tronzo closed the paper, folded it crudely, and dumped it into Paul's trash can. "I know what I'd do if it was me, that's for sure." He pumped his eyebrows, gave a couple licks to an imaginary cunt.

Paul took a few careful strokes with the plane the length of the core, the thin shavings curling up over the top of the tool, then released the block of wood again from the vise, eyed it carefully close to his face. "What makes you think she was pretty?"

Tronzo looked surprised, as if surprised that Slater was paying that much attention. He was a short, squat man with a tonsure of salt-and-pepper hair and olive skin who sweated a lot, was always damp. Like Paul, he wore brown coveralls, though Tronzo's drooped and sagged, baggy around his ass, his crotch almost down to his knees, the pants legs bunched up around his ankles—Paul's fit as if they were tailored, a perfect and off-the-rack 42-Long.

Paul took a piece of fine sandpaper, wrapped it around a dowel slightly smaller than the circumference of the core, and carefully sanded the sides of the radius. Tested the smoothness with his finger. Blew the remaining sawdust away. Then looked at Tronzo who was looking at him. "It never said the girl was pretty."

"Who said she was?"

"You did. Couple of minutes ago."

"Oh. Well, I just figured she must be. Pretty."

"Because nobody'd do that to an unpretty girl?"

"No. Well, I mean, I guess—"

"If she was ugly, would you still be so interested?"

"Who said I was interested? I was just telling you what it said in the paper." Tronzo squinted at him, as if trying to make him out against a glare. "Jeez. You got a weird turn of mind, Slater, you know that? A weird turn of mind."

He left the entrance to Slater's cube and was headed back across the aisle to his own work space when the horn blew through the shop, the lunchtime whistles and sirens of the mill sounding outside. Tronzo shifted gears, grabbed his lunch bucket from the table in his workspace, disappeared down the aisle toward the lunchroom.

Paul checked the radius of the core with his tri-square one more time, measured the dimension with his inside calipers, tested the smoothness of the finish again; the core block was ready for the end sections to be fitted and glued, the grooves cut along each side and fitted with a spline, the assembly shellacked.

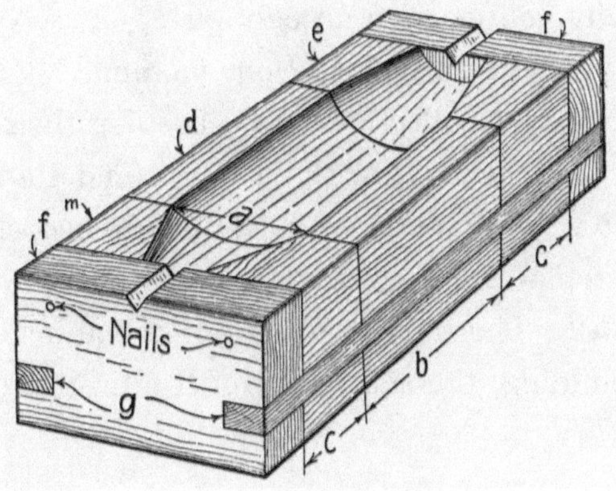

He would have liked to stay in his work area, eat his lunch while finishing the piece, not have to talk to anyone, but he didn't want to call attention to himself, didn't want to appear standoffish or as if anything was bothering him; nor did he want the shop steward calling him out for doing too much, thinking he was trying to make the others look bad. Reluctantly he left the core block on his worktable, took his lunch pail, and headed down the aisle.

In the washroom he urinated, washed his hands at the large circular sink in the center of the room, splashed cold water up over his face, rubbed it through his close-cropped hair, and continued on into the lunchroom. The usual card game was in progress; as usual he took a seat at the end of the long metal table, close to the others but not among them. Tronzo looked up from his hand as Paul got settled, opened his lunch box.

"Hey Packy, while you're up turn on the TV," Tronzo said. "Slater will want to see if there's any news about the murder of that ugly girl in Schenley Park last night."

"Who said she was ugly?"

"I thought they said she was beaten to death."

"Ugly girls can get beaten too."

"Yeah, but with an ugly girl how can you tell?"

"Is that why you married an ugly girl?"

"That's no way to talk about your momma."

The group gave a collective groan, keeping their attention on the cards in their hands. On the TV Bill and Patti Burns, the father-daughter news anchors on KDKA, talked silently. Their images were replaced by grainy footage that bore the title THE FALL OF SAIGON. The same photograph of the helicopter on the roof of the building, the same trail of frantic refugees trying to get aboard.

"Turn it up, turn it up."

Bill Burns was saying, "While Marine helicopters evacuated the remaining officials from the US embassy. . . ."

That's an Air America Bell 204, Paul thought, and that's not the embassy, that's the Pittman apartments, a few blocks away, where the CIA was, or at least where it was back then, we weren't regular army, we were Department of Defense and got our orders there. . . .

"Shit, look at that."

"They've been running that same photo over and over. It's depressing."

"Awful. Just awful."

"Whatcha got?"

The footage switched to images of a Sikorsky Jolly Green Giant coming in on the deck of a carrier, its doors releasing groups of Vietnamese women and children, then a shot of US sailors pushing a Huey over the edge of the deck into the sea, the chopper flopping over like a wounded beast as it disappeared over the edge, its blades like upraised arms.

"Your tax dollars at work."

"Pathetic. The greatest country on earth and we got our asses whipped by a bunch of slanty-eyed little—"

"We should have bombed them into oblivion while we had the chance."

"What the hell was it all for anyway?"

"You want this Twinkie?"

"I'll give you a Twinkie."

"You going to deal those cards or just shuffle them all day?"

Paul stared straight ahead for a few moments, then put his uneaten sandwich back in his lunch box, poured his soup back in his Thermos, and left the room. Behind him he heard someone say, "Give me two."

Without knowing he was going to do it beforehand, without having ever done anything like it before, Paul went to his locker, took off his coveralls and hung them up, put on his windbreaker over his khakis and polo shirt, and without telling anyone what he was doing—he barely knew himself—punched out at the time clock and left the shop. The pattern shop was in an old brick building in the middle of the Allehela Works of Buchanan Steel, a building that dated from before the Civil War, the large integrated mill growing around it, absorbing it among the Bessemer converters and later the facilities for the basic oxygen furnaces, the great metal buildings of the slabbing and blooming mills, the rolling mill and pickling shop, the mill stretching for a mile in either direction along the curve of the river. He got in his truck parked in the small lot beside the shop and drove through the mill, waiting at a crossing while a train of slag cars, waves of heat still rising above the empty ladles, trundled past on its way to the blast furnace, then continued out of the shadows of the massive complex and into the sunlight near the front gate, nodding to Bill and Charlie in the guardhouse as he passed through the fence. Out.

At the stop sign on the short access road, he looked up the hill at the streets of Furnass, the town climbing the lower slope on this side of the valley—on the other side of the river the valley wall rose sharply, tree-covered bluffs of granite and sandstone— he could see the roof of his house a few blocks away, on the steep side street below the main street. The small frame house on a slant where he grew up; the house where he watched his father every workday walk down the hill in the mornings and come back up the hill in the evenings from his own job at the mill; the house that, after he and Sharon were married as soon as Paul came back from Vietnam, they decided that it only made good sense to take over after his parents retired to Florida. If he turned up there now, at midday when he was supposed to be at work, he knew Sharon would be concerned—he could see her worried face, her searching eyes, always full of care whether it was for a damaged husband or simpering child or lost dog—asking him the same questions he was asking himself—Why? What's wrong?—for which he had no answers. "I can't do it," he said out loud, under his breath. He turned onto Third Avenue, loose gravel plinking up against the underbelly of his truck, and along the cyclone fence of the mill, past the soot-covered buildings and the railcars unloading at the tipple and the man-made mountains of coal and iron ore, through the venting clouds of smoke and hissing steam—in his mind's eye he saw his truck being tracked by someone on a rooftop in the town above on the slope (from his rooftop?), saw his truck in the crosshairs of a sniper scope as if he were doing the tracking, the truck in and out of view between the buildings that lined that side of the street as he sped along until he was out of range—until he circled up the ramp to the bridge that spanned the end of the valley and he joined the traffic on Route 65 heading upstream along the Ohio River toward Pittsburgh.

Two

Like most of the mill workers of Furnass, which is to say most of the men who lived in the town, Paul was in the practice of spending a few hours each evening after dinner at one of the men's social clubs—it would have seemed strange, if not almost un-American not to; his father had done so, as well as Sharon's father, his uncle, both his and Sharon's grandfathers, mill workers all—the Turner's Athletic Club or the VFW, Polish Falcons (even though he wasn't Polish) or the Sons of Italy (even though he wasn't Italian either) or the Sons of Allehela, the Elks or the Eagles or the Moose (though he tended not to like the clubs with animal names, not that he had anything against animals but those clubs were frequented more by merchant- and office-types rather than the workingman), for a couple of beers and to play a few numbers, check in with the guys he had known all his life. But in the years since he'd returned from the service, he found he had less and less to say to people, found he was more and more impatient, intolerant even, of the small talk, the talk that went on night after night on the same subjects, how the Steelers or Pirates were doing, the latest girl around town who was said to put out and who was thought to be doing her—and increasingly of late, if there were going to be layoffs at the mills, if the mills were going to close. So for the past few months, he still left the house after dinner, after he talked to Sharon for a while and spent time with his kids—Stephen, eleven, and Mandy, seven—but then instead of making his normal round of the clubs, at first a couple nights a week, and lately most nights, he headed through town to Ohio River Boulevard and drove the ten miles or so into Pittsburgh. Away from Furnass.

He had lived this close to Pittsburgh most of his life, but in fact the place was as foreign to him as the cities—Manila and Jakarta, Seoul and Tokyo, and of course, Saigon; always Saigon— he had spent time in during his years in the service. When he was a kid, he went up to Pittsburgh—it was always "up" when you went to Pittsburgh, even though Furnass was north and Pittsburgh was "down" if you were looking at a map—with his family a few times to Forbes Field to see the Pirates or Steelers play; in high school he went by bus on a field trip to the Carnegie to see the dinosaur bones and a bunch of old paintings they were told were important. After they were married, he drove Sharon and the kids into Pittsburgh occasionally, to the department stores downtown, Kaufmann's and Gimbels and Joseph Horne's, when she couldn't find the clothes the kids needed at the shopping centers. But his destination on these recent evening forays were the clubs in Oakland and Squirrel Hill and Shadyside he had heard about, read about in the papers or saw on television, where young adults went to hear music and hang out and enjoy themselves.

It was curiosity, really. He wondered what went on in such places, what it was like to go to such places. After all, he wasn't that much older than they were, the people who went to these clubs, he was only in his early forties, he still thought of himself as young, he certainly didn't think he could be considered old. But he had missed out on nightlife when he was that age, enlisting as soon as he graduated from high school, then getting married as soon as he returned, suddenly a family man with two children. He didn't kid himself, though, he knew he didn't belong in the rock clubs like the Decade and the Spotlight Lounge, even the disco bars like Zelda's Greenhouse or Peter's Pub, all he had to do was look around and see that he was a lot older than most anyone there, he didn't fit in. The truth was he probably wouldn't have gone to such places when he was younger even if he had had the chance. But now several nights a week, he would find himself on the fringe of a crowd of twenty-year-olds pogoing up and down to earsplitting guitars in some grungy club, sitting at a bar with a beer that cost three times what it was worth watching a young girl in a cage wearing white leather boots and not much else perform a dance that looked like she was pounding sand.

But neither his late evening ramblings nor his occasional shopping trips with Sharon prepared him for the press of traffic on the freeways, the lane closures and traffic merges of getting into downtown Pittsburgh solo, without a spotter, someone calling out the signs, at noontime on a workday. When a bridge off-ramp dumped him onto Fort Duquesne Boulevard he thought he recognized a few landmarks but quickly got turned around and into unfamiliar surroundings, almost running over several pedestrians in the crowded crosswalks and jaywalkers who took sport in dodging among cars in midblock. If these idiots had any idea how little I know where I'm going, he thought, they'd think twice before running out in front of me. Or maybe not, because they're idiots. It would serve 'em right if I. . . . When he found himself circling for the third time the open quadrangle of Market Square, he pulled his truck into a yellow zone and parked. And allowed himself a big sigh of relief. What the hell did I think I was doing?

He got out and stretched, looking around at the older two- and three-story brick buildings that lined three sides of the square; in the opposite corner a crane with a wrecking ball, swinging like a pendulum, was busy reducing a number of buildings to rubble, clouds of brick dust exploding periodically as another section of a wall disappeared. The area was busy in the early afternoon, businessmen in suits hurrying by in earnest conversations, secretaries in high heels and tight skirts trying to negotiate the ballast-block paving stones. But mainly the open space seemed a drain trap for the city's homeless, blacks with nowhere else to go, with a sprinkling of winos and drunks and addicts. In a small patch of grass in one of the quartered sections, half a dozen old men passed around a bottle in a brown paper bag, laughing raucously and ribbing each other; an old woman in a babushka and wrapped in half a dozen blankets despite the sunny day sat on a bench sorting through her bundles in a shopping cart; on another bench a plump woman slapped at the three children on leashes playing around her bare toes.

This wasn't the kind of thing he had in mind when he thought of coming to Pittsburgh, though he couldn't have said what it was that he did have in mind. On the corner of an alley was the white tile facade of the Original Oyster House; a sign in the window said it was the oldest bar and restaurant in Pittsburgh. Why not? You said you wanted to do new things, go to places you've never been to before, he thought as he pushed between the swinging doors. The long narrow room was busy, a curious mixture of business executives and more of the riffraff from the square. The tables along the wall were all taken; it was too late to turn around now; he found a place at the long galvanized metal bar and got settled. A workman beside him, apparently a regular, ordered a glass of buttermilk and a couple of breaded oysters. Paul ordered the same and was surprised when he liked them. He waited until the place cleared out a bit, studying the photos on the wall of boxers from the '40s and '50s and Miss America contestants in their ball gowns, the stuffed fish leaping across the walls and the image of himself in the mirror behind the bar, sitting among it all, before he paid and left.

He felt he had accomplished something as he walked across the square and took a side street that led toward the Point. He was approaching Stanwix Street when he heard the screech of tires, an engine revving too high. Across the busy intersection two cars were speeding toward him from the direction of the river, one chasing the other. The first car made the turn onto the street leading to the Fort Pitt Bridge but the second, a police car, cut the corner too tight and went over on two wheels, then all the way over, rolling onto a concrete divider and bursting into flames. Paul was running before he was aware of doing it, dodging through the cars stopped to watch what was going on, thinking the officers might be trapped, he had to get them out before it exploded, he had to help—at the same time he became aware of the people standing around watching, there were crowds roped off along the sidewalks, some of whom were applauding. What the hell was going on? He stopped behind a group of onlookers along a police barricade.

In the street a fire truck had been waiting for the accident. Firemen were already rushing toward the smoking car, spraying it with foam as the driver and his companion scampered out of the windows of the upside-down vehicle, giving each other high-fives like athletes who had just scored. As the crowd continued to applaud, the two men did exaggerated bows as they laughed and headed off toward a camera truck.

"Did you think it was real or something?" the guy beside Paul said.

Paul shook his head, still trying to grasp what was going on.

"The way you came running up there," the guy said. "Looked like you were going to try to save somebody."

"I didn't know," Paul muttered. "I had some medical training in the army. . . ."

"The age of heroes isn't dead."

The guy was watching him, grinning at him, almost as if he were encouraging him about something. He was a tall skinny guy—Paul at first thought he was a kid, then realized he was much older, maybe close to his own age, it was hard to tell—with long hair in ringlets down to his shoulders, wearing a black Jack Lambert number 58 Steelers jersey, jeans, and the high-top sneakers kids wore when Paul was growing up and Paul always hated. Around his neck was a large pewter peace symbol on a beaded necklace; a worn leather bag with long fringe hung from his shoulder. Go to hell, weirdo, Paul thought. He turned away, turned his attention back to the street.

The guy beside him turned his attention to the street as well, but kept talking as if continuing a conversation he and Paul started earlier. "It's an easy mistake to make these days, confusing the fake with the real. Because the media, the entertainment industry, the government, they all want you to be unable to tell the one from the other. News isn't news nowadays if it isn't entertaining and the stars of our entertainment have to generate news if they want to be a success and they're usually more entertaining than the movies they produce. And the government wants you to confuse the two because if people really understood what was going on they'd take to the streets. Like they did to stop the war."

Paul looked at him. I have to get away from this guy before I do something. He moved a few yards down the sidewalk and mingled with another group of people watching the firemen checking out the car, the movie crew checking their equipment and starting to clear the scene. But the guy was still beside him.

"The thing is, the general population would much rather see the simulacrum than the real thing anyway. They would much rather visit Disney World to see a fake mountain than go to a real mountain, see fake animals nod their heads and bare their fangs than experience the real animals. Of course, the real problem with real animals is that they can eat you. For real."

The guy flashed a disarming grin when Paul turned to him again. "Hi, my name's Sam."

People along the curb were looking at them, starting to move away, a widening circle around them.

"You want something?" Paul said.

"We all want something, dude," Sam said and smiled.

Dude? Are you kidding me? From the street came the sound of someone yelling. Paul and Sam both turned to see what was going on. A broad, stocky man in an open safari jacket who was noticeably shorter than those around him, with a shrub of salt-and-pepper hair covering his head, a matching shrub of salt-and-pepper beard hiding most of his face, was screaming at some technicians on the opposite curb tending the banks of lights and reflectors, apparently including anyone within range in his rant.

"Ah. Nicoletti," Sam said.

Paul shrugged; the name meant nothing to him.

"The director. The great man himself," Sam said. "It is his special province to be able to yell at everybody else."

Nicoletti had turned his attention to a young woman in a tight chino skirt and low heels standing close by the technicians. She hurried forward to Nicoletti, looking through a sheaf of papers in her arms as the director continued to berate her about something.

"Is she one of the actresses?"

"Her?" Sam said. "Not hardly. She must be doing an internship or something with the production. Poor Suzy. I'm sure this isn't what she signed up for."

"You know her?"

"Only in passing, as they say. I see her every once in a while out in Oakland, she goes to CMU. Suzy Two Quarters. That's what she always gives me. I may forget a lot of things but I never forget what a person is good for."

Paul looked at him. What is this guy talking about?

"Panhandling. As in . . ." Sam held out his hand, palm up; when Paul didn't get the message, Sam presented his palm a second time. No go. Sam shrugged and grinned and looked back at the scene in the street. "Oh well, it was worth a try."

Nicoletti had moved on, turning his attack first on the crew on the camera truck, then to another film unit farther along the sidewalk, leaving the girl standing where she was in the street, still looking frantically through the sheaf of papers in her arms. She looked like she was about to cry.

"There's no call for that," Paul said under his breath. "He shouldn't be allowed to yell at people like that."

"The law of the jungle," Sam said, his hands folded behind his back, rocking slightly on his heels. "The way the world turns, the way the cookie crumbles. Dog eat dog, or I guess in this case dog eat pussy."

Paul glared at him. Sam's face lit up.

"Wow, must have touched a nerve. I get it, you're a champion of the little guy, the underdog, or I guess the underkitty, if the other term offends you. . . ."

Paul was afraid he was going to hit him. What the hell am I doing here, listening to this freak? Get me out of here. . . . He pushed by the few people along the curb and cut across the street, away from the scene with the upturned car and the firemen and the film crew and the girl still looking through her papers. One of the policemen on crowd control started to say something to him, but Paul looked at him and the policeman let it go.

Three

Paul left the noise and confusion of the street and entered the parklike setting of Gateway Center, drawn in by the peaceful tree-lined walkways, the pattern of walks separated by flower beds blossoming with tulips and daffodils, arrangements of reds and yellows and purples in the dappled sunlight, the stainless-steel facades of the office towers glistening overhead through the branches of the trees. He sat on a bench for a while until he collected himself—Why did that guy start talking to me? Why can't people let other people alone?—then he continued on, watching the plashings of a fountain for a while, listening to the water, until too many people came out of Gateway One, standing around chatting and smoking. Paul turned away, heading toward the open area between the Hilton and Gateway Towers, crossing the street into Point State Park.

He was feeling calmer now, the open green spaces of the park lifting his spirits, the full sunlight on his face, making him glad he had decided to come here today. Right now, I'd be standing in my cubicle, the other guys would be heading to the lunchroom for their break or maybe Tronzo would decide he wanted to tell me something about something, maybe more about the murdered girl in the park or whatever the hell was on his mind, and always the noise of the grinders and the belts and generators and the whine of the motors and the Bridgeport milling machine, the smell of burning wood and hot metal and oil. . . . On the bluffs across the Monongahela apartment towers lined the ridgeline, the rose window of a large church caught the sun, the cross on top of the church glinting like a diamond in a tooth. He followed the trenches and breastworks cut in the grass, the remains of Fort Pitt, reminders that this peaceful setting was once a battle-ground, then through a tunnel under the bridge ramps and out into the farther reaches of the park, toward the Point, the joining of the Allegheny and Monongahela Rivers to form the Ohio, the confluence marked by the tall fountain at the apex of the park, the city itself.

His good mood had returned, he felt happier than he could remember. Glad to be alive. Across the Allegheny was the bowl of Three Rivers Stadium, he had to remember to bring the family up here for a Steelers or Pirates game sometime, the way his dad used to take him to Forbes Field when he was a boy, he didn't know why he hadn't done it before this. An outing with the family, he had to do more of that. Across the Monongahela the toy-like cars of the incline made their way slowly up and down the slanted track, the cars from this angle looking briefly as if they might collide at the midpoint, then passing harmlessly by one another. Down the Ohio beyond the tall plume of the fountain a riverboat pushing a load of barges made its way downstream, heading toward the Mississippi several states away. It occurred to him that soon the boat would be passing the mouth of the Allehela, the view of Furnass beyond the viaduct across the en-trance to the valley. His home.

I should be getting back. Sharon'll wonder what happened to me. I think she wanted to go to Holy Innocents tonight too, some meeting or other, or maybe it was a novena, she'll need me to watch the kids. . . .

He retraced his steps, back across the open plains of the park, back across the street into Gateway Center again, the pathways between the rows of flower beds, the cross-shaped office towers above the trees buttery in the lowering sun. He knew the afternoon was growing late but he didn't want the day to end, he wasn't ready to surrender just yet. At the Hilton there were tables and chairs outside on the plaza, in front of the restaurant, though at the moment there was no one there. He took a seat and, when a waitress appeared, ordered coffee and—because he wanted a treat, wanted the day to last as long as possible—a piece of carrot cake. A few sparrows bounced among the legs of the empty tables and chairs; he tossed a few cake crumbs their direction and watched as they sprung about like some kind of children's toys. He didn't see her coming along the walkway until she was on top of him, threading her way through the empty tables toward the restaurant entrance, scattering the birds.

"Oh dear, I scared your little friends away," she said to him.

"That's okay." Unable to think of anything else to say.

It was the girl from the movie company, Suzy Two Quarters the hippie called her; she smiled but wasn't really looking at him, her gaze focused at some point fifteen degrees off to the side of his head. As she continued on inside, she brushed past his table, her thigh sheathed in the tight tan skirt almost touching his arm. Paul busied himself with his coffee, finishing his carrot cake.

In a moment the birds were back and Paul flicked the remaining crumbs at them, making a game of it, trying to see how close he could come to them, wondering if they would try to catch the crumbs on the fly—when the girl came out of the restaurant and scared the birds away again.

"Oh my goodness, I did it again, didn't I? I scared your little friends away. You must hate me."

She was trying to arrange a couple bags of takeout in her arms along with a stack of papers; one of the bags was starting to drip and she looked as if she was about to lose the whole armload.

Paul stood up and took the leaking bag from her and put it on his table.

"Here, let me give you a hand with that."

"I can get it. I mean I thought I could. They're wonderful little birds, aren't they? So cheerful and full of life, I just love them. Oh, I've dripped all over your table."

"It's okay."

He opened the bag and set the lid on the coffee cup properly, then held the bag until she got the rest of her load arranged. "Sure you can get it okay?"

"Yes, yes, I'm fine now. I'm only going over there," she nodded at Gateway Towers on the other side of the narrow plaza. "Francis—Mr. Nicoletti is working late and told me to pick him up something. Of course he couldn't get it himself."

She rocked her head from side to side, rolled her eyes to punctuate the point. Her eyes were startlingly blue, like two small holes in a fence with a cloudless sky beyond, though they met his own eyes only briefly, moving away quickly again to the fifteen-degree point beside his head. This close to her he could see that her complexion was slightly pimply and pockmarked under heavy makeup; her cheeks were knobby, her chin small and pointy, and there was a faint line across it, off center, an old scar.

"Well, I'm off," she laughed suddenly, a kind of bubble. "You're a very kind man to help a lady in distress."

Then she was gone, threading back among the tables, across the narrow plaza, walking among the beds of tulips and daffodils—she walked like a dancer, or the way he thought a dancer would, pointing her toes so she appeared to glide, as if she were making her way carefully across a surface that was slippery or one she was afraid to disturb—watching the flick of her ass in the tight skirt, and into the entrance of Gateway Towers, the long tall building rising like a wall blocking the late afternoon sky. He pushed away from the table and wandered back through the gardens of the office center, back into the rush and tussle of the downtown, thinking, I should have offered to help her with those bags, it would have been a natural thing to do, she probably thinks it's strange I didn't, You're a very kind man, I wonder what else a pretty young intern has to provide the director, she seemed like a really nice girl. When he got back to his truck, he found a parking ticket on the windshield.

. . . the young woman identified as Sandra Love has been dead now approximately sixteen hours, her body lies in the Allegheny County morgue on Fourth Avenue, the squat stone building designed if not to match then at least to complement the Renaissance-Romanesque fantasies complete with towers and turrets and minarets of Henry Hobson Richardson's County Courthouse and Jail complex nearby, on a table slightly tilted for viewing in the orangish-yellowish tiled room called the Cooler, where the newly dead are displayed for viewing, where teenage Pittsburgh boys traditionally brought their prom dates to show them the stiffs and maybe get some extra cuddles, extra feels from the squeamish girls, a practice that the officials finally got wise to and belatedly stopped a decade or so earlier, the young woman lying alone this evening because it has been a slow day here for the dead . . . as at his desk in the squad room of the Public Safety Building a couple of blocks away on Second Avenue, Lieutenant Nathan White looks through his notes one more time from their visit earlier in the day to Sandra Love's apartment and their canvassing of her neighbors, goes over for the third time the reports of the uniformed officers from the night before of witnesses at the crime scene and the preliminary report from the medical examiner's office, still unable to come up with anything that looks like a lead or a clue, feeling pressured more than usual by the case, aware that there are elements of the young woman's death

that could indicate the beginning of a string of serial killings or a series of copycat murders, but aware that it's more than that too as he looks out the window, the traffic slanting up at eye level on the ramp of the Boulevard of the Allies heading out of downtown toward Oakland and the eastern sections of the city, he's aware that the eyes of the department and the media and the city are on him, this is a high-profile case—a young white woman brutally assaulted in a public park—and he's a black police lieutenant, Stan the coroner's assistant at the crime scene wasn't unique in his questioning of the racial disparity between victim and investigator in this case, Stan was only the first, White all too aware that though he is not the first African-American lieutenant in the Pittsburgh police department he is close enough to stand out, a disposition that is reinforced by the department and the city when they trot him out for benefits and public appearances, standing him in the background at press conferences and photo ops that have nothing to do with either him or his investigations, thinking There's got to be something here, what am I missing, I've got to do well on this case, I've got to, I've got to show those bastards once and for all that I'm as good, as capable, as anybody, as anybody white, I've got to show those bastards . . . while in Oakland, in the attic of an old house converted into apartments on South Bouquet Street a few blocks from the University of Pittsburgh campus, Sam Connor sits at the kitchen table in his apartment counting through the change and crumpled dollar bills that he collected today—thinking Nineteen dollars and eighty-five cents, not bad, not bad at all for a Thursday, it isn't even the third of the month when the welfare checks come out and everybody's got some loose change—goes to his refrigerator and takes out the Dutch oven of corn and rice and pinto beans that he fixed for himself earlier in the week and has been working his way through ever since, heating it on the stove as he listens to the unavoidable sounds of the students who live in the apartments of the house below him, a cacophony of radios playing Top 40 and stereos blasting the latest hits by Tony Orlando and Dawn or the Ozark Mountain Daredevils, Elton John or Earth, Wind & Fire or, heaven forbid, Barry Manilow, until he can't take it anymore, thinking Forgive them Lord, they're children, they know not what they do, and while his dinner continues to warm on the stove he goes to his own stereo and puts on the Grateful Dead's Aoxomoxoa and turns up the volume to sonic levels, opens his dormer windows to share this music of the gods with the neighborhood, smiling to himself as he thinks Lord Jerry smiles upon us, children, and all's right with the world, prepares to eat his supper and take his usual evening nap in preparation for making his rounds of the clubs and nightspots in Oakland and Shadyside and Squirrel Hill, playing air guitar with Garcia for a few bars on "St. Stephen" as he anticipates the coming evening, the treasures of new experience the night will present to him . . . as on the twelfth floor of the Gateway Hilton hotel, a young man recently enrolled at Allegheny College named Jeff Berner stands at the corner window of the room for which he had to pay dearly, the room that the desk clerk was reluctant to give him when he checked in two days earlier until Jeff said he wanted it for a month and would pay in advance—it wasn't a great hardship, he was using his father's credit card, and besides he'd probably need the room for that long at least when he got a role in Nicoletti's new movie—ignores the view of Point Park and the fountain at the confluence of the two rivers into a third, the view of the hills and rivers and the sky to the west starting to turn toward evening, in favor of the smaller window to the side, the view of Gateway Towers across the narrow plaza, the building where he's learned Nicoletti has his production office, holding back the gauze curtain for a better view as he scans the windows of the building opposite as he has repeatedly the last two days, looking for a clue as to which of the windows belong to Nickolodeon Productions, when he sees movement in the plaza below and watches a young blond woman in a tight chino skirt carrying a stack of papers and several white bags make her way among the planters of flowers along the walkway to the door of the Towers and disappear inside, thinking that he saw her earlier today at the filming near Stanwix Street, she works for Nicoletti, his assistant or something, and watches the windows opposite more intently, hoping to see where she goes, a light turned on or a curtain pulled back, but can't determine anything, the windows seem permanently streaked and murky, or depending on the placement of the lowering sun shining up the river valley, to reflect the windows of the hotel back at him, though he continues to keep watch undeterred just on the chance when after fifteen minutes or so he's ready to call it quits he happens to see a light flick off in a window on a lower floor of the building and waits and in a few moments the girl reappears, coming out the doors and into the plaza, and before she disappears below the edge of his window, he sights down the barrel of his finger-gun and thinks Gotcha . . . as later that evening on the eighth floor of Gateway Towers, in the temporary offices of Nickolodeon Productions, Francis Paul Xavier Nicoletti, commonly known as Nicko, sits in the dark of the conference room he's converted into a small theater where he can review the daily rushes, drinking the cold cup of coffee that has dripped over today's notes and eating the cold sandwich the intern Suzy picked up for him, thinking Another Reuben, every night she gets me a Reuben, she must think I like them and is afraid to get me something else, either that or it's the only thing she knows how to order, sitting beside the projector in the dark room fast-forwarding through one of his earlier movies entitled Blood Truth *until he comes to the scene he's looking for, where the lovers are in the park late at night, the skyline of the city beyond a line of dark trees, so close and yet so far, as the couple kisses and the girl laughs as the guy pretends to chomp on her neck, then takes hold of her arms and puts them behind her back, the girl looking at him quizzically but suggestively as if to say Oh yes? What did you have in mind? and pins her arms behind her as he kisses her again and then backs her slowly in a kind of dance a few steps against a small tree and eases her down till she's sitting and he's kneeling in front of her between her legs, her skirt hiked up to accommodate him there, then takes a piece of silk rope from his jacket pocket and she laughs again as if to say You think of everything don't you, as if she's seen it before, as if this is not new to her, and he takes hold of her arms again and places them behind her around the base of the tree and ties her wrists together and she speaks for the first time in several minutes, saying "Not too tight" but he gives them an extra tug regardless and when she starts to protest he covers her mouth with his mouth and she's lost for a moment in the kiss and then he pulls back from her and pops a ball gag into her mouth, the girl surprised now, her eyes wide and questioning as the guy rests back on his heels for a moment, studying her as she's trying to say something to him, it's apparent this is rougher than she intended and he stands up and takes a gun from his jacket pocket and hits her with a heavy downward blow that knocks her head to the side and she only gets a quick look at him before the second blow comes and then again and again as the special effects turn her face to mush and the camera moves slowly away, up and away from the violence to focus on the skyline and the nearby city, so close and yet so far, then the scene fades to black as Nicoletti turns off the projector and turns on the light to look at this morning's newspaper again, the story of the murder of a girl in a local park and thinks Wow, that's really spooky, and really terrible for the girl too of course, but I got to say it's great publicity . . . and in Furnass, ten miles up (or down) the river, after Paul Slater arrived home from his afternoon in Pittsburgh in time for dinner, his wife Sharon none the wiser about how he spent his afternoon—Paul stopped at a*

The Pattern Maker

McDonald's and emptied his lunch box into a garbage can, poured the soup down a storm drain—made his usual small talk at the dinner table—it meant he had to make up some stories about what went on in the shop today but that wasn't something entirely new, he has made up stories in the past to make a day seem interesting when it fact it had been deathly slow and uneventful— helped Sharon with the dishes as he often does, and then, while Sharon got Mandy into her bath and into her pj's and got herself ready for her novena, played catch with a baseball and gloves with Stephen in the alley beside the house—they couldn't do it in the street in front of the house because if whoever was on the downhill side of the steep street missed, the ball could roll all the way down the hill five blocks to the fence at the mill—and after seeing Sharon off to Holy Innocents and making sure that Stephen is doing his homework at the dining-room table, he goes upstairs to Mandy's room and sits down beside her on the floor, watching the television with her, watching as she draws on the pad of paper in her lap, the child the size of a seven-year-old but with the eyes, the face of someone much younger, someone who would never develop beyond the age of two or three, watching the child watch the screen as a police car careens through a warehouse district and crashes into a stack of crates—for the briefest instant on some level of his mind Paul thinks of seeing the filming today in Pittsburgh, the police car rolling over and catching fire, the on- lookers on the curb applauding, the crew looking on impassively, but the memory is gone just as quickly—then scribbling furiously on her pad of paper, after a moment Paul saying, "Can Daddy see what you're drawing?" and the little girl looks up at him, her head loose and floppy on her shoulders; he cups the back of her furry head and studies the piece of paper: "What is it?" he asks and the little girl tells him in her own language, the only words he recognizes being "Chair . . . and the, and the . . . fly bird," she chatters and laughs; "Is it a bird?" he asks and she looks puzzled; he cocks his head for a better view, there is indeed a creature of some sort on the paper but it's one he's never seen before, a beast whose body consists of a series of lopsided rings, with a great horned head and numerous stick legs, the creature surrounded by other jagged designs, waves or flames, and Paul says "That's very good, Mandy. Very good" as the child holds the drawing out to him, for him to take, his, though she continues talking, relating a troubled narrative that he can't understand but that seems to fill the child with sorrow and fear; she searches his face as she tells her unintelligible story, and, not finding what she is looking for in his reactions, appears as though she might cry or scream; "It's all right, Mandy," Paul assures her, "it's all right, Daddy's here, Daddy's here" and Mandy says, "Tree bird fly Daddy Daddy car is . . . is?" then her mind moves on again, the child reaching for another crayon and begins to draw again, chortling happily to herself and Paul decides to sit there for a while longer in case, just in case, eventually taking her in his arms and carrying her over to her bed and laying her down, tucking her in and turning off the overhead light but continuing to sit there beside her bed in the glow of the night-light, watching as she falls asleep, sitting there in the half dark until he hears Sharon return from church, never once thinking about having to go to work tomorrow or the afternoon he spent today in Pittsburgh, never once thinking of what might be going on in Saigon at this very moment as the North Vietnamese set up their government and settle old scores or of the girl he talked to briefly today named Suzy. . . .

Friday, May 2, 1975

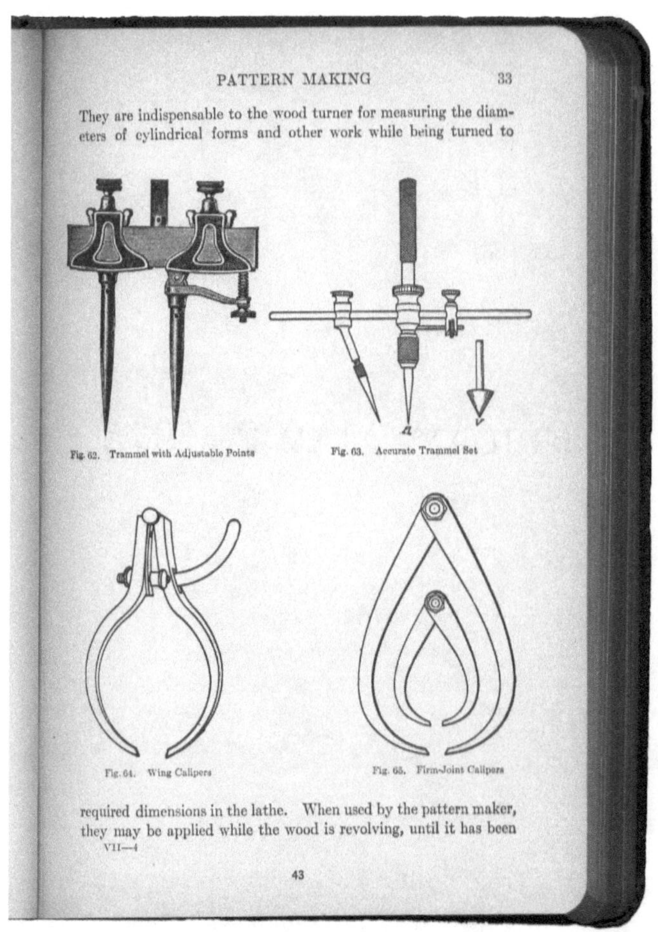

Measuring Tools

Modern Shop Practice

Four

"Finish your Pop-Tart, Stephen," Sharon said. "You'll be late for school."

"Tommy isn't here yet," Stephen said. Not looking up from his comic book spread on the table in front of him.

Captain Marvel, thought Paul. Christ.

"You want to be ready before Tommy gets here," Sharon said. Sitting beside Mandy, ready to put another spoon of strained applesauce in the child's mouth.

"I will be," Stephen said.

"Your mother told you to get ready," Paul said. Drinking his coffee, leaning against the drainboard.

Stephen looked at him, as if ready to say something smart, then, seeing the look on his father's face, thought better of it. The boy ate the remaining bite of Pop-Tart, closed the comic book, and headed upstairs to finish getting ready.

"And here's Tommy," Paul called after Stephen as the boy appeared at the screen door.

"Come on in, honey," Sharon said, "if you want to. Would you like something to eat?"

"No, ma'am. I'm okay."

"He'll be right down," Paul said, turning back to the television on the counter now that the string of commercials was over. On the screen was the same photograph of the helicopter on the roof of the building in Saigon, the same footage of the helicopter being pushed off the deck of a carrier into the South China Sea; this time they added footage of a number of sampans and other small craft bobbing in the choppy water between American destroyers, the upturned faces of the refugees pleading to come aboard the larger ships.

"Where will they go?" Sharon said, the spoon poised a few inches in front of Mandy's mouth, the little girl straining forward to meet it.

To hell, one way or another, Paul thought. Which their lives will be no matter what happens now. I wonder if Freddy made it out. We said we'd take care of him and his family if he'd translate for us but we probably never did . . . I got to get going.

Paul put his coffee cup in the sink and went to get his windbreaker from the closet, passing Stephen in the narrow hall—"Will you come to baseball practice tonight?" "I'll try to, unless I have to work late"—kissed Sharon on the cheek and Mandy on top of her head—"Fly, Daddy, fly?"—palmed her head a few extra seconds as he met Sharon's eyes, then followed the boys down the back steps to his truck in the paved parking spot in his backyard.

With his two good-bye toots to Sharon, he pulled out of the alley and headed down steep Thirteenth Street toward the mill, sitting along the river, the long soot-black buildings encased as always in their clouds of smoke and steam, four blocks away, the cross streets marking his progress down the hill like treads of a stair, the sounds of the mill getting louder, the constant rumble of the machinery like the undergrowl of the pounding surf, the warning sirens and safety bells, the hiss of steam, steel ringing on steel, the whistles of the switch engines moving railcars, and the smells, coke and oil and smoke and sulfur and something else he couldn't name, not burning flesh but close. Then he stopped. He pulled over abruptly before he got to Third Avenue and watched the spread of the mill before him, watched the other cars and trucks pulling into the parking lots in front of the mill, the men in twos and threes crossing the street and moving through the fence, passing the guardhouse, on their way into the mill. He remembered his dad used to walk down here to work every day, snow or rain, those killer hot days in summer, and more to the point, walk up the hill again after a full day's work. And here he was driving it. Pathetic.

What happened to me? How did I get soft? We used to hike

twenty miles a day, thirty sometimes, seventy-pound packs, through jungles, over mountains. No, it wasn't soft, it was something else. Careful. Too careful. Easy. Safe. There was the time he took Freddy upcountry, they couldn't use the rivers because it was too dangerous, no one was to know they were there, that he was there, not even his own people, the CIA rep said if you're caught we'll disavow any knowledge of you, up to the border and beyond, he left Freddy at the border because he didn't know the language in Cambodia anyway and if they caught him they'd flay him alive, following the trails and streams deeper into the bush but never on the trails and streams themselves, a week or more until he got to the plantation and set up his position in that rubber tree, two days without movement as he watched the house through his scope, got to know the rhythm of the household, got to know how the plantation owner beat the houseboy for stealing food and took the servant girls any time he felt like it so it made it easier somehow, watched in the evening light as his potbellied form came out afterward and sat on the porch, the glow of his cigar periodically lighting his face in the crosshairs till Paul could make the positive identification, squeezed off the round and the man's face exploded into a red mist . . . no.

He sat a few moments longer until he could feel himself growing calm again, did the breathing exercises they taught him those many years ago, then, when he could feel his center return, put the truck in gear and drove on down the hill. Except at the stop sign he couldn't do it. He even wanted to, knew that he should, and couldn't. Instead, he turned right and headed toward the bridge and the rush-hour traffic into Pittsburgh.

Five

Francis Paul Xavier Nicoletti burst out of the door of his bedroom, showered and dressed and ready for his day, anxious to tell Fran his exciting news, what he had discovered the previous evening by going through some scenes of his previous films, anticipating the delighted look on her face—but there was no Fran. He expected her to be sitting at the counter in the kitchen having her coffee reading the paper as she always did in the mornings, but the kitchen was empty, there was no one sitting at the counter, there was no sign of her. What the hell? Did she leave for the office already? Without saying anything? He went back down the hallway and looked in the door of her bedroom, stepped in and checked the bathroom, the walk-in closet just to be sure. No Fran.

Nicoletti stalked back down the hallway and into the kitchen—then on a hunch went over to the doorway to the solarium. Fran was sitting among the rubber plants and Norfolk pines, at the spindly table on one of the spindly chairs, reading the *Post-Gazette*, wearing a white satin-and-chiffon peignoir. He stood in the doorway for a moment, waiting for her to look up from the paper, but she kept reading as if she didn't know he was there, or if she did know, didn't care to admit it. What's she doing out there? Could be a trap. She must be up to something, the woman's always up to something. Maybe I better rethink how I'm going to approach her on this. . . . Nicko dug his stubby fingers into his salt-and-pepper beard, scratching as if he fingered arpeggios, still hoping for some sign of recognition from her, before turning back to the kitchen to fix himself an espresso.

Twenty-three years of marriage taught me this too: Don't ask for trouble. It'll come around easily enough on its own, thank you very much. . . .

It was a Spanish-style house, swirly stucco walls and exposed vigas across the ceilings, corner beehive fireplaces, alcoves here and there, and archways over the doors, totally out of place and incongruous in the Squirrel Hill area of Pittsburgh. The owners had decorated it accordingly with massive dark wood furniture and tile floors; on the walls were mosaics of saints and carved crucifixes of Christ in agony—Nicko knew for a fact that the owners were Jewish, but they summered in Majorca—pikes and spears and gauntlets covered with sharp studs; sitting in a corner of the living room was a chain mace said to date from the Crusades. Fran rented the house for them when they set up shop in Pittsburgh to start filming, she thought it important for appearances' sake to keep their living arrangement apart from the offices she rented at the Golden Gateway; Nicko would have preferred to set up housekeeping in the penthouse she also rented on Grandview Avenue overlooking the downtown, but she insisted that was for visiting studio execs and the stars he hoped to attract for cameos. All of it was based on her theory that to be successful they had to appear successful. How's that working for us lately, my love, Nicko thought as he made his espresso, taking time to steam the cup before he started, making sure the brew foamed to his liking. After a few sips, both to get himself revved up and to make sure he didn't spill it—it wouldn't do to give her a ready-made opening for whatever she had planned, the chance to carp at him about a dripping cup—he took a deep breath and crossed the room to the solarium.

Fran was still reading the paper, still giving him no notice. Beneath the glass-topped table, her legs were crossed, exposed to the thigh between the skirts of white satin. They are certainly among the great legs of the Western World, even at fifty. If I had legs like that I wouldn't want to cover them up either. One white mule, a large pom-pom at the toes, dangled from the end of her foot; she slapped it occasionally against her heel with a scrunch of her toes, a comment on something she read. Nicko leaned on the doorframe and sipped his espresso. After another minute, without looking up from the paper, Fran said, "Aren't you going to ask me what I'm doing?"

"I figured you'd tell me when you were ready."

"You're no fun at all. I expected some typically caustic Nicko remark about bad imitations of Gloria Swanson."

"I was thinking more of Jean Harlow."

"I'll take that." Fran sighed and put down the paper. "I've always wanted to sit here in this solarium wearing a peignoir in the morning, having coffee and reading the paper. It always sounded so elegant. So I thought I better go ahead and do it, before we lose this place."

"Where'd you get the peignoir?"

"Millie in wardrobe. Your female lead, whom you still haven't named, or incidentally found anyone to portray her, gets murdered in it, at least in the last treatment I read."

Nicko ignored her sarcasm, the dig. "We're not going to lose this place, if that's what you're getting at."

Fran gave him a look that said That's how much you know. She was a tall lean woman with green eyes and a mask of freckles across the bridge of her nose and across her cheeks; her short blond wavy hair clung to her skull like a swimmer's cap. Nicoletti grew animated again as the newspaper reminded him of what he wanted to talk to her about.

"Did you see the story in yesterday's paper about that girl?"

"Which girl, Nicko?"

"The girl they found murdered in the park."

"Oh yes, that was terrible." Fran tapped the folded paper under her elbow. "There's more about it today."

"What does it say?"

"Not much. Just going over it again, the way newspapers will. . . ."

"Did you catch it? They said her face was beaten beyond recognition. And that she was tied to a tree."

Fran just looked at him.

"That's what happens in *Blood Truth*, remember? I just looked at it again last night."

At the end of her crossed leg, the white mule with its

pom-pom slapped against her heel. Nicoletti raised his eyebrows to encourage her to go on. After a moment Fran sighed.

"Are you saying you think whoever killed the girl in the paper was like a character in your movie?"

"Or maybe the movie gave somebody the idea. Maybe it was a copycat of some kind, you know, with us being in town making a film and all. . . ."

Fran got up and started collecting her coffee cup, the paper. She was shaking her head. "I think that's a pretty obscure reference—"

"I know. That's what I'm getting at."

"What are you getting at, Nicko?" Fran said on her way to the kitchen. She was half a head taller than her husband and looked slightly down at him as she passed. For a moment he was engulfed in the scent of Joy perfume, stirred up by the breeze from the chiffon peignoir.

"I know it's an obscure reference," he said. "That's why I'm thinking we need to call it to somebody's attention. You know, the media. . . ."

Fran stopped halfway through the doorway. "You want me to send out a press release? Saying the girl's murder was a copycat of your movie? Or maybe call the police and tell them? You're not serious, tell me you're not serious."

That look. She could stop a charging rhino with an eyebrow. "You said yourself that we need as much publicity as we can get for this movie. And people are starting to get interested in my work again—"

"It's a pathetic idea and I don't want any part of it. Besides, as far as this film is concerned, that's all been decided for us. I told you yesterday, it's over."

She went on into the kitchen. He could hear her washing her dishes at the sink, cleaning up, as he continued to stand there looking out through the murky glass at the backyard, the fence surrounding the house on the opposite side of the block. Beside him was the tall crinkly trunk of a potted palm, the fronds at eye level. It wasn't that bad an idea. *And I'm standing here talking to a palm tree, an artificial one at that. Why would anyone have an artificial tree in a solarium . . .* then remembered the most important thing he needed to talk to Fran about this morning. He caught her as she was putting her cup and saucer in the dishwasher, the sleeves of the peignoir pushed up to her elbows. Nicoletti put down his espresso cup and leaned like an A-frame on the central counter across from her, working up as much enthusiasm as he could into his voice, the enthusiasm he used to sell his ideas, make his pitch. "It's not over till it's over."

Fran turned off the water, closed the dishwasher, and turned to face him, leaning the small of her back against the sink, as if bracing herself. "What's that supposed to mean?"

He mugged, pumped his eyebrows, his best I-know-something-you-don't look.

"It isn't a threat this time, Nicko. The studio was quite clear, quite definite. They have pulled out of the project, once and for all. We're officially in turnaround. It's over. We'll have to give up this place, the Gateway Towers office, the penthouse on Mount Washington, we might as well head back to LA, though I don't know where we're going to live. . . ."

"Did they give a reason? I mean, they can't just throw away a project like this without a reason, what about all the money they've sunk into it already?"

"They have a host of reasons, unfortunately. Mainly they aren't satisfied with what you've shown them in the dailies. They mentioned words like 'scattered' and 'no clear concept.' Oh, and 'a piece of shit.' Sorry."

"I told them how I was going to shoot this movie. The whole idea is to let the story line develop as we go along. To let the character development determine what happens. When I told them about it originally they loved it."

Fran rolled down the sleeves of the peignoir. "You don't get it, Nicko. They gave you the money to make this movie because the movies you did in the past showed a lot of—again, the studio's words—'tits and blood.' Not only that, but you developed a following who like your particular brand of 'tits and blood.' But that's not the kind of stuff you're giving the studio now in return for their money. They were paying you for more 'tits and blood.'"

"But I'm trying to get away from doing that kind of stuff. You know that. That's why I wanted to make this movie in the first place. I want to try to do something better." He straightened up, started to walk away down the counter, then came back, looking at her under the pots and skillets hanging over the central island. "I was looking at *Blood Truth* again and some of my other things, and it was there, Frannie, it really was there all along, people just didn't recognize it back then, what I was saying about human nature. Okay, okay, I was wrong for a while there, I know that now, I was showing too much skin, too much blood, special effects for the sake of special effects. But my basic message is still true, the terrible things people do to each other, all in the name of love. And I'm older now, I know more what I'm doing now."

Fran straightened up and moved away from the counter, looking around to make sure everything in the kitchen was in order, then looked his direction again, blinking slowly as if bored. "That's all very impressive, Nicko. But we have no money."

"There's got to be something." Nicoletti wagged his head. Grinned.

"You're not thinking of trying to go ahead with it, are you?"

"I'm shooting this morning over at Pitt. The only reason I'm still here is that I couldn't get the Cathedral of Learning until after nine. And I wanted to talk to you."

"You scheduled a shoot after I told you we're in turnaround?"

Nicoletti rubbed a spot on the granite countertop with his index finger, watched his finger for a moment, then met her eyes. All business and determination. "I've worked too hard for this to give up without a fight. Not until I've tried every possibility to keep going. Even those things I might otherwise detest."

"Nicko, don't do this. Please."

"We'll find a way. We've always found a way. You and me. We've been in worse shape than this and somehow always managed to find the money to go on."

She studied him a moment, evaluating him, then shook her head slowly as if regretting her conclusion. "Thorsten."

For a moment neither one said anything. Stood there looking at each other. Listening to the hum of the refrigerator, the distant sound of a garbage truck on another street. Fran lowered her head and started to leave, then stopped at the end of the counter and looked at him again. She crossed her arms, holding herself in the white peignoir, supporting her heavy breasts as if they were an offering on a plate.

"When the studio agreed to back this film, I thought you were the one who told me that I wasn't to see Thorsten again. Under any circumstances. I thought you were the one who demanded that I break off all contact with him. Now you want me to see him again?"

"This is different. Thorsten's a businessman, he's always looking for a good deal. And we always made money for him. Some money, at least."

"Isn't this a little too much like pimping? Even for you?"

She didn't seem angry; no, if anything it was as if she were bemused at the irony. He moved closer to her, close to the end of the counter. Close enough to touch, though he didn't reach out for her.

"I'm scared, Frannie. For the first time in my life I'm really scared. I'm scared I'll never get another chance to make another movie. And I admit it, I have no idea how I'm going to finish this one, even if I—we had the money. Maybe I've been kidding myself, trying to do something more 'significant.' Maybe all I'm good for are those—"

"Stop it! I won't listen to any of that." She walked a few steps away, toward the hallway and their separate bedrooms, then stopped and looked back at him, her voice under control again.

"I won't listen to this—"

"Frannie—"

"I said I won't listen to this. You're right, we'll find a way." She picked through the leaves of a spider fern in a planter stand, then looked at him again. "I already called Thorsten. Last night. He's flying in late this evening, I'll see him first thing tomorrow. But don't get your hopes up. Not everybody you screw is anxious to get back into bed with you."

"Obviously the same can't be said for those who want to climb back into bed with you."

"You son of a bitch."

He watched her turn and sweep out of the room and down the hallway, the heels of her mules clacking on the tiles, the white chiffon peignoir billowing in her wake like a cape, like a cloud. *Why on earth did I ever say that? She's doing exactly what I want her to do, need her to do. And she knows me so well, she went on ahead and contacted Thorsten, has already arranged to see him. Ah Frannie.* He felt the energy draining from him, his puffery all gone. *Am I really going to do this, send my wife to her lover so we can get the money we need to finish this film? I guess so. Don't blame me, Frannie. Please. I've got to do anything I can at this point. I'm dying here. If something good doesn't happen soon, there won't be enough of my career to save. Though I suppose I shouldn't feel too bad about it, we both know there's something in it for both of us when the angel from Minneapolis comes to town.*

He went back along the counter, drained the dregs of his espresso. Come on, Nicko, old son, get yourself together. Hey, even Coppola looked like he was a goner at one point, he could barely scrape together the money for the first *Godfather*, had to mortgage everything he owned to finish *Apocalypse Now*, then almost blew it all on *One from the Heart*. I can make it yet, I know I can, I just need a break, a little help. . . .

Beside his espresso cup on the counter was the newspaper. The story of the girl found murdered in the park. What did I say to Fran there, the terrible things we do in the hunt for love? Maybe that's my title, *For Love*. He toddled his stubby fingers into his salt-and-pepper beard, this time as if digging for something, folded the paper under his arm, and went to get ready for the day's shoot.

Six

The garbagemen were out on South Bouquet Street. Sam stood on the curb in the early morning light watching the large blue truck work its way toward him along the narrow street, the men in their orange coveralls appear from behind the truck, gather up the bags and trash cans and disappear again behind the truck, the sound of the compactor whining against the facades of the tall narrow houses along the street, Sam taking it all in. As the truck got closer, one of the men came forward along the sidewalk to gather the bags near Sam; the man looked at Sam as if to say What the hell you looking at, hippie?

"Hi," said Sam. "Thanks for doing this."

"Fuck you," the man said, gathering up the bags and disappearing behind the truck. As the cab pulled beside Sam, the driver, a beefy black man with an arm like a weight lifter's dangling down the side of the door, called to him.

"Hey Sam, you seen D'Angelo this morning?"

Sam shook his head. "Just getting started, James. Haven't

seen anybody yet. Just you guys."

One of the men at the back of the truck shouted, "Yo!" and the driver pulled ahead, looking at Sam in the tall side-view mirror. "You see him, you tell him I'm looking for him, okay?"

"Got it," Sam said.

The guy who looked at Sam earlier gave him another look, as if to say I don't care if you know James or not, stay out of my way. Sam smiled at him and nodded. "Peace out, brother."

He started to move on—the guy looked like he thought Sam just said something dirty to him—when he saw Carla coming down the sidewalk. Swinging along in her fringed leather jacket, tight jeans, and Cossack-style boots. He could guess how this would play out. He hurried down the sidewalk to meet her then walked along beside her, between her and the men as they approached the truck. As he expected, the men stopped what they were doing to watch her pass.

"Hey, baby, where you goin' in such a hurry?"

"You want some of me, baby?"

Sam skipped along beside her, walking sideways, grinning at the men, trying to block her from them, saying, "Gentlemen, gentlemen, please. A little courtesy, please."

"Get out of the way, faggot."

As he and Carla passed the cab, James, his muscled black arm still hanging down the door, shook his head. "You stirring up the animals, young lady."

Carla's face was hard-set, looking straight ahead, she hadn't even acknowledged Sam as yet. They were half a block down the street, Sam dodging around the garbage cans and stacks of trash trying to keep up with her, before she slowed her pace a little and glanced at him.

"Thanks, Sam. I appreciate it. I'm in no mood for that kind of thing this morning."

"I can see that. How about if I buy you breakfast up at the

O? Or you buy me breakfast, seeing as how I don't have any money yet this morning? Or maybe you buy your own breakfast and I'll sit there and look hungry? What do you say?"

They stopped as a delivery truck backed out of a driveway. Now that he got a good look at her, he could see her eyes were bloodshot, as if she had been crying or sleepless or both, but she smiled at him despite herself. "That's sweet, Sam. But I'm not hungry."

"I'll show you how to make clouds in your coffee."

"I've got enough clouds in my life as it is. I have to go see somebody."

"You don't seem too happy about it."

"I have to see Ianni."

With the delivery truck gone, they resumed their walk, Sam back to hurrying to try to keep up. "Sounds ominous," Sam said.

"One of his goons said Ianni wants me to work a private party tonight. I told Ianni when I started that I wouldn't work any private parties. That's what Sandy started doing, and look what happened to her. No way."

"And you're on your way to find Jimmy Ianni and tell him so."

Carla scuffed along in her low-heeled boots; the fringe on her jacket and the fringe on Sam's shoulder bag swung in unison.

"I'd be careful," Sam said. Across the street were the backs of buildings on the Pitt campus, the school of law. The sidewalks began to be crowded with students, more obstacles for Sam to dodge, bicycles chained to the racks in the parking.

"Why? What can he do? If he fires me I'll go to another club, that's all."

"I don't think you want to find out what he can do. Ianni strikes me as a man who doesn't take rejection well."

"Thanks for the advice, Sam, but that's his problem. I'm not going to do a private party and that's that."

Sam pulled up when they reached Forbes; he was headed downtown. "Good luck," he called after her. "I'm always around if you need something."

She fluttered her fingers at him above her shoulder without looking back. Sam watched her as she jaywalked at an angle in front of Hemingway's and headed across campus to Nirvana.

Yeah, good luck, girl, you're going to need it if you try to buck a guy like Jimmy Ianni. I better look her up later, see how it went. Kids, goddamned kids, don't know what they're getting into, waving their ass around for money, they think all they have to say is I don't want to and the whole world will stop, they don't know what these guys are capable of. That's not the way of the world. . . . He waited until she disappeared among the crowds of students close to the student union, then continued up the hill to Fifth Avenue to catch his bus downtown. He had his rounds to make.

Seven

Jeff Berner left his room at the Gateway Hilton, made sure the DO NOT DISTURB sign was secure on the doorknob so it wouldn't fall off, so there was no chance the maid would go in by mistake, and took the elevator down to the lobby. He thought of eating his breakfast in the hotel restaurant—it was certainly convenient, charging it to his room, even the tip—but he decided he was tired of that, he wanted something new, he had eaten in the restaurant every morning so far, to say nothing of lunches and dinners, he was here to have adventures and start a new life for himself, if he was going to be a star he had to get used to doing new things, handling himself in new situations. He proceeded through the hotel to the doors opening into Gateway Center and headed down the walks toward the business district.

Jeff was small for his age but of an athletic build, with blond hair that continually slipped down over his forehead in a cowlick—a feature he decided to cultivate because it gave him what he thought was an all-American look, an image he thought would be helpful in the movie roles he wanted. He had pulled out of Allegheny College a week or so earlier, before his finals, so he wouldn't be able to graduate as scheduled, too impatient to begin his acting career to wait even another month after he heard that Nicoletti was in town making a film. But despite his best efforts, there was nothing about him that would make him especially memorable to the casual observer, other than this morning, among the well-dressed people heading into the offices in Gateway Towers, the men in suits and sport coats and ties, he was wearing a red nylon anorak, chinos, and Docksiders without socks—he had read that the really cool actors in Hollywood didn't wear socks.

Nicoletti certainly wouldn't be his first choice for the director of his film debut—he was no Coppola or Lucas, Arthur Penn or Sam Peckinpah, even though his early work was compared with the others in the late 1960s and early '70s, specifically for the use of graphic violence. Nicoletti's reputation had gone downhill the last few years—a "pornographer of violence," one critic dismissed him—but Jeff thought that would work in his favor; Nicoletti would be more approachable and willing to give an unknown a break. After breakfast, Jeff thought he'd go to Nickolodeon's office and make an appointment for a screen test or whatever was needed.

He emerged from the calm and shade of the Golden Gateway into the bright sun and noise and bustle of the downtown. He crossed busy Stanwix Street and headed up Forbes into Market Square. Parked around the square were trucks making deliveries at the restaurants and bars; several semis with open trailers idled beside a demolition site for a new high-rise; and in the far corner of the square a white school bus, decorated with crudely drawn symbols in black, triangles and spirals and stars, as if someone had taken a housepainter's brush to the flat surfaces of the old bus. Near the bus was a group of young people, sitting on raggedy blankets on a section of the grass. The girls wore long dresses made from unbleached muslin; most of the young men wore tunics made from the same cloth, and all wore heavy homemade sandals. A few children, toddlers, wandered among them. Some of the group were drinking wine, others had the faraway look of druggies; the several young men of the group—there were twice the number of girls—wore curved knives on their belts. Jeff angled their direction for a closer look, he had only heard about hippie communes, he had never seen one in the flesh before. Wow, like something out of the '60s. Maybe I can get some ideas for characters.

Eight

The first thing Sam noticed when he got off the bus from Oakland in Market Square was the oddly painted school bus sitting in the far corner, the figures in white spread over the patches of grass. Normally he would have welcomed the sight, the invasion of the counterculture into the heartland of the ordinary, a breath of something different in a world of sameness, but even across the square something seemed amiss, there was a bad air about them, Sam's sensors told him they were trouble. He approached them warily, the same way he would if he suspected they were alien invaders or beings from another dimension—he wasn't discounting either of those possibilities—or zombies.

On the sidewalk in front of a section of grass, at an intersection of one of the quarter squares of the park, one of the group was putting on a show for the others. He was larger and appeared older than the rest, a bear of a guy; he wore a red top hat decorated with red and black streamers, the ribbons weighted at the ends with small bells dangling down around his shoulders, with a red vest open over his naked chest—his upper arms were massive—cutoff jeans and sandals. His face was mainly covered with a black thicket of a beard, and his hair, in dreadlocks, tangled with the streamers from his hat. He was playing a jagged, uneven rhythm on a headless tambourine as he sang meaningless syllables in a singsong voice, dancing on one leg and then the other. He ignored most of the people who passed by, but whenever a businessman or a group of men in suits and ties came by, he ran at them, singing into their faces, "Business! Business! Business! Business!" following after them, threateningly, then running back to resume his one-legged dance in front of his friends.

Standing off to the side was a young man in a red anorak, watching, a half smile on his face as if eager to join in the fun. After a few minutes, the Hatter noticed the Kid watching him and flew at him, waving his tambourine and shaking his head so the bell-tipped streamers danced in front of the Kid's face, screaming, "Business! Business! Business! Business!"

"Busy-ness! Busy-ness! Busy-ness! Busy-ness!" the Kid said back at him, grinning.

The Mad Hatter straightened up, a wild look in his eyes. "Hey, motherfucker, you making fun of me?"

The others of the tribe stopped what they were doing to watch. The Kid was taken aback, blinking as if he were just waking up. "What?"

"Don't 'what' me, cocksucker." The Mad Hatter shook his head to send the bells and streamers and dreadlocks flying.

The Kid stared at him, a sickly grin on his face; now he was aware of what was happening, and aware that it was too late to get out of it, his expression a mixture of enchantment and fear. Sam walked over to them and stood on the other side of the Hatter, hands clasped behind his back, smiling appreciatively.

"Dude, I dig your hat. Where'd you get it?"

The Hatter snapped his head around to look at him. "Who are

you talking to, freak? Who the fuck do you think you are?"

"I'm the Ghost of Hippies Past," Sam said and smiled, all charm, to the several young women sitting on the grass nearby. A couple of them smiled back. He was hoping one or two were friendly, before this was over he thought he might need all the support he could get.

"You fuck with me, ghost, and I'll send you back to rock-and-roll heaven." The Hatter was proud of that one; his bells jingled in self-congratulation.

"I don't doubt it for a second," Sam said.

The Kid was still dumbstruck with fear, more vulnerable than ever; the frightened expression on his face was an open invitation for more trouble. Sam eased himself around so he was between the Hatter and the Kid. "Where you folks from?"

"Upstate New York," said one of the girls sitting on the grass. "We're the Jackal Commune. Maybe you've heard of us."

"Yeah, we're the Jackal Commune," the Hatter said into Sam's face, spittle flying, jingling. "We came to check out Pittsburgh."

"Poor old Pittsburgh," Sam said.

The Hatter looked at him, unsure how to take the remark. Sam smiled disarmingly. The Hatter looked around at the girls for a clue as to how to treat this guy. Sam smiled at the girls too.

"We're trying to unite all cultures, you know?" another girl said. She had the remnants of what appeared to be a black eye and wore a hand-knit blue sweater, the yarn full of dried grass and snags, over her de rigueur muslin dress. As she spoke, a baby boy without a diaper or pants toddled over to her, the backs of his legs stained with feces; the mother, if that's who she was, was perhaps eighteen. "Like, to spread the best of all cultures, from one to another, you know? So people will, you know, learn to get along better in the world."

"Yeah, and we're the jackals because we live off the leavings of the lion," the Hatter said, looking around at the taller buildings beyond the Square, the demolition site.

Sam caught the eye of the Kid, nodding for him to take off, get out of here. The Kid looked at him questioningly.

"We're all for peace and love here in Pittsburgh," Sam said, trying to keep the Hatter distracted.

"Peace and love," the Hatter laughed. He picked up one of the jugs of wine lying around on the grass, tossed back his streamers and bells and nattydreads, and took a long pull. The girl was trying to clean up the baby with pieces of old Kleenex that she pulled from her sweater sleeves. The Hatter went over and sprawled on the grass beside her, his bells jingling; he claimed her dirty ankle, wrapping his hand around it like a shackle. "Fuck your peace and love, dude."

Sam nodded to the Kid again, and this time the Kid turned and started across the Square—for a brief second Sam could have sworn the Kid appeared as a darkly luminous egg, an oblong collection of dark fibers that somehow emitted a pulsing luminescence—heading out of the park down Forbes toward Stanwix.

"Keep the faith, brothers and sisters, keep the faith," Sam said, giving them the peace sign all around in farewell, and started to edge away in the same direction as the Kid. He had a momentary fantasy of trying to rescue the young mother, whisking her and the child away from the others, running through the alleys of downtown hand in hand, Sam carrying the baby, the three of them pursued by howling, scimitar-wielding muslin-clad figures—and gave up the idea just as quickly. What makes you think she'd want to come away, my friend? She probably thinks what they're doing is groovy. When he was sure the Hatter was settled and wouldn't come after him, Sam turned and hurried after the Kid.

When he got to Stanwix he saw the Kid dodging through

moving traffic on Liberty and Penn, almost getting hit by a bus—Where's he going in such a hurry? Was he that scared? It sure took him long enough to realize what was going on—walking quickly into Gateway Center. And what the hell is it with Gateway Center all of a sudden? That's where that guy watching the filming yesterday disappeared into. Holy sanctuary? Fool's paradise? Where would he be going? Sam ran to keep up, to keep the Kid in view. He followed him half a block behind along the walkways and promenades, past the office towers, watching as the Kid entered the plaza entrance of the Hilton. Sam hurried after him, following him inside and through the maze of ground-floor corridors in time to see the Kid get on an elevator. He's staying here? Far out. Hardly looked old enough. Maybe he's with Mummy and Daddy. Either way, there's got to be some money involved. What would he be doing in town all by himself staying at the Hilton? His speculations were interrupted by a guy who was obviously a house detective coming toward him across the lobby. Sam gave him the Hindu abhayamudra sign—right hand upright, palm facing out—to reassure him that he understood, bowed and took several steps backwards, then turned and hurried back the way he came, bursting out the doors into the sunlight and shadows of the plaza, thinking It's a world of wonders, a world of wonders. . . .

Nine

It had occurred to Paul lately—not as a completed thought, it was more like a suspicion, a vague notion—that much of his life seemed to have happened without him. Or rather, maybe it was that his life seemed to have happened *to* him, without his having much to say in the matter. After graduating from high school he didn't know what to do with himself, so he took a guidance counselor's offhand comment that, "Well, you could always join the army." Once he was in the army he tried to do his best, as he always did with everything, and ended up a paratrooper. Once he was a paratrooper, he was qualified to become a Ranger; once he was a Ranger, he was qualified to become a Green Beret. Along the way he progressed up through the ranks, to sergeant and then master sergeant; because he figured his primary job in the army was to fire a rifle, he wanted to do it as well as he could so he enrolled in sniper school. Eventually they sent him to a little war that few people knew was going on in Southeast Asia, years before his government would acknowledge that he or any other military personnel were there. In Vietnam he performed what were classified as special projects while spending much of his time living on his own in the mountains with a tribe of Montagnards. He became so assimilated into the life of the village that the elders gave him his own tribal name; he collected, though he wore it only on special ceremonial occasions, when it was expected of him, a necklace of ears.

As he looked back in midlife, it all seemed more a matter of chance, not choice. The same was true when he returned to the States, at the time when other young men were just leaving to go to what he heard them call The Show. He tried college for a while, at the local community college, but he was older, in more than years, than the other students and felt badly out of place. When some of the students found out he had been in Vietnam, they called him baby-killer, sometimes behind his back, sometimes to his face. When Paul wouldn't deny it—that such things happened distressed him more than his detractors could ever know—others avoided him completely, but he was secure in the knowledge that he had had a job to do, and he had done whatever the job required and done it well. He was ready to drop out anyway when his father told him he could get him a job at the mill. Though his father had worked all his adult life on the pickling line, he wanted better for his son and called in some favors to get him an apprenticeship in the pattern shop.

In a way, taking a job at the mill was a true homecoming. He had grown up with the presence of the mill dominating every facet of life in the town, attuned as much to its cycles of changing shifts, its sights and sounds and smells, as he was to the hills that overlooked the town, the river in its S curve flowing past it—that he would end up working there seemed inevitable, as immutable as a fact of nature. And from the first day he was at home in the shop environment; he felt comfortable working with the machines and tools of the trade. He applied himself as always to learning everything he could about his newfound craft, and the work was challenging enough to keep his mind occupied, to keep him from thinking about things he was trying to forget.

Even love in his world seemed to follow the laws of inevitability. He and Sharon grew up together—if she wasn't exactly the girl next door, she was at least the girl in the next block. They went to the same grade school; they didn't necessarily walk together up the hill to junior and then senior high school but the friends they did walk with were never more than half a block away from each other; they were part of the same group of kids that hung out on Seventh Avenue after school and all summer long, in front of the Blue Room or the Rexall drugstore or Mikey's All-Niter; when it came time for the senior prom, it was understood that he would take Sharon, though they had never dated before—each other, or anyone else for that matter—and he never remembered actually asking her.

The first week he was in basic training, her letters started to arrive, and they kept coming regularly, enough so that he came to expect them, and more to the point, miss them when for some reason they didn't arrive. When he returned from the service half a dozen years later, he found that she had grown into a sturdy girl with a broad, open face—not pretty exactly, but attractive— a pleasant, solid young woman with dark brown curls and unclouded green-gray eyes; it seemed only natural that they would start going out. She told him that, whenever she saw him when he was home on leave, the sight of him in his uniform—the green beret cocked at an angle, the black shiny paratrooper boots, the braided cord over his shoulder—made her toes curl. He supposed that was what love was—wasn't that the way a girl was supposed to feel about a guy? Why wouldn't he love a girl who felt that way about him?—and they were married within the year.

Everything fell into place like the tumblers in a lock. His parents wanted to fulfill their lifelong dream of retiring to Florida, so Paul and Sharon bought their house, the same house Paul grew up in, on the corner of the alley on Thirteenth Street, a block and a half below the main drag. Soon after they moved in, Sharon became pregnant with Stephen, and four years later, Mandy. They knew all their neighbors, of course, having either grown up around them or from Holy Innocents where they went to church, and had a small circle of friends, mainly Sharon's friends, girls she knew all her life and their husbands; Paul's friends consisted of the men he saw in the evenings at the VFW or Sons of Allehela or the Polish Falcons, guys he grew up with as well as their fathers and uncles though he had never been especially close to anyone even back in school, there was no one he hung out with, watched ball games with or met for a drink, he didn't know why, people seemed different since he returned, or they treated him differently—he couldn't even talk with the younger guys who went in the army when they came back, his experience there so much different from theirs—he found he had nothing to say to anyone, nothing anyone would understand.

But he wasn't thinking any of this at the moment as he crept along in traffic on Ohio River Boulevard—Route 65, Killer 65, as locals called it, from the number of high-speed accidents that occurred because of its narrow lanes, cars passing inches from each other, though you'd never know it at the moment from the slowness of the rush-hour traffic—he was functioning on pure instinct, the mechanics of the journey, making sure he was in the right-hand lane beyond the McKees Rocks Bridge, on the elevated section with its glimpses of the city ahead staying left past the turnoff for the North Shore, bearing right again into the lower deck of the Fort Duquesne Bridge and making the complicated merge across lanes to the ramp leading down into the city. And it was pure instinct, a reflex action, without realizing he was doing it, as he turned onto Stanwix Street and started looking for a place to park, his truck at a red light engulfed by pedestrians streaming across the crosswalk, when he reached under his seat and touched the .45-caliber automatic pistol, just to make sure it was there.

Ten

"Listen to this, Nathan," Sergeant MacCarron said, sitting beside him in the car, reading a paperback novel.

His hand quivered as he reached to touch her, then he ripped the soft, delicate gown from her breasts. His mouth covered hers, his hands sliding down and peeling her from the gown, branding her with a white-hot intensity that made her knees give way. His mouth slid down to her neck, then down to her breasts, his teeth biting gently at her skin while she shivered, her eyes closed.

"Does he make you feel this way?" he asked in a thick, raw voice, licking and kissing her until he thought she would lose her mind. . . .

"Great stuff, huh?" Mac said, holding up the book so White could see. "I keep telling you, Nathan, it's all right here. A good romance novel will tell you everything you need to know about the human heart and why people do what they do." MacCarron used an unopened stick of Doublemint gum as a bookmark and put the book on his lap, a canted smile on his face that Nathan could never read. "So, where's your boy?"

"Don't know," Nathan said, blowing across the top of his coffee. They always made it too hot to drink, why did they do that? "This used to be one of his regular stops, this time of morning. We'll wait a little while to see."

They sat in the unmarked car at the corner of Forbes and Stanwix, beside the McDonald's, watching the flow of traffic, the pedestrians on the sidewalks. Mac took his coffee out of the paper bag and took a large gulp of it, unfazed. How does he do that? Nathan thought. Must have a throat lined with asbestos.

"What do you know?" MacCarron said after a few minutes, nodding at the windshield toward the Point.

Sam was coming from the direction of Gateway Center, making his way from traffic island to traffic island through the complicated intersection, holding his shoulder bag close to his side.

"I'll go talk to him," Nathan said, putting his coffee cup in the holder and starting to get out.

"Figured that," MacCarron said, taking up his book again. That smile again. "He's your friend, not mine."

Nathan stood at the apex of the corner in front of McDonald's, his suit jacket open, hands in his pants pockets. Sam didn't see him at first, started through the busy traffic toward Liberty, then noticed him and came over, a large smile on his face.

"Hey Nathan—I mean, Lieutenant."

They touched the backs of their right hands, an old greeting from the days they played clubs together, both students at Pitt though Nathan a few years older, in the late '50s and early '60s, when the clubs were blues clubs tucked away on side streets in Oakland and the Hill District. Sam looked like he wanted to give him a hug but thought better of it.

"What brings you out and about? You on patrol?"

"Looking for you, actually."

"I don't know whether to be flattered or nervous. Should I be cleaning out my bag before we say anything further?" Sam was grinning, but Nathan was sure he meant it.

"Let's stand over here where we can talk," Nathan said and led the way out of the flow of pedestrians, closer to the wall of the building. As he joined the lieutenant, Sam leaned down and waved to MacCarron in the car. MacCarron just looked at him.

"Not really a friendly guy, is he?" Sam said.

"Mac doesn't like you," Nathan said.

"I've gotten that impression. And after all the information I feed you guys too." Sam leaned over and toodled his fingers at the sergeant again. "Which I'm guessing is what you're looking for now."

"You still make the rounds of the clubs at night," Nathan said, more of a statement than a question, studying the face of the other. Sam would meet his look occasionally, but then his eyes would dance away. Is he on something now? I can't tell. He was always good at that.

"Somebody has to keep track of what's going on. These kids nowadays don't appreciate the music, they have no idea what was going on back then, somebody has to keep the flame alive." When he noticed Nathan was having none of it, he shrugged. "Yeah, I hit most of the clubs. There's nothing like a sentimental drunk pining for the good old days if you want a handout."

"The girl who was murdered the other night in Schenley Park."

"Sandy Love," Sam said, shaking his head, his big hair a beat behind. "Yeah, that was really awful."

"You knew her?"

"Not in the biblical sense," Sam said, trying for a joke, then pulled it back. "Not that I wouldn't have liked to, with all due respect to the dead. Yeah, I kinda knew her, we talked a few times, but I didn't know her very well."

"Heard anything about it?"

"Not much. The girls aren't talking about it much, but it's sure freaked them out."

"Ever see anybody hanging around acting suspicious?"

"They're bars at midnight filled with drunks, Nathan, everybody looks suspicious. You remember."

Nathan had to smile. "Yeah, I remember."

"Do you still play?" Sam asked.

Nathan shook his head. "I haven't touched it in years. When Alexa had the baby. . . ." He didn't want to think about these things. "You?"

"Nah. Sometimes I think I should break it out and show these three-chord wonders what it's all about, but you know. . . ."

Yes, Nathan did know. But he wasn't going to think about that either. "Well, if you think of anything, or see something you think would be of interest, let me know." He took a twenty-dollar bill from his pocket and gave it to him.

"You know," Sam said, "the more I think about it, I did hear something about Sandy working some private parties lately. I'm not sure that's what she was doing the night she got it in the park, but I know Ianni was farming her out."

"Where'd you hear that?"

"A girl named Carla. I think it's Carla Brunnel, something like that. She worked at Nirvana with Sandy. Ianni wants to farm her out for private parties too but she said after what happened to Sandy she wants no part of it. Which leads me to believe there was some connection."

"You know where we can find this Carla?"

"I know she was headed to Nirvana this morning. She lives on South Bouquet, somewhere beyond Bates. I've been there but never noticed the address. It's down in the basement, you go between houses to find it."

"If we don't find it, we'll ask you to help."

"Uh, wouldn't want to do that. Ruin my good name, you know? Everybody knows Sam, everybody loves Sam, everybody can trust Sam. . . ."

Nathan looked at him and thought This could be me. If I had chased that musician dream far enough. Alexa saved me from that, all right, but then had to save herself. Afraid I'd pull her down. Drown her in the dark world of cops. I'm not going to think about this. "Here's my card, if you think of something or you need to contact me."

"Apparently you already know how to contact me."

As Nathan went around the car and got in, Sam went over to the closed window and gave MacCarron a wide smile, blew him a kiss. Mac started to open the door and Sam scurried down the street and around the corner. The sergeant laughed, a slightly evil cackle that suggested pleasure from questionable sources, stuck his book back in the glove compartment, got himself settled again.

"So what did Captain Airhead have to tell you? Anything worth anything?"

"I think we need to talk to Ianni again. Seems like there are a few things he didn't tell us the first time, such as that Sandy Love was doing private parties."

"No shit. Ianni keeping secrets from us. Imagine my surprise. Yeah, let's go see ol' Ianni again. I'd really like to bust that bastard for something. Just on general principles."

Nathan started the car and pulled around the corner onto Liberty. As they passed Sam scuffling along, MacCarron pointed a finger at him. Sam grabbed his chest and sunk to his knees as if mortally wounded, totally bewildering the pedestrians around him.

Eleven

Francis Paul Xavier Nicoletti buried his head in his hands.

Worked his fingers up into his bushy hair, feeling for his scalp, then scratched vigorously at his thick beard like a man digging for fleas. It was such a simple scene: Warren and Natassia come out of the doors of the Cathedral of Learning, walk across the stone balcony and come down the steps, talking earnestly, Warren telling his female colleague about his wife's infidelities, setting the stage for their own infidelities later; they should have wrapped the scene an hour ago, and yet here they were, about to do another take. But something about it just wasn't right.

"We are losing the light, my friend," Helmut the cinematographer said.

"Give me one more, only this time I want an angle from the bottom of the steps."

"I cannot. The light will be gone before I get the camera moved." Helmut nodded toward the Gothic-style building towering over them that was about to block the midmorning sun, throwing the scene into deep shadow. "To shoot it then, I would have to totally relight it, bring in the kliegs, I don't think the Kinos would cover it. We'd have to talk to Mark. More time."

Nicoletti turned away. Truth was he was having trouble keeping his mind on the scene. His thoughts kept turning to his discussion with Fran this morning. That the project was officially in turnaround, he shouldn't be shooting at all today, that according to Fran they didn't have the money to pay for the day's cast and crew and equipment; he had no idea if the studio would pick up the expenses now that they officially had withdrawn from the film. But that wasn't it. No, as bad as all that was, it was only another variation of the ever-present financial pressures he had faced on every film he had ever made. It wasn't even the wondering if Thorsten, his financial angel from Minneapolis, would come to his rescue one more time.

No, what was bothering him was the idea that Fran thought to contact Thorsten before Nicoletti suggested it to her. That she was that willing, undoubtedly that eager, to see Malcolm again, to resume their get-togethers, their little tête-à-têtes, she probably had already reserved a room for them at the William Penn. He started to picture them in bed—Stop it now. What the hell are you trying to do, drive yourself crazy? What has to be has to be. I just wish she was as eager to help me as she is to see Thorsten. During the filming of *Apocalypse Now*, Eleanor Coppola kept a journal of what Francis was going through, she published it as a book afterward, even made a documentary film out of it. That's the kind of support an artist needs. If Frannie ever cared for me like that, maybe I could have—Stop it! This wasn't like him, feeling sorry for himself. He wasn't the kind to get sad, he was the kind to get even. To try harder. Show the bastards. Helmut, a dark gaunt figure who looked as if he were plucked from a painting by El Greco, was waiting.

"What are you looking for here, my friend?"

"I want . . . intensity. That's it. I want this film, everything about this film to have the intensity, the same kind of punch to the gut as . . . like that story in the news about that girl they found in the park the other night. I want this movie to hit the viewer the same way."

The answer surprised him, but he supposed it was true in a way. He turned to face the man, digging his fingers deeper into his beard.

"What girl in what park?" Helmut said.

"You didn't see it? It was all over the news the last couple days. They found a girl murdered in Schenley Park the other night. She was tied to a tree with her head bashed in. You should keep up with these things."

Helmut shook his head decisively, one arm clasping the other. "I don't want to know about reality. What can reality teach me? I make stories, I shoot stories."

"Then imagine that kind of intensity."

Helmut shook his head all over again. "It's two different things. What you describe, and what you want to shoot here. This is just two people talking. But how can I say 'just'? This has its own kind of intensity. What is more important in the world than two people talking?"

Helmut spread his hands as if displaying stigmata. Nicko turned away. Maybe that was the problem right there. What did he know about a man and woman talking as friends? If he was honest with himself, he had never talked to a woman as a friend in his life, only as a precursor to sex. Or to see if there was the possibility of sex. Or to flirt for the fun of it as if there was the possibility of sex. The one exception turned out to be Fran. Their relationship together was only about the sex at the beginning, but over the years she had become his best friend—his only friend, truth be told—his buddy, his confidante. The friendship growing stronger it seemed as the sex drained away from them. Though sex still seemed alive and well as far as Fran and Thorsten were concerned. A sobering thought.

Now he was not only sad, he was getting depressed. He looked around quickly. The young production assistant was standing at the bottom of the steps trying to look like she knew what was going on. Before he even knew he was going to do so, Nicoletti walked away from Helmut, caught the girl's eye, waved her over to him. She came like a puppy.

"Do you have a car?" he said quietly to her, leaning toward her, talking into the side of her hair.

"Do you mean here?"

Of course I mean here, you silly twit. "Yes, do you have a car here?"

"I thought maybe you meant just in general." She leaned a little away from him, flustered, realizing he didn't want explanations. "Yes, I have a car. It's in the parking lot over there, by the museum."

"Go get it," he said taking her elbow to pull her close again, so she wouldn't lean away, speaking quietly to her. "Yes, I mean right now. Meet me over there at the corner. And don't tell anybody what you're doing. Just go. Now."

She looked startled—he almost swatted her bum to get her started—but she tottered off on her low heels, her ass working diligently within her tight chino skirt. What the hell is she doing wearing one-inch heels on location? And a skirt she can hardly walk in? She doesn't have a clue. He looked back. Helmut was watching him; the crew was watching him; Warren and Natassia were standing halfway down the steps watching him. Everyone waiting on his word. He went back to Helmut.

"What do you want me to do with it, Nicko?"

Nicoletti looked at him for a moment, not saying a word.

After a full minute, Helmut shrugged, wagged his head from side to side. "I'm sure, my friend, after twenty takes, you have something you can use."

My friend. No, I'm not your friend. You're my cinematographer. I'm your employer.

"What do I want you to do with it? I want you to shoot it again. A twenty-first time." He looked past Helmut and shouted to the cast and crew. "You heard me! We're doing it again! Now, right now, while there's still light!"

The scene exploded into activity, Warren and Natassia hurrying back up the steps, the makeup artists clustering around them as they went back inside the doors, the grips and gaffers making their last-minute adjustments, the PAs talking earnestly into their walkie-talkies. All except Helmut; he stood where he was a moment, then walked slowly back to the camera, giving his instructions to the cameraman and the grips. When he got the nod from the assistant director, Nicoletti said, "Action!" The clapper board sounded and the AD gave the cue in his walkie-talkie for Warren and Natassia to start. After a few seconds, the couple came out the door, talking animatedly among themselves, came across the stone balcony and started down the steps. But Nicoletti had already turned and walked away.

Twelve

Nirvana was in a strip of storefronts and businesses—a beer distributor; a plumbing-supply; an insurance agency—near Centre and North Craig, in an area that was neither the student district of Oakland nor the Italian neighborhood of Bloomfield, a plain stucco-faced building that, perhaps at night with the neon lights on, might convey a certain boozy promise, but in the flat light of day looked only run-down and seedy. The sidewalk cellar doors were standing open, a metal slide slanting down into the depths of the basement, but no one was around. MacCarron tried the padded, studded leather front door and found it unlocked. He stepped back and, bowing slightly, twirling his hand with a flourish, held it open for White, a smile not quite playful. Nathan gave him a sarcastic look—See? Here it is again. What's he getting at?—and led the way inside.

When they were here the day before, the lights were on as an elderly black man mopped the floor, a bartender took inventory behind the bar. Now there were red and blue and yellow strobe lights flashing in the darkness and disco music pumping away through the empty club. On the elevated stage, under the spotlights, a lone dancer, a tall girl in a green thong bikini and sheer green chemise, was dancing with her eyes closed, wrapping herself in various configurations around a brass pole. No one else seemed to be around. White and MacCarron stood beside the stage for a couple of minutes, looking up at her but the girl, if she saw them at all—she seemed in a trance with her own movements—ignored them. Finally, MacCarron looked at White, flicked his head, reached down to the lip of the backlighted glass stage, and pounded with the flat of his hand. The girl stopped and looked at them.

"Jeez," the girl said.

Nathan held up his badge. "Can we talk to you a minute?"

"You don't need the badge," the girl said, cocking her leg at him. "I knew you were cops when you came in."

"Down here please, miss," MacCarron said. "And could you turn down that music?"

"I was practicing my new routine," the girl said by way of explanation. She model-walked to the back of the stage, disappeared behind the curtain, then reappeared on their level.

"Practicing?" Mac said to Nathan as they watched the girl come toward them. "What's there to practice? Waving their ass around is the most natural thing in the world for these girls."

"Is Ianni here?" Nathan said to her as she approached.

"Nah. He left a while ago. And don't ask me when he'll be back. Funny thing, Ianni never checks in with me about where he's going and what he's doing."

"What's your name?" Mac said, hands in his baggy pants pockets.

The girl looked at him as if he were stupid, then swept her hands down over the front of her skimpy clothes. "What else? Chartreuse."

"Of course it is," Mac said.

"What's the name on your driver's license?" Nathan said.

"Charlotte Miller," the girl said. "Except I don't have a driver's license."

"I'm sure there's always somebody who's more than happy to give you a ride," Mac said, "anytime you want to go someplace."

"What's that supposed to mean?" the girl said, though smiling, knowing full well what he meant.

This is off to a rough start, Nathan thought. Hard to play good-cop bad-cop when we both look like dumb-cops.

"We're sorry to bother you . . . miss"—he couldn't get himself to say Chartreuse—"but we need to ask a few questions—"

"About Sandy Love, right?" the girl said.

"We heard you were friends with Sandy," Nathan said. He noticed MacCarron was looking at him sideways, wondering what was going on. They hadn't heard any such thing, but Nathan figured he'd get a reaction one way or another.

"Where did you hear that?" Chartreuse said, concerned.

Nathan thought the best answer was no answer.

"I knew her, all right, but we weren't friends or anything. Ianni likes it better if he thinks the girls are at each other's throats."

"And why's that?" Mac said. "Ianni afraid you girls will become lovers?"

Chartreuse looked at him as though she expected he'd think something of the sort. "He likes to think that at any moment the backstage will break out into a catfight. I think it gets him off or something."

"What about a girl here named Carla?" Nathan said.

"What about her?" Chartreuse said.

"That's unfortunate about your mouth," Mac said, looking at her with concern.

"What about my mouth?" Chartreuse said, touching her lips.

"It shoots off when it's not supposed to."

"Funny man," Chartreuse said. "Carla's the one with the mouth, boy. She's always giving Ianni grief about one thing or another. She was here earlier, talking back to him, saying she won't do this or that. She gets Ianni in a bad mood and then he takes it out on everybody else."

"Today, when she got into it with Ianni," Nathan said, "was it about working private parties?"

Chartreuse looked at him as if wondering how he knew that. "Yeah, I guess Ianni wants her to work some parties, now that

Sandy's gone, and Carla, she doesn't want to do it. Not after what happened to Sandy. She was friends with Sandy, so she knew what she'd be getting herself into."

"Do you think what happened to Sandy was the result of one of these private parties?"

Chartreuse looked around the dark room, as if wondering who might be in the shadows, who might be listening. "I wouldn't know anything about that."

"Who takes part in these private parties?" Mac said.

"Friends of Ianni, I guess. Business associates, you know."

"You guess," MacCarron said and laughed. "Like you've never been the nightly special for one of Ianni's little soirees."

"That's right," Chartreuse said, and nodded once for emphasis. "I don't have to, I'm protected."

Nathan didn't understand. Mac looked at him and grinned. "She means she's the nightly special for Ianni himself or one of his lieutenants. I'm sure she gets enough of a workout that way, don't you, Charleroi?"

"The name is Chartreuse."

"Yeah, right," Mac said. "Charleroi is probably where you're from. Somewhere down the Mon Valley."

The girl's eyes narrowed, slits of hatred. Oh good, Nathan thought, now we've really alienated her.

"Do you know if Sandy was working a private party the night she was killed, and who it might have been with?"

Chartreuse laughed. "Like I'm going to tell you something like that. If Ianni wants you to know that kind of information, he'll be the one to tell you, not somebody like me. And Ianni would be the only one who knows because he never writes anything down, he keeps it all in his head."

"A regular Einstein," Mac said.

The girl had no idea what MacCarron was getting at. Nathan took out his card and gave it to her. "If you think of anything else, please contact me. We don't want what happened to Sandy Love happening to anybody else."

Chartreuse took the card and looked at it, laughed. "White. That's funny. You don't often see a mixed couple of cops. What are you, some kind of affirmative action thing?"

"You see?" Mac said to her. "That's what I meant about your mouth."

"Come on," Nathan said, and started back through the empty club. He got to the door before he realized the sergeant wasn't with him. MacCarron was still back with the girl, holding her by the arm close to him, saying something into the side of her face. In a moment he came back through the darkness, the strobe lights isolating his progress in red and blue and yellow flashes. As they headed back outside, the daylight making him squint, Nathan said, "What was that about?"

"Miss Charleroi's probably right," Mac said as he climbed into their car and got settled, smoothing the front of his already rumpled suit jacket, clicking the seat belt. "Ianni's not going to be forthcoming about his private parties. And he's too smart to write anything down so a warrant wouldn't get us very far."

"No, I meant what was that about, with you and the girl back there?" Nathan said as he started the engine.

"Oh that? I was just making a date with her for later. Giving her something to look forward to."

As he pulled out into the traffic on Centre Avenue, Nathan didn't know if Mac was serious or not. Was it another one of the sergeant's jokes? Or would he really do such a thing, use the power of being a cop to get himself some action on the side? Nathan thought he was going to have to keep an eye on him.

Thirteen

The sidewalks and walkways of the campus were crowded with students coming and going with the change of classes; across the street on the opposite corner a vendor selling Pitt T-shirts and sweatshirts from open-air racks was doing a brisk business; traffic along Forbes Avenue and Bellefield was busy; a helicopter was coming in low, heading toward Presbyterian Hospital. But no Suzy and her car. If Suzy was her name, he couldn't quite remember. Something like that. He looked back across the campus at the Cathedral of Learning, the forty-two-story Gothic Revival skyscraper rising improbably in this part of town, at the cluster of lights and cameras and technicians gathered around the side entrance. Hoping they couldn't see him from there. I just walked away. Ha ha, just like that. Wonder what Helmut thought when he looked around for the order to cut and it didn't come. Ha ha, he might still be shooting. He looked around one more time for the girl and her car; he guessed he would have to go back to the shoot, though he had no idea what he'd say to them. Hell, he didn't have to say anything, he was the director. He took a couple steps toward the path between the hedges when there was a screeching of tires and a yellow 280Z roared around the corner and braked sharply at the curb. The girl behind the wheel.

"This is yours?" Nicko said, working to squeeze his girth into the passenger seat.

"I'm sorry I'm late," the girl said, "but traffic is all jammed up. Yes, this is mine."

"Remind me to tell bookkeeping that we're paying you too much."

"You're not paying me at all, I'm an intern." Then she looked at him and laughed gaily. "Oh you, you're a big tease, aren't you? Where do you want to go?"

I'm a big tease. I've been called a lot of things but. . . . "Downtown. To Gateway Towers. I need to go to the office."

She nodded, looked over her shoulder at the oncoming traffic, then floored it, roaring off in front of a UPS truck, slamming her way up through the gears to Fifth Avenue, then whipping around the corner to beat a yellow light, scattering a few Pitt students heading toward the student union.

"Yes, this is mine. Daddy got it for me while I was teaching in Peters. He was worried about me driving around on these Western Pennsylvania freeways in my trusty old Beetle. Actually I wanted a Porsche or Corvette, they're much more in these days, but Daddy has a friend who owns a car dealership and got a good deal. I guess I should say 'my father,' 'Daddy' makes me sound like a little girl, doesn't it? I've been trying to watch that, it's just a habit, you know, calling him that, but sometimes I slip up—oh damn you!"

They were speeding down Fifth, past the student district and the facilities of the medical center, weaving in and out of traffic, beating the yellow lights at each corner, when an older sedan came into her lane and started to block her. She whipped around the car, the bus beside them blared its horn—Nicoletti got only a glimpse of the offending driver, an elderly man in a battered Adams hat and Steelers jacket—before a red light finally caught her. As they waited at the intersection, she glared at the old man in her rearview mirror.

"If there's one thing I can't tolerate, it's incompetence."

"There seems to be a lot of it going around these days," Nicko said, feeling a little touchy on the subject. *She better not be referring to me . . . she isn't, is she?*

"I know, and there's no excuse for it. I'll bet you didn't notice my license plate, did you?"

Nicko was taken off guard. "Er, well, no. . . ."

"HYT. People think they're initials, but they're not. It stands for Help Yourself, Tootsie. That's my mantra. In this world with all these incompetent people," she said, looking at the elderly driver in the rearview mirror, "that's what you have to do, help yourself, because no one else is going to do it for you."

The bus she cut off had pulled up beside them in the bus lane;

the driver, a shovel-faced African-American, glared down at Nicoletti. He started to shrug to the man to show that he wasn't complicit when the light changed and she floored it and they leaped forward again, sweeping down the hill on Craft and then a hard right onto a ramp, never stopping as they merged with traffic, heading down to the freeway next to the river toward the downtown, past the Soho Works of J&L Steel between Second Avenue and the river, the rows of material silos and the blast furnaces and the battery of smokestacks belching smoke—Lord, he thought, the people here really live with this stuff, take it for granted, proud of its dirt and its grime and their ability to live with it—her arms straight and elbows locked, her version of a race-car driver, humming three notes of a song to herself, the wind through her open window splaying her hair. Nicko pulled the tails of his safari jacket out from under him and braced himself against the armrest; he wished he had thought to buckle his seat belt, but it was too late now. Don't want to look like her driving is bothering me. . . .

This was crazy, he knew. He left forty people, actors and technicians, caterers and teamsters, and Lord knows who all else, standing around back there at the Cathedral of Learning, waiting for him to tell them what to do next. Forty people just standing there. The idea made him giddy all over again. But he had to get out of there, get away, clear his head, there was too much crowding in on him, he couldn't get his thoughts together, about the movie or anything else. And the only place he could think to go was back to the office, maybe seeing Fran would help him get his perspective back, she had always been able to do that for him, see things clearly, put him back on track. Because he had realized as he was standing there at the shoot—the shoot he shouldn't be doing in the first place, the shoot he was pushing to do even though he probably didn't have the money to pay for it—that the reason he kept filming the same scene over and over today was that he didn't have the vaguest idea how to set up the scene that would follow it. All his technique, everything he thought he knew about making a movie, seemed suddenly to have left him. He was bereft of ideas. Adrift in his own mind.

They were speeding along Parkway East toward the downtown, beyond the noise and the smoke of the mills now, weaving in and out of traffic, the girl talking about something that he couldn't quite hear with the wind whipping in the open windows and that he didn't care about anyway. He supposed he could shoot the scene following the one of the couple coming down the steps from the Cathedral of Learning as a simple A-B sequence: A and B, his would-be lovers, walking along across the campus. There would be an establishing two shot, medium-long, low angle perhaps, the master shot that set the scene, then half a dozen exchanges of the A-B cycle as the two walk along, to create identity and intimacy for the audience. Shots of A and B never the same size, eye contact between characters maintained with a five-degree cheat, a variety of camera angles so the shots aren't always face-on . . . it was textbook stuff. Except that none of it made sense to him; it all seemed hopelessly boring and pointless; it needed the words to carry the scene, and he didn't know what the words were. He had sold the movie to the studio on the idea that the characters and dialog would develop as they went along, and the plot would develop accordingly. But the truth was he knew nothing more about the characters, or the story he was trying to tell, than when he started.

He was called back to present reality when Suzy—Is it Suzy? Shit, I wish I had paid more attention—put the 280Z into a slight four-wheel drift as she made a high-speed turn from the left-hand lane up a short ramp and shot out onto Stanwix, dusting the heels of a businessman who just made it to the center island in time as they crossed Fort Pitt Boulevard. After straightening out of the turn, fishtailing slightly when she overcorrected, the girl glanced over at him and batted her pretty blue eyes. He was about to say something but she got busy again, downshifting heel-and-toe for the stoplight at the Boulevard of the Allies.

An interesting girl. For all her showing off, she was a good driver. He was used to riding in sports cars with Fran, though his own taste ran to Mercedes sedans. Fran always made a place for herself in traffic, wherever she wanted to be; things seemed to know to get out of her way, with cars as with everything else. Suzy—I'm going to call her Suzy whether that's her name or not, I'm her boss, for God's sake—was wilder but more opportunistic. Fran was direct but never took chances; Suzy was a taker, fitting in here and there. He could appreciate that. As they waited at the light Nicko remembered what he started to say.

"I apologize for not spending more time with you. I've been meaning to ask you how the internship is going."

"Oh fine, just fine. It's all very exciting."

"Everyone treating you okay?"

"Oh yes."

"And you feel you're getting something worthwhile out of the experience?"

She nodded. "Mm-hmm."

It was not the unqualified enthusiasm he expected. Or hoped for. "I mean, that is the purpose of this, to give you the chance to learn what the movie business is all about. It's not just so I get a cheap gofer. Ha ha."

She was watching the traffic signal, as if she were watching the countdown lights at a drag strip. Ready, set, red, yellow. . . Nicko braced himself. "Well, anytime you have questions—"

Go! The light turned green, but instead of sending the car lurching forward, Suzy eased through the intersection. He looked at her to see what was wrong; she kept her eyes straight ahead but smiled, aware that he was watching her. Is she playing with me? Interesting girl. Interesting thighs too.

"Well, there is one thing I have been curious about," she said thoughtfully.

"What's that?"

"Before, in your earlier films, your camera work was always very fluid. It's one of the things you're known for. But I've noticed in shooting this film you've been keeping the camera static. I'm curious why you decided to change your style." She glanced at him, as if afraid how he might take what she said.

He studied the side of her face as they stopped at another light. It wasn't the kind of question he expected. The girl seemed to have a number of surprises.

"Give me an example of my fluid camera work."

"In *A House Turned Red*, when the woman is tied to a chair and the man beats her head in, the camera circles from a low angle and spirals up, then dissolves into another shot of the same thing, spiraling up again. I've heard a lot of people talk about the special effects in that killing scene, how realistic they are and everything, but I've always thought the camera work is what's important there. That's what makes the scene extraordinary."

They waited while a tractor-trailer made the corner before continuing on. She glanced over at him again.

"I feel stupid talking to you about this."

"Don't, please. I'm very interested. Why do you think the camera work in that scene is so important?"

"It mitigates the violence of the scene. Other directors would have shown it in slow motion or something, made the audience dwell on it. But you kept it in real time, while lifting it out of real time too. You made it lyrical, almost delicate."

"I've thought about that, actually. I've wondered if it's wrong, even immoral, to show that kind of violence as lyrical. Violence isn't that way, you know. It's a terrible, horrible thing, to beat someone that way."

"It's not wrong. You transformed it into something lasting,

something above the horror of it. It's the same thing you did with the sex scenes. That's why your early films are so important, that's why I think they influenced other directors. The problem was that the mass audience missed the point and picked up on the sex and violence as ends in themselves."

"Where did you get all these ideas?"

She lowered her eyes briefly, watching her finger trace back and forth along the bumps inside the rim of the steering wheel, thinking carefully about what she wanted to say, as they waited for the light. After she made the turn onto Penn and joined Liberty Avenue, she said, "Nobody told them to me, if that's what you mean. They're my own, I wrote a paper once on your use of the camera."

"I'd like to see it."

"You don't have to be polite."

"It's not very often somebody accuses me of that." He smiled ruefully, then reached over and patted her leg. "And I didn't mean to slight you when I asked where you got your ideas. It's just that you're the first person I've talked to in a long time who seems to have some idea of what I was trying to do in my work."

"You're not serious."

"That's what a lot of critics have said about me too." He laughed, but it seemed hollow and faraway, even to himself. The girl was full of surprises, all right. He thought he was going to dazzle her, give her a big thrill by asking her to drive him back to the office, give her the chance to be with the Important Man himself, but there seemed to be more to her than that; she made him feel that he could open up to her, that she was an intelligent, sympathetic listener interested in the things he had to say. He looked past her, at the traffic going by as they waited to turn right onto Commonwealth and circle the Golden Gateway, but his attention was focused deep within himself, talking as much to himself as to her.

"I was always amazed that so many people missed the point of what I was doing in those early films. It always floored me. With a moving camera shot, you have to be careful how you use it, how you establish it in the sequence of shots and how you resolve or anchor it at the end. At the time I did *House*, most directors would have ended that sequence with a close-up, or at least a medium shot. But I kept the camera circling, then floated it right out the door and down the hallway and out the front door into the night, with the beating still going on so you never see the terrible results. I'm not saying I invented that shot—hell, Hitchcock does something similar in *Frenzy*—the important thing is I was using the camera there to help tell the story. I wanted the camera to work as hard as the actors."

There were so many things that he had started out to do with his career, how did he get sidetracked so badly? There was a joy in working with the camera, making the visual elements work as part of the structure of a film, using the camera as something more than just a passive recorder of a scene. He understood how to make those visual elements work, understood them as well as Coppola or Scorsese or anybody, if only the studio would give him a chance. He wanted to keep working, to make a movie that would put him up there with the other significant directors of his generation; he *had* to keep working, it was the only time he was truly happy, it was the only thing that made all the other crap in his life tolerable. Talking to Suzy, he felt excited about his work again, he remembered all over again what he had set out to do with his art and why he had given up so much to keep working. Why he had even risked having Fran see Thorsten again. Oh there's still so much I want to do, so much. . . .

They pulled into the driveway in front of Gateway Towers; Nicoletti motioned for her to pull into a space marked NO PARK-ING, and Suzy turned off the engine.

"Are you all right, Mr. Nicoletti?" She was looking at him, concerned.

He blinked, slowly coming back, slowly focusing on her. "Yes. Yes, of course. Suzy, my dear, you're wonderful."

"Oh, you."

"No—oh you!" He leaned over and kissed her on the cheek. He was surprised again: she smelled like cinnamon. "Come on."

He hustled out of the car and around to her door to help her out, then led her by the hand toward the front door—the uniformed attendants smiled, nodded their recognition, one of them opening the door for them—almost dragging her. Suzy hurried to keep up, laughing. Nicko laughed too as he pulled her close to him to usher her across the lobby to the elevator, singing close to her ear, "What's the word, what's the word, my pretty little bird. . . ."

Fourteen

Back in his room at the Gateway Hilton, Jeff lay on his bed, trembling, still shaken by his experience that morning in Market Square, going over and over in his mind what had happened, why it had turned so terribly wrong so terribly fast, why the guy in the hat with the bells singled him out—what did the guy have against him? Jeff hadn't done anything to him—the threat of violence in the air, violence toward him. The guy flew at me, waving his tambourine and shaking his head so the streamers tipped with bells danced in front of my face and screaming, "Business! Business! Business! Business!" and I thought he was making a joke, I grinned at him and repeated it, "Busy-ness! Busy-ness! Busy-ness! Busy-ness!" but then the guy straightened up, a wild look in his eyes, "Hey, motherfucker, you making fun of me?" and all his friends lying around on the grass stopped what they were doing and started watching us, watching me, and all I said was "What?" trying to figure out what was happening but the guy said "Don't 'what' me, cocksucker" and he shook his head and sent the bells and streamers and dreadlocks flying and I thought he was going to hit me at any second and then that guy in the Steelers jersey with all the wild hair sort of stepped in between us and said just as calm as could be, "Dude, I dig your hat, where'd you get it?" and the crazy guy was taken aback for a moment and I took the opportunity to get away, I ran away from the trouble, I was afraid like a little kid like I've always been afraid and I ran away. . . .

He lay on his bed in a kind of daze—a waking stupor, not aware of time passing, somewhere between fear and grief and self-loathing—for one, two hours before he finally was able to roust himself, sitting on the edge of the bed for a while, hunched over, his elbows resting on his thighs, his gaze unfocused on the rug in front of him, a double vision, finally getting to his feet and walking tentatively across the room to the large front window, parting the drapes and the white sheers.

Eight stories below, taxis and cars were busy moving in and out of the driveway in front of the hotel, under and away from the marquee at the main entrance; across the street there were people walking on the sidewalk that circled the open park that fronted the Point; beyond the elevated freeway that joined the two bridges, one to the left, the other to the right, arcing away from him like wings, he could see the spout of water from the fountain at the Point, the apex of the city, the confluence of the Monongahela and Allegheny Rivers, the Ohio beyond stretching away; across the Mon, traffic streamed through the tunnel midway up the bluffs of the hillside, the toy-like cars of the incline climbing away from each other on the slanted track, there was the glint of sunlight from a car traveling along the crest of Mount Washington. Life went on.

And why shouldn't it? Nothing happened to any of them this morning, nothing changed their world. But what was he talking about? What was this big, momentous event that supposedly affected him so deeply? So a guy confronted him in Market Square, so the guy came at him and called him a cocksucker and motherfucker, acted like he wanted to hit him. The guy didn't hit him, the guy didn't do anything to him but talk to him, say a few harsh words to him. Big deal. It wasn't as if the guy actually did something, hit him or something. The thought made him depressed all the more. What was wrong with him? Why did little things like this affect him so much? Nothing happened; he had to keep telling himself that: nothing happened.

He had to get over it, forget about it, move on. Sitting on the desk, among his spare change, room keys, car keys, wallet, brochures for sights and events around town, was his copy of *Dramatic Readings for Auditions*—he still hadn't decided which selection to use for his audition or screen test at Nickolodeon, when it came up. He leafed through the pages of the well-worn paperback, remembering readings he had done in drama classes at Allegheny College:

O, what may man within him hide,
Though angel on the outward side!
How may likeness made in crimes,
Making practice on the times,
To draw with idle spiders' strings
Most ponderous and substantial things!

He tossed the book down again, feeling ridiculous and embarrassed, then laughed at himself. He better be careful, someone might see him from the street or somewhere, think he was a crazy man. But he was feeling better, feeling better about himself, about the world in general, he couldn't let what happened in Market Square get him down.

He had planned to go to Nickolodeon's offices today, now he

was determined to do so more than ever; he'd go across the plaza to Gateway Towers, find out what floor their offices were on, sign in or do whatever was required, take care of the paperwork before he talked to them about an audition or screen test, make his presence known to them, let them know he was available. Yes. He pulled his red nylon anorak over his head—no need to get dressed up for this, he was only going to find out some information—felt happy again, happy to be doing something, on the road to making his career happen. When he left his room the door closed behind him with a resounding thud.

The sun was high in the sky now, flooding the plaza between the hotel and the Towers with light, the elevated flower beds crazy bright with reds and oranges, tulip heads nodding in unison with a slight breeze, rippling along the line. An elderly man in a tweed cap and tweed jacket sat on a park bench, arm out-stretched as if welcoming the day or anyone who might happen along; Jeff smiled at him, said, "Good morning, sir." The man just looked at him. Maybe he's deaf, didn't hear my greeting, to hell with him. Jeff walked on, watching his reflection growing in the glass doors of the Towers.

As he entered the building, across the lobby on the street side, Francis Nicoletti was coming through the doors, escorting the pretty blond girl Jeff had seen before coming in and out of the building. Nicoletti was draped over her, holding her close as if ready to engulf her, absorb her, like a bear or yeti, his hands on her shoulders, guiding her this way and that, as if she were unable to move on her own. The elevator doors opened just as Jeff met them halfway across the lobby and Nicoletti moved the girl inside the open car, turning her around at the back of the car to face him, so that Jeff could see her face in the mirror lining the back of the car, both Nicoletti and the girl looking at him. He could see himself in the mirror too, and for an instant he saw himself as they must see him, standing there in the lobby, a hopeless figure in a red nylon jacket, looking lost, uncertain.

"Well, you coming?" Nicoletti said to him.

"No . . . go ahead," Jeff said, feeling a wave of embarrassment wash over him, turning away.

Nicoletti shrugged and the doors closed. As the car ascended he heard them laughing together, the sound growing distant in the shaft, rising into the building. Jeff knew they were laughing at him.

Fifteen

Fran Nicoletti heard them before she saw them. Heard the elevator doors open down the hall, the two of them giggling, then Nicko's hushed voice saying that they should keep it down. That brought another round of giggles. Fran leaned away from her desk so she could see the doorway through the outer office. Nicko was coming in from the hall, framed by the open doorway, leading Suzy by the hand; when he saw Fran, he stopped so suddenly that Suzy bumped into him. To Fran's way of thinking they were acting like schoolchildren. Like lovers. He certainly didn't waste any time, did he? As soon as he knew I would see Malcolm again. . . .

But it didn't surprise her. Nicko couldn't help himself when there were attractive young women around, attractive young women who invited him to explain things to them—he who was always so good at explaining things. She should know, she was one of them herself, once upon a time. As Fran went back to the papers on her desk, Nicko sent Suzy on some errand in the other office—with a pat on the ass? She didn't want to know. He came into her office doing his little-boy-humble routine.

"You're here," he said.

"Of course I'm here. I'm always here. All of me," she said, turning toward him slightly and displaying her chest—then hated herself for it, hated to have him think that she was in any way competing for him. Turned back to her papers. "And I thought you were on location at the university."

"I asked Suzy to bring me in." Then he stage-whispered, "That's her name, isn't it?"

"Yes, Nicko," Fran said in an equally phony whisper. "That's her name."

Then he continued to just stand there, looking at her, his hands buried deep in the pockets of his safari jacket.

"And?"

"I had to get away for a while."

She turned in her chair to put a folder in the hanging file in her desk drawer, turned back again, focusing her attention on the papers and folders in front of her. Come on, Nicko, out with it.

"So, here you are. The both of you."

"Yes. Well." He laughed a little.

"I can see the shoot getting along without her. But I would think it might be a little difficult without the one calling the shots." She didn't look at him, she wouldn't give him that satisfaction, busied herself with her papers. Then she sighed and looked at him after all. Furious with herself for weakening. "What do you want, Nicko?"

"Nothing. I don't know. I was having trouble on the set, figuring out what to do next. I thought maybe you might have some idea—"

"Maybe that's what the studio was trying to tell you all this time. Free-form might sound good in a pitch, but it's ideas on paper that gets things accomplished."

"Those bastards. If they'd only give me more time. . . ." He started to turn away, wrapped up all over again in his anger, then turned back to her. "Any word from Thorsten?"

"So that's what this is all about. Why you apparently just walked off a ten-thousand-dollar location shoot, that we can't pay for anyway, and brought your pretty little thing in here to flaunt her in my face. . . ."

Suzy appeared behind Nicko in the doorway. Smiling. Watching the two of them like a spectator at a tennis match.

"I just thought maybe you heard something from him."

"You mean like a little singing telegram saying he's on his way?"

"Jesus fucking Christ, Frannie!" he exploded. "This is no fucking game! I need to know if he's going to come in on this movie!"

There you are, Suzy dear. An example of the famous Nicoletti temper. Sure you want to get mixed up with it?

"I told you this morning at breakfast. He gets in this evening, and I won't know anything until I talk to him tomorrow. Until then we both have to wait. Even though I know how much you hate to wait for anything." She looked at Suzy and raised her eyebrows.

Nicko looked at the floor, glanced over at Suzy and back at the floor again. "I just to need to know, that's all. . . ."

Fran swiveled a few degrees to the left, a few degrees to the right, then back again. Thoroughly, she had to admit, enjoying herself. How does it feel to be the powerless one for once, husband o' mine? Then Nicko's head snapped up, ready with his next idea.

"Is there anything I can do? Should I call him tonight when he gets in?"

"I can assure you the last person he wants to talk to at this time is you. If things go well, we'll see later on. I suspect he'll probably just want to deal with me, as he has in the past. I still have to convince him that he can make money on the deal, even coming into it this late."

"You'll see him at his hotel?"

Fran didn't say anything. Volley, serve.

"So I can assume you'll be indisposed the rest of the day. Tomorrow night too."

"You bastard, Nicko," Fran said, not loud but with venom.

"This is what you wanted, you got me into this—"

"Careful," Nicko said, nodding to Suzy in the doorway. Aware that Nicko meant her, the girl became absorbed studying the movie posters on the wall.

"Oh yes," Fran said and smiled at her. "Must be careful of the children."

Nicko came across the room quickly—Is he going to hit me?— but it was only Nicko being Nicko, excited at his latest idea.

"Well, it doesn't matter whether he wants to see me or not. We'll have a party in his honor, a reception, we'll invite all those Pittsburgh society folks who are always inviting us to their charity balls and events. All those hangers-on and wannabe movie folks from Squirrel Hill and Fox Chapel—"

"Nicko, don't—"

"Don't what, Frannie? Don't keep trying to work every angle we can so we can make this film? Not on your life." He looked at Suzy standing in the doorway, her worried, anxious, unsuspecting face. "Not on your life too," Nicko said to her.

Suzy broke into smiles, having no idea what they were talking about, only knowing that she was included, that Nicoletti had included her. The man could break your heart, Fran thought. Her heart went out to him, he was trying so hard, he always tried so hard. And for a brief instant it occurred to her that maybe they could start over, just the two of them. They had been through so much, maybe they could rebuild what they once had together. Nicko still got offers occasionally to direct other people's projects, maybe she could round up more of those for him, and they could do commercials, TV productions, promotion videos. In time, if things went well, they could resurrect this film, or do another one that Nicko was more sure of. In that instant she saw the two of them again when they were younger, kids really, bundled up in sweaters and blankets and anything else they could find to keep warm, sitting on the bed in the cheap hotel where they lived while making his first film, *Death Dealer*, Nicko working on the script while she worked on the production schedules; in that same instant, she saw them putting their work aside and rolling together giggling over their papers. She wanted to go to him, to stand and walk into his arms and hold him and tell him how much she loved him—and she would have too, if Suzy wasn't there. But that was the point, wasn't it? She was there.

"We stopped talking to those people and going to their affairs months ago, and we weren't very nice about it either, because you thought those people were phonies and you didn't want to talk to them, to answer all their inane questions and comments about your films."

"Well, I'm ready to talk to them now," Nicko said, looking at her and then to Suzy and back again. "We'll make it a celebration of starting out on our own. It won't be a wrap party, it'll be an unwrap party. A celebration of saying 'Fuck the studios.' And Malcolm, our angel from Minneapolis, will be the guest of honor, whether he decides to come or not. By the time we chat up all these Pittsburghers, get them interested in the film and let them know we're looking for a few select investors to come in on it with us, they'll be fighting among themselves for a chance to get a piece of it. Who knows, before we're done we might not even need Thorsten's money. Wouldn't that be a corker?"

Nicko laughed to Suzy and clapped with delight. The girl beamed back at him, wide-eyed with admiration. Fran reached for her pack of cigarettes then didn't have the strength to take one out. The man, the man.

"Even if you can get anybody there at this late date, I won't have people spilling drinks all over that beautiful house. We can't afford to pay the damage when the lease runs out."

"Then we'll have it at the apartment. That's even better, it'll help justify it as a production write-off."   ·

"It's certainly appropriate, because we're about to lose it too."

She felt so tired she could barely keep her eyes open.

"Good. We won't have to worry if the neighbors complain we're making too much noise. And Sunday we can take a couple of the most likely prospects up to the cottage at Seven Springs. I suppose we're losing that too."

"I'm not going."

"To Seven Springs?"

"To any of it." She regarded him from her position, slouched back in her desk chair, the picture of exhaustion. Then she roused herself and got busy again, shuffling through the papers on her desk, though she could feel him watching her; he wasn't the only one who could go on, business as usual. "I'll make the calls to set it up, if you want me to. But the party you're describing sounds as phony as the phonies you hope to bilk. And I'll tell you right now, Malcolm not only would not come to a party like that, if he hears about it he'll also think less of you as a person than he already does."

She thought this time Nicko was going to hit her for sure. Go ahead, do it, get it over with, you'll feel better for it. I'll feel better for it. But after a moment, his eyes like two gun slits, he looked away, down at her desk, absently, not really seeing it at first, the in-box, then focused on the pink slip of paper on top, the while-you-were-out message addressed to him, picked it up and read it.

"I'll take care of it," Fran said.

"Who's Janet Rawlins?"

"*Rolling Stone.* They were going to do an interview."

He nodded as he remembered. "When?"

"Tomorrow. That's probably what she called about, she was supposed to get back to me to confirm. I'll give her some excuse."

"Excuse? For what?"

Fran looked at him. "They were planning a feature on the film."

"So?"

"Nicko—"

"Tell her I'll see her here tomorrow morning as scheduled. That'll be fitting—I'll do the interview with her while you're doing your thing with the angel from Minneapolis. Perfect."

Before Fran could say anything, Nicko whirled around, grabbed Suzy by her upper arms as if trying to compress her, and moved her toward the door, speaking into the side of her hair though looking at Fran over his shoulder, making sure Fran heard him. "Come, my little chickadee, we're going to make a movie."

Sixteen

He parked his pickup in Market Square, as close to the spot where he had parked the day before as he could get, though this time he made sure he wasn't in a commercial zone, and retraced his steps to the corner of Stanwix and Liberty where he had watched them filming the day before. But there was no sign of Nicoletti's movie company, no sign of the crew or the staged accident, no sign that anything had ever happened there. On the chance that he might run into the girl again, he crossed the street into the Golden Gateway and followed the tree-lined walks, the flower beds crazy with tulips, past the fountain to the Hilton, stood at the table where he'd had his coffee the day before—the sparrows still bounded between the tables looking for crumbs, he liked to think that they were the same ones he saw then—watching the entrance to Gateway Towers, searching the wall of windows for a glimpse of her, knowing it was foolish, knowing he was being stupid, until a waitress came over and asked if he wanted something. He muttered no and, his head down, embarrassed, hurried back up the paths to the sidewalk again.

From there he began a systematic search to see if they were filming somewhere else in the downtown, following instinctively the methods he used in another time in a far-off country for another purpose entirely, moving in concentric arcs radiating out from the Gateway, back and forth from one side of the Golden Triangle to the other, from one river to the other, verifying that one sector was clear before moving on to the next, through the busy midmorning streets until he was certain Nicoletti and his crew were nowhere around and he was back where he started.

Across the street was a McDonald's—he could smell it from here—wedged into the point of a complicated seven-way intersection. Suddenly he realized how hungry he was, as if he hadn't eaten for days. Sharon always packed him a midmorning snack in his lunch box, but he didn't want to go back to his truck, for one thing he was afraid he'd be tempted to give up and head back to Furnass, back to work, as if nothing had happened; besides he wanted something different, this was supposed to be a day for differences, for doing something out of the ordinary, the unexpected, he couldn't remember a time when he had been to a McDonald's without his family, especially at this time of the morning when he was supposed to be at work.

But the moment he stepped in the door he wished he hadn't. The place was full of the same riffraff who took over the benches in Market Square, the homeless and down-and-outers, druggies and dealers, bag ladies and drunks. He hadn't taken off work and come to the big city for this. But he was here now, he didn't know where else to go, and when a tired black teenage girl behind the register looked at him and said "Next," he ordered an Egg McMuffin and coffee and took them to a table next to the window, as far from everyone else as he could get. He was getting settled, had his first sip of coffee, opened the wrapper of the sandwich, when the guy he saw yesterday at Nicoletti's shoot, the weirdo in the Steelers jersey and long hair, Sam, put a coffee cup on the table and slung his shoulder bag with the long fringe over the back of the chair across from Paul. The bag started to slide off; Sam reset it, giving it a stern look and pointing a finger to order it to stay put. The bag slid off regardless. Sam shrugged and made a face as if to say, Well, what did you expect? and set the bag on the seat. He looked around at the other tables for something, then said to Paul, "Don't go away. I want to show you something."

The guy threaded his way through the tables back to the counter. As he stood in line, he called to Paul, "You want anything while I'm here?"

Paul tried to ignore him, as if he didn't know who the guy was speaking to. He considered getting up and leaving before Sam returned but was conscious that people would notice and think it odd. I just want to be left alone. Why can't people leave me alone. . . ? He worked to get control of himself, the techniques that were second nature to him now, box breathing, four seconds deep inhale, four seconds deep exhale, he could feel his center coming back to him, one hand resting on the other as if holding it in place, waiting to see what Sam would do next.

"Here we go," Sam said, returning with an aluminum cream pitcher. He sat down opposite Paul and got himself settled as if preparing for a presentation. "Funny people. They were guarding this cream pitcher like it was the only one in the world. They should know the world is full of cream pitchers. I know, I know, you're going to say, 'Maybe they only have the one cream pitcher.'" Sam leaned forward, squinting with one eye, pirate-style. "Aye, matey, and right you'd be too. But then we'd be talking about their lack and not the world's, *n'est-ce pas*? Watch this."

The guy hunched down until he was almost on a level with the paper coffee cup and slowly poured in some cream along the edge. He watched it for a moment before straightening up again; he sat back with his arms folded, obviously disappointed.

"Hmm. It's usually better than that. Maybe the cream isn't cold enough. Or maybe it's too cold. Or maybe the coffee's not hot enough. Or maybe it's simply a case of it's not supposed to be. Maybe it's a manifestation of God's intervention into the most trivial affairs of mankind. And womankind. On the other hand, maybe it's an example of divine providence, maybe it was never supposed to happen in the first place, or maybe it's proof that God is really the Great Blind Indifference after all. Who knows? That's why they call them mysteries. I'll bet you never thought a cup of coffee could get so complicated, did you?"

Sam smacked his lips and looked at Paul.

I'm not going to say anything, I'm not going to do anything to acknowledge him and maybe he'll go away. . . .

"Well, as long as you're not in a hurry, let me try it again."

He hunched down a second time and slowly poured in some more cream. Paul, against his better judgment, watched what he was doing. The cream appeared as a dull tan layer beneath the surface of the coffee.

"That's something like it, but it's still not very good. The world is fraught with disappointment, pilgrim. Fraught, fraught."

Paul had only a vague idea what the word "fraught" meant—was the guy trying to make fun of him? He was watching Sam with cold blue eyes; Sam seemed to take it as encouragement.

"See it? See the way the cream's churning around in there, rolling over itself? Sort of looks like clouds rolling across the sky, doesn't it, the way storm clouds roll in sometimes? Has to do with the coffee being hot and the cream being cold, the opposition of natural forces or some such thing, laws of thermodynamics. You have to be careful adding the cream, but sometimes it'll go on that way for a couple of minutes. I figure that's where the line from that song came from, 'I got clouds in my coffee, clouds in my coffee. . . .' You know the song I mean?"

Paul gave a slight shake of his head.

"If I'm not mistaken, I believe I saw a little movement there, a little twitch of a response, a chink in the great stone face. Am

I to take that as a negative?"

Despite Paul's efforts to ignore the guy, he was amused by Sam's antics and oddball enthusiasms; and it wasn't his nature to be impolite. *The guy seems harmless enough, he's just a little kooky. . . .* "I don't keep up with popular music."

"No, I don't suppose you would. Too frivolous for a serious type like you."

"It's not that—"

"You don't have to explain. The world needs all kinds. And it's good to know there's somebody out there balancing out the superficial guys like me. Still, I would have thought you were the right age for that song." Sam suddenly learned forward and pointed to the bracelet on Paul's wrist, a simple brass ring with hash marks in a crude design. "That's the real thing, isn't it? Degar."

That he knew the less familiar name for the Montagnards impressed Paul—*What's this guy want? What's his angle?*—but he stayed cautious.

"I've seen a lot of imitations, but that's serious shit." Sam straightened up, looked at Paul differently. "Well, yes, that would explain a lot. Yes, it would. Bet you got that before they became a cliché. I don't even want to know."

Sam closed his eyes and put his hands up, waving them beside his ears. Then he was all smiles, a different Sam.

"So, you here again to watch them filming?"

"They're not around today."

"Which means you've already checked. Interesting. You don't look like the film-buff type. Oh, wait, I get it. You're not here to watch them make a movie, you're here to watch Suzy."

Paul stood up quickly, sending Sam juking backward.

"Whoa! Must've touched a nerve there."

I got to get out of here. I'm going to hurt somebody. As Paul started toward the door, Sam called after him, "They're at Pitt today, out in Oakland."

Paul, at the door, looked back at him. Sam shrugged. "Just in case you're interested. Hey, you mind if I eat this?" he said, pulling the wrapper with the Egg McMuffin toward him.

Seventeen

"I'm sorry you had to hear all that," Nicoletti said as he got into the car on his side, Suzy on hers.

"It's okay," Suzy said. As they leaned in to get settled in the confines of the car, their heads brushed each other. Making them both smile.

"That's Frannie for you," Nicko said, buckling up. "She sounds all high and mighty about not coming to the party. Truth is she never liked the apartment to begin with, even though she was the one who pushed for it to present a certain image. The same with the place in Seven Springs. Well, for once I'll put these places to good use, why we spent the money for them in the first place."

He looked at Suzy but the girl only pumped her shoulders once as she started the engine and began to pull out of the driveway. Having no idea what he was talking about. "Turn left, turn left," Nicoletti said, almost reaching over and helping her turn the wheel. Suzy followed his direction and at the end of the block headed back down Commonwealth in front of the Hilton. At the red light, he pointed to the windshield, to the bluffs across the Mon, the row of buildings along the crest line, the spire of Saint Mary of the Mount, the apartment towers. "It's that one, the white one right behind the incline. The view is tremendous, I'll get people at the party who just want to see the inside of the place." Nicko thought a minute, then put a hand on Suzy's leg. "And how about you, young lady? Would you like to see the view from the top?"

When the girl just looked at him, puzzled, Nicko thought,

Good grief, do I have to explain everything to her? Wonder what else I'll have to explain.

"I'm asking you to the party on Saturday night. I want you there, you can be my date. Seems like my wife has her own plans for the weekend."

"Are you sure it'll be all right with Fran?"

"What do you care?"

Suzy smiled prettily, batted her eyes at him, and floored it when the light turned green to beat the oncoming traffic, heading up the Boulevard of the Allies back to Oakland.

Eighteen

When she heard, a short time later, the elevator return to the floor with its telltale *Bing,* heard the doors open and someone step out—there was a loud *Clack!* as a heel caught on the metal threshold—she didn't really think it was Nicko coming back to see her, to talk to her again, to try to set things right between them, she didn't really hope it was Nicko, coming back, feeling sorry or bad or simply that he wanted to see her again, and yet she did too, she did hope, somewhere in her mind, that it was Nicko, thinking instead that it was undoubtedly someone else, one of the secretaries or executives from another office on the floor, coming back from lunch, or a delivery boy or messenger— in fact she barely thought about it at all, barely acknowledged it, thinking it was nothing to think about, about who might have gotten off the elevator, and went on with her work, looking over her list of possible big-money donors in Pittsburgh, the list she made for herself when they first came to Pittsburgh, just in case of an emergency such as this, the people in the local arts scene whom she might contact for Nicko's party at this late date, the culture vultures who might be starstruck and desperate enough to want to drop money into Nicko's charity pot, until she realized that she hadn't heard anything after whoever it was got off the elevator, hadn't heard anyone come down the hallway or go into another office, hadn't heard any movement at all. She looked up and listened. Nothing, no one. The building was silent. Beyond the large window beside her desk, the traffic on the ramps to the bridges at the Point moved silently. She leaned back so she could see the patch of hallway through the open door; the only sound was the squeak of her office chair. She wondered if there was anyone in the offices farther down the hall, if anyone would hear her if, for some reason, she called out. Called for help.

You're being silly, little girl. Maybe someone got off on the wrong floor and hopped right back on the elevator again. She was just jumpy today, exhausted, that was all. It wasn't every day your husband loses his project, goes ahead and spends thousands of dollars he doesn't have, pimps you out to an ex-lover, and then introduces you to his latest plaything. She started to go back to her work when one of the shadows in the hallway moved.

"Hello?" She caught the apprehension in her voice; she made sure her voice was firmer when she spoke again. "Can I help you?"

The shadow, having shifted once, didn't move again.

"Hello," she said again, starting to get angry. Was someone trying to play a joke on her? Nicko? He used to love to play jokes on me. . . . She pushed her chair back from the desk; with the sound of the squeaking casters, the shadow moved, came toward the door, the figure of a man. Fran's stomach felt as if it were in her throat. What's the matter with me? I never get uneasy like this, I must really be tired. A young man appeared in the doorway.

Fran laughed out loud.

The young man—he looked more like a boy dressed-up pretending to be a young man—blushed.

"Can I help you?"

"I'm looking. . . , the boy-man hesitated, "for Francis Nicoletti's office."

"With an *i* or an *e*?" Fran said sarcastically, relieved.

"Huh?"

Huh, Fran thought. "Fran*cis* or Fran*ces*?" She exaggerated the enunciation of the words, mouthing them at him, aware that he was embarrassed and confused but unable to stop herself from making it worse for him.

The young man forced a smile while he tried to figure out what she was talking about.

Her own fear gone, Fran relaxed, in control of herself and of the situation again. The young man was wearing a light blue corduroy leisure suit, the jacket more like an overshirt, with small buttons up to the neck and flap pockets, worn open to show the shirt underneath, the sleeves rolled up once to show the lining; his matching bell-bottom trousers dragged on the floor at the heels of his brown platform shoes. He was either parodying being dressed up, or worse, he thought he was being serious about it; these were probably his good clothes while he was in college, for going to discos and parties, something he bought at Sears or J. C. Penney, and he wasn't aware that they weren't appropriate for business occasions. She couldn't help it, she laughed again.

Corduroy Boy looked around helplessly.

She thought again that she was alone on the floor; they were going to have to do something about that, they couldn't have people wandering in this way, someday it could be somebody dangerous.

"I'm Mrs. Nicoletti and these are Nickolodeon's offices," she sighed, weary of playing with him. She arched her eyebrows and closed her eyes. "Maybe that will help you out."

"I came to audition . . . to read for Mr. Nicoletti."

"Oh." She opened her eyes again and stared down at her desk. Nicko hadn't told her that the casting agency was sending someone, he was forgetting to tell her what she needed to know to run the business. That explained why the young man looked like this,

Nicko must be casting for a nerd. She started looking through her piles of papers for her employee records. "They didn't tell you to go out to the location?"

"No, I—"

"Well, let me see your slip," she said, extending her hand. The young man just looked at her.

"I don't have a slip."

"Didn't the agency give you a slip?"

"I didn't come from an agency. . . ."

"Then who are you?"

"My name is Jeff Berner. Jeffrey Berner."

"Who sent you?"

"Nobody."

"You mean you just walked up here and thought you'd get an audition?"

Jeff looked around; then he grinned at her, trying to be charming. "No, actually I rode up in the elevator."

Fran leaned back in her chair and laughed again, throaty, hard, showing her bad teeth, aware that she was laughing at him and unable to stop herself. It felt good to laugh, she felt better than she had all day.

"Oh dear," she said, pretending to wipe a tear from her eye. "Let me see, I suppose you were in a couple of plays in college, and you've seen a couple of Francis Nicoletti films, and you heard he was making a movie here in Pittsburgh. So you came here because you thought it would be easier to break into movies here than in Hollywood. Am I right?"

She had turned sideways and was leaning back in her chair, her legs crossed outside the well of her desk. From where he stood in front of her desk, the young man kept glancing at her legs. If he wants a show. . . . She uncrossed her legs and crossed them again, taking the opportunity to hike her skirt a little higher, exposing her mid-thighs. Pretty legs, little girl.

"I think Mr. Nicoletti is a great director—"

"I doubt that. Even I don't think he's a *great* director. But no matter, directors choose their actors, not the other way around. Unless you're Paul Newman or Robert Redford, and for the time being I don't believe you're on that level."

"I didn't know how to go about—"

"You get yourself an agent and you get a portfolio of publicity photos and you start going around to casting agencies and try to find parts, like everybody else. You don't wander into a production company and say here I am, I want to be a star."

"I didn't say that."

"Well, it amounts to the same thing."

She laughed again but she noticed Jeff Berner wasn't smiling now. He had become solemn, withdrawn, as if his eyes had receded into the youthful puffiness of his cheeks, an angry child of a size to do something about it.

"I don't think you should laugh at me. I didn't know how these things worked."

"I'm sorry if I hurt your feelings. But you better get used to that, there are a lot of hurt feelings in this business. Sometimes I think the only thing this business does is hurt people's feelings. Look, you run along and get your act together and maybe in ten years or so Francis Nicoletti will call you. But until then I suggest you learn how this industry works before you go around taking up anyone else's precious time. At least learn enough not to come around during lunch hour. And for heaven's sake, unless you're trying out for the part of a car salesman, get yourself some decent clothes."

She tucked her legs back under her desk and busied herself with her papers again, dismissing him. It's for his own good, she told herself, he has to grow up and get into the real world. They'll eat him alive. . . . He stood there a moment staring at her. When she glanced up at him, his eyes had narrowed to slits, no longer angry but something else, something blurred and undefined. Then he turned and left.

She waited until she heard the elevator return to the floor, heard the same *Clack!* as he dragged his heel over the threshold, heard the doors close and the elevator descend again, before she got up and went to the door. The hallway was empty; there was no one there. She walked down to the elevators to make sure. There was nobody there, he was gone. She laughed out loud as she went back to her office, her laugh echoing hollowly down the narrow corridor, in and out of the empty offices. Little girl, you need a drink. But a deep shudder ran through her.

Nineteen

He thought he'd probably have to drive around Oakland awhile to find where Nicoletti was filming at the university. But coming up Forbes past the main campus he saw the crew set up beside a walk between the Cathedral of Learning and Heinz Chapel. He circled the block until he found a space near the line of equipment trucks and Winnebagos parked along the curb beside the expanse of lawns. As he walked between two of the trucks, one of the crew was coming across the grass carrying a light stand, the heels of his cowboy boots sinking in the grass.

"That asshole doesn't know what he wants," he said to Paul. Paul nodded, the understanding between workingmen about the nature of bosses.

He followed the trail of cables and electrical wires across the grass to the top of a terrace overlooking the shoot on the level ground in front of the chapel. Along the walk were several batteries of lights, microphones, a camera on a dolly, and two dozen people standing around, centered around a man and a woman, Paul assumed they were actors, looking like college professors, the man with a pipe, the woman with an armful of books, talking to Nicoletti. The director was gesturing animatedly, taking turns at what seemed to be making fun of the way each of the actors had been walking, then demonstrating how he wanted each to walk, how he wanted them to relate to each other; the couple watched Nicoletti without comment though their body language said they weren't happy. As Paul watched Nicoletti got out of the way and motioned them to try the scene again. Suzy hovered near Nicoletti, holding a clipboard but with apparently nothing else to do. After fifteen minutes or so of the crew taking light readings and adjusting the banks of lights and reflectors, makeup women dashing into the scene and out again applying a touch of powder here, wiping a bit of sweat there, they were finally ready to roll. At the call of "Action," the actors started down the walk again, talking to each other, as the camera off to the side rolled along a few feet in front of them, everything going along well until the camera rolled off the tracks on which it was mounted and nearly tipped over.

Paul could hear Nicoletti's swearing all the way to where he was standing on top of the bank. He grinned to himself; so much for all your carefully laid-out plans. Situation normal: all fucked up. Paul watched a few minutes as Nicoletti stomped off toward the cathedral and the crew tried to right the camera, but it was obvious nothing was going to happen for a while. Suzy stood with a number of others as the camera crew struggled to repair the tracks but there seemed no way for Paul to talk to her. What did you think, fool? That you were just going to walk up to her and say, "Hi, remember me? I saw you last night on your way back to your office." He shook his head at himself, took one last look at the proceedings and was starting to turn away when Suzy broke away from the group and waved in his direction. He looked around, thinking she must be waving to someone behind him, but no, she was waving at him, her arm extended straight up over her head, her hand flapping like a semaphore, as she came toward him and up the steps to the top of the terrace. Me?

"Hello there, I thought it was you," she said, walking across the grass from the steps, a happy smile on her face. "You're the nice man who helped with my drippy bags yesterday."

"I didn't think you'd recognize me."

"Of course I recognize you. You were very nice to help me."

She was dressed the same as the day before—tight tan skirt, a blue checked blouse with a white sweater over her shoulders held in place by the top button, low-heeled pumps—he wondered if it was a requirement for her job. There was a breeze and she tossed her head to keep her hair out of her face, shielded her eyes with her hand as she squinted up at him at an angle. Paul glanced around, afraid to look at her too closely, afraid he might scare her away. Several robins were working the grass a few yards from them.

"I see you're still making friends with the birds," she said. "I'll try not to scare them away this time."

"I don't think you have to worry," Paul said, noticing the birds for the first time. "They seem pretty busy with robin business."

"Robin business, that's cute. What are you doing here in this part of town?"

Careful. "I was just driving by and saw all the equipment trucks, and thought it must be you—I mean, not you, it must be the same . . . filming. . . ."

"Yes, it's us, all right. Sort of hard to keep us hidden, isn't it? So, you must have seen us yesterday, before I saw you. Did you see the accident, the car overturning and bursting into flames and all? Wasn't that wonderful?"

"It was something, all right."

She looked around. "Well, why don't we walk? It's going to take them a while to get the camera set up again, and Francis— Mr. Nicoletti—is in one of his sulks. He gets those when things don't go the way he wants them to. He can be such a baby at times."

She raised her eyebrows as if to say, Shall we? and started across the grass away from the terrace. Paul fell in beside her. They had only gone a few steps when she stopped again.

"Would you hold this a minute?" she said, handing him her clipboard. Then she braced herself on his arm—even through the cloth of his windbreaker her touch made his breath catch in his throat—as she slipped off her pumps, hooked them in her fingers, and took the clipboard again.

"That's better," she said, skating a few steps across the grass. "You're probably not supposed to walk on the grass but I don't care. Do you?"

"Not at all. Seems that's what grass should be for."

"That's what I think too," she said, nodding her head once for emphasis, looking pretend-stern for a moment then smiling broadly again. "So tell me about—there you are, I don't even know your name."

"It's Paul. Slater."

"I'm Suzy Konecki. It's very nice to meet you, Paul."

She presented her hand formally as if she were just learning business skills; when he shook it, he was surprised at the softness of her skin, that he could feel the sinews and bones within the flesh. They continued on, the sun glinting through the leaves of the trees as they moved, winking at him. He thought quickly of something to ask her, he didn't want her to ask any more questions about him.

"You sound like you're very close to . . . Nicoletti."

"What makes you say that?"

"Well, you called him Francis."

"Oh that. Well . . . yes, I guess you could say I am rather close to Francis. Of course, on a shoot like this it's rather unavoidable, you know? You're thrown together day and night. And my position calls for me to work very closely with him."

"What is your position?"

"Officially, I'm the graduate student production assistant." She laughed a little, looked at him as if to see his reaction. "It sounds grand, doesn't it? I'm in the film department at Carnegie Mellon and there was an opening on this crew. It's quite an honor, if I do say so myself."

"It sounds like it." Paul watched the tips of his shoes moving through the grass, her bare feet skimming along beside him. Feeling himself starting to get depressed. Feeling increasingly the world of difference between them. Don't be a fool, she's just being nice, polite, friendly to the guy who helped her. Too friendly, killing time, she doesn't know, they never do. . . .

"It really is, quite an honor. I was out of school for a while, I taught grade school for a couple of years before I decided I wanted to get my master's degree and go into film. It's a wonderful opportunity for me, working this closely with a man like Francis. He's teaching me the business from the ground up. It virtually guarantees my career later on."

They had come to a small parking lot beside the Cathedral of Learning, blocking their way. "I guess I should be getting back," Suzy said, "in case Francis is ready to go again."

They started back, across the grass, the way they came, the sun now behind them, the patchwork shadows of the leaves like a moving carpet, the shadows of the two people merging all the shadows into one. Think. Think. What can I ask her?

"You doing anything special this weekend?"

"No, not much," she said, shaking her head, watching her feet as she placed them in the grass, he thought again as a dancer would, pointing her toes. "Same old, same old. How about you?"

Paul saw himself puttering around the backyard, digging up the soil for Sharon's vegetable garden, working on Stephen's bike. Driving Sharon and the kids to the mall. "No."

"Saturday mornings I usually play tennis over at the PAA."

"PAA?"

She looked at him and smiled, then turned back and pointed across Fifth Avenue at an imposing block-long Renaissance-style stone building. "Pittsburgh Athletic Association. They have some glass-enclosed tennis courts up on the roof."

"Looks fancy."

She shrugged. "I guess. My father's a member so I get to use their facilities. It's very nice."

Paul took another glance at the building. "Yes, I would think. So, you're from around here. Originally."

"Oh yes. Sewickley. Actually, Sewickley Heights. You?"

It seemed ridiculous to say it. "Furnass."

"Really? We're almost neighbors, that's very close."

Worlds apart.

"Oh, and on Saturday night I'm going to a party with Francis," she said, clasping her clipboard to her breasts, her shoes dangling like accessories. "He's entertaining some movie people and local bigwigs and wants me there with him. I'm really excited about it."

Worlds and worlds. As they approached the place where they'd started, they stopped to watch an ROTC platoon on the lower terrace, in shirtsleeves and garrison caps, led by a red guidon, going through their basic paces, left face, right face, about-face, open ranks, close ranks, mark time. . . . Suzy was enthralled watching them below.

"Oh aren't they splendid? I think they all look so handsome, there's nothing like a man in uniform." Then she realized that Nicoletti was back with the crew, the camera was back on its track, and they were about ready to start shooting again. She hurriedly put on her shoes and ran for the steps, calling over her shoulder, "It was nice to see you, I have to go. . . ." And was gone, skipping down the steps and running across the grass, joining the group around Nicoletti, talking to those around her, laughing with one of the technicians. As if she'd been there the whole time. He waited a few moments in case she looked back his direction, then turned away and headed back across the grass to his truck. His face burning as if he'd been slapped.

Twenty

"The other policeman we talked to," Mr. Love said.

The statement hung there until it became a question. "Sergeant MacCarron?" Lieutenant Nathan White said.

"Yes," Sandy Love's father said.

Another question in the form of a statement. Now Nathan got it. "He's taking care of some other matters. I'm in charge of the investigation."

Mrs. Love apparently understood what her husband was getting at as well, and tried to smooth the awkwardness. "You see something like this on television or in the movies, but you never think it can happen to you. Or to someone you. . . ."

From somewhere in the maze of subterranean rooms came the sound of a distant radio, an insistent clunking in the warren of pipes overhead. A brief whirr of a power tool. Someone cutting through bone? Opening a skull? Nathan tried to put such thoughts out of his mind. The three of them stood in the basement hallway of the county morgue, waiting. As impersonal as it seemed, Nathan thought it better than taking them into the Cooler to view their daughter. The Meat Locker as the attendants called it. But he could tell already that there was nothing he could do to help the girl's parents get through this. Particularly her father. Nothing he could do to change the fact that solving the murder of his precious baby girl was in the hands of a black man.

"I'm sorry to have to put you through this. . . ."

"No, we understand," Mrs. Love said. She was a plumpish

woman in a dark blue suit, her red hair the same color as her daughter's though the older woman's was styled into an unfashionable bob. Nathan thought of the pictures he had seen at the club of Sandy, her impressive body. Except for the hair, it was hard to believe that mother and daughter came from the same gene pool. Is this what Sandy would have looked like if she had grown old in Saint Louis? Did her mother start out looking like Sandy when she was younger? And was immediately ashamed for thinking such things at a time like this. Maybe everything her father's thinking about me is justified, maybe I shouldn't be handling this investigation, not with all this media attention, no wonder Mac bowed out for the identification. . . . His thoughts were interrupted by the sound of the creaky doors of the freight elevator and an attendant in white getting off and wheeling a gurney down the hall toward them. On the gurney a white sheet covered a human-shaped lump.

"I need to prepare you," Nathan said. "I'm afraid there . . . isn't enough left of her face to make an identification. But you said there was a small birthmark on her left shoulder. . . ."

"I understand, Lieutenant. But you don't have to worry. I'd recognize her if I only saw her arm, her fingers."

Nathan nodded, appreciating the sentiment, even though he knew better from past experience. He asked the attendant to roll the body over and lower the sheet so they could see the back of the right shoulder. Sure enough, there was a small strawberry patch on the girl's shoulder blade. She must have covered it with makeup when she danced.

Mrs. Love nodded. "Yes. That's Sandy."

Her husband moved forward to have a look as well, grimacing slightly. He was a tall distinguished man who put Nathan in mind of Fred Astaire or Joseph Cotten, a matinee idol from the '30s or '40s, looking decidedly out of time and place, his hair heavily pomaded and furrowed into distinct rows. The girl probably adored him, her daddy. Nathan nodded for the attendant to cover the girl's body again.

"Can we see her anyway?" Mrs. Love said. "I mean her face."

"I really don't think that would be a good idea."

"No, we want to." She looked at her husband. He didn't say anything, but some understanding seemed to pass between them.

Nathan nodded to the attendant, who rolled the body on its back again, making sure the sheet was tucked in discreetly around the top of the girl's breasts.

Her face had been cleaned up since he saw it at the crime scene, but that only served to show its total destruction. It looked like a broken mask, the features in places where they shouldn't be, a face made from modeling clay that had been kneaded and stretched and pulled into fantastic shapes so that it no longer appeared at all human, a slit here that might have once held an eye, a few teeth there sticking out of what might have been a cheek. The man and woman stared down at the remains of their daughter without expression.

How can they stand to look at it? Someone they loved?

Nathan tried to imagine what he would feel if this had happened to someone he loved, but the only one who came to mind was his ex-wife, Alexa. He knew himself well enough, knew the human heart well enough from all he had seen over the years, to suspect that there must be part of him that wished to see Alexa lying there, broken and destroyed, for leaving him and running off with someone else. Maybe the fact that he thought of her at all in these circumstances meant he pictured her there. But he didn't think so. Mainly what he felt was a great sadness. For all of them. He looked away, trying to regain control of himself, putting himself into a policeman's frame of mind, reading over and over a hand-printed sign that someone had taped to the wall: REMEMBER TO RETURN HEAD BLOCKS.

Still looking at the body, Mrs. Love said, "You're going to get the monster who did this to Sandy, aren't you?"

Nathan tried to shift the conversation in another direction. "Did Sandy ever talk about anyone? Anyone she was seeing, or who maybe was giving her trouble?"

"I was trying to think, after we got the news of what happened. The only one she ever mentioned was somebody she called the Big Yawn, I guess because she thought he was so boring. That was Sandy, always the 'big' this, the 'big' that. I supposed it was short for John, or maybe even Juan. I never quite understood—"

"Could it have been Ianni?"

"I suppose so." She glanced at her husband, who seemed frozen somewhere between outrage and shock. "I'm afraid Sandy didn't tell us that much about what she was doing, and we . . . I was afraid to ask. When she stayed here after graduating from Pitt, it wasn't under the best of circumstances. We were hoping she'd decide on someplace closer to home, but, well, you know young people, that only made her want to stay here in Pittsburgh all the more. We tried to be content that she finally seemed to have found herself, that she seemed to have friends here, and was going to law school and all. I didn't want to pry too much into her private life, I didn't want to make her stop talking to us altogether. Now I wish I had pried a little more."

They don't know their daughter was a dancer, that she worked in the sex clubs. They don't know she was probably turning tricks. And it's going to be up to me to tell them.

"You about done here, Lieutenant?" the attendant said, anxious to put the body back in its locker and end his shift.

Nathan looked at Mrs. Love, who nodded. Her husband continued to stare at the mangled face on the stainless-steel cart.

"Mr. Love?"

He regarded Nathan with a look of total befuddlement on his face. "I don't know what I'm supposed to do."

Richard Snodgrass

None of us do, Mr. Love. None of us.

. . . and the sunlight turns golden, buttery, as the day wears on toward evening, casting a romantic, melancholy glow over the city, the sun on its westward trek seeming to shine straight down the Ohio River like a spotlight covered with a yellow gel at the fountain that marks the confluence of the two rivers to make the third, casting strong thoughtful shadows over the grass of Point State Park, its lawns and knolls, the outline of Fort Duquesne and the bastions of Fort Pitt thrown in sharp relief, the plaques that commemorate the violence and bloodshed on which the city was founded, the light and deep shadows continuing past the parks and buildings of the Golden Gateway, the golden facade of the Gateway Hilton, on down Liberty and Penn and the other streets radiating out from the Point, over the crowds along the sidewalks rushing to their cars and buses to begin the trip home, the streets approaching gridlock with traffic, the end of the day at the end of the week, the anticipation of the coming weekend palpable throughout the city, the promise of good things to come, as much a presence as the yellowish light, a city encased in amber, fixed in its time and place and the minds of the characters of our story . . . as at the Public Safety Building on Grant Street, police lieutenant Nathan White sits at his desk looking up at his boss, Joe Ciampa, the head of the homicide squad, who says, "Let me get this straight, you actually told the parents of a murder victim that you thought there was a good chance we'd never find out who killed their daughter?" and Nathan says, "I'm pretty sure I didn't say a 'good' chance, I think I only said there was a fair chance," and Sergeant MacCarron sitting at his desk that fronts his partner's says, "Good one, Nathan," and Commander Ciampa says, "Why in the hell would you ever say that?" and Nathan says, "After they identified the body the father was pushing me to promise that we'd get whoever did it, and I couldn't do that, I wouldn't

· 116 ·

do that," and Commander Ciampa's face goes red, "This case is getting more media attention than any case I can remember and you—" and Nathan says, "You know as well as I do that if the killer isn't a member of the victim's family or a friend or acquaintance, statistically there's more than a fair chance we won't find who killed her, I didn't want to give them false hope," and MacCarron nods and shrugs, makes a conciliatory face, "He's got a point, Joe, this could be random, somebody who just saw her dancing at the club and grabbed her, even a serial—" and Commander Ciampa says, "Don't even think the words 'serial killer,' that's all this department needs, but you better fucking be checking known MOs just to make sure," and Nathan says, "We already did that, the first thing," and the commander says, "Well, then check them again," and turns away, heading back down the aisle between the rows of desks muttering to himself, "Tell the mother of a murder victim we can't find her daughter's killer . . ." and MacCarron looks at his partner and says, "The commander seems a little peak-ed this evening," and Nathan says, "You know what I mean," and Mac says, "I do indeed, and I agree with you, but maybe your timing for soul-baring truth was a little off," and Nathan says, "So I guess we check MOs again," and Mac says, "Not tonight, partner, I'm out of here, and if you have any sense you'll get out of here too; funny thing about work, it'll all be waiting for us tomorrow," and Mac gives Nathan a knowing look and heads off down the aisle of the rapidly emptying squad room but Nathan continues to sit there for a while, thinking *What did he mean if I have any sense? Does he think I'm stupid or something? Or is this just another part of the race thing, Sergeant MacCarron, oh I'm sick of this whole business, I'm beginning to think Sam had the right idea after all, just say to hell with it all, I should never've stopped playing my axe, I got to get out of here . . .* while in her office at Nickolodeon Productions in Gateway Towers, Fran Nicoletti looks out the window beside her *desk, beyond the traffic backed up on the ramps to the Fort Duquesne and Fort Pitt Bridges, at a diesel tug pushing a string of coal barges upriver against the current, hears the door to the office down the corridor click shut and the voices of the dental hygienists talking among themselves, leaving for the weekend and thinks that pretty much empties out the floor, thinks that means she's probably alone on the floor, thinks You're pathetic, little girl, you've watched too many of your husband's spooky movies, but can't help it, has to admit to herself that she's spooked being there in her office without someone else on the floor, the visit from Corduroy Boy unhinged her, something about the way he looked at her, the way he seemed to slink around, making her uneasy the rest of the afternoon, as if she had been visited by a harbinger of something dark, evil with a baby face, Okay, that's enough for today, I've made as many phone calls as I can to set up Nicko's spur-of-the-moment party tomorrow night, there's nothing more I can or am willing to do, it all depends on Malcolm now, and my talk with him tomorrow morning, our angel from Minneapolis, what I can convince him of, and she turns off her typewriter and turns off the lights in her office, takes one last look around and closes the door behind her, listening for the tell-tale click, and takes the elevator down to the lobby, feeling at once relieved and unburdened and more like her feisty self, steps out the doors into the golden light of the late afternoon, the plaza between Gateway Towers and the Gateway Hilton and looks beyond the hotel at the line of buildings along the ridgeline of Mount Washington across the Monongahela River, the white apartment building where Nickolodeon rents the penthouse and where Nicko insists he's going to have his party tomorrow night, thinks The man, the man, he's going to be the death of me, he's certainly dragging me with him into the sinkhole of his career, I hope his pretty little life raft Suzy is enough to keep him afloat until I can get us some more money, and turns and heads along the walks lined with planter boxes of tulips and daffodils toward the bar in the restaurant of Three Gateway Center, the Foundry, telling herself Cheer up, little girl, there's nothing to be afraid of, nothing that a drinkie-poo can't take care of . . . as at the Gateway Hilton Jeff Berner wakes from an unscheduled afternoon nap to find his room full of golden sunlight, lying on his bed where he fell asleep after returning from his disastrous interview with the bitch at Nickolodeon, Mrs. Nicoletti, crying himself to sleep still in his good blue corduroy outfit, it never occurring to him beforehand that it might not be appropriate for all occasions, remembers the interview all over again and thinks She should never have talked to me like that, there was no call for her to do that, make fun of me like that, I'll show her, I'll show her all right, gets up slowly and goes to his window, looking down at the plaza between the hotel and the office tower and sees, like the answer to a prayer, like a sign from the universe, Fran Nicoletti coming out the door of Gateway Towers and starting down the walk toward him—for a moment she appears to look up at the hotel; Jeff steps back from the curtain, Did she see me? How would she know I'm here? Maybe she's looking for me, maybe she knows what she did was wrong and wants to make it up to me, wants to offer me a role after all—but then she turns and heads up the plaza toward Stanwix Street, walking out of his line of sight and he experiences the pain and disappointment all over again, the end it seems of all his hopes and dreams of getting into the movies, and sits back down on the edge of the bed and takes off the blue corduroy outfit, the clunky platform shoes, and takes his suitcase from the closet and wads the clothes into the suitcase until he can think of someplace where he can throw them away permanently, puts on his jeans and button-down shirt again but before ordering a pizza goes to the dresser and removes the nickel-plated four-inch-barrel Colt Python .357 that he's kept hidden under the pile of his underwear, the revolver he took from his father's closet the last time he was home—his father's pride and joy, the Rolls-Royce of Colt revolvers, as his father never tires of referring to the weapon, though as far as Jeff could tell his father had never fired it in his life, just loaded it and stuck it up there behind his old sweaters in case of a break-in someday—weighs the gun in his hand momentarily then places the barrel against his temple, feels the cool metal zero against his skin, holds it there for a half a minute or so, but thinks No, that's not it, this isn't what I want to do at all, lowers the revolver again but decides he'll keep it handy from now on, places it on top of the dresser, just in case . . . and the afternoon wears on into evening, the golden light that covered the city disappearing as quickly as if someone had flicked a light switch, the last vestiges of the sun finally falling behind the westward hills, the streetlights coming on and the neon signs casting their parti-colored glow over the sidewalks in Oakland beyond the university district, the rough business district near the corner of Centre and North Craig, where Sam Connor, wearing his Steelers jersey and a peace symbol around his neck and hair like a bearskin hat gone electric, ditty-bops along carrying a scraggly bunch of daffodils he liberated from a municipal planter on Baum Boulevard, but instead of Carla sitting on the stool in front of Nirvana finds the long-legged dancer named Chartreuse, "Gee, Sammy, for me?" Chartreuse says between snaps of her gum, "You shouldn't have," and Sam says, "I didn't, where's Carla? She's usually at the door at this hour," and Chartreuse says, "Not tonight"—Snap! Snap!—"she has to work a party at Ianni's house tonight," and Sam says, "I thought she was going to tell Ianni she wasn't going to do that," and Chartreuse laughs and pumps her leg, "Oh sure, tell Ianni she's not going to work a party for him, that's rich"—Snap! Snap!—and Sam is about to say something more when a dark shape moves behind the beaded curtain in the doorway, a very large dark shape, one of Ianni's bouncers who practically fills the doorway and Sam says, "Oh, gotta run" and*

*skips on down the sidewalk though behind him he hears Char-
treuse say, "Ow! That hurt! I didn't tell him nothing," and Sam
thinks Not good, not good at all, dumps the flowers into a trash
can and scurries on, his head filled with images of effecting a
rescue, bursting into a party in an exclusive house in Squirrel Hill
or Schenley Farms and finding naked couples strewn over the
furniture in every room, crashing through the rooms until he finds
Carla in the midst of a gang bang and grabs her hand and pulls
her away, back through the house to safety, the two of them running down the dark lawn together, Carla still naked, Sam's arm
around her protectively as he promises her she'll never have to
work a party like that again, that he'll take care of her forever
and ever, but even he knows it's nothing but a fantasy, there's
nothing he can do tonight but go back to his room in the attic on
South Bouquet Street and sit on his mattress on the floor listening
to the Dead as he gets stoned and tries to forget, forget it
all . . . as in his rented house in Squirrel Hill, back home after
the day's shoot on the Pitt campus, Francis Nicoletti wanders
through the downstairs and then the upstairs, turning on the
lights, hoping that maybe Fran is here after all, that maybe she
got home early and fell asleep on the couch or their bed or in a
chair reading, but no, the house is empty, no Frannie, ends up
standing at the kitchen counter where he had his talk with her
this morning, his attempt he thought to get her to approach Thorsten to take over the financing of his film, only to find that she
had already made the call to their angel from Minneapolis without
his having to say anything to her and that Thorsten was on his
way, that Fran would see him tomorrow morning, see him and
probably fuck him if he knew Fran and Thorsten, knowing their
long relationship together—she said, "Isn't this a little too much
like pimping, even for you, Nicko?" and I said, "I'm scared,
Frannie," and she said, "Stop, I won't listen to this"—looks
around the kitchen at the deep shadows created by the indirect*

lighting, the lights over the sink and under the range hood and above the rack of pots and pans hanging over his head at the counter, thinks even a banal, placid house like this can look terrifying if you know what you're doing, thinks again of what Suzy said in the car today, that he didn't get enough credit in the industry for pioneering so many of the techniques used today— Did she really say that, or did I just infer it?—and leaving the kitchen goes downstairs to the finished basement where he has set up an editing room for himself, goes to the rack of film canisters and takes out the one labeled Death Dealer *and threads it into the flatbed Steenbeck editing table and zeros out the counter and fast-forwards the whirling tape until he comes to the part he's looking for, watches on the small screen as a man in a business suit walks across the floor of a parking garage late at night, the floor almost deserted, only a few cars here and there, pushes the elevator call button impatiently, and when the elevator doesn't come right away, ducks through the open door to the stairwell, the camera tracking him as he descends two floors to a lower level, the only sound his footsteps on the concrete stairs, tires screaming on a distant ramp, distant voices, a car horn, a single beep, far away, then out the door and across the floor, with only a few small isolated patches of light among the deep shadows, walks between the few remaining cars to his own car and starts to unlock the door when a tall figure appears between the cars, in front of him, in the darkness, and the man in the suit says, "Oh, it's you, you scared me," and laughs a little uncomfortably, the close-up of his eyes showing that everything is not right at all, the figure after a moment moving closer, into a patch of light, the light revealing a terribly disfigured face, the features smeared as if they are made of melted wax and are dripping from his face until it's apparent the man is wearing a stocking mask, and holding a gun, "No, you don't understand. . . ," the man in the suit says, but the figure motions him back toward the stairwell, pushing him when he hesitates, back toward the doorway marked* EXIT *where the man in the suit starts to head up the stairs but the figure grabs him and pushes him down, down on his knees at the foot of the steps, pushing his face to the floor, "My wallet's in my pants, you can take the whole thing, please," he says wild-eyed, filled with terror as he tries to shift his head, his face scrunched against the concrete, the gun behind his ear, sweat rolling down his forehead into his eyes, stares across the expanse of floor—the concrete is filthy, littered with debris, oil stains, wads of chewing gum pressed into hard black spots—his eyes dilated, fixed on something, then his face going out of focus as into the foreground, bumping along almost comically, across his field of vision, comes a large black bug, scurrying along, a dung beetle following the trail of beetle scent they'd left for it (it had taken days to get that right, to get that damn beetle—it wasn't the one they started with; after the first one got sidetracked and went every which way, Nicoletti himself ended its budding stardom with one swift blow from the side of his hand, the crew at first shocked and surprisingly horrified then exploding into hoots of laughter (he went around for days trying to wipe it off, rubbing his hand repeatedly against his pants)—to bump across the floor just that way), the face of the man on the floor looming out of focus behind the insect like some distant landscape as the gun goes off, a geyser of blood erupting from behind his ear and gushing down his neck onto the concrete, the river of blood sweeping the bug away, the face, the man going limp, collapsing like a sinkhole falling in upon itself as the blood rushes forward across the floor and laps up against the screen and the screen goes red . . . and Nicko turns off the machine and leans back in his chair, in the circle of light from his desk lamp, and thinks Yes, that was a wonderful scene, and totally unappreciated as the girl said, what all goes on there, the circling camera and the use of selective focus, including the beetle in front of the victim's face, the reference to Castaneda and how can we be sure of the world we live in, there being worlds within worlds, it was brilliant, gets up slowly and turns off the lamp and finds his way in the dark back up the stairs to the first floor and decides to go on to bed, Fran will get home when she gets home, there's nothing to say between them now anyway, taking solace in the anticipation of the party tomorrow night, there won't be anyone there who appreciates him for his true worth either, including little blond Suzy-girl for all her fawning, but at least people will be paying attention to him as if they do . . . and ten miles downstream from Pittsburgh, Paul Slater has returned to his home in Furnass, after having stopped by the ball field beside Buchanan Steel and watched Stephen at his Little League practice, after the practice loading up the bed of his pickup truck with a bunch of Stephen's friends and driving each of them home, up and down the streets of the hillside town, waiting to make sure each boy gets into his house okay because it's a dangerous world and you can't be too careful, you can never tell when something bad might happen, then goes on to his own house on Thirteenth Street and parks his truck in the paved space beside the alley, follows Stephen into the house and kisses Sharon on the cheek as she sautés vegetables on the stove, on the drainboard leaves his lunch box that he emptied out again at a service station on Ohio River Boulevard on his way home and goes to check on Mandy sitting in her playpen in the living room watching television—when she sees her daddy she points at an animated mouse on the screen and says something unintelligible to him; Paul listens to her intently, says, "That's right, isn't it?" cups her head in his hand, bends down and kisses her hair—and goes upstairs to get ready for dinner, the meal uneventful with its usual small talk though Paul is careful not to volunteer anything of his day, then afterward as Sharon redds the table and cleans up in the kitchen Paul turns on the television again in time for the evening news, but whereas the last two days there seemed to be endless stories of the fall of Saigon suddenly there is next to nothing, there's a mention that the Communists have reported the takeover of Vietnam is complete, but most of the coverage is about President Ford vetoing a farm bill and an upcoming meeting between Ford and Anwar Sadat in Austria and Paul turns off the news in favor of a game show and sits in the living room for a few moments, watching Mandy watch the contestants on the screen, adding her drooly comments to the proceedings, turning to him occasionally for verification—"That's right, Mandy, you got it"—watching a young blond woman in a ball gown point out the various prizes to be won and sharing in the banter with the host, then finally gets up and goes into the kitchen and gives Sharon the news that he has to work tomorrow—"Oh Paul, on Saturday? I wanted to go out to the mall and look at wallpaper for here in the kitchen," and he makes a regretful, tight-lipped face and says, "I'm sorry, babe, you know it's out of my hands, if the work needs done . . ." and Sharon says, "I know, I'm just disappointed, that's all, I was thinking we could take the kids to Red Lobster afterward. . . ," and Paul shrugs his regret again and goes out the back door into the backyard, the night sky alive at the moment with one of the Bessemers at the mill in heat, lolling in its berth and sending flames fifty feet in the air, the sky roiling yellow and orange with steam and smoke and the scream of the sirens and warning bells and Paul goes to his truck and takes the pistol from underneath the seat, the Detonics Mark V Combat Master, a smaller version of the .45 caliber Colt automatic he had with him in Nam, carries the gun over to the side door of the house and down to his workbench in the basement, turns on the bank of lights overhead, unloads the weapon and sets about to clean and oil it as he does every week, appreciating all over again the workmanship of it, the brushed-steel finish, the slightly bobbed hammer spur so it won't catch on your thumb . . . the flat Pachmayr-like mainspring housing for a good grip . . . the high profile of the fixed rear sight—*

he ticks off the features to himself as if reciting a litany—and when he's done pulls back the slide a couple of times, listens to the action, the movement of precision part on precision part, before reloading it again, weighs it in his hand, sights down the barrel at an imagined target, then turns off the lights and goes back up the steps and out the side door into the night, the sky calmer now that the heat is done, a layer of gray smoke over the valley, the mill a galaxy of pinpoint lights that takes the place of the unseen stars, returns the pistol to its place under his seat, in the holster he's rigged to hold it in place so he can grab it easily if he ever needs to, locks his truck and returns up the steps to the back porch, taking a moment to watch Sharon, in her Furnass Stokers T-shirt, her comfortable fit jeans and bare feet, as she putzies happily around her kitchen, his wife, the mother of his children, before opening the door and joining her, sitting on the kitchen stool as she finishes up, "I'll be done here in a minute and we can watch some TV, 'kay?" and he says, "'Kay," aware that, in his heart of hearts, for reasons he can only guess at, things are anything but . . .

Twenty-One

When Lieutenant Nathan White finally left the Public Safety Building, the last thing he wanted to do was to have to cook for himself tonight. Going home to his apartment on the North Side was bad enough, there being nowhere else he could think to go, the lesser of all possibilities, nowhere that he could tolerate after the day he just had, but then on top of that to face another dinner of scrambled eggs and ham—the only alternative in his cooking repertoire was steamed zucchini with penne pasta in marinara sauce, but he knew he was out of fresh zucchini, penne pasta, and canned sauce—was too much to bear. Plus, even though he was achingly tired, he wanted something special, he yearned for a treat, a reward for all his efforts. On his way through town, he got the idea to stop at the Foundry to get something to take out; it had been a favorite place while he was married, close to where Alexa worked at Joseph Horne's; they would meet there after work, the chicken parmigiana his favorite meal—he actually liked the veal version better, but wouldn't eat veal after he found out how calves were treated before they were slaughtered.

He parked on Liberty and walked back to Gateway Three. But as soon as he stepped in the door of the restaurant, he knew he had made a mistake. It was *their* place, not *his*, why on earth did he ever think he would be comfortable in a place that did nothing but remind him of *her*, of *them* as a couple, their marriage that failed? But he was here now, he might as well go through with it, he frankly didn't have the energy to turn around and walk out again and think of somewhere else to go. He took a seat at the bar, ordered his takeout and a Jack Daniel's on the rocks while he waited. Thankfully the place on a Friday night wasn't busy, happy hour over an hour or so earlier, only a few hangers-on left after the business executives and secretaries cleared out on their way home to get ready for the weekend—he remembered what it was like, that excitement, the anticipation. The lounge was dark, most of the illumination coming from the lighted glass mural behind the bar, a copy of the large mural called *The Puddler* that was on the front of the Pittsburgh Press Club on Wood Street, complete with twinkling lights to simulate sparks from the molten metal. He had been sitting there a few minutes when a waitress came over and told him that the woman in the back booth wanted to buy him a drink. Nathan thought it must be a joke, but when he looked where the waitress was pointing, a blond woman sitting alone in the banquette raised her glass to him. Nathan took a large swallow of his drink, told the bartender where he'd be when his food arrived, and made his way toward the back.

"The lieutenant doesn't recognize me, does he?" the woman said as Nathan approached the red leather booth.

"No, ma'am. I'm afraid I don't."

"'Ma'am.' I guess I'll never get used to handsome younger men calling me 'ma'am.' It seems so . . . final." She took a sip of her wine. "I'm Fran Nicoletti. Have a seat, join me."

Nathan sat down across the half circle from her but remained cautious. "I'm afraid I'm still drawing a blank."

Fran sighed, leaned her chin on her hand, being patient. One side of her face appeared to glow from the cigarette between her fingers. "We met last year at a film festival dinner at the DoubleTree. My husband and I had recently moved here, and you were in all the papers because you solved some case or something. As I recall we talked about what it felt like to be trotted out for media events, you because of racial diversity and me because I was the wife of a quasifamous man."

"Of course. Mrs. Nicoletti. I'm sorry, I meet a lot of people, and it's dark in here—"

"You don't have to apologize, Lieutenant. Though it's sweet that you want to. I probably wouldn't have remembered you either, except that you're very handsome and I was flattered you talked to me that night. Actually I was both flattered and grateful. I was in need of some company and you came to my rescue, whether you realized it or not. Come to think of it, I'm in need of some company tonight as well. And here you are again. Do you believe in fate, Lieutenant? Or coincidence?"

"In my line of work I try to keep focused on facts. They get me in enough trouble as it is," he said, thinking back on what he told Sandy Love's parents today about the chances of catching their daughter's killer, and the commander's reaction to it.

"'Just the facts, ma'am, just the facts,'" Fran said, lowering her voice and trying to sound official. When Nathan looked at her questioningly, she said, "Sergeant Joe Friday? *Dragnet?* The

TV show? Don't tell me you're too young to remember."

"My family didn't watch much television when I was growing up. And the few times we did, we didn't watch shows about white policemen."

"White policemen," Fran giggled, more like a sneeze, into her wineglass. "That's who I'm talking to right now, isn't it? A policeman named White?"

"I think you may have had a little too much to drink, Mrs. Nicoletti," Nathan said, studying her for the first time since he sat down. Though she was probably ten years older than he was, she was still a good-looking woman, all blond and glamorous and full of the self-assurance that seemed to come naturally to media and movie people. There was a brassiness about her too, a no-nonsense quality that he liked, though there was also a hardness that tended toward the brittle, a carapace of sorts around her that he thought might shatter all of a piece if the wedge were applied at the right crack. "How about if I get you a taxi home?"

"Now, now, don't be that way. All policeman-y. Nathan—it is Nathan, isn't it? Do you mind if I call you Nathan? Well, I'm going to do it anyway. Thank you for your concern, Nathan, but this little girl is doing just fine. Just fine. If there's one thing I've had to do it is to learn my limits. For a lot of things. How much. . . ." She thought about something for a moment, her expression turning faraway, then she was back again, a woman of smiles. "Besides, here's one of those coincidences for you. I was all set to call someone in your office today but didn't get it done because of a bunch of last-minute silliness for one of my husband's parties. But now I don't have to call your office, because here you are."

"What were you going to contact the police about, Mrs. Nicoletti?"

"Fran. You must call me Fran. Especially if I'm calling you Nathan, Nathan." She smiled, the coquette, and sipped her wine.

"You know that young woman they found murdered in the park the other day? The one who was tied to a tree?"

"I do, very well. That's the case I'm working on."

"So there you are. Fate. Coincidence. We're brought together through the workings of the universe. The Great Scriptwriter in the Sky."

"What about the murdered young woman in the park?"

"Well, personally I think it's a cockamamie idea, a shameless ploy of my husband's to drum up interest in his failing career, but so be it, the man does what he has to do. Anyway, Nicko, my husband, has this idea that whoever killed that girl was doing a copycat of a murder that happens in one of his gory movies, one called *Blood Truth*. I know, I know, don't say it, I think he's completely—"

"Why does your husband think they're similar?" Nathan was beginning to wish he had brought his drink with him, he was needing something to do with his hands, and he could stand the alcohol at this point.

"Well, I guess because they are. Similar. Silly man. I'm not sure there whether I meant Nicko or you." She giggled, raised her eyebrows, took another sip. "Both young women were tied to a tree in a park, both young women were beaten to death about the face, almost beyond recognition. The girl in *Blood Truth* was beaten with the butt of a gun, is that what happened to this girl?"

"We're not releasing that information at this time," Nathan said. Thinking quickly.

"Which probably means she was, from the expression on your face. Oh don't worry, Nathan, I'm not going to go running around telling people. What do you think of me?"

The fact was he wasn't sure what he thought of her. Besides that she was getting drunk. As he was considering what else he should ask her, the waitress, a raven-haired girl dressed like a disco dancer, knee-high white boots and short shorts, even though the place had no disco, came over with a plastic bag containing his food. He looked at the check, gave her the cash and told her to keep the change. She smiled broadly at him and sashayed away.

"The lieutenant has a way with the ladies, doesn't he?" Fran said. "Will you use your charms to call her back? I need another glass of wine."

"I think you've had more than enough, Mrs. Nicoletti."

"Fran."

"Mrs. Nicoletti." Nathan looked around uneasily. He knew what he should do, he should stay and make sure she got home okay, but he was weary of the day, if not of her, he wanted to go home and have his dinner and try to forget there was a world where young women were beaten to death and people became rich and famous making movies about them.

"You're in a quandary about me, Nathan. That's very sweet. But don't worry about this little girl, I'm going to have another glass of wine, which I can handle very well, thank you very much, and then I'm going to my car and drive home and I'll be just fine. Considering what all I have to face tomorrow and what all I have to do, all in the name of my husband's supposed art, there's no way I'm going to mess myself up drinking the night before. You run along, have your dinner, though I appreciate your concern. On the other hand, if you're down this way tomorrow evening, that's a different matter. I'm going to be here drowning my honor and pride as much as I can. Then you could be a real service to the community by keeping me off the streets."

Nathan stood up, gathered up the bag of food, and looked at her again. "Thanks for the tip about that movie."

"You're not going to do a thing about it, are you? No, of course not. Good night, Nathan."

She gave him a little sideways smile, then looked around for the waitress. Nathan headed back toward the front of the lounge. As he passed the bar, he stopped and showed his badge to the bartender, a young man with a *Viva Zapata* mustache. "That's enough for the woman in the rear booth."

"Mrs. Nicoletti? She's a good customer, and seems to be able to hold it pretty well. . . ."

Nathan leaned closer and gave him his best Sergeant MacCarron shark's grin. "You didn't understand me. I said the woman in the rear booth has had enough."

"Got it. Officer."

SATURDAY, MAY 3, 1975

Core=Box Construction. Several methods of constructing the master pattern for the core box may be utilized. As only two castings are required—one for each half of the core box—the quickest

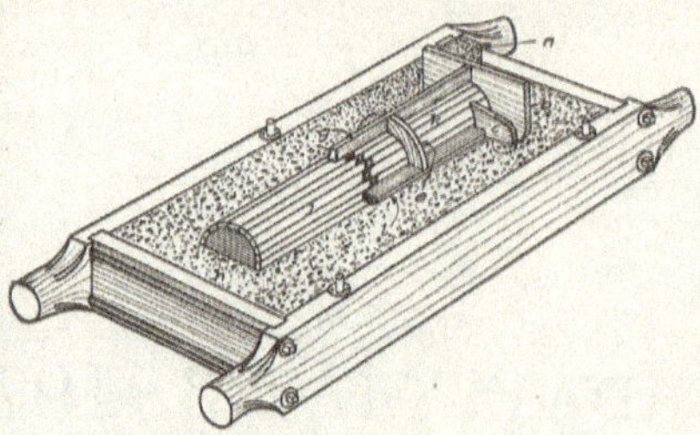

Fig. 295. Pattern Assembled on False Cope Ready for Ramming Cope Mold

method of constructing the pattern should be used, provided the results are accurate. A nailed and glued pattern using a green-sand core for molding the inside would produce the smoothest casting, Fig. 294. The pattern, however, would be very fragile, and a form

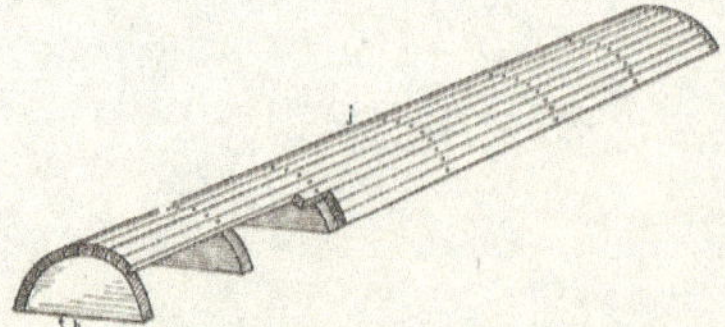

Fig. 296. Wooden Form

should be made to fit the inside to hold it in shape while ramming the drag mold.

Use of Form. The construction considered will be to furnish the molder with separate flanges and lagging, and assemble the parts on a wooden form, Fig. 295, or a dry-sand core can often be used in place of the wooden form.

VII—13

Twenty-Two

From the sidewalk in front of the building, the stone facade of the Pittsburgh Athletic Association looked more imposing than it had from across the street the day before when he was walking with Suzy. Who would design an athletic club to look like some kind of Renaissance temple? Paul thought. Somebody who wasn't that serious about athletics, that's for sure. Must have been someone who was very serious about telling other people they didn't belong here. The stone stairway to the front doors was divided in two, one set of stairs to the left, one to the right, meeting again at the front door. More confusion, I guess, make you choose which one to take. The original design for battlements made them easier to defend this way, bet your average businessman walking up here never thought of that, just knows it intuitively. Keep out, you. We don't want your kind. You're not one of us. Paul chose the left-hand side and entered the large oak doors.

Beyond the vestibule and another set of doors, Paul stepped into a marble lobby that had seen better days, with tall ceilings and flat lighting. An older man in an ill-fitting blue uniform, with a tonsure of gray hair around a shiny pate and a bushy gray mustache that appeared off-kilter, sat at a desk behind a counter. As Paul started to walk past, the guard called, "Excuse me. Can I help you?"

"I'm a guest of Suzy Konecki. She told me to meet her up at the tennis courts."

"Well, let's just see what I have written down here," the guard said, looking at the ledger in front of him. "No, I don't see anything listed here. . . ."

Paul walked over to the counter, leaned in close. "You know Miss Konecki's father, don't you? He's on the board of directors, and I doubt that he'd be happy to hear that one of his daughter's invited guests was given a bad time when he tried to enter."

The guard sat straighter. "I don't mean to give you a bad

time. But it's my job to check—"

"And I'm sure he appreciates it. But how would I know she's at the tennis courts if she didn't invite me?"

Paul didn't wait for an answer. He turned away and headed down the corridor toward a brass plaque that said ELEVATORS, not venturing to look back, his Green Beret training kicking in. Be the result, soldier. This ain't nothing but a thing. Blend in, no one can see you. When he pressed the Up button, the doors opened immediately and he was gone, doors closed, the car lifting up through the building.

When he stepped off the elevator at the top floor, the sound of bouncing balls kept up a steady tattoo within the greenhouse-like structure, punctuated by an occasional grunt or someone making a comment, and the squeak of rubber-soled tennis shoes dragging on the playing surface. Only a couple of the half dozen courts were occupied; he saw Suzy on the far side, toward the back. He walked around the perimeter of the large empty space, skirting the playing areas, and took a seat beside her court, on a bench with his back against the wall, on her side of the net. Her opponent was a handsome young man, dark-skinned or deeply tanned, with a long face and lots of black curly hair. The sight of them laughing and talking between volleys gave him a pit in his stomach, but he stayed put. After a few minutes, she was ready to serve when she happened to look his direction. She went back to the game, held the ball ready to serve, then looked at him again, as if to make sure it was really him, her expression non-committal. Paul gave a little wave; Suzy didn't smile. She played the rest of the game without acknowledging him again, but he didn't think she played as well. When the game was over she met her opponent at the net and the two of them walked to the side-lines, the net between them, and gathered up their equipment and sweaters. They appeared ready to leave when Suzy looked at Paul and held up her index finger, indicating that she'd be back, to wait for her. Her companion looked at Paul questioningly but Suzy took his arm and guided him to the elevator. The two of them laughing at something. He told himself that it wasn't about him.

He sat there for close to half an hour, long enough to wonder if she was coming back; and wonder whether the police would be with her if she did come back. This was crazy, crazy. What did he think was going to happen? That she'd be happy to see him, that they'd spend the day together, doing things around town, go to lunch or a walk in the park somewhere, go to a movie— that she'd suggest they go back to her place? He must have scared her out of her wits, of course she'd get away as fast as she could, he'd be lucky if he wasn't arrested, what would he ever tell Sharon, how could he ever explain why he'd come here today when he wasn't sure himself—and then the elevator doors opened and there she was again, alone, coming toward him across the empty courts, her face still flushed from the exercise and her shower, in a clean tennis outfit, a white dress with a tiny pleated skirt that showed most of her thighs, a white sweater thrown about her shoulders like a short cape. She came over to him and sat down on the bench beside him, not close but not far away either, businesslike, without smiling, keeping her oversized straw purse on her lap, holding it in front of her like a shield. She smelled of soap and cinnamon.

"What are you doing here, Paul? That is what you said your name is, didn't you? You can't say this is a coincidence."

"No, of course, it's no coincidence," he said, unable to meet her eyes for very long, looking down mostly at his hands. "You told me you played here Saturday mornings. So I took a chance. I wanted to see you."

"How did you get in?"

"I told the guard I was your guest. And when he started to question it, I said your father wouldn't like me being questioned."

"You did? But you don't know my father. Do you?"

"No. I said he was on the board of directors. Is he?"

"No," she said, but instead of being angry she giggled. "You said that? And he let you in?"

Paul shrugged, and chanced a smile. Suzy giggled again, reached over and slapped at his arm. "You're a wild man, aren't you? A wild man. What was so important that you wanted to see me about?"

"Nothing special. I just wanted to see you. To talk to you, you know. . . ."

She looked as if she might smile, then caught herself. "Don't you think that's rather presumptuous?"

"Presumptuous? I'm not sure what—"

"I mean, suppose I had another date or something? Suppose there was somebody else waiting for me?"

"Do you?"

"Do I what?"

"Have another date? Or something?"

She laughed, like a kind of burp, and looked away. In a moment she said, "No, not really." Paul smiled, relaxed a little. "But I might have," she added.

"Is there someplace here to get coffee? Or a drink?"

"There is, but I'm afraid I can't. I have a million things to do today."

They sat uneasily for several long moments, watching or pretending to watch the game going on in another court. Finally Paul said, "Did you win?"

"Win what?"

"You know—your game."

"Oh that. Well, as Francis says, the winning isn't always in the score. The important thing is that you feel like a winner."

He tried to ignore the reference to Nicoletti, but it made him out of sorts. "In other words, you didn't win."

"Well, I almost won a couple of games," she said and laughed at herself. She crossed her tanned, pretty legs and sat forward, leaning toward him. "I'm a very competitive person, in case you didn't know. As a matter of fact, when I was in college I won the title of America's Most Beautiful Majorette."

"Is that right?"

"That's right," she nodded once for emphasis and sat back again, looking away for a moment. "I almost won Best Twirler too, but I only came in second. That nearly broke my heart. I wanted it very much for my grandfather."

Paul shook his head to show he didn't understand.

"My grandpa," she glowed. "He used to take me to all the twirling competitions, clear back to when I was a little girl. He was always my biggest fan. He even drove me when I was in college. My mother and father never cared that much about it, though they paid for my lessons of course. But Grandpa would always sit in the very first row, and then afterward we'd go somewhere and get something to eat, just my grandpa and me."

Her voice had become increasingly like that of a little girl, or rather an adult's imitation of a little girl. Then her voice was normal again, only quieter, and her eyes looked like they could tear up. "Grandpa was always very proud of me."

The display of emotion made Paul uncomfortable; he wondered all over again why he had come, what he thought he was doing here. What he expected her to do. This was stupid, stupid. He wanted to forget the whole thing, to get away from here as quickly as possible; yet as he watched her fiddling with her purse and acting as if she was getting ready to leave, he was desperate for her to stay.

"Well, I guess I better be running along. Thank you, Paul, it was nice to see you again."

"Are you sure you wouldn't like a drink or something?"

"No, no, I better not. As I said, I've got an awful lot to do today. . . ."

"Such as?"

She laughed but was taken aback. "Well, if you must know, I've got some laundry to do, and I need to go to the market, and I've been meaning to wash my car . . . now don't tell me you're going to follow me around to all those places too. You're just crazy enough to do something like that, aren't you?"

She had no idea how crazy he felt. "You said you don't have a date today."

"What?" She looked around quickly, as if ready to bolt. "Maybe not today, but tonight there's a very important party at Francis' apartment. . . ."

He felt a wave of despair and anger at the mention of Nicoletti again, but he pressed on. "I mean today, right now, this morning and afternoon. You don't have anything you were going to do with that guy you were playing with, do you?"

"Who, Raoul? No, no, nothing like that. Raoul's a sweet young man, but I'm afraid his tastes are for other sweet young men." She looked away, became thoughtful for a moment, almost as if she forgot Paul was there. "It's funny, I actually haven't made many friends here at the club, not like I thought I would. I admit that's why I started coming here, I thought it would be a good place to meet people. . . ."

"I find that hard to believe. A beautiful young woman like you. . . ."

The statement seemed to snap her out of it. She turned to him abruptly and swatted at him again, though what he said obviously pleased her. "Oh you, you're a big tease, aren't you? I'll bet you knew about Raoul all along."

He had a choice: it was laid out in front of him: it came down to this moment: he knew if he didn't come right out and ask her now, if he didn't try, he would never have another chance, because he would never put himself in this position again. Never. "Would you like to do something with me today?"

He blurted it out as she was about to stand up; she stopped dead. She tried to smile, fussed with her purse. "There, you see? You're a big tease. . . ."

"I'm serious. I'd like to go somewhere with you or have something to eat with you or anything you'd like to do. Look, I was never any good at this kind of stuff. I see all these guys on TV, they always have such good things to say, but I. . . ."

He closed his eyes for a moment, his hand working in front of him as if he were physically reaching for the right words. Then he clenched his hand into a fist and squeezed it, hard, and locked it into the other, his mouth pulled tight as a knife slit. He sat hunched over for a moment, his eyes still closed, then raised his head and looked at her, speaking to her in a soft measured tone. "I don't know what I'm supposed to say to you right now. But I'd really like to do something with you today. I'd really like to be with you."

She stared at him wide-eyed, blinking, visibly moved, though apparently unable to decide what to do. When she didn't respond after a full thirty seconds, Paul said the only thing left he could think to say. "I'm not going to hurt you."

"Oh, I know that," she laughed gaily. She looked around as if looking for something, anything. Then back to Paul, fifteen degrees off the side of his head. "Well, maybe we could go for a little drive. . . ."

Twenty-Three

The apartment was off South Bouquet Street, a few blocks from Sam's attic room, tucked away under the rear of the building, at the end of a dark passageway between the buildings and down a few steps. From the apartment windows overhead along the narrow passageway came the sound of a radio, a guy yelling at someone, the smells of tomato sauce and soap; directly above him, in an open kitchen window in the building next door, the sill lined with dirty glass jars of cuttings and bulbs, a calico cat peered down at him, watched him pass. Don't go knocking any of those jars down on my head, Puss-Puss. Sam knocked on Carla's door; the door fit badly in the frame and rattled at his touch, it would be easy to knock it down, easy for someone, not for him. No answer. He knocked again. The apartment window, looking out into the passageway, was curtained with a brown towel. How now, brown towel? There was no way to tell if anyone was inside or not. He knocked again. Nothing.

He sighed, loud enough to be heard on the other side of the door if anyone was listening, and scuffed back along the passageway past the window and up the steps. Then tiptoed back. Above him, the calico cat hunched down on the sill, thinking Sam was playing a game, its bright spotted face budding between the sprouts and jars. It could be this way, or it could be that, right, Calico-Puss? We're all mad. In a moment, just as he hoped, the edge of the brown towel peeked away from the window, and quickly dropped into place again. Sam walked back to the door and knocked again.

"Carla. It's Sam. Come with good tidings of great joy. Well, maybe just your basic run-of-the-mill joy. Matter of fact, I guess I don't have any specially good tidings either, just a cheery good morning."

"Go away, Sam."

"Now is that any way to treat a visitor? After I went to all the trouble to find where you live?"

"I can't see anybody now." Her voice sounded distant and small but not as if she was far away from the door; it sounded as if she had her face covered, as if her head was buried in her arms.

"Maybe there's something I can do to help."

"There's nothing nobody can do now. Nobody."

She sounded a little louder—as if she'd raised her head? It was a good sign, it meant at least she was paying attention to him—but her voice sounded slurred or drugged; that worried him. He sniffed the door but couldn't smell gas; if she was still this coherent, there was probably still time to help her, even if she was trying to overdose. He was glad he came when he did, he could probably break down the door if he had to. She was quiet for a long time. He wanted to keep her talking, in case she tried to do something now.

"Can't you let an old friend in? And I'm not just anyone. Sam I am, the guy who brings you flowers when you have to sit on the stool, the guy with never a discouraging word."

"Just go away, Sam. Please."

"Then I guess you better get used to the sound of my voice through this door, because I'm not going anywhere. Could get a little messy in regard to toilet facilities, but if you don't mind I don't. . . ."

"Why are you doing this? Why can't you just leave me alone? I want to be alone now."

He could barely understand the words.

"Because I heard what happened. About you having to work Ianni's private party. And I can guess what all happened. Come on Carla, open the door. You need somebody right now, and I'm probably the best you've got."

It was quiet inside for a moment. Then he heard her stirring, getting up—had she been sitting, lying on the floor?—and coming across the room. She hesitated on the other side of the door.

"It's okay, Carla," he said softly.

The chain was lifted out of the slot, the bolt pulled back; the door opened a few inches, then stopped. He waited; when the door didn't open any farther, he pushed it open slowly and stepped inside. The girl, in the wedge of dim light from the door, was on her way back across the room, toward the bed.

He closed the door—the wedge of light went out—and he stood where he was until his eyes got used to the darkness. The only illumination in the one-room apartment came from the curtained window looking out on the passageway and another window he could see through the open door to the bathroom. Gradually he could make out that the room was in total disarray: there were dirty clothes and dirty dishes everywhere, a couple of open suitcases on the floor, the dresser drawers and closet open. Carla sat on the bed, huddled back in the corner, her legs tucked under her, as she tried to light a cigarette. She was wearing a threadbare multistriped bathrobe; she pulled at her hair, which had sweated out of any of its curl, her loose and springy perm, and lay lifeless against her head, tried to pull it down to cover the side of her face.

Sam, when he could see well enough, picked his way through the things on the floor, dumped a pile of clothes off one of the straight chairs at the table and carried it over beside the bed, and sat down. He opened his peacoat, put his shoulder bag down on the floor beside him, leaned forward on his elbows. Carla was trying to smoke, trying to hold the cigarette between her torn and swollen lips. It was worse than he feared, than he ever imagined. Cuts and bruises covered her face, her face swollen more on one side than the other so it appeared wrenched off center, the girl almost unrecognizable. It took everything he could muster to remain calm and nonchalant, matter-of-fact, though he felt his crotch clench, felt slightly nauseated.

"Well now," he said, smoothing his long hair, bringing his hands together to his forehead and sweeping them over the top and down either side to his shoulders. "Anything broken that you know of?"

She shook her head carefully, not looking at him.

"Okay. That's good. Teeth all in place?"

She nodded.

He sighed his relief. "Have you done anything for. . . ?" he gestured toward her face.

"Some ice." She pointed to a couple of towels, now only wet, lying in a wad on the floor. When she talked she tried not to move her lips—he thought it was a wonder that he understood her at all through the door.

"But nothing for the cuts. Let me see what you have," he said, starting to get up, to check the bathroom for first-aid supplies.

"You heard . . . what happened?"

He sat back down again. "None of the particulars. And nothing about . . . this. I just heard you were working the private party, after you said you wouldn't, and I knew it couldn't be good." He waited a moment before continuing. "Have you taken any pills or anything?"

"No."

"I need to know."

She shook her head again.

He reached in his shoulder bag on the floor and pulled out a small bottle of Courvoisier. "Well then, how about a drink of this?"

"No, that's okay."

"Now darlin', I broke some of my rules to get this, I even hit on a couple of out-of-towners." He threaded his way over to the sink and brought back a couple of fairly clean-looking glasses. "I even let them photograph me with my arm around a guy's wife, I'll be immortalized in somebody's plastic album in Omaha as the time Aunt Martha met a real live hippie. The least you can do is have a little drink with me."

She looked at him as though she'd like to be mad at him but didn't have the strength. He handed her a glass and she drank from the corner of her mouth, trying to keep it away from the still-bleeding cracks on her lips. He poured himself some in the bottom of the glass but didn't touch it. Some of the Cognac must have found its way into her sores; she cried out a little and put her hand to her mouth, the liquid running down over her chin and through her fingers, dripping down on her robe. Sam handed her a towel and she dabbed at the robe, at her chin, and he poured her a little more. She drank more slowly this time.

"That helps a little now, doesn't it?"

She nodded, unsure, and held the glass on her knee, staring at it, not looking at him, thinking about something, remembering.

"Now then, I think you better let me have a closer look at the damage."

"No."

"Yes, baby girl, yes."

He reached over and turned on the small bedside light, an art deco pixie lamp—its dancing bronze harlequin balancing a silver globe on her outstretched toe—that provided only speckled illumination. Carefully, with two fingers barely touching the bottom of her chin, he lifted her face to look at him, brushed the strands of hair with the same two fingertips back from her face, and she let him. The sight of the bruises covering her face, her black eyes, the gashes from a ring or belt buckle or both—My god, the bastards, the bastards—got him in the groin again but he was careful not to show it, not to show anything. The wounds appeared clean and not too deep though there were a couple that should have stitches.

"Let me help you get dressed and get you to a hospital."

Her look said no and it was obvious she meant it this time so he didn't press it

"Well, it was just an idea," he said, lisping and flopping his wrist, and she smiled a little, it was enough that she let him help her at all. The bastards. Nor had she tried to do anything foolish or fatal, such as try to check out. Good girl. He went to the bathroom to see what she had in the way of bandages and antiseptics—nothing—and came back with a washcloth and a bowl of hot water. From his shoulder bag on the floor, looking at the moment like a lumpy fringed pillow, he pulled out a box of cotton, some bandages, and a bottle of hydrogen peroxide.

"You just happen to have some stuff with you, right?"

"Yeah, well," he shrugged. "You never know when it might come in handy. Let's see what we can do for you."

Twenty-Four

She stepped out of her dress, then her slip, leaving them like puddles on the floor, squirmed out of her pantyhose and dropped them over a chair arm, stepped back into her high heels—he always liked her this way, in her panties and bra and high heels, it always turned him on—and walked over to the curtains, to the center of the floor-to-ceiling drapes across the windows and parted them a little ways, split them apart with the edge of her hand, looking out over Mellon Square eighteen floors below, laid out on top of an underground parking garage, the harlequin pattern of the paving, the rows of planters and fountains, only a few scattered people occupying the granite benches on a Saturday morning. Along the cornice of a high-rise building cattycornered to the park, a row of crouching stone Atlas figures held up the roof. The sunlight, as she stood in her underwear, in the parting of the drapes, was warm on her arms and shoulders, warm as a lover's touch.

"He doesn't know what he's doing with the movie, does he, Fran?" came the voice behind her. "I'll bet he doesn't even have a shooting schedule at this point."

"I gave you a copy. It was in the packet of things I left at the front desk for you."

"Then he isn't following it. You sent me some of the early rushes, remember? He's not shooting at all what he said he was going to. I don't see how he could even have a story line at this point. It's no wonder the studio pulled out."

She kept her back to him, though she could see Thorsten lying on the bed in the reflection in the glass; the bar of sunlight, the sunlight coming through the opening of the drapes, fell across the dark room like a glimpse of another time frame, a slice from another world. Let him get a good look at me. My ass. Let him get a taste for it. God I hope it still looks good enough to want. Now's a fine time to think of it.

He was in his early sixties though he appeared no older than Fran except for his styled and layered gray hair; he had a long, lean runner's body—he still ran three miles a day—and a deep tan that he maintained even through the long Minnesota winters. A truly handsome, distinctive man, even more so as he got older. He lay propped up on the pillows, still in his suit pants and blue oxford cloth shirt, his regimental striped tie and tasseled loafers, hands folded across his stomach, watching her. She knew him well enough to know that he would want to clear away the business at hand before considering anything else. But he could certainly see what she was offering in the bargain. Good for you, little girl.

"He's got a basic story line. The idea was to expand on it. Let the characters build on it as he goes along."

"Come on, Frannie. Remember who you're talking to here."

Guess I better parade it around a bit too. She let the drapes fall closed again—the bar of light went away, the room once again in darkness, in the dark glow from the drapes. She went over to the dresser, to her purse, and took out a cigarette, lit it, blowing the smoke at the ceiling.

"He's trying to go beyond what he's done in the past, he's trying to do something better. He's tired of being labeled as only a Grade-B porno-thriller director. He wants to show he can do a film that's in the same league with Coppola or Penn any other mainstream director. I can't blame him for that."

"I can't either. The problem is, the studio thought they were paying for a mainstream porno-thriller."

"He knows that. We've talked about it."

"The trades say he can't even decide on a title for it." Thorsten adjusted his glasses, the thin squarish white-gold frames, with two precise fingers. "I'm not a fool, Frannie. Please don't try to treat me like one."

She regarded him, her right foot tilted back on her stiletto heel, cradling her breasts as she picked an imaginary piece of tobacco from the tip of her tongue. No, he was certainly no fool, she had known that for a long time. What she tended to forget was that he knew her as well as she knew him.

Their families had been close friends in Minneapolis, her father a doctor, his father a real estate investor; the two families even shared a vacation cottage in the lake country for many years. Malcolm was often around while she was growing up; she had had a crush on the older boy for as long as she could remember, but he never seemed to know that she existed. Then after she graduated from Northwestern and moved to LA, after she settled in Hollywood and got a job with Roger Corman, Malcolm called, out of the blue, saying he was in town on business and wanted to take her to dinner. As it turned out, he wanted more than that. He had inherited his father's fortune and had decided to invest in movies; he wanted Fran to teach him about the industry, and put him in touch with the right people. And he wanted her too. She found that he had always been aware of her back in Minneapolis, he was only waiting for her to grow up. At the time, his calculating nature attracted her to him even more; it was only later that she began to understand the depth of those calculations, and that it might be something other than love that would make a man wait until a young girl became ripe.

"Nicko isn't the major talent he always wanted to be and thinks he is," she said. "But he is a good director and writer, he's better than just competent, and that's more than you can say for a lot of the people in this industry. He was on the same wavelength as Coppola and Scorsese and Peckinpah, and he was on it long before all the imitators picked up on it. He did it on his own, he tackled subjects and visual imagery no one else would touch, he was original. And he should have the chance to make the film that he feels is in him."

"Coming from you, Frannie, that's almost touching. It almost sounds like marital loyalty."

"Screw you."

"You're a remarkable woman."

"We made a lot of money for you," she said, still standing at the dresser, smoking. *This isn't going well. If things don't improve pretty soon, I'm going to feel like a damn fool standing around here in my underwear.* She went over to one of the easy chairs and sat down, crossing her legs, swinging her foot in his direction.

Thorsten pressed his fingertips together to form a kind of temple, then considered the architecture. "You know, here's something I never thought about before. I always thought I was the one who singled out Nicko. I always thought I got interested in him because of what you told me about him, and that I asked you to put me in touch with him. It never occurred to me that maybe Nicko was the one who singled me out, after you told him about me. That he asked you to get me interested in financing his first film. Interesting."

"You asked me if I knew any promising young filmmakers. And I did."

Thorsten was pursuing his own line of thought. "It would certainly explain a few things. I've always been curious how Nicko rectified it in his mind that you and I were lovers. I would sit across from him in meetings and think surely he must know I'm screwing his wife. How could he bring himself to talk to me? But it never seemed to faze him."

"To be honest, I don't know whether he ever knew for certain or not. He always suspected it, and that was enough for Nicko. After that, it didn't really matter to him whether we were actually lovers or not. He's an artist, to that extent at least, his own version of reality is the only one that interests him. I frankly don't think he would want to know for sure. It would destroy the suspicion. The illusion, the fantasies. The only thing that really matters to Nicko are the pictures going on in his head."

"You may be right. I always supposed he simply chose to ignore it, afraid to say anything because he didn't want to upset the arrangement and lose his financing. What I never considered was the possibility that Nicko more or less sanctioned our affair. That it was all according to plan, as it were."

"What difference would it make? You got what you wanted, which was me. And you got your investments. I'm the only one in the arrangement who could object, I was the one being used."

"Don't pretend to be a victim, Frannie, it doesn't become you. If anyone ever uses you, it's only in ways that you find are to your advantage."

She felt herself blush; this man knew her so well. She wondered at times if she chose the wrong one to be the husband, the wrong one to be the lover. She married Nicko, but it often felt as if Malcolm were the one she loved. "You still didn't say what difference it would make to you."

"I didn't say it would make a difference. If I'm concerned at all, it's in the realm of control. Control determines the taker from the taken. It's essential to know the difference, if one is going to do business."

"Ah yes. Everything comes down to business, doesn't it?"

He shrugged noncommittal, not wishing to pursue the point.

"Nicko was good business for you," she went on. "He made a lot of money for you."

"You said that before. And you're right, he did. No question about that. On the other hand I gave him a lot of money so he could continue to live out his fantasies up there on the screen."

"You gave him a lot of money so you could live out your fantasies, too. So you could be involved with the glamour and excitement of a world that you could never be included in otherwise. Don't kid yourself, Malcolm, you needed Nicko at least as much as he needed you. Maybe more so. Because Nicko was the one doing it, he was the one who was actually making the movies. Maybe he did live out some of his fantasies through what he put up there on the screen, but at least he didn't live out his fantasies through someone else's life."

Thorsten, not angry, simply matter-of-fact, swung his legs over and sat on the edge of the bed. "You want me to take over the financing of this film, is that right?"

"Yes."

"I said you are a remarkable woman, and I meant it. And you're intelligent enough to know what my answer is going to be. You must know my answer, because otherwise you would never allow yourself to say the things you just did. Frannie the businesswoman would have kept her emotions to herself."

"Malcolm, I—"

He waved his hands in front of him; and as if he were a magician, she became silent.

"I don't know why you made your deal for this movie with the studio instead of me. . . ."

"We knew we were talking bigger money than the other—"

"Stop it!" This time he cut her off with the slice of his hand; it was the first time she had ever seen the anger she always suspected he was capable of. "You also knew that I would want a piece of it. But that's not the reason I'm going to pass on the offer to take it over now."

He closed his eyes for a moment as he regained his control. When he finally looked at her again, his blue eyes behind the metal-frame glasses were neither warm nor cold.

"You said it yourself, Frannie. I'm a businessman. And you're a businesswoman. You know that write-offs can only go so far. I want fair return, in some way or other, for the money I invest. Maybe Nicko made money for me in the past, but I don't see how he can do that for me now, not with this property. If this film is supposed to be his big story, he's showing me that he doesn't know what his big story is. But it's not a question of aesthetics. It's purely business."

Fran tilted back her head and aimed a thin blue shaft of smoke at the ceiling before crushing out the butt and getting up from the chair. Showtime, little girl. It's now or never.

Twenty-Five

"This is where it all started, right here in this little machine," Nicko said and jumped up from behind his desk, hurrying over to a bookcase and taking down an old Keystone 8mm movie camera. He flipped out the wind-up key from the side and gave it a few cranks, then put the camera to his eye, going through the motions of taking footage with it, pretending, making a show of it; he panned the room, squatted down to get a better angle, framed various images, his desk, his chair in front of the windows, slowing down as he swept over the clutter on top of his desk—he thought of the long panning shot around the room as Jack Nicholson played the Chopin Prelude in *Five Easy Pieces*, the slow pan over the photos on the mantel and family mementos, giving the background of the entire story right there, or as much as you needed to know of it, setting the stage for the Nicholson character's personal crisis—God what a lovely scene, what a lovely use of the camera, delicate and haunting and like a kick in the balls at the same time, I doubt that anyone ever did it better; God how I wish I had done it—then began to take what he was doing more seriously, got caught up in it, began to actually watch, study, the images as they became framed in the view-finder, the desk cluttered with manuscripts and books, stained coffee cups, his small porcelain owl, the Dundee orange marmalade jar full of pens, a handkerchief wadded into the cushion of his chair, a storyboard for the scene at Pitt on the wall, the balls of crumpled worksheets having missed their mark in more ways than one on the floor around the wastebasket, repeating to himself as if addressing a class of admiring film students, A long panning shot primarily establishes continuity; in a large landscape it establishes the scale, in close quarters it sets a mood of intimacy; the shot creates a flow that, depending upon the pacing and subject, can create a feeling of tension or calm, depending also on the skill of the director, seeing in the tiny yellowed viewfinder the office of if not a successful man then at least a hardworking one, a man who was certainly trying. Then he remembered himself, lowered the camera. Janet Rawlins, a pretty young woman in her early thirties with long layered brown hair, dressed in a wine-colored wool suit, pink blouse, and oxblood high-heeled boots, sat in the chair across from the desk, legs crossed, watching him, a bemused expression on her face.

"Sorry," Nicko said, giving her his best little-boy expression. "I guess I got carried away."

"No, no, that's fine," Janet Rawlins said, circling her hand to encourage him to go on.

"It's just that this is where it all started, this little camera. Using it is how I first learned that I had something to say with a camera, even as a kid. I used to make monster movies in my backyard with all the neighborhood kids as actors—and, I might add, then sell them tickets so they could see themselves on the screen."

"That's maybe where it started," Janet Rawlins said. "But I'm curious where it's going now."

Nicko looked at her, moved his tongue to the side of his mouth, a shrewd look to acknowledge her shrewdness; he snapped the wind-up key into place and placed the camera back on the shelf.

"I don't suppose, Miss Rawlins," he said, going back to his desk, but not behind it now, sitting instead on the front of it, leaning the backs of his thighs against it, "that this is going to be one of those interviews where the interviewer takes the interviewee apart when she gets him in print, is it?"

"You told me that I should call you Francis, or Nicko. You should call me Janet."

"All right then. Janet."

"And do you really think," she said, cocking her head at him, standing her pen on end for a moment on her notepad, "that I'm the kind of person who could do such a thing?"

Nicoletti looked first at her tape recorder, then, between the tops of her boots and her skirt, her lovely knees, then at her eyes. "Young lady—Janet—I get the distinct feeling that you could do just about anything you set your mind to."

"I'll say this, I think you're a bit of a flatterer."

"For a moment I was afraid you were going to say I was a tease," he said, leaning in her direction. "A great big tease."

"A tease?" she laughed. She flipped her pen on its head and back again a couple of times. "No, I might call you a number of things, but a tease isn't one of them."

"What then? Name one."

"You're a manipulator."

He raised his eyebrows, as if mildly surprised. "And what did I do to make you think I'm a manipulator?"

"Well, for one thing, you're trying to turn this interview around so that I'm the one answering questions."

"The terrible thing," he said laughing, "is that I'm succeeding."

"Yes, I know," she laughed again. Reaching back and lifting her hair off her collar, the back of her neck.

"Remember I am a director. And director is another name for manipulator."

"You're also a writer and producer."

"That was nice of you not to sneer."

"Why would I sneer?"

Nicko shrugged, shook his head, washed his hand down the lower part of his face and dug deep into his beard momentarily. Then pushed off from the front of his desk, walked around, and sat down behind it. Studied his hands folded on his blotter for a moment. "I think there are a number of people who would argue the validity of using those terms in regard to yours truly. At least in terms of success."

"Your films in the late sixties were very successful."

"Oh yes, financially that's true, but looking back at it now it seems a rather dubious distinction, or at least ironic, to have your work so completely misunderstood, to see it become so popular for the wrong reasons. What I meant when I said 'in terms of success' was artistic success. Whatever that means. I think there are a lot of people who would dispute that in regard to my work. Of course, let me say right here and now that *I* consider those movies artistically successful, as far as I was allowed to fulfill my vision for them by the studios. Now I want to grow beyond the view of the world those films presented."

She looked quickly over her notes, then appeared to abandon whatever was written there and charge ahead on her own. "So, if, when you started, you were interested in making . . . let's call them meaningful films, why did you start to make porno-horror films? Why did you decide to do *A House Turned Red?*"

"Are you suggesting that I only did *House* for the money?"

"There you go again," she said, uncrossing and recrossing her legs—her knees flashed at him—"trying to turn it around so I'm the one answering questions." He didn't nod this time, he just looked at her. "The question is whether *you* think you did it only for the money. You obviously liked all the fame and money you got with films like *House* and *Death Dealer*, anybody would. So isn't that really why you started to make sexploitation films?"

He studied her for a moment, looking at her from under his heavy eyebrows; he wanted to take out his glasses and get a really good look at her without the fuzziness—he carried them in his jacket pocket for emergencies only, though he was supposed to wear them for distance all the time—but his vanity kept him from it. He had misjudged her, underestimated her, this was no ordinary young woman, this one was harder, or if she was ordinary, in her flutterings and flirtations she had an instinct for the jugular. Which made her genuinely attractive to him for the first time. He blew a little breeze up through the ends of his mustache, a soft hiss.

"You may find this hard to believe—Janet—but I thought at the time I did *House* and those other films that I was in the creative vanguard of things."

"Well, I know that's what the critics say about them now. But is that really what you had in your mind then?" She smiled at him.

She not only finds the jugular, he thought, she likes to suck on it too. He felt suddenly drained, weary—she wasn't in fact asking him anything that he hadn't asked himself, over and over again; or rather, had used a great deal of energy over a great deal of time to keep from asking himself—for that very reason he forced himself to his feet and moved back to his perch on the front of the desk, leaning away from it, toward her, like a bushy-bearded gargoyle in a rumpled corduroy suit, forced his juices to start flowing again, the energy to start flowing again, to go on, go through with it.

"It may be hard for someone your age to understand—I'm making a point about age because you are younger, a lot of things you may take for granted weren't always that way—but when things opened up in the sixties and the mores started to change, it was as if we all threw away the yoke not only from the fifties and forties or even the thirties, it was as if we came out from under the weight of the entire Victorian era, the whole stifling atmosphere of Protestantism and Puritanism, it was as if the arts and society were picking up things again we had lost all the way back to the Renaissance. Everything was changing, clothes for instance—it was suddenly all right for guys to look fancy again, how long had that been?—music, politics, everything; it really felt like it was the dawn of a new age. And movies changed, suddenly you could show things that before you always had to cover up. It actually seemed for a while that major Hollywood stars would soon be doing pornos, though of course then they wouldn't be pornos, they'd be legitimate, they'd be art or they'd be plain old movies. Brando did *Last Tango*; people began to take the Mitchell brothers' films seriously; they even talked about Marilyn Chambers or Linda Lovelace as if they were truly actresses. It really began to look like a filmmaker would be able to show the sex life of his characters, and that was a tremendous step, a challenge, a person's sex life is a pretty big chunk of their character, after all. That was all forbidden before that, verboten, you could never show such things. It was a very exciting prospect. And I thought I was taking it to its next logical step, I thought I was extending the medium."

"By showing a man tormenting a woman, raping and torturing her in every conceivable way, and then bashing her head in?"

"By explicitly showing the ties between sex and violence, by showing the audience what might be going on in some level of their minds."

"Are you sure you weren't just showing what might be going on in some level of your mind? Are you sure you weren't the one who primarily liked the fantasies involved?"

"Well, of course they were going on in my mind, that's what

I'm getting at, that's what I thought filmmakers could, and should, show. Yes, they're inside me, they're inside all of us, they always have been and most likely they always will. Wait a minute, I was reading something the other day . . . where is it?" He made a halfhearted search through a few of the piles of papers and magazines close at hand, then dismissed them all with a wave. "Well, it's around here somewhere. Anyway, there were some woodcuts of Kublai Khan's invasion of Japan in the thirteenth century, I was thinking of what a hell of a movie that would make, if you wanted to do some kind of epic, there were something like five thousand ships, incredible for that age, incredible for any age. I suppose that's wishful thinking on my part, Christ, I can't even get financing for this little picture. Anyway, it seems that when the khan's troops raided the outlying villages, after they killed all the men and raped the women, the soldiers cut slits in the women's hands so they could thread ropes through them. Then they strung the women up on the bows of their ships as they returned home, showing off their trophies."

Janet Rawlins visibly shuddered. Nicko leaned back from his perch on the edge of the desk, watching her intently, her reaction to what he was saying. Sure that he was dazzling her with his perceptions and understanding of the human condition. It was a familiar pattern to him, what he found with his movies: when he talked about the most disturbing sexual acts, people might cringe, might even turn away momentarily, but they always came back for more, they couldn't help themselves, they couldn't get enough of it—and in regards to pretty young women, they couldn't get enough of him either. It was too bad he already told Suzy he would take her to the party tonight, he would have liked to take this Janet Rawlins instead, it would be good for her article to show him in action. And it was obvious the way she was watching him that she was interested in him for more than just a magazine piece. He leaned closer to her again, his hands clamped on the edge of the desk, his face inches from hers.

"People try to tell you about the good old days when life was simpler. Fact is, their atrocities were simpler and more to the point back in the good old days too. But you tell me the difference between that and the businessman who walks around with a young dolly on his arm and shows her off at a trade show or a convention or something where everyone knows he's been upstairs pumping her in his room. Or, walking into a restaurant with a trophy wife on your arm, be it your own or somebody else's, all the better if it's somebody else's. It's a matter of degree, not kind. Man has a natural tendency toward dominance, to want to kill all the men in sight and get all the women, and then show off his success and his rapes to other men. It's a fact of human nature. You might want to change it, it might offend your feminine or humane instincts, we all might want to change it—I want to change it, for Christ's sake, why do you think I'm doing these movies?—but first you've got to recognize that's the way the world is."

Twenty-Six

They drove, in her yellow 280Z, around the city for several hours, through the rest of the morning and on into the afternoon, played tourist, circled the city on the Blue Belt, dipping in and out of neighborhoods—they made a game of it, looking for the white signs with blue circles on the unfamiliar streets—from Homestead to Bellevue, McKees Rocks to Aspinwall, places neither one of them had ever been, crisscrossing back and forth over the three rivers, grateful for the signs to follow because Paul didn't know any place particular to go and because Suzy seemed afraid to stop. As he rode beside her, he could smell her, clean and cinnamony. The warm air from the open windows played up her arms and ballooned the loose top of her tennis dress until it barely touched her shoulders; through the armholes of the sleeveless top he caught glimpses of her bra straps and her tanned skin, the beginning curves of her breasts, that excited him as much as if he were a teenager. In the confines of the tight car, his leg was inches from hers and when she rested her hand on the gearshift knob their arms, on turns, brushed against each other. The pleats of her tiny white skirt spread like fingers over the tops of her thighs; he noticed her tan was uneven, that the fronts of her arms and legs were slightly darker than the backs, and there was a vapor of light blond hair on her arms that haloed the softness of her skin. He could imagine touching skin as soft as hers for hours at a time, just running his hand over her. He could not imagine ever growing tired of her.

As they drove, they talked about little things, the weather and the day and things they saw along the streets, talked about anything (and nothing) it seemed, simply to keep talking, though over the course of several hours, in bits and pieces and without Paul ever asking her, he learned the following about Suzy: that she took one hundred thousand units of vitamin A every day to make sure the acne didn't return that appeared on her face after the first time she slept with a man; that the dermatologist who prescribed the vitamin A therapy was in Philadelphia and that she flew there once a month to see him; that she went to the dermatologist after she tried going to a psychiatrist who didn't clear up her face, he only messed up her mind; that the dermatologist put her on a diet that consisted mainly of broccoli and broiled chicken for the evening meal; that the reason she and Francis didn't see each other more often, he swore, had nothing to do with the broccoli and broiled chicken; that she was jealous of her sister Jean, who she thought was much prettier than herself even though Jean had two kids and cellulite; that she loved dogs, hated cats; that someday she wanted to paint and learn modern dance, and maybe write a book, a book of children's poetry; that her favorite color was white, then blue; that the funniest joke she ever heard was the one about the man with a banana in his ear; that her idea of style was to walk into the Duquesne Club with two Afghan hounds; that her idea of class was to walk into the Duquesne Club with two Afghan hounds and not be flustered when they said dogs aren't allowed and asked her to leave; that her idea of having made it was to walk into the Duquesne Club with two Afghan hounds and be allowed to stay anyway; that she considered people who pick their noses to be mentally retarded; that she had to run water in the sink, and sometimes hum a little tune, before she could tinkle; that she considered being physically fit a moral imperative, whatever that was; that she considered working-class people to be more honest because they were so basic and down-to-earth; that she never wanted to live anyplace that didn't have a swimming pool; that she loved her current apartment even though it didn't have a swimming pool; that she thought plants are our friends; that she felt America was the only country in the world that was close to God; that she didn't know whether God existed or not but that she thought there had to be Something up there; that she had to agree with Rauschenberg, or maybe it was Jasper Johns, that the American flag was really a work of art; that she always thought Tom Petty's "American Girl" was written about her; that the only reason poor people are poor is because they don't try hard enough to better themselves; that people can do anything they want to with their lives; that people can be anything they want to be, if they want it badly enough; that a Mercedes is actually a better car than a Rolls; that Puffs tissues are better than Kleenex because they don't have so much lint; that men look sexy in tennis shorts but that sweat turns her off; that she thought the arms race and the threat of nuclear holocaust were really serious problems but she was sure the president and the generals knew what they were doing; that she would never marry a man like Francis, even if he asked her.

When he asked her if she had been following the fall of Saigon, she said she saw it was in the news but it was all just too de-pressing, that she changed the channel whenever such news came on. That she thought it was important to keep a positive attitude toward life.

She never asked a thing about Paul and his life, and Paul never said.

Only once did his curiosity get the better of him. He asked, "How's Nicoletti?"

"He's fine," she glanced at him warily. "He's very busy with this new film. . . ."

"No, I mean how are you two getting along?"

"Why do you ask?"

"Just curious."

She smiled, tossed back her head and downshifted. "We're fine, just fine. We have our ups and downs, but you have to expect that. Especially in an open relationship like ours. He's free to do his thing—he *is* married, after all—and I'm free to do mine. But thanks for asking."

He wondered what she meant exactly by an open relationship, but was afraid to ask.

In the early afternoon, after she announced that she was tired of driving and needed something to tide her over until dinner, they drove to the Strip District and joined the weekend crowds shopping for fresh produce and meats. At the Pennsylvania Mac-aroni Company they bought containers of pasta salad and Italian vegetables and a warm mini baguette—Susy insisted that she pay—stopped at a state store for a couple bottles of red wine—Paul insisted it was his turn to pay, and Suzy conceded, reluctantly—then drove to Schenley Park where they sat at an overlook sharing the containers of food and drinking the wine from paper cups—she produced a corkscrew from the glove com-partment and the paper cups from behind the seat; he thought she must do this with Nicoletti, have picnics with him, that's why she knew where to buy the food, where to go in the park—watching the runners and families at a playground and half a dozen guys playing Frisbee. When there was still some wine left, she suggested they take it back to her apartment to finish it.

"Your apartment?" The wine had made Paul heady, he wasn't sure he heard her correctly.

"Why, Paul, you're blushing," she said, and patted his knee. "You don't have to worry, I promise I won't seduce you or anything. I only want to show you something, that's all."

As she backed out of the parking space, she winked at him, scrunched her shoulders and giggled at a private joke, then slammed the gearshift into first and popped the clutch, sending the 280Z careening down the winding road amid screeching tires and pinging gravel. Paul's senses reeled.

Twenty-Seven

He bent over her and held her face with one hand, dabbing carefully at the cuts with the washcloth and wads of cotton; the hydrogen peroxide fizzled in the cuts, in the still-open sores around her mouth and cheeks. She stared, wide-eyed, he thought at his forehead or maybe at someplace far away; then her eyes brimmed.

"I know, I know," he said, trying to be more careful. "This must really hurt—"

"He wanted me to do all his friends. There were all these guys there, all his friends, and he had this table with stirrups like they do in a doctor's office—"

"It's okay, baby girl. It's over now—"

"I wouldn't do it but they made me do it anyway, they held me down and they all took turns, they just stood around and laughed and looked at me, and then they wanted me to do other stuff too and I wouldn't and Ianni beat me up in front of them and then some of them did things to me anyway. . . ."

"It's over now, Carla, I promise it's over."

"How do I know they won't get me again? How do I know they won't come here after me?"

"Because I'm going to stay close by until you get your strength back, and your face stops looking like a beach ball, and then we're going to help you get someplace where you'll be safe."

He cradled her face in his hand again and tried to position her better in the meager illumination from the pixie lamp as he went back to work on the wounds. She mumbled something, a word, that he didn't understand, meant more for herself he supposed than for him; he waited a moment, for her to volunteer what she had said, waited to see if she needed to talk about anything.

"Columbus," she said.

He stopped dabbing and looked at her and went back to dabbing again. "As in Christopher? As in finding a new world?"

"No. Ohio. That's where I'm from. Columbus."

"I would have said the eastern part of the state, there's more of an Appalachian twang in your voice, the kind you get toward West Virginia."

"My grandparents lived in West Virginia, near Wheeling. I used to spend summers there."

"Your favorite grandparents," he said, and waited for her nod. "The Talmud says—at least I think it's the Talmud—the reason grandparents are so special to us is because they're the enemies of our enemies. Nice, huh? This is going to sting a little . . . hold on. Look, how about a little more Courvoisier before we go on with this? I don't know about you, but I sure need some."

He poured more into the water glasses and they each took a couple of swallows before he went back to work. She gripped his left arm in both her hands, holding on to him as though he were a pole in a world that has a tendency to tilt, holding him, he thought, not only because of the pain of the cuts.

"Columbus," he said, patting at the wounds as if putting on the finishing, careful touches to his creation. "Nice town,

Columbus. Fairly clean, as I remember, not like Cleveland or Cincinnati. Let me see: you probably tried Ohio State but didn't like it."

"Too close to home."

"So you transferred to Pitt and stayed on afterward. A familiar story."

"I got interested in theater and took some classes at the Playhouse. I thought if I got good enough maybe I could get into the CMU graduate program."

"And to earn money you started dancing at Nirvana."

"I tried the temp agencies for a while, but I couldn't stand being cooped up in an office all day."

He sat back to look at her, admiring his handiwork. "There. That's as good as I can do. We'll just have to watch to make sure they heal okay. Otherwise, my girl, hi-ho, hi-ho, it's off to the emergency room we go."

She was sitting on the bed in much the same pose as she sat on her stool in the doorway of Nirvana, one leg balanced out over the knee of the other, swinging her foot a little, her multi-striped cotton robe falling open at the thigh, the pale leg covered with bristle, her foot dirty, or maybe it was just the pallor of her skin, the sole and up the sides and heel red, as if she'd stepped in something, watching him watching her. "Why are you doing this?"

He chuckled. "Maybe because there's a little bit of Columbus in us all, Ohio as well as Christopher—"

As he spoke, he reached to clear a strand of her hair that was stuck in one of her wounds but she grabbed his hand, stopping him.

"That's not what I meant, and you know it. Why are you doing this for me? Why do you want to help me?"

She held his hand in both of hers, looking into his face. He started to pull back, started to chuckle but then stopped to look at her in the glow of the lamp, this pale and unlovely, damaged girl, her hair, limp and stringy now, that didn't look right even after it was set and never would, her skin that would always be blotchy and coarse, and her features that would never be beautiful or even pretty, this girl, for that matter, who would probably never be loved, for that matter though she would probably be fucked enough because she would never be attractive enough or intelligent enough or have enough money to make the best of what good qualities she did have—all that, of course, before someone had tried to turn her face into pulp and almost succeeded— and he broke.

"Because we all have to help each other. Because the world is such a terrifying place, even under the best conditions, and we're all responsible for each other and we have to help each other try to get through this shit, we have to try to make it better for each other if we can, we have to try to do what we can, there's evil in this world, there's evil. . . ."

She pulled him gently from the chair onto the bed and he lay beside her, his head in her lap, crying, his face, his cheek resting against her bare leg, his tears tracing down her thigh, as she stroked his hair, ran her hand down his long hair, comforted him, rocked him gently back and forth.

"Ah, Sammy," she said, bending over him as best she could, speaking softly into his ear. "I was the one that got beat up, and you're the one that's hurting."

Twenty-Eight

She unhooked her bra and let it fall to the floor, pulled down her panties and stepped out of them. She went over and stood in front of him as he sat on the edge of the bed, still in her high heels. The way he always liked her.

Malcolm put his hand on her thigh, ran his fingertips up the curve of her thigh and over the ridge of her pelvis and down again, almost as if he were appraising her. For a moment he watched his hand, his fingertips moving over her skin, lost in thought or memory or the sensation itself. A chill ran through her. He smiled, tight-lipped; then he patted her twice with the flat of his hand. Like patting the flank of a horse.

"You're also intelligent enough to know this is over."

"That's the funny thing," Fran said, looking down at him. She touched his gray hair. For the first time she was aware that the room was chilly, as if the chill air on her body outlined her, defined her. "I think that's why I could stand to try to sell myself to you one more time."

Thorsten thought a moment, then eased by her and went over to the table and started putting his papers back in his briefcase. "If you'll excuse me. I can still catch a plane back to Minneapolis this afternoon."

Fran stepped out of her shoes and sat down on the edge of the bed. She touched the spot on the coverlet where Malcolm had been sitting, then lay back on the pillows. "I think I'll stay here for a while. If you don't mind."

Malcolm looked at her as he put on his suit jacket. "Won't Nicko think we were sleeping together, even though you didn't make the deal?" Then a look of recognition came over his face. "Oh, I see."

She smiled at him in return; he understood her so well. Suddenly she felt very very tired; she turned on her side, away from him. Malcolm came over and folded the other half of the coverlet over her. He bent down and kissed her hair.

"I'll miss you, ballsy lady."

She tucked the pillow under her head as she heard the door close behind him, rolled in the blanket as if it were a cocoon, felt herself starting to drift away. Ballsy lady. I guess that's me, all right. Except in Nicko's mind it's another way of saying "castrating bitch." Oh Malcolm, I've missed you so much over the course of my life, I've even learned to live with it. . . .

Twenty-Nine

Janet Rawlins was feeling slightly sick to her stomach. She watched Francis Nicoletti watching her, thinking of how many of her impressions of him she could include in her article. There were tufts of silver hair springing out from the side of his head, tufts of hoary hair sticking out of his ears, a hair poking out of a nostril and winding up around the tip of his nose; his knuckles looked oversized and wrinkly as they curled around the edge of the desk, like they were made of dough; the backs of his hands were covered with hair, the veins on the backs of his hands like blue worms, like the veins and bulges of a flaccid cock. He looked every bit like what she had heard about him, even from her editor on the phone when they first talked about the project, that Nicoletti was a man who never lived up to his potential. She had already formulated her opening sentences, before coming here today: *Francis Paul Xavier Nicoletti looks tired. The man who made and subsequently lost a fortune during the late '60s in X-rated movies sits in his office looking like the subject, possibly the victim, of one of his own porno-horror epics. . . .* But it was more than the physical presence of the man that was getting to her. He looked at her as if he planned to make her his latest prize, looked at her as if she were one of the trophy rapes he had just described, a piece of sexual meat to be slung on the bow of a conqueror's ship after being staked out spread-eagled, for any man to enjoy. She had come into this interview with a distaste of the man—not the man himself necessarily, she had never met him before, knew only what she had heard and read about him in her research for the article. But now, having spent time with him, she could say she truly disliked him. Him and everything he stood for.

"So that's what you consider your movies to be about? To

show the world as it really is? That's very noble and all, but I have to say the world as you perceive it to be is pretty jaded. Because the world you portray is nothing but brutality and sexual dysfunction. There isn't any room for beauty or kindness or even basic human decency. There's no room for love, as far as that goes, in the world according to Francis Nicoletti."

"You find the world boils down to only a few basic stories. And most of those stories aren't very nice, to say the least. 'The horror, the horror,' as the man says. It's the horror of the horrible things we do, and want to do, to each other for our own preservation and self-interest. What I tried to show were characters who took their drives and emotions and wants to the limit, to their furthest conclusions. They are characters who are trying to break through."

"Break through?" she laughed derisively. "Break through what?"

"You can go ahead and think those movies were only made for the money if you want to, but the truth is they weren't, they were trying to say something."

"You keep saying that, you've said it before, that you're trying to say something. Just what do you think you're trying to say?"

He leaned toward her again, his voice soft, almost a whisper, but with a rasp, insistent. "That we're all desperate, desperate to reach out."

"Reach out. To what?"

"Every one of us knows in our heart of hearts, whether we can voice it or not, that our bodies are not only our prisons but our executioners too, that long before most of us are ready to die our bodies are going to do us in, either from disease or accident or plain old age, that this goddamn human flesh that gives us all these wonderful pleasures and makes us feel so good at times is also going to make us stop all the pleasure and goodness too, and in the process it's going to make us go away forever. We're all desperate to reach out of that, to get out and away from that somehow, to reach out of ourselves, the mortal shell that encapsulates and condemns us. Sex is the ultimate way to reach out, of course, for a man to reach out to a woman, to enter a woman, or for a woman to include into herself, to take into herself a man. But the terrible thing is that for some people the only way they can reach out is through violence. The only way. And more often than any of us would like to admit, the sex and the violence are mixed. More often than any of us would like to admit, they're indistinguishable."

"And are those the ways you reach out? Through sex and violence?"

He folded his hands, down at arm's length, in front of himself, his hands forming a kind of cup. He looked down at the cup, studied his hands for a long moment, then looked up at her again, a small smile on his face. "Some people might think so. Might think that's all there is to it. But the sex and violence are only incidental. I try to reach out by making movies. It's all I know how to do."

Thirty

Suzy's apartment was on South Highland Avenue near fashionable Walnut Street, on the third floor of a stately redbrick house with white trim, at one time somebody's mansion but now divided up into rental units, with hedges out front and pine trees on either side to help separate it from the houses too-close next door. Beyond the foyer, he followed her up the carpeted stairs, past an open door on the second floor where a young man watched a basketball game on television, his Barcalounger positioned so he could keep an eye on the hallway. Suzy waved to him and they went on up the steps to the third floor.

"That's Brandon," Suzy whispered, leaning close to him, her lips brushing his ear. "I think he has a crush on me and likes to keep track of my comings and goings."

Paul wondered how often there was somebody with her on these comings and goings.

Her apartment was in the front of the house, with a window overlooking the street. She had decorated the living room in what she called her film motif—white walls and black shag area rugs, black canvas director's chairs, a white couch with nearly a dozen black throw pillows, and floor lamps that looked like small spotlights. In the low bookcases, which were alternately painted black and white, were hardbacks and paperbacks about films; on the walls were framed movie posters—*Dark Passage, Laura, A House Turned Red.*

"Make yourself comfortable," she said, motioning vaguely around the room before disappearing somewhere in the back.

Paul felt anything but comfortable. What the hell am I doing here? He moved tentatively about the room, as if afraid he might break something simply by looking at it. On top of a bookcase was a snifter the size of a basketball half filled with matchbooks from bars and restaurants; on the mantel of the blanked-out fireplace was a parade of framed family snapshots and photographs; on the floor in a corner was a two-foot-tall stuffed giraffe. I wonder if Nicoletti comes here, if they make love here. He tried to sit in one of the director's chairs but it felt flimsy as if it might tip over; he stood in the open space near the front window where he thought he was safe from damaging anything. Why did she bring me here? What does she want to show me? He imagined her coming back into the room naked, he imagined her stretched out on the bed in her bedroom waiting for him; he snapped his head back and forth to clear away such images. Am I supposed to be doing something? What's taking her so long?

Then she called him from somewhere in the rear of the apartment. He followed the sound of her voice down the long hallway— "Paul, oh Paul," she kept calling, her voice distant, almost as if she weren't there at all—passed the rooms laid out one after the other, bedroom, bathroom, dining room, and on into the kitchen. But she wasn't there. He stuck his head into the pantry. Gone. Is she playing some kind of game? Hide-and-seek? In his mind's eye he saw her flitting naked from room to room. Stop that! "Paul, oh Paul." The back door was standing open; as he started down the narrow winding steps in the alcove that separated the front of the building from the back, he heard someone running ahead of him, the sound of soft shoes on the wooden steps. "Paul, this way, Paul. . . ." He followed the passageway under the rear of the building into a tiny backyard.

The yard was rimmed by the backs of other buildings, a patch of grass hidden in the center of the block, the sky three stories overhead, a rectangle of blue between the rooflines, like looking up from a well; in one corner was a small grotto with a weathered Virgin, in another an empty birdbath. Suzy stood in the center of the yard, poised on one leg, still in her tennis outfit, her tiny white pleated skirt, her other leg cocked seductively in front of her, cradling a baton. She smiled and tilted her head and made a little face, as if to say "Well, what do you think?" then began to twirl, spinning the baton in front of her as if it were a propeller, then wrapping it about herself, down her torso and through her legs and up again, almost faster than he could keep track of in the shadowed light, leaping and whirling and throwing the metal rod as high as the buildings and catching it again on her fingertips, all to the beat of some music that only she heard; then she snapped the baton up on her shoulder like a rifle and bowed before she assumed her beginning pose again, her leg cocked in front of her, aimed right at him, though she was a little shaky by this time, out of breath, a light sheen of sweat on her face and a proud look in her eyes. Paul was transfixed.

"I used to be better," she said happily as she walked past him, nodding for him to follow, leading the way back through the passageway, under the rear of the building, and up the steps. "I used to be able to do two batons at once."

"I can't imagine anything better than what I just saw," Paul said, his head down, keeping his eyes on the winding stairs so that he didn't trip.

Suzy stopped—Paul almost ran into her—and looked back down at him. She stood with one foot on the next step, her legs spread; he looked up into her crotch, above eye level, up at her white cotton panties trimmed in lace under her tennis skirt, the soft mound of her twat.

"You know, Paul," she said, still a bit winded but looking at him intensely, very sincere, "you're really a wonderful man."

Back in her apartment, they sat side by side on throw pillows on the floor of the living room—her idea—finishing the wine and listening to records she wanted him to hear, music he had never heard before, or if he had heard them hadn't paid attention to, songs by groups called the Spiders from Mars and Queen and Styx. "Where have you been?" she looked at him incredulously, curled beside him, her legs folded under her on a black pillow, her soft shiny knees staring at him like twin accusations; he wondered as well. And she told him more stories about herself.

"I used to have this terrible dream all the time when I was growing up. I'd be riding in the backseat of the car with my family, and we'd get halfway across that big bridge from Sewickley over the Ohio River, and all of a sudden the bridge would start to collapse. It was strange because I was never afraid of the bridge in real life, in fact I loved it—I always looked forward to going across it when we went to the airport or somewhere. Besides, a big bridge like that doesn't just fall down, does it? But in my dream there would be this great crunching sound, and all the girders would start to buckle, and the road would open up in front of us and down we'd fall. But the really terrible part was that I always landed in this thick slimy mud, I'd be covered with it. Ew . . . it makes me shudder to think about it. I don't think the dream would have bothered me so much if the water was nice and clean."

Soon enough, the late afternoon sunlight filtered through the louvered shutters and hanging plants, coating the room with a warm buttery glow. As they talked, or rather, as she talked and he listened, his hand stalked hers along the bluffs of the black pillows—her hand was elegant, long-fingered, long-nailed; his own was hard and he thought shell-like, the dark creases and whorls etched in his skin despite his nightly fifteen-minute ritual scrubbing, the tip of one finger permanently cracked up the center where a metal plate once fell on it; a workingman's hand: did it bother her? It bothered him—edging closer, near enough to touch, before hers would fly again, landing someplace new, and his hand would pick up the trail again, slowly of course, following hers in careful stages, through the snags and underbrush of the black shag rug, then back up to the heights of the pillows again, her hand always within reach but his never quite reaching, Paul unsure whether she wanted him to or not. He touched her only once, and that was by mistake or accident: she reached over to pour the rest of the wine and his wrist touched her arm. Her skin was so cool and soft that the sensation shot through his body like an electric shock. From the way she sat back and looked at him, he expected her to say, "You're a big tease, that's what you are," but thank heaven all she did was smile.

They had been sitting quietly for some time listening to the music when she stood up abruptly, all smiles and hurry.

"Thank you, Paul, it's been such a lovely day, but I really must get ready now, oh I'm so excited about the party tonight, I don't know what I would have done without you to help me take my mind off it. You've been such a dear, but you've got to understand I have these other things to do. . . ."

She helped him to his feet and escorted him to the door before he could say anything. Then as soon as he was standing outside in the corridor, she changed again; he gazed at him intensely, affectionately, resting her cheek against the edge of the door. "You're such a nice man, Paul. I always feel so at peace when I'm with you." She smiled and closed the door inches from his face.

. . . and as the afternoon in early spring turns to evening, Janet Rawlins sits in a lounge area at Pittsburgh International Airport, waiting for her plane back to San Francisco to board, watching the large Alexander Calder mobile dangling from the ceiling in the central rotunda, the arrangement of floating yellow and green petals turning slowly, stirred occasionally by the currents of the air-conditioning and people passing below and a wayward breeze from outside the automatic doors, her notepad on her knee as she cleans up her notes from her interview this morning with Francis Nicoletti, thinking perhaps she can use the trope of the slow turning mobile in her piece about Nicoletti, something on the order of what goes around comes around, or ain't karma a bitch, that he's exploited sex and shown human conduct at its lowest level to raise up his career and now he's being dragged down, pulled under, by that very same reputation that got him to whatever heights he achieved in his heyday, that will teach him, the son of a bitch, try to hit on her, will he, oh there was nothing overt of course, nothing she could ever cite as harassment or make an official complaint about, but it was there, all right, she's even come up with a title for her piece: "Francis Nicoletti: Stuck in the Mold," hears her plane being called for boarding and gathers up her notes and purse and carry-on and clicks across the floor of the rotunda in her high-heeled boots toward her gate, across a large inset figure in the marble floor showing the points of the compass, smiling to herself, sure that she's going in the right direction, sure that this article is going to make her career . . . as in Carla's

basement apartment on South Bouquet Street, after fixing her a dinner from the things he found on her shelves, peanut butter on Ritz crackers and tomato soup—the ultimate in comfort food to his way of thinking; he could rarely afford such luxuries—Sam Connor putzies around the kitchen area cleaning up, washing the dishes piled in the sink and sweeping up the crumbs on the floor that give walking around the room a particular kind of crunch, then tries redding up the rest of the apartment, collecting the dirty clothes strewn around the floor and furniture but determines there's really no place to put them and finally dumps them back on the floor again, checking periodically on Carla asleep on the bed in the corner until it's obvious that the girl won't be waking up anytime soon, adjusts the blanket over her so she won't catch a chill, collects his shoulder bag and leaves the apartment, closing the door carefully behind him so it doesn't click, realizing as he does so that he doesn't have a key to get back in but decides it's just as well, he doesn't want to bother her again this evening, he'll come back tomorrow, and heads up the street to Fifth Avenue to get a bus downtown, thinking he hasn't been on his rounds all day, that there's still a chance to hit the Cultural District, the fashionable couples coming and going to the theaters and restaurants, it's all well and good to minister to the afflicted but a guy has to earn a living . . . as in the area of the city known as Shadyside, Paul Slater stands in the hallway of Suzy's apartment building, staring at the door Suzy closed inches from his face, wondering what she'd do if he punched a hole in it as he's thinking of doing—"Oh Paul, thank you, you're such a wonderful man, I needed a window there"—then finally after several minutes turns and goes back down the stairs to the street, his training in finding his way in enemy territory kicking in, directing him up the street for half a dozen blocks until he comes to Fifth Avenue and continues on the couple of miles to his truck where he left it this morning parked near the Pittsburgh Athletic Association—it feels *like lifetimes ago—and drives down Fifth out of Oakland and through the Hill District to the downtown, parking once again in Market Square and going in search of the weirdo called Sam, the only thing he can think to do, to get the information he needs, thinking Sam's always shown up when I don't want him around, let's see if the guy will show up when I do . . . as in his room at the Gateway Hilton, Jeff Berner lies on the bed waking slowly for the sixth or maybe the eighth time today, coming back reluctantly from the chemically induced stupor brought on by the Nembutals he took from his father's supply in the bathroom cabinet on the same visit home when he took the Colt Python from his father's closet, checks the progress of the trapezoid of light across the ceiling that he's been tracking through the day when he wakes from these dreamless sleeps, though already his thoughts are turning again to the memories that leveled him in the first place, that made it impossible for him to either get up from the bed or to sleep without the aid of the pills, memories of his shameful response to his confrontation with the Mad Hatter in Market Square—I ran away, like a little kid, like a girl, I ran away—and his embarrassment at Nickolodeon's offices when he went for an interview—she laughed at me, she made a fool out of me, she shouldn't have done that—unwinds from the covers and drags himself across the room to the bathroom where he has to lean against the wall to stand and piss, decides that one more Nembutal won't kill him, he wants to extend this state of bliss as long as he can, takes the pill and staggers back across the room and collapses on the bed, searches through the tangle of covers until he finds the pistol again and curls himself around it like it was a pet, a child, a lover, slipping away into the safety of his cloud of unknowing . . . as across the Golden Triangle at another hotel, Fran Nicoletti wakes in Thorsten's room at the William Penn, the suite she booked for him thinking it would be their love nest, or at least an upscale version of a bordello, but instead has been the site of the first good eight hours of sleep she's had in months, stretches luxuriously, enjoying the feel of the crisp sheets against her flesh, remembering briefly what it felt like to be young and sexy and oh so alive, gets up and goes to the bathroom to take a shower and remembers Malcolm's hand on her flank earlier today and then his removing it again, turning her down both as a lover and as a business partner, thinking as the hot water pounds down on her, Well, little girl, I would have been happy at this point to take the one as the other, unclear which her first pick would be, gets dressed and leaves the hotel, walking proudly through the grand lobby where afternoon tea is being served to a few out-of-towners and after thinking of walking it, decides No, little girl, there's no value in skimping on expenses now, you're worth whatever the market will allow and then some, takes a taxi the half dozen blocks to the Foundry at the Golden Gateway to keep her date with half a dozen Tanqueray martinis and whatever or whoever else happens along . . . and in the squad room of the homicide division at police headquarters, Lieutenant Nathan White, having spent his day off in the office cleaning up a week's worth of paperwork because it needed to be done and because it was easier than sitting around his apartment all day thinking there must be something he could do to enjoy himself, turns off his Selectric typewriter and takes his suit coat from the back of his desk chair and collects his car from the underground parking garage and leaves the Public Safety Building, facing once again the dilemma he had the night before, and most nights if the truth be told, what to do for dinner, thinks what he really wants is the chicken parmigiana from the Foundry—Lord, that's sad, an entire city full of restaurants and I can't come up with anything else to eat except the same thing I had the night before, I'm pathetic, but it's what I want—remembers Fran Nicoletti telling him that she'd be back there again tonight and wonders if that has something to do with his wanting to go back there, but dismisses the idea, tells himself she was drunk when she said that and it doesn't matter whether she happens to be there or not, she's not the dish he's after, drives across town and parks again along Liberty Avenue and goes inside the restaurant, the bar as empty as it was the night before, is about to order a drink and his food to go when the bartender with the* Viva Zapata *mustache nods to the back and says, "She's back there," and Nathan walks down the length of the bar to the banquette in the back where Fran Nicoletti watches him approach, a growing smile on her face, raises her half-empty, half-full martini glass and salutes him, "My White knight, come to help a lady in distress. . . ."*

Thirty-One

He parked again in Market Square and set about to reconnoiter the area, clearing first the Cultural District—there was a symphony concert at Heinz Hall, a play at the Nixon, a rock concert at the Stanley—but there was no sign of Sam among the people milling about along the sidewalks. When the crowds began to thin, he decided he was wasting his time and headed back to his truck. Then, purely on a whim, he detoured to Stanwix Street and went down the steps into the McDonald's. Sam was seated at the same table by the windows where Paul had talked to him before; he was slouched over talking earnestly to a young Asian teenager dressed all in black, his black hair swept back into a ducktail, sitting across from him. As Paul approached, Sam looked up, looked back at the boy as he continued talking, then back at Paul again, quizzical. The teenager took one look at Paul and was gone, out the door. Sam chuckled.

"You seem to have made quite an impression on my young friend there, dude." Sam pressed his palms together and raised them to his forehead—for a second Paul thought Sam was about to give him a Buddhist greeting—but it was only to smooth his long hair back over his head. "Easy to see why. You've got a look on your face like you're ready to off everybody in the place, though I've seen you with that look before. Are you generally in a killer mode, or is it something you can turn on and off?"

Paul ignored the question as he took a seat across from him. "You seem to know a lot of what goes on around here."

Sam shrugged. "Amazing what you can learn when you keep your eyes and ears open."

"Where would Nicoletti hold a fancy party?"

"Ah. Methinks this is more a question about Miss Suzy Two Quarters than about Nicoletti. Though maybe not, the more I think of it."

Paul just looked at him.

"Yeah. Well. There's the place he's renting out in Squirrel Hill. That's been in the papers a couple of times—"

"She said it's an apartment somewhere."

Sam looked ready to make another comment, then thought better of it. "There's the offices in Gateway Towers but I never heard there were any living arrangements there."

"It's supposed to be someplace special they keep for parties and functions. It's supposed to have a great view—"

"Of course. I've heard about it, but never been there. In fact that guy you just ran off told me once he's made some deliveries there. And we're not talking UPS, if you know what I mean."

"So where is it?"

"Now, that bit of information is going to cost you. Sorry to put it in such a mercantile framework but I've recently come into a situation that's going to require some extra resources—"

He was interrupted by Paul taking out his wallet and removing sixty dollars and laying it on the table. "Will that do it?"

"That's funny. The police only give me twenty, and I always considered that generous. I didn't realize how valuable I am. Yeah, that'll do it. C'mon, we need to take a walk."

Sam collected his fringed shoulder bag from the back of his

seat and led the way out of the restaurant into the warm evening, Paul a reluctant few steps behind, following the black number 58 football jersey with LAMBERT on the back, the two of them in a loose single file, guide and follower, crossing Stanwix and following Liberty a couple of blocks past the Gateway Hilton, across Commonwealth and into Point State Park, following the circular walk around the dark lawns toward the Point, leaving the lights of the city behind them, a wall of lighted buildings, like a stage setting with cutout buildings and neon glows, the sounds of traffic growing distant. Midway around the circular walk Sam stopped under a streetlight near what appeared to be a trench dug into the dark grass.

"You're a military man, you'll appreciate this. It's one of the original bastions of Fort Pitt, carefully preserved to remind us all that Pittsburgh is a city built on violence and bloodshed."

Paul looked where Sam was looking, shielding his eyes with his hand to block out the light from the streetlight, but all he saw was a dark cut in the earth lined with brick, zigzagging away into the darkness, the mounds of dark grass above. As Sam continued on he maintained a monologue, like a tour guide.

"Unlike most of the cities of the Republic that were built on trade, Pittsburgh's origins were in blood, it was a military establishment before anything else, not a fort built to protect a settlement, first Fort Duquesne for the French and then Fort Pitt for the British, a bulwark against the wild frontier, all the dark terrors stretching out across the uncharted continent, the town growing up outside the walls only an afterthought, shelter for the camp followers who trailed after the soldiers, the settlers who trailed after them. Ah, now there were some real lowlifes. People think that pioneers were such great people but the journals of the day say the early people of Pittsburgh were nothing but thieves and whores and cutthroats. A place known for its violence. And, by the way, exceptionally dirty, lots of rats and vermin. Charming."

The walk led to an underpass beneath the freeway connecting the two bridges arcing away into the night. The floor of the underpass humped over a reflecting pool, rows of small spotlights under the water illuminating the tile roof. Sam started through the tunnel but Paul stopped at the entrance. What the hell am I doing, following this weirdo who knows where? Now's the time I should have my weapon with me, it's right in the truck, I know better, I was taught better. I won't make this mistake again. When Sam realized Paul wasn't behind him he stopped and looked back.

"You don't have to be afraid, dude. I won't attack you. That's pretty funny—the soldier is afraid of the pacifist." Sam lifted the peace medallion off the chest of his Steelers jersey and jingled it at Paul.

"Where the hell are you taking me?"

"You want to know where Suzy is or don't you?" Sam shrugged and continued on through the underpass, resuming his monologue. Paul again wished he'd brought his pistol with him, but continued after him.

"When Fort Pitt was under siege during the French and Indian War, the settlers who made it to the fort in time hunkered down behind the walls and listened to the screams of the settlers who didn't make it as the Indians tortured them to death across the river. Burned them alive, cut off their fingers and stuffed them in their mouths, poured molten lead down their throats. Sometimes flayed them alive or ate chunks out of their bodies in front of them. Both men and women. I guess it never occurred to anyone hiding in the fort to go rescue them. Yes sir, a bloodthirsty place, right from the beginning. Right where we're walking now. Though I have a feeling you'd get along just fine. There."

The underpass opened out into a large flat area, rows of dark trees on either side, tracing the banks of the two rivers, angling toward the fountain at the Point some six hundred feet ahead, the column of white water plashing in the darkness. Beyond the fountain the cut of the Ohio River into the distance formed a dent in the dark hills; above the hills, smoke-gray clouds drifted against the blue-black sky reflecting the glow of the mills farther down the river, pulsing orange and yellow as if the sky was something alive.

"There," Sam said.

"What the hell are you talking about?" Paul said, looking around at the night. "There's nothing here."

"Like I was saying about opening one's eyes and ears. Up there."

Sam walked a little farther into the darkness, then pointed back beyond the superstructure of the Fort Pitt Bridge toward the hills on the other side of the Monongahela River. Along the ridgeline, close to where the incline terminated at the top of the bluffs, there was the spire of a church spotlighted against the night sky, the lights of a number of private homes, and a multi-story white apartment building glowing in the darkness. The lights of the top-floor apartment spilled out onto a balcony where tiny figures could be seen silhouetted against the interior of the apartment.

"Yep," Sam said. "I'd say that's a party, all right. And your girl was right, that must be quite a view on a night like this. Though personally I'd love to see the view on the inside. Now that would be something—"

"She's not my girl," Paul said, standing as if transfixed at the vision in the night.

"If wishes were horses, beggars would ride, as the saying goes," Sam said. "But whatever. Anything else you want me to show you? I noticed there were still some bills in your wallet."

Paul looked at him, Sam's face barely visible in the darkness. Thinking, He's not worth it. Keep your eyes on the objective, trooper, your life depends on it. The man who would lead must know why and how. He turned and headed back through the underpass, back toward the lights of the downtown.

"That's okay," Sam called after him. "I'll find my way back, don't worry about me. . . ."

Thirty-Two

"This is insane," Nathan said under his breath as he crawled on his hands and knees under the conference-room table in Nickolodeon's offices, in the dark, naked, looking for his clothes.

In the darkness, from on top of the table above him, Fran giggled. "What's the matter, Lieutenant? Lose something?"

"Where did you toss them?" He gave up on this side and crawled over the heavy bracing under the table—his knees ached from the hard surface of the table, his right knee was rubbed raw and bleeding slightly—pushed a couple of chairs out of his way and found a pile of his clothes beside a potted plant. He rose carefully and lifted the edge of the translucent drapes along the row of windows. Across the plaza was the Gateway Hilton, the checkerboard of lighted rooms like visions of hotel rooms in the night. He ducked back down again and sat on the floor to put on his clothes. Fran leaned over the edge from where she lay on top of the table, her face moonlike in the darkness, watching him.

"Why, Lieutenant White," she said in a false southern drawl. "I do believe you're embarrassed."

"This is insane," he hissed. His head was throbbing, his stomach full of quicksilver that, whenever he moved too quickly, threatened to squirt out of him at one end or the other; the room, if he looked at any one spot too long, had a tendency to slide down the walls. "Somebody's going to hear us."

"Nat, Nat, Nat. Nobody's going to hear us."

"My name is Nathan."

"You're right. Nathan," Fran said, leaning back and stretching out on the tabletop. "A gnat is one of those pesky little bugs that you want to wave away. And you're certainly not that."

Her body with its dusting of freckles was luminous in the half-light from the windows; she was still a good-looking woman, her breasts full and pointed at the ceiling, her flanks and ass firm, even if she was ten years older than he was. He looked away, he had to get out of here.

"I don't know what I thought I was doing," he said, struggling to pull on his pants.

"I can tell you. We were talking about my husband's theory that his movies had some connection to that girl's murder in Schenley Park. So we came up here because I thought I had copies of Nicko's films here I could show you . . . and then some other nice things started to happen and we ended up on this table. Ended up ended up, I might add."

Nathan checked his service revolver in its holster, his badge in his suit coat, both draped carefully over the back of one of the wheeled conference chairs. Thank heaven he had had enough sense at least to take care of them properly. Then he hazily remembered that it was Fran who took his suit coat and holster and draped them over the chair. As she was undressing him. He put on his socks and shoes.

"And you certainly knew what you were doing when we fucked an hour or so ago, before we fell asleep."

"Is that how long I've been here? Christ."

"Actually, you've been here longer than that," Fran said, becoming a bit sullen.

Nathan got up on his knees so he could pat his pockets to make sure everything was there—keys, change, handkerchief—before he stood up.

Fran raised up on her elbow. "Look, Nathan, we're not kids.

We both know what goes on in the world. You see the terrible things people do to each other every day, the way they hurt each other, and I see it too. What's so wrong with two people being nice to each other once in a while?"

He stopped and looked at her in the darkness. She must have been a beautiful woman once, she was probably beautiful still; but now in the half-light, his stomach queasy and his balance none too steady, she seemed almost grotesque, her freckles like polka dots and her flesh with an unhealthy sheen like something you'd find on decaying fish. He shook his head to clear it and turned toward the door.

"I have to get out of here. . . ."

She was up off the table and holding him, her face broken, dissolved in tears. "Hold me, please hold me. . . ."

He couldn't have held her if he wanted to, her arms wrapped around him pinned his arms to his sides. After a moment, he eased himself out of her grasp and left the room, finding his way through the dark offices and down the elevator to the plaza. Outside the night air hit him in the face and he breathed easier. *Jesus, what was I thinking? I wasn't thinking, if a reporter ever got hold of this—.* His thoughts were interrupted by a voice that said, "Hey, dude."

Thirty-Three

Sam was sitting on a bench in the plaza, his legs folded under him in a loose lotus position, when Nathan, slightly favoring one leg, came out the door of Gateway Towers, muttering to himself. Sam waited, wondering if the lieutenant would even notice him— he didn't, walked right past him—before he unwound his legs and called after him.

Nathan spun around, his hand under his suit coat on his holster.

"Whoa, man!" Sam said. "Don't shoot, Hornet. It's only me."

Nathan looked at him a moment, still not registering who it was. Finally he made the connection with Sam, but he didn't relax any.

"What the hell are you doing here? That's a good way to get yourself shot."

"I can see that's true, if you try to speak to an old friend with a gun."

Nathan realized his hand was still on his holster. "Yeah. Well. Okay. But that still doesn't tell me what you're doing here in the middle of the night. You following me?"

"Coincidence. Chance. Fate. Who knows? I was just walking through here from the Point when I saw you go into the Towers. That was Mrs. Nicoletti, wasn't it?"

"So what if it was?"

"Easy now. Just seems a little funny, that's all. The reason I was at the Point was to show a guy where Nicoletti himself was having a party tonight. Then I come along and happen to see you with the Mrs. It's a funny ol' world. Seems like the night is full of movie-star-crossed lovers."

Nathan moved closer to him, all cop now. "What are you talking about, lovers? The lady was drunk and I was escorting her back to her office."

"Hey, I'm all about love, you know that. I'm all in favor of that other guy mooning over a girl he barely knows. And as for you and Mrs. Nicoletti, the way she was leaning on you, I doubt very much if you were discussing parking tickets. Besides, that was two and a half hours ago. That's a heck of a lot of parking tickets."

"And from what you're telling me you waited all that time out here to see me. What do you want, Sam? What angle are you working this time?"

"Heh heh. Good one. But no angle this time. I just have some information for you. Remember? You told me to contact you if I found out anything about Sandy Love."

"So?"

"Jimmy Ianni."

"What about Jimmy Ianni?"

"I'm sure Jimmy Ianni was responsible. If he didn't do it him-self, it was one or more of his goons."

"What makes you so sure? Is there a witness or some evidence?"

"Well, all the girls who work for him are convinced he had a hand in it."

Nathan ran his hand over his hair and down across his face. "So it's just hearsay. We talked to Ianni the first day of our in-quiries, and talked to the girl, Chartreuse, at his club after you told us about your friend . . . Karen?"

"Carla."

"Carla. But we didn't find anything that would lead us to think Ianni was involved. No matter how unsavory a character he is."

"Unsavory," Sam said. He wanted to spit.

"You have to give me more than just a feeling or a dislike of the guy, Sam. Look, I'm tired, I need to get home. . . ."

"They beat up Carla. Really bad. They may have been trying to kill her. After they gang-raped her."

"Who's *they*?"

"Ianni. And a bunch of other guys. I got the idea Ianni wasn't one of the ones who beat her up, but it was his men under his orders. And Ianni was one of the guys who raped her."

"Is she willing to press charges against him? And testify, when it comes to court?"

"I haven't talked to her about it, but I'm sure she would."

"That would enable us to bring him in for questioning, and get a warrant to search his club and house. Otherwise, our hands are tied."

"I'll talk to her about it tomorrow and let you know."

"Is she all right otherwise? Well, no, of course she isn't. But does she need anything, we can get her to the hospital. She needs to go anyway to have herself examined and get some blood and semen samples."

"I tried to get her to go but she wouldn't hear of it. But maybe when I see her tomorrow. . . ."

"When did all this happen?"

"Friday night."

Nathan grimaced. "It's probably too late for semen samples. But there would undoubtedly be signs of the assault. The hospital report will be critical for a trial. And to back up the warrant for his arrest."

"She was asleep when I left her. She was pretty shook up, as you can imagine. Almost in shock, so I can't push her too much or she'll close up completely."

"Do what you can, as soon as you can," Nathan said. He started to leave, then turned back, digging in his pocket for his wallet and offering a twenty-dollar bill. "Thanks, Sam. Here."

Sam shook his head. "No thanks. I'm good. I more than made my quota with this evening's other acolyte of love."

Nathan looked at him sideways, still offering the bill. "Take it anyway. We'll call it a special gift between old bandmates, to help you forget you ever saw me this evening. By myself or with anybody else."

"I don't know what you're talking about, mister. I'm not that kind of guy," Sam said grinning. But took the bill anyway.

. . . and in his room at the Gateway Hilton, Jeff Berner sits on the air-conditioning unit just below the window in his room, the unit blowing cold air under him, up between his folded legs, trying to get awake from his chemically induced sleep, sensing that if he doesn't stop it now he might slip into a place from which he can't

come back, wondering as it is if he's hallucinating as he looks down at the plaza eight stories below and thinks he sees the police lieutenant he saw on the news reports the night they found the body in the park come out the door of Gateway Towers and begin talking to the hippie in the Steelers jersey Jeff encountered in Market Square when he had the run-in with the Mad Hatter, watches the two men talking for a few minutes and then the police lieutenant give the hippie some money before the two men go their separate ways, the policeman toward Liberty Avenue and the hippie toward Stanwix Street, the two figures moving along the walks in and out of the circles of light until they're both gone and Jeff wonders What was that about? Did I just see that? I never should have taken that last pill, continues to sit there for a few minutes hoping his head will clear when out the same door of the Towers comes Fran Nicoletti who takes the walk toward the turnaround beside the building and gets into a red sports car and roars off into the night, and Jeff thinks So that's it. That bitch called the police on me, that cop must have been there to see her about me, and the hippie is working for him, he's paying the hippie to keep an eye on me, and things that have happened to him recently begin to make sense, he sees how the world is stacking up, and he gets down from his perch on the air-conditioning unit and goes across the room and picks up his father's Colt Python revolver that he's been keeping handy on top of the dresser, carries the gun over to his red anorak that's thrown over the back of the desk chair and places the gun in the zippered kangaroo pocket, wondering if it's too apparent through the nylon fabric but decides it's not too bad if he keeps his hand in his pocket on that side, the casual observer won't be able to tell it's a gun, decides he's going to take the gun with him from now on . . . as in his small brick house on a slanted brick street in the Lawrenceville neighborhood, police sergeant Frank MacCarron, after waking from a few hours' sleep, finally admits to himself that he's not going to get back to sleep anytime soon, probably not until it's his normal time to get up at six o'clock, which he will regardless that it's Sunday morning, gropes around in the dark on his nightstand, and turns on a small reading lamp, looking over at the mound of his wife beside him to make sure he hasn't disturbed her—his wife of thirty-nine years, Madelaine, or Panda as he calls her, her hair in curlers under an opaque shower cap, a woman who over the years has grown increasingly to look like Mac, or Mac has grown increasingly to look like her, as red-faced as he is though not from once being a heavy drinker, her body as rotund and rather formless as his own, though it is a joke between them that he has a better set of tits—reaches over and adjusts the covers around her shoulders to make sure she's warm enough and then opens his book, hoping to finish Love Rogue *so he can start the new Harlequin romance he picked up at the drugstore this evening when he stopped for the prescription for his diabetes, becoming aware as he lies in the small circle of light in the darkness of the bedroom that he's not going to be able to read either, unable to stop thinking about—which means worrying about—Nathan, his partner's seemingly endless ability to get himself into difficult situations, the latest being shooting off his mouth to the parents of Sandy Love, saying that there was a good chance they'd never find their daughter's killer, all true of course but not something you should say out loud, particularly not so your commanding officer can hear it, now all that has to happen is for the media to get hold of it and Nathan will find himself handing out parking tickets for the rest of his career, the lieutenant already under Commander Ciampa's scrutiny for what appears to be inappropriate relationships with women involved in some of Nathan's recent cases—there was the mother of a pair of missing twins whom Nathan seemed to spend an exorbitant amount of time comforting; and then the wife of a murdered advertising executive whom Nathan was photographed escorting to a charity event—*

Mac is certain that nothing improper happened in either case, just coincidence and bad timing on Nathan's part, examples of Nathan's basic nature to want to help, to make people feel better, protect them, but police officers can't chance being compromised, particularly not with the press scrutinizing Nathan's every move because of his race and his unique position on the homicide squad, Nathan's problems starting a few years earlier before he and Mac were partners when Nathan's wife left him, talk starting that it sent Nathan off the deep end as far as women were concerned, not from any evidence of such activity but simply from other men's expectations and assumptions and projections of what they'd do or like to do if it happened to them—and then, of course, Nathan was black, you see, good-looking, trim, well-dressed, well-mannered; what else could he be?—a reputation foisted on him of being a hound, Nathan's then partner asking to be reassigned so he wasn't painted with the same brush, after which Mac was assigned as Nathan's partner supposedly to provide a steadying influence and moral balance—a joke, that, to anyone who knew Mac's soft-porn proclivities—to try to settle the younger man down, though the most disturbing thing Mac found in working with his new partner was the inability to talk to Nathan about any of it, false accusations or no, the way partners need to talk about pitfalls and problems, the one time Mac broached the subject Nathan muttering something about Mac keeping his prejudices to himself and then not speaking to him the rest of the day—hell, if prejudice was the issue Mac knew all about it; he grew up in the projects of Aliquippa where, as a Caucasian, he was the minority—he considered taking his concerns to Ciampa but knew he'd only alienate Nathan further, on top of everything else his partner had the reputation as a hothead, as it was no one else in the department wanted to partner with him, no, there was nothing to do but keep an eye on the lieutenant to make sure he didn't do anything to foster the bad impression, including going off half-cocked, and hope for the best, Mac drifting off with his book folded open on his chest, in his waking dream following a bouncing orange ball down a wooded hillside, through the brush and trees, across a stream and down a fathomless canyon, down and down . . . as in a penthouse apartment on Grandview Avenue on Mount Washington, on the ridge overlooking the city, Suzy, wearing the white satin-like sheath dress she purchased specially for the occasion, a glass of Champagne in each hand, wends her way through the crowd of Pittsburgh socialites and illuminati and wannabes, smiling to the actors and technicians she recognizes from the crew, to where Nicko is standing against the wall talking to someone—she thinks he's the CEO of a local gas company but she's not sure, a tall man with a shaved head and a British colonel's mustache and a beautiful blue blazer who makes no effort to hide his appraisal of her, looking her up and down, the expression on his face, his half smile, suggesting that he expects Nicoletti to offer her to him—and Nicko takes one of the glasses of Champagne and says "Thanks, babe," and puts his arm around her, rubbing his hand over her bare shoulder proprietarily, slipping his fingers underneath her spaghetti strap while continuing his conversation about gross over net and percentages off the top, keeping her close to him until the other man gets the message or loses interest in her and Nicko gives her a couple extra see-you-later rubs and a pat on the ass and sends her off again, and she walks back through the groups of laughing talking smiling people to the door of the balcony and goes outside to where there are only a few people, the night clear and beautiful and warm in late spring, the breeze coming down the Ohio River, and stands along the railing, takes a sip of her Champagne and looks out over Grandview and the slope of the hillside down to the Point and the three rivers, the lights of one of the cars of the incline beginning its descent while at the bottom of the tracks its twin car begins its ascent, the lights of the two cars as she watches meeting

*halfway up or halfway down and continuing on their way, as far-
ther along the base of the slope galaxies of pinpoint lights outline
the mills along the black river on the South Side, the glow of the
furnaces and coke ovens and the locomotives shuttling white-hot
ladle cars between the buildings looking like toys from this height
and distance, and thinks No, this isn't the way she thought it
would be, wanted it to be, when she dreamed of being at a party
like this, she always saw herself as more of an equal with everyone
else, she thought she would meet interesting people and have interesting conversations about films and books and other interesting subjects, she thought she would be more than a bauble on
someone's arm, but if this is what she has to do to gain access to
this way of life, so be it—Help Yourself, Tootsie—lifts her face
to the night and shakes out her hair and thinks the world, her
world, is a wonderful wonderful place . . . as below on Grandview
Avenue, Paul parks his pickup truck in a space half a block or so
down the street from the tall white apartment building, gets out
and walks up the street, steps out onto the mushroom-shaped observation platform beside the station for the incline just as the
car arrives from the bottom, the light from the windows spilling
out over the brush and the rock face of the hillside, as cheery as
a circus wagon or carnival ride, the lights of the city at night
across the river spread below him like an infinitely detailed model
of a city, something you might see spread under a Christmas tree,
the lights of an airliner overhead descending the black sky on its
way to the airport, but he turns away from the view and looks
back at the building across the street, the lights of the penthouse
apartment more visible here, figures moving about along the railing of the balcony, watches for a few minutes until he's convinced
he wouldn't recognize Suzy regardless from this distance, turns
back to the railing of the overlook and relieves himself down the
hillside, then returns to his truck, stretches out on the passenger
side of the bench seat, leaning against the door so he can look out*

the back window at the apartment building, where someone might appear from the entrance at street level or where a car might appear from the underground garage, settles back to wait as long as it takes, the patience to wait not a problem for him from his training and experiences in-country, keeps his vigil, the lights of a tall communications tower rising behind the building flashing red and white warnings through the night, until the black sky turns by stages sea green then blue above the roofline of the building, the lights of the apartment still burning, the doors to the balcony still open, though there is no one along the railing now, the draperies sucked outside the sliding doors, playing along the edges of the doorframe, by the morning breeze, and Paul falls asleep, without meaning to, the back of his head resting against the cool glass of the side window, his Detonics Mark V Combat Master automatic pistol, taken from its holster under the driver's seat, resting on his lap, under his folded hands. . . .

Sunday, May 4, 1975

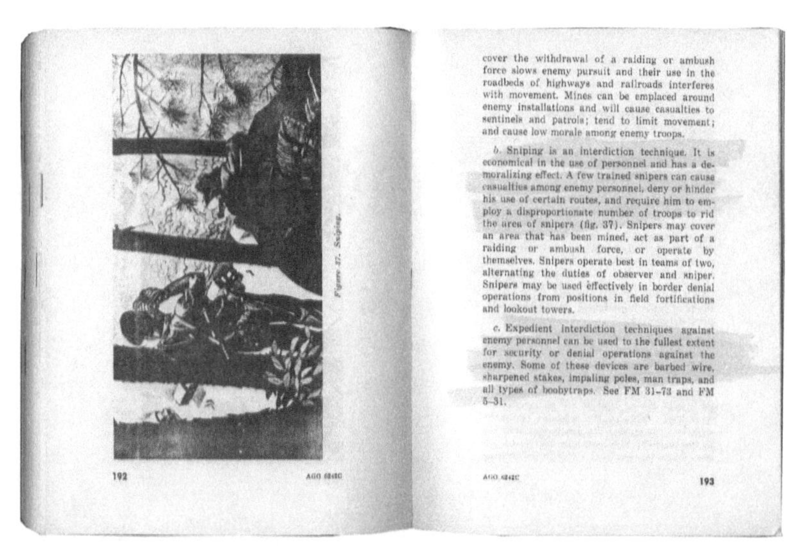

cover the withdrawal of a raiding or ambush force slows enemy pursuit and their use in the roadbeds of highways and railroads interferes with movement. Mines can be emplaced around enemy installations and will cause casualties to sentinels and patrols; tend to limit movement; and cause low morale among enemy troops.

b. Sniping is an interdiction technique. It is economical in the use of personnel and has a demoralizing effect. A few trained snipers can cause casualties among enemy personnel, deny or hinder his use of certain routes, and require him to employ a disproportionate number of troops to rid the area of snipers (fig. 37). Snipers may cover an area that has been mined, act as part of a raiding or ambush force, or operate by themselves. Snipers operate best in teams of two, alternating the duties of observer and sniper. Snipers may be used effectively in border denial operations from positions in field fortifications and lookout towers.

c. Expedient interdiction techniques against enemy personnel can be used to the fullest extent for security or denial operations against the enemy. Some of these devices are barbed wire, sharpened stakes, impaling poles, man traps, and all types of boobytraps. See FM 31–73 and FM 5–31.

FM 31-20
Department of the Army Field Manual
Special Forces Operational Techniques

The dog's head filled the window. Paul woke staring up into its face, a large grayish-white shaggy face with rheumy eyes, a malamute though it wasn't well cared for, the hair matted around its ears and under its jowls; the dog didn't seem unfriendly, just concerned, puzzled perhaps, worried at this break in the normalcy of things, the order of its world: a man asleep in the cab of a pickup truck. A woman in a housecoat and curlers—a gauze scarf floated around her head like a pink cloud—stood on the sidewalk tugging at the dog's leash—"Come on, Tige, come on boy"—as she also tried to look in the window, look at the man in the cab of the truck, a break in the normalcy of things, the order of her world too, relieved and maybe somewhat disappointed to find that Paul was actually alive and only sleeping, afraid too of any man who would dare do such a thing and in such a good part of town too. Paul raised up and glared at them; the malamute ran its large rippled tongue up the glass until the woman almost strangled it pulling it backwards, trying to get away before the crazy man in the truck came after her. When they were gone, there was still a large wet streak in the middle of the window, blurring the center of the window, a thin trail of saliva sliding down the glass and puddling at the bottom of the sill.

Paul looked around, his head throbbing, a pain in his neck, in his back; his right arm, the one he was lying on when he woke, was numb and wouldn't move the way he wanted it to. His pistol had slipped off his lap onto the seat beside him; he stuck it in the pocket of his windbreaker. It was cloudy though warm, glimmers of sunlight breaking through the overcast, catching on the facades of the buildings. He looked at his watch. Eight forty-five. There were a few people along the sidewalk, tourists, early morning runners, no one on the observation platform. Across the street at Nicoletti's apartment, several people stood along the balcony, leaning on the railing, talking among themselves, admiring the view. So they stayed there all night, at least some of them, I didn't miss them by falling asleep. I wonder what they did up there all night, those who stayed, but I don't have to wonder, do I? He recognized Suzy, in white shorts and halter top, with Nicoletti, her arm in his; as they talked she leaned back her head and laughed. In Paul's mind, he could hear her say You're a big tease, that's what you are. A big tease. . . .

When Suzy, Nicoletti, and the others moved indoors, Paul climbed out of the truck—stiffly, barely able to move at first; I'm getting old—and walked down the sidewalk to the station at the top of the incline and used the men's room to urinate, splash water on his face, straighten his clothes after sleeping in them. Outside again, he bought an Italian sausage sandwich and a Coke from a vendor just setting up his cart and carried them back to the truck, taking up his vigil again. After an hour or so there was a flurry of activity in front of the building, the doormen hustled around, bringing cars up from the garage, parking them on the apron in front of the building, six of them, a couple of Mercedes and several foreign cars Paul didn't know the names of and Suzy's yellow 280Z. In half an hour a group came out of the building together and divided themselves up into the cars. Suzy and Nicoletti got in her 280Z, Nicoletti driving, and took off first, making a U-turn in the street—Paul ducked down in the seat as they passed him—waiting at the corner until the others fell into line behind them, then squealed off, leading the way, the other cars hurrying to catch up, along Grandview toward McArdle Roadway down the face of the bluffs. Paul slid over on the seat and started his truck and sped after them.

Thirty-Five

"Sit down if you want to, dude. Take a load off." Sam looked up at the kid in the red anorak and nodded to the other end of the bench, and went back to slicing around the circumference of an avocado with his Swiss Army knife. Thinking *You might as well sit down, you've been watching me for the past fifteen minutes across the square, might as well get a good look up close.* "I'm between services, I won't be here much longer. My name's Sam, by the way. You should know who you're talking to, if you're going to stare a hole in me."

"Sam Bytheway."

"Good one. Actually I have a last name but nobody knows who that is. Everybody knows me just as Sam, in case you're ever looking for me. And you are?"

"Jeff. Berner." The kid sat down cautiously at the far end of the bench, keeping a good distance between them. "What kind of service? Is that some kind of department thing?"

"Department? Don't know what kind of department you're referring to. No, I'm between church services. I just finished up the Catholic mass at Saint Mary of Mercy down the street there, and I'm waiting for the trifecta to let out."

He has no idea what I'm talking about, but of course he's not going to say anything. Didn't think so. Sam wiped the blade of the knife across his tongue, carefully, then wiped the blade on his pants leg and put it in his shoulder bag. He held up the fruit to the kid as if to say *Watch this,* then twisted the two halves in opposite directions and separated them, revealing the stone. *Voilà!* The kid looked unimpressed. *So much for magic.*

"The trifecta being, in case you were wondering, the First Presbyterian Church and Trinity Cathedral over on Sixth Avenue, and the United Church of Christ around the corner on Smithfield. When those churches let out, it's a panhandler's dream. All those folks full of the Holy Spirit, and I'm happy to give them an outlet. I wouldn't have come downtown at all today, except I have a number of regulars who would sorely miss practicing their recharged faith, alms to the poor and all that."

"So that's your cover? You're supposed to be a panhandler?"

"Nothing supposed about it, dude. You're looking at the genuine article."

"Yeah. Whatever."

Sam had balanced the half avocado with the stone on his thigh and proceeded to turn the other half inside out and gnaw a bit on the flesh, ending up with some on the end of his nose. He wiped it off with a finger, checked it to make sure that's what it was, and then licked it off. *Wonder who or what he thinks I am? He hasn't a clue, as naive as they come. Babe in the woods. This could be fun before it's all over. I need a diversion today, so I don't think about. . . .*

"These things aren't really that good by themselves. But it's a little difficult to steal the rest of the salad to go with it. The lettuce tends to get soggy in your pocket, and the oil and vinegar runs down your leg."

He finished the half and dumped the skin into the waste bin at the end of the bench, took the other half and dug out the stone and flicked it in the bin as well. The kid just looked at him and looked away again. Market Square was nearly empty on a Sunday morning, a few winos on a bench near 1902 Tavern. A woman walking a dog. But the kid didn't seem to be looking at any of it, it was more like staring into space. *Yep, definitely something on this guy's mind. Maybe shake him up a bit.*

"So. Did you recover from your run-in with the Jackal Commune and the Head Jackal the other day?"

"What?"

"I was there, remember? I like to think I created the diversion that got you away in one piece from that guy."

"The cops. Do they bother you much?"

Sam looked at him. Finished nibbling on the avocado and threw the skin away. *It's like he's in his own world, on his own planet. Earth to kid, earth to kid, hello? Like he's either on some trip or coming down from a big one. Is that a gun in the pocket* of his anorak? Far out.

"No, the cops don't bother me much. Do they bother you?"

It took a minute for Sam's question to register with him. "Huh? Me? No, why should they? Why'd you ask that?"

"Just wondering. Just wondering why you were wondering why the cops would bother me."

The kid squinted at him, trying to follow the "wonderings" of the sentence. Sam rubbed his hands together and leaned forward, resting his elbows on his thighs.

"You know, you remind me of a guy who used to hang around here a couple of years ago. Peter something-or-other, I probably never knew his last name. Always wore nice clothes, like you, somebody said he came from a wealthy family on Long Island or someplace. Anyway, it turned out that this guy Peter thought he was the Angel of Death, sent down from the Lord to claim a soul—he had the revelation during an acid trip. The problem was he couldn't remember the name of the person the Good Lord sent him after. It was driving him nuts. I mean, you can see his dilemma: when the Great Dispatcher in the Sky sends you on an errand, you don't want to return empty-handed. The unemployment benefits for a laid-off angel can be hell, if you know what I mean. So Peter sat here in this square every day, on this very bench as a matter of fact, hoping he'd remember the name or recognize the person if he or she walked by. A funny guy. He was around here for a good while."

The kid pumped his shoulders once, noncommittal, looked away. Across the square an elderly black man started dancing to a boom box, a kind of one-person tango, with his friends on the nearby benches clapping time. Sam and the kid watched the man for several minutes.

"So dude, what, or who, did you come here looking for?"

"What makes you think I'm looking for anything?"

"People are always looking for something. There's

undoubtedly some reason why you're hanging around. Though I have to say, whatever or whoever you came for, it sure seems like you haven't found it yet. You've got the look of somebody who's been having a rough time."

It was evidently the right thing to say; the kid's attitude changed with the prospect of having a sympathetic listener.

"I'm an actor. Or I guess I should say I want to be. I've been trying to see a director about a part—"

"Don't tell me. Francis Nicoletti."

"Yeah. How'd you know?"

"A wild guess."

"I went to his office but I couldn't get past his gatekeeper."

"One of the oldest stories known to mankind. The gallant young knight on a quest meets a dragon guarding the entrance to the cave."

"She was a dragon, all right."

"A she-dragon then. The worst kind."

"His wife."

"Ah, the other Frances Nicoletti. Don't know the lady myself, but I get the idea she can be quite a handful. Maybe even quite an armful." As Sam leaned forward, the peace medallion around his neck hung down like a plumb bob in front of his chest. He swayed from side to side a couple times to set it swinging, then straightened up again, stretching out his arms along the top of the bench like a crucifixion, open to the day. "Well, if Mrs. Nicoletti wronged you, you should go to her and tell her so, show her she made a mistake about you, that you are a young worthy and that she should let you in to see the great man. If you don't stand up for yourself, these women will walk all over you. Use you for a doormat and scrape the mud off their psyches onto you."

"You think so?"

"Absolutely."

"Maybe you're right, maybe I should go see her," Jeff said, considering something. "She shouldn't have talked to me the way she did. She laughed at me. Too bad it's Sunday and the office is closed today. . . ."

Sam watched a flock of pigeons leave the safety of a patch of grass, take flight and circle the square, settling again in the cobbled street. Stupid birds. Rats with wings. Now they're right in the way of the next bus that comes along, the weakest of the weak will end up a hood ornament. A patch of feathers on the paving bricks. The end of it. They never learn. He was fed up with the kid beside him, his whining, his petty troubles about getting an audition. Wants to be an actor, don't make me laugh. What you really want is to be famous, you don't want to act or learn the craft that makes characters come alive. Stupid kid.

"Then you should go to her house. She upset your life, didn't she? Why shouldn't you upset hers a little? Show up on her doorstep: 'I'm here, I'm here! Open up the gates!'"

"I don't know where she lives."

"Squirrel Hill."

The young man looked at him questioningly.

"I don't know the address but I know it's out there somewhere. A resourceful young man like yourself should be able to find it. I could show you the apartment Nicoletti has on Mount Washington but I don't think that would do you any good. No, your best bet is the house in Squirrel Hill." Sam stood up. "I got to go, I've got some church services to catch."

"Wait. You didn't finish your story. About the guy who thought he was the Angel of Death."

"Peter whatever-his-name-was? That's a sad case. Poor Peter decided to take another acid trip to help him remember the name of the person he was sent for. But that acid must have been worse than the first, because once he got out there on his trip, the only name he could remember was his own." Sam shook his head, shrugged.

"That's the end of the story?"

"That was the end of Peter's story. He never came back down to earth again. The last I heard he was in a mental institution somewhere, probably still there to this day. Guess he saw something out there among the stars that he liked better than down here. Or maybe, once he was out there, really out there, he saw something down here among the everyday that he didn't like at all. Hard to say. Whichever, given the nature of the world, I can't say I blame him. What do you think?"

"I think Peter sounds pretty dumb."

"Come on—the story wasn't that bad. I've got another one about on upholsterer, a housewife, and a popcorn machine, maybe you'd like that better. . . ." But Sam's heart wasn't in it, he was getting tired of putting him on—the game was wearing thin. He kept thinking of Carla, he needed to get back to Oakland to see how she was doing, find out if she'd be willing to press charges against Ianni and his crew. The only reason he hadn't gone to see her already this morning was that he wanted her to move in with him and he would need extra money to make it happen; it would be safer for her, he could look after her, take care of her, keep her away from the clubs and guys like Ianni. And who knew? Maybe in time, after the healing, they could be lovers, be a couple. It was about time he settled down, got a real—Gasp!—job to support them. This way of life he'd been living, he'd always considered it just a phase, a put-on to the world, a game to see how long he could make it work, get by, but he didn't want to play it so far that he couldn't come back in again. He turned away and started across Market Square.

"Hey, is that all there is?"

Sam stopped and looked back at him. "This is all there is, dude," Sam said, spreading his arms to signify himself, the world.

"What more could you want?"

"But aren't you going to question me or something?"

Sam was about to give him one of his typical facetious answers—I question you enough as it is—but thought better of it. That was then, this is now. Best not to say anything at all. This is the new Sam. Sam in the world. Responsible Sam. Sam in love.

Thirty-Six

The little parade of cars, with Paul following in his pickup, made its way across Liberty Bridge, then the Boulevard of the Allies along the uptown bluffs past Duquesne University and onto the Penn-Lincoln Parkway, heading out of the city. The order of the cars got scrambled somewhat getting through the tollbooths for the Turnpike, then regained their order as they sped east. An hour or so later, they turned off the Turnpike at the Donegal exit and took the county road into the mountains toward Seven Springs Mountain Resort. Paul dropped back as they turned into the stone gates at the entrance, keeping the caravan in view as it circled around the basin toward the collection of buildings.

The resort in springtime looked like an abandoned outpost on a far frontier. The acres of parking lots were empty, the chairlifts and T-bars stood like antennas up the slopes of the hills, the ramps and buildups exposed. The hillsides were bare, patches of grass beginning to show on the rough earth. Past the main lodge and the residence towers, Nicoletti's little caravan turned off the main road and climbed a secondary road away from the main complex into a small valley dotted with cabins on the slopes among the trees. They pulled into a cul-de-sac in front of a large log cabin with a veranda, made to look rustic but obviously new, the cars parking in a line along the side of the road.

Paul watched from a distance as the group got out of their cars and made their way up the slope to the house. The group was obviously divided up into couples now, Nicoletti with his arm around Suzy as he ushered everyone inside. Paul drove on, the curve of the road circumventing the base of the small hill and parked in the turnoff to a fire road. With his pistol tucked in the pocket of his windbreaker, he set off into the woods, climbing through the trees and scrub brush a mile or so over the crest of the hill and down the other side until he was fifty feet or so from the cabin. He took up a position on an outcropping of rock where he had a full view of the deck at the rear of the house and the large windows that showed much of the activity going on inside, the partygoers pouring themselves drinks, dancing in the living room, taking turns bending over the kitchen counter to sniff what Paul figured were lines of cocaine. The sounds of the stereo playing swing music, of tinkling glassware and laughter, drifted up the barren slope. Paul made himself as comfortable as he could in a niche of the rocks and settled down to wait.

Thirty-Seven

"Look out!"

Jeff, still on the bench after talking to the hippie, juked as an orange Frisbee sailed by in front of his face, followed by a gray dog, upright, suspended in midair for what seemed like seconds, jaws open, its tongue hanging out, a dog floating in space, at the level of his eyes, almost colliding with him before landing and running on, followed by a guy Jeff's age, the dog's owner, chasing after animal and disk.

"Hey, watch what you're doing!" Jeff shouted after him.

The guy looked back over his shoulder at Jeff as he ran, an expression on his face that said Go fuck yourself.

Go fuck yourself, Jeff thought, watching the guy and his dog disappear down a side street, in the same direction Sam went. What was all that from the hippie about some guy on a bad acid trip, and then that Jeff should stick up for himself with Mrs.

Nicoletti? Just go beat on her door. Demand that she be nice to him, give him a chance. Teach her a lesson. That was easy enough for Sam Bytheway to say. And why did he say all that if he was working with that policeman after Mrs. Nicoletti complained about his visit to her? Maybe it was a trap. He got up from the bench and crossed the square, heading down narrow Graeme Street to Fifth and over to Liberty. Whatever, Sam had given him an idea. He stopped in the CVS on the corner of Sixth; he was looking for women's stockings, but all they had were pantyhose though he supposed they would do the trick. When he paid for them the young Asian guy behind the counter winked at him and grinned, but Jeff ignored him. On the sidewalk he took the pantyhose out of their protective plastic egg and stuck them inside his anorak's hand-warmer pocket along with his father's gun and continued on toward the Allegheny River, roaming.

He was still groggy from the Nembutal, the forced sleep of the day before; and still shaky from the run-in with the Mad Hatter. He just couldn't spend his life being afraid, he just couldn't. He didn't know what he was so afraid of, he could take care of himself, if nothing else he had his father's gun, just to make sure. He could go anywhere he wanted to. When he got to Fort Duquesne Boulevard he crossed over the Tenth Street Bypass and headed down the steps to the river walk, heading toward the Point. The Allegheny was brownish, the waves lapping up against the edge of the concrete walkway a few feet away to his right; beyond a low barrier to his left cars sped along the bypass toward the ramps lifting to the Fort Duquesne Bridge ahead. Under the ramps rising above him, the walkway narrowed, the walls of the tall bridge piers closing him in on one side, the river frighteningly close on the other. Out on the water several racing shells from the rowing club swished along to the rhythmic chant of their coxswains, the multi-oared shells like giant insects skimming along the surface. Ahead, in a niche at the base of the bridge piers, along the narrowest part of the walk, were two teenagers, one black, one white. The boys stopped talking when they noticed Jeff.

Jeff hesitated, then stopped and turned around and headed back the way he came. The boys laughed, and then he heard their footsteps scuffing along behind him. He picked up the pace, there were cars streaming along on the bypass, the rowers out on the water, passersby crossing the ramp to the Sixth Street Bridge ahead, surely the boys behind him wouldn't try anything here, would they? He thought of the gun in his pocket but was more afraid to pull it out, suppose they grabbed it, took it from him, would he really have enough courage to use it? He was nearly running when he reached the steps to Sixth Street, he could hear the boys behind him, closer now, laughing, talking about something, laughing at him. At the top of the steps, he hurried over to the curb at the red light and turned around. The boys were behind him all right, but they stopped at the top of the stairs, looking at him, sneers on their faces. One laughed to the other and said under his breath, "Dumb motherfucker. You better run." Then they turned and headed across the bridge toward the North Shore, probably their destination all along. The light turned green and Jeff headed back into the downtown, back to his room at the hotel. Mortified. More ashamed than ever. Shaking with fear.

Thirty-Eight

Sam carried the bag of groceries along the passageway between the buildings and down the three steps to Carla's apartment. After making his rounds of churchgoers downtown and collecting his quota for the day, he stopped at the Giant Eagle on Forbes for provisions—more canned tuna, tomato soup, the things he'd need to make chicken soup. Overhead, the calico-puss sitting among the jars of bulbs and cuttings barely paid attention to him, glancing down once and closing its eyes again. That's right, Puss-Puss, just me. You better get used to it, I'm going to be a regular occurrence. Carla had told him where she hid a spare key in the shed for the garbage cans, but he decided to knock anyway, to make sure he didn't take her by surprise, she was probably still concerned about Ianni's men coming after her. But something was wrong. There was no response when he knocked. He tried to look in the window beside the door but the brown towel blocked the view. He knocked again, and realized the door seemed loose, flimsy. He tried the knob and it opened without the key.

The apartment was empty. All Carla's things were gone—the clothes hanging from the rod in the corner, the few books and knickknacks, her art deco pixie lamp beside the bed. All gone. The place didn't look ransacked but he couldn't tell for sure, there wasn't enough left to tell if her disappearance was forced or not. If someone had taken her or if she went on her own. No, it was on her own. She played me. She must have known she was going to cut out last night when I was here. She let me fix her up, take care of her, let me go on about the terrible things people do to each other. Knowing as soon as she had a chance, as soon as I was gone, she was going to leave.

Sam put the bag of groceries down on the bare table and stood there for a while, looking around. Well. So be it. I shouldn't be surprised. The way of the world. Don't get your hopes up, dude, karma going to get you if you don't watch out. And she knew how I felt about her. I would have done anything. . . . But that doesn't matter now, does it? They're all the same. All the same. Life goes on. The fucking bitch.

Thirty-Nine

At dusk, the pines lining the ridge behind the house spiked against the ball of the sun before swallowing it whole. Lights came on in the house; the music became slower, dreamier, and couples danced, wrapped in each other's arms, out on the deck, silhouetted against the lights inside. As the evening wore on, the couples moved off the deck, their arms still around each other, into the farther reaches of the house. One couple—Paul didn't know them, he only knew, cared about, that the girl wasn't Suzy—came down the steps and up the slope toward him, he was afraid they might come to the rocks where he was, but no, they lay together in the darkness on the grass less than ten yards from him, squirming and rooting around, the young woman moaning softly, "Oh help me, Bob, help me, Bob. . . ." Later, toward ten o'clock, activity picked up in the house again. There was laughter from the front, voices calling "Good night," "Good night," the sound of cars pulling away into the night. For a while, after everyone else was gone, Suzy and Nicoletti walked back and forth across the lighted windows, cleaning up a little, gathering dirty glasses, emptying ashtrays, picking up napkins. Then they disappeared again, somewhere deeper in the house, all the lights still burning. As Paul lay among the rocks, there was only the sound of the wind in the pines, the occasional cry of an owl.

When ten minutes passed and they hadn't reappeared, he took the .45 from the pocket of his windbreaker. Tapped the bottom of the handle sharply against the heel of his hand to ensure the clip was all the way home. Clicked off the safety. Pulled back the slide to make sure the first round was in the chamber, the gun now in battery. Then he stood, brushed the dirt from his pants, and made his way carefully down the slope toward the rear steps. The coals in a hibachi glowed at the far end of the deck; the soft music was playing inside the house but he still didn't see anyone. He eased up the steps and across the deck. The sliding glass doors were open. He flicked the safety of the .45 again with his thumb to double-check that it was off and held the gun up in the ready position as if he were the one on guard against an intruder. Keep that weapon up, soldier, you don't know where your enemy is.

When he was sure no one was about, he stepped into the kitchen.

The sink and counters were piled with dirty dishes; liquor and wineglasses were everywhere, there was a container of dip upside down on the floor that no one had bothered to clean up. Pigs. But what would you expect. . . ? He waited, listened, then moved on, across the room to the doorway of the living room. There was a fire in the fireplace, a few lamps turned low, but no one was there. Remember, in making a house-to-house sweep, the only secure area, the only area you can count on, is the area you have cleared yourself. Your enemy's prayer is that you'll take something for granted. . . . Beyond the picture windows at the far end of the room, the pines were silhouetted against a rising moon.

Then something moved, on the floor beside the couch; there was a murmur of voices, something stirred. Paul stepped into the room. They lay on an Indian rug in front of the fireplace, Nicoletti's bulk, braced on his outstretched arms, working over her. His naked back was covered with black curly hair all the way down his spine, the soles of his feet were bright pink, his ass flabby like twin white purses; Suzy's legs were wrapped partway around his middle, her feet making little circles in the air as Nicoletti pumped her, her face obscured from this angle. Paul moved closer, standing beside a bookcase, fifteen feet from them. Suzy turned her head slowly and for a moment stared at Paul, her blue eyes at first uncomprehending, then full of sympathy and apology, doing nothing that would give him away. The first round opens up the back of his head, splattering fragments of the brain pan across the room like pieces of a burst balloon, Nicoletti's body continuing its rhythm for a second or two as the blood and brains start to empty out of the half shell of his skull, before he bucks wildly and Suzy screams both from the realization of what is happening and from the pain of his lurching inside her before Nicoletti drops on her like a sack of flour and the second and third rounds slam, rip away at the flesh and muscle of his back. . . but only in his mind's eye. Paul watched for a moment longer as Nicoletti groaned softly, mounted over her like a tripod, and she turned her attention back to her lover, looking up at him, reaching up and running her fingers through his hair, murmuring, "It's okay, baby, it's okay, come now, come in me now, oh. . . ." Paul turned and retraced his steps out of the room, out of the house, back across the deck and up the slope into the black trees, the gun limp at his side, back through the woods, his way lit by a quarter moon, crashing through the brush and the low-hanging branches, up over the crest and down to where he had left his truck.

. . . and Paul drives through the night, out of the resort and along the winding road through the trees, the lights of an occasional house set back on the hillside, driving faster than he should and he knows it, eighty, ninety miles an hour, almost blind with tears and rage and he doesn't know what all else, finally coming to his senses long enough to pull off, skidding into a turnout, coming to a full stop, gravel pinging up against the frame of the truck, his headlights absorbed in clouds of dust, and he slams the truck into neutral and steps on the emergency brake and bursts out the door, retching, stumbles across the turnout to a line of trees as his body tries to throw up but there is nothing there, only bile and a little water, standing there in the grass bent over with dry heaves until he's afraid he'll cough up an organ, until it finally stops and he continues to stand there bent over, panting, bracing himself with his hands on his thighs until he can finally stand upright again, looking off into the dark woods in front of him as his breath slows and deepens and he's himself again, after several minutes takes the gun from the pocket of his windbreaker and looks at it, pulls back the slide to eject the round in the chamber, the bullet leaping out of the ejection port like an insect set free and disappearing into the dark brush at his feet, then weighs the gun in his hand

for a moment, the brushed stainless-steel finish of the Detonics Mark V Combat Master glimmering in the moonlight, thinking What the hell was I thinking? What the hell did I think I was going to do? Kill them? Kill Nicoletti? For what? For fucking a girl that I barely know and know she doesn't give a shit about me? Oh my God, what did I almost do? I must be crazy, crazy, pulls back his arm and is ready to throw the pistol as far as he can into the woods when the lights of a passing car stop him and he waits until the car is gone, the glowing eyes of its taillights receding into the night, and he looks at the pistol again, pulls the slide back a couple of times, listens to the action, the movement of precision part against precision part, then snaps the magazine back into the handle, closes the safety, and carries the gun with him as he returns shakily to his truck . . . as in a rented house in the Squirrel Hill area of Pittsburgh, Lieutenant Nathan White lies naked on a king-size bed while Fran Nicoletti, in her white peignoir, lights the last of nearly four dozen candles she has placed around the room—votive candles, utility candles, long slender tapers, a Twelve Days of Christmas candle, enough candles that he thinks they've probably raised the temperature of the room a couple of degrees, at least he's sweating as if they have—her back to him saying, "Did you really think the reason you came all the way out here at this time of night was to see my husband? You silly man," as Nathan, lying there in the reddish flickering light like some sacrificial offering, thinks This is crazy, crazy, suppose her husband comes home, Oh hi, I wanted to ask you about a murder, Fran turning to him as she blows out the double strands of dry spaghetti she's been using to the light the festival of lights, saying, "You're beautiful, you know that, Lieutenant? And you're blushing all the way down to your cock, ha ha. Ah Nathan, that's why I want all these candles, I was afraid I'd never see you again and then here you turn up on my doorstep tonight. I want this to be a celebration, a celebration of the mature hump, the bringing together of two adults who want nothing more than to use and please each other, or, as they say in the vernacular, to fuck each other's eyes out, ha ha. Wait a minute, my love, let me go put on some music, have you ever done it to 'The Rite of Spring'?" as she sweeps out of the room, her peignoir stirring currents of air, setting one of the santos on the mantel to rocking momentarily, a sound like tiny applause, in the candlelight its glazed wooden eyes twinkling at him as he thinks I have become the kind of person I hunt down for a living, a man who can't control himself, a man who will do something against all consequences, a man who can't be trusted, and I know all that and I know I'm going to do it anyway. Alexa was probably right about me, right to leave, there are times I wish I could leave me too, I guess that means I forgive her, now I wish I could forget her. So what does that tell me about the human heart? What the human heart is capable of? Nothing that I like knowing, as suddenly he is surrounded by the sound of blazing brass, pumping percussion, the Stravinsky piece seeming to burst out of the walls as Fran rushes back into the room, an eager, hopeful look on her face as if she is afraid he wouldn't still be there, then smiling broadly as she gazes at him, standing at the foot of the bed, pulling off the peignoir in one grand motion, standing naked in front of him, making a production of tossing the garment aside, the gown sailing across the room like a flimsy ghost, causing all the candles to dip in unison so that for an instant the room, the world, seems to tilt . . . as at the Greyhound bus terminal in Youngstown, Ohio, the destination of the first bus she could get out of Pittsburgh when she decided what she had to do, Carla sits in her buckskin jacket and Cossack-style boots, ignoring the stares and come-ons of the late-night loiterers, her few hastily gathered things around her, on one side her old cloth suitcase, on the other a large brown Giant Eagle bag containing her one prized possession, her art deco pixie lamp, found in a Hill District secondhand store, having fled her apartment on the spur of the moment, before any of Ianni's men can find her and finish what they started with her— she knows Sam said he would protect her, but she also knows that Sam is no match for the kind of men who might come for her; besides, Sam offers another kind of danger to her, a love she doesn't want, that she knows would only drag her down into a way of life that she wants to get away from now—her ticket in hand, determined to make a new life for herself, determined never to let anyone like Ianni or Sam or anyone else take advantage of her or use her again, proud of herself or at least a new pride growing within her, waiting for her connection home to Columbus . . . as on Commonwealth Plaza between Gateway Towers and the Gateway Hilton, Jeff sits in the dark slouched on a park bench, bitterly disappointed with himself, with always being afraid, with people pushing him around and never taking him seriously, his dream of becoming an actor falling in pieces around him, when he sees a yellow 280Z at speed pull into the turnaround beside the Towers and slide to a stop, the passenger leaning over to give the girl driving a quick kiss on the cheek and then climb out, Nicoletti in his safari jacket looking back through the open window as he says something to the girl and the girl says something in return, both of them laughing as the girl peels rubber around the half circle and fishtails out onto Fort Duquesne Boulevard and away, Nicoletti watching her go and then turning and heading down the walk toward the Stanwix Street Garage, and Jeff has a sudden idea, he was going to do the audition piece for Mrs. Nicoletti, take Sam's advice and force the issue with her, reenact the garage scene from Death Dealer, *make her take him seriously, but why not do it for the Man himself, this is his chance to show Nicoletti himself what he can do, and do it in an actual garage, it will be perfect, Jeff checking in his anorak pocket to make sure the pantyhose are still there along with the pistol as he gets up and follows the figure down the walks between the dark office towers. . . .*

Forty

Nicko pulled up the collar of his safari jacket against the night air, but it was more for effect than anything else, the night being warm. Was there someone behind him? He glanced over his shoulder but didn't see anyone, the walks of the plazas between the office buildings were deserted. He decided he was just tired, that's all, no one was up at this late hour except clandestine lovers and scavengers. Sometimes it's hard to tell the difference. I wonder which one I am. He had every right to be tired, he told himself, he had had a long a day, a long couple of days, what with the party and all. Beating the drum for his movie. All he wanted right now was to go home and go to bed, get some rest. No, more than that, the truth was all he wanted right now was to go home and see Fran. Tell her how the party went, that a couple of the money people in town might be interested in backing them. Tell her that maybe there was hope for the film yet.

Oh Frannie. Frannie. Make a lap, Frannie, he used to say to her. Make the Big V. He stopped and wheeled around; he was sure he saw something out of the corner of his eye, but the sidewalk was empty, the lampposts with their circles of light standing like silent sentinels. Ha ha, must be a guilty conscience. He walked on. He loved Fran, of course, she was the love of his life. Maybe he didn't desire her as much anymore, but he respected who she was, there was a real person there. She did what she said she was going to do, and did it without a lot of fuss and bother. And she was the only one who understood his work, what he had been trying to do all this time. She was the only one who understood how badly he had failed. He wondered if he could make things up to her in some way, all the lost or failed connections. I'm not making a very good start at it, am I, spending the weekend screwing Suzy? No, that was dumb talk. Fran would never expect such a thing from him, a piece of jewelry or something as a peace offering—or piece offering, in this case. That wasn't her style. A classy lady.

He walked around the fountain in front of One Gateway Center, the water turned off now, the basins full of standing water lit from below, then headed down the walk toward Stanwix, rounding the corner of the parking garage and into the gaping entrance, walking up the ramp to the second floor where he arranged to keep his car. The ramps on the lower floor were brightly lit, but there was no one in the collection booth, most of the cars on the first floor belonging to the rental agency, there was no one around. The second floor was darker; his Mercedes was in a row of cars along the back, sitting in the shadows. He started toward it when he heard something behind him; he turned and caught a glimpse of someone moving quickly among the parked cars. He hurried to his car and tried to unlock the door but the key wouldn't fit in the lock and someone came from between the cars and stood in the shadows beside a pillar.

"What do you want?" Nicko said.

The figure didn't say anything. Stared at him. Then moved closer. It was a man, his face pulled down into a grimace, the features smeared—a stocking mask.

"Who are you?"

"I've got a gun."

He did indeed. On one side of the gunman's head was what appeared to be a large goiter, he was terribly disfigured, a flap of loose skin. Then Nicko burst out laughing.

"It's pantyhose! That's pantyhose over your head! That's hilarious, who are you? Is that you, Warren? You're always kidding around. . . ."

Whoever it was became confused. "No, this is real . . . I mean, I'm an actor. . . ."

No, it wasn't Warren, he was too young, he was almost a boy, it wasn't anyone he knew. It didn't matter, he wasn't going to put up with it, whoever it was, no one was going to try to threaten him. He lunged forward and grabbed him, the boy stumbling backwards, almost pleading, "Wait . . . wait a minute," then there was a loud sharp noise and the incredible pain then more noise as he collapsed on the ground and felt as if someone were kicking him and he thought That story I told that girl reporter, that was Spielberg's story, not mine, Frannie found that camera in a junk store, I only wish . . . and then there was nothing at all.

Monday, May 5, 1975

as many turns of the worm to produce one turn of the gear shaft as there are teeth in the gear.

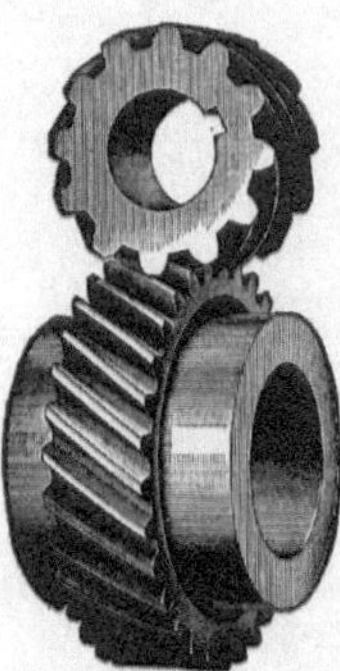

Fig. 125. Helical Gears

Helical Gears. Helical gears are a modification of the ordinary gearing in which the pitch surfaces may be cones or cylinders, Fig. 125. These gears work very smoothly and quietly as the teeth have always two points touching in the plane of the axes, besides being stronger than those of ordinary wheels.

Train of Gear Wheels. Gear wheels are often used in a train, Fig. 126, so as to increase the mechanical advantage. In the case illustrated, there are two pairs of gears, each pair having 24 and 11 teeth, respectively. Either pair has, therefore, a mechanical advantage of $\frac{24}{11} = 2\frac{2}{11}$; and the two pairs taken in series have a mechanical advantage of $2\frac{2}{11} \times 2\frac{2}{11} = 4.76$. Hence, *in any compound machine the final me-*

Fig. 126. Train of Gear Wheels

chanical advantage is equal to the product of the mechanical advantages of the separate machines.

Compound Machines
Practical Physics
Modern Shop Practice

Forty-One

There was a pain in the center of his back, along the spine, between the shoulder blades only a little lower, an ache but a sharp ache, a pressure, like a large hand pressing its fingertips into him.

"You okay?" Sergeant MacCarron said.

"Yeah, just a little twitch," Nathan said, working his shoulders, trying to shake it off. He rang the bell again, looked at the intercom above the mailboxes: nothing. He checked the name on the mailbox again, to make sure he had the right number: S. KONECKI NO. 6. He rang the bell again, tried the front door again. He shrugged to Mac and turned to leave.

He turned too quickly: he was dizzy, he leaned a hand against the archway of the building to steady himself, glad that Mac hadn't seen him. What was wrong with him? He didn't think he was ill, only wobbly. Since the call came to his apartment early this morning that Francis Nicoletti had been murdered, he had been in something of a daze, walking through the steps of the investigation as if by rote. Almost afraid of what he and MacCarron would turn up next. What would he do if it came out that he had been having an affair with Nicoletti's wife? He supposed he could call it an affair, though it wasn't that, really. No matter, the papers would have a field day. And worse than that: someone could say he had a reason himself to kill Nicoletti. For most of Sunday evening he had an alibi, if you want to call screwing the murder victim's wife an alibi; but he left Fran's before the time Nicoletti was killed, and no one could vouch for his whereabouts the rest of the night. I barely knew what the man looked like until I saw the crime-scene photos, why would I want to kill him? Not for Fran, but people wouldn't know that. . . . As he walked down the steps of Suzy's apartment building, his back and shoulders ached more than ever, as if the hand of pain were weighing too heavily upon him, pushing him down. The trouble with being sensitive is that all your nerves are exposed. Except Alexa didn't think I was sensitive enough. At least not to her. There was a time a few days ago when I could see myself killing her too. . . .

He had reached the car parked in front of the building when he heard a voice call from above, "Hello?"

He turned too quickly again; the pain gripped him so he could raise his head only so far. Suzy was leaning out a window on the third floor, holding it open with one hand and her robe closed with the other. "Are you the police?"

"Yes, ma'am," MacCarron said, reaching in his suitcoat pocket and holding up his badge. "We need to talk to you."

"I thought you would eventually. I'll buzz you in," she said and left the window.

"You hear that, Nathan?" Mac said to him as they headed back up the steps, Mac in the lead. "She thought we'd need to talk to her eventually. I think we've got a live one."

Nathan didn't respond, he was afraid to say too much, in addition to trying to hold it together until the pain in his back settled down, there was the added pain of looking up. Until the Big Hand relaxed its hold on him. *A Big Hand digging into my back. As in Let's give the lieutenant a Great Big Hand? The ramblings of a crazy man, or a man going crazy. I've got to watch it.* Mac reached the buzzing front door just in time and Nathan followed him in.

Considering the weight of the Hand, not to mention the pain every time he jostled it the wrong way—he made a mental note that the Hand was vindictive and not to push it the wrong way— he considered that he made it all the way up the steps quite an accomplishment. Suzy was waiting for them at the railing on the third floor and led them in the open door to her apartment. She was wearing a blue terry-cloth bathrobe and blue fuzzy slippers; her hair was unwashed and tangly, her face pale and blotchy without makeup, her underlying acne quite apparent. Mac looked at him and cocked his head as if to say *See, I told you,* as the two men followed her into the living room. She motioned for them to sit in the black canvas director's chairs across from the glass-topped coffee table; she sat on the sofa, where she apparently was sitting before the bell rang. On the coffee table were dirty glasses, a cereal bowl, a half-eaten box of chocolate chip cookies; magazines and newspapers were strewn about the floor. She sat across from them, her legs crossed, her blue robe open far enough to show her lovely thighs.

"If you were expecting us," Nathan said, taking out his notebook, "you must know why we're here."

"Yes, I saw it on television. And in the paper." Suzy motioned vaguely to the sections of newspapers scattered around the room.

"We're both sorry for your loss—"

"My loss?" she said, and laughed a little dismissively. "What loss? Mr. Nicoletti was my employer, and what happened to him was tragic, of course, awful, but it's not like he was a relative or anything. . . ."

At that, MacCarron raised his eyes from the bit of leg she was showing and looked at her dead on. "Miss Konecki, we know you were having an affair with Francis Nicoletti. We know you were with him most of the weekend, including time at a rented cabin at Seven Springs with several other couples."

"Who said that? Who were you talking to?"

"Mrs. Nicoletti among others," Nathan said, trying to get control of the interview again.

"So you'd do us all a favor, and make it a lot easier for yourself, if you'd be straightforward and tell us the truth about what was going on," Mac said.

"You don't think I'm a suspect or anything. Do you?" Suzy leaned forward and covered up her exposed leg. Mac looked at Nathan and made a face as if he was sorry to see it go away.

"We need to ask you some questions as part of our investigation. Such as, when did you last see Mr. Nicoletti?"

"I dropped him off last night at Gateway Towers around ten thirty or eleven, I guess it was. He left his car in the Stanwix Garage there, he got out and . . . I never saw him again."

"Where did you go from there?" Mac said.

"I came home."

"Can anyone vouch for that?" Nathan said.

Suzy thought a moment. "Well, yes, as a matter of fact. The boy downstairs—I call him a boy but he's actually a young man— he was coming in when I did and asked me over to his place for a drink."

"And you went?" Mac said.

"Well, yes, he's very nice. He's always trying to date me or something, but he's very young, I mean he's my age, but he's rather immature."

"You prefer a more mature man," Mac said.

"Well, yes . . . no, I mean—"

"So you didn't really like this guy—what's his name?"

"Brandon, but—"

"You didn't really like this Brandon but you went into his place and had a drink with him anyway," Mac said. "How long were you there, a couple of hours? You'd need to be if you're using him to vouch for your whereabouts while Nicoletti was being killed."

"I don't know what you're insinuating," Suzy said.

"I'm not in-*sin*-uating anything," Mac said. "I'm just establishing a timeline for you on Sunday. You spent the day with one guy who you apparently spent the night before with, and then you come home and spend another couple hours drinking with a guy you don't care for that much. You have quite an interesting social life."

Suzy looked like she was about to cry. Nathan had to admit that Mac was good at Bad Cop, Good Cop. "Miss Konecki, if Brandon can verify the time you spent downstairs, then you have nothing to be concerned about. But I do need to ask you, do you know of anyone who might want to kill Mr. Nicoletti? Anyone that you've been working with, for instance?"

"No, I don't think so. I mean, Nicko—Mr. Nicoletti could be difficult at times. He'd yell and scream at people, but he was only trying to get the best work possible. I know people would say bad things about him, but they didn't mean them. Not like that, anyway, not like they'd kill him or anything."

"Have you noticed anyone hanging around where you were shooting? You know, anyone acting strange?"

"I don't think so," Suzy said, and sat back again, exposing her thigh again. "Well, there was one guy, his name is Paul. He's been around the set the last couple of days. But that was because of me."

"Because of you?" Mac said, not bothering to take his eyes from her bare leg.

"To see me. He came to see me. He's a friend of mine, I mean he became a friend of mine. He would come by the set to see me."

"Paul? Paul what?"

"I'm not sure . . ."

"And he's a friend of yours? Another friend?" Mac said.

Nathan shot him a look to shut him up. "Can you describe Paul?"

"Oh, he's about forty, maybe mid-forties. Tall, well built. Good looking, he almost looks like he could be in movies. A strong chin. He seemed to always wear a tan windbreaker—but this is what I mean. I know lots of men, I have lots of men friends. With Mr. Nicoletti it wasn't like I was his mistress or anything. . . ."

MacCarron hooted in spite of himself.

As they pulled away from the curb and continued down South Highland, MacCarron said, "So. What do you make of this Paul guy? That's the first we've heard anything about him."

"I don't know. I suppose it's possible. Guy has a thing for Konecki and doesn't like Nicoletti screwing her and gets revenge."

"Hard to imagine that little girl inspiring so much passion."

"What are you talking about?" Nathan said. "You couldn't keep your eyes off her legs."

"Hey, partner. If she's cheap enough to show 'em, I'm cheap enough to look at 'em."

As they approached Walnut, Nathan pulled over into a yellow zone. "There's a pay phone. Hold on while I check our messages."

He hated to use public phones but didn't want to use the radio in case there was a message from Fran; if Mac suspected something or thought it was odd, he didn't say anything. The phone was as dirty as he feared, the recess of the earpiece caked with muck, the grille over the speaker covered with who knew what. He used the Kleenex he carried in the car for such emergencies and cleaned the instrument as much as he could—then of course he had a filthy piece of Kleenex he didn't know what to do with. He rang into the office and listened to the messages, then carried the tissue with two fingertips over to a waste bin before returning to the car. Mac watched him as he climbed in.

"Mr. Clean. You're more fun to watch than my wife cleaning the toilet."

Nathan gave him a sarcastic look as he started the car.

"Anything going on?" Mac said.

"Matter of fact, we got a message from Sam."

"Your hippie friend? He want to sell us some dope?"

"I think he wants to sell us some information. He wants to meet me at the O."

"If nothing else, maybe we'll get some cheesy French fries out of it."

Forty-Two

"Look at them, Nathan. They think they know it all. And the fact is they don't know a thing."

Sam sat with the edge of the counter pressed into the small of his back, facing away from the windows in the back room of the O. Then turned on his stool to look at Nathan.

"We thought we knew it all too, at one time," Nathan said.

"I wonder if we were this bad. I mean, look at them. Like lambs to the slaughterhouse. And they vote. They would gladly elect their own slaughterman, and go happily down the chute to their destruction singing campaign songs." He watched a couple of Pitt students go by, carrying their trays of hot dogs and baskets piled high with French fries covered in cheese. "If you want something to eat, go on ahead."

"I'll pass. My partner wants me to get him some of those cheesy fries, but I refuse."

"A guy has to have some standards in this world, right?"

"I'm sure you didn't call me to discuss the dietary standards of the Dirty O," Nathan said.

"Yeah, how about that? When you gave me that card, I thought you were kinda putting me on or something. But I called and here you are."

"So, why'd you call?"

"There's a guy you should be looking at for Nicoletti's murder. He's a young guy, named Jeff Berner, he's been staying at the Hilton for the last week or so, maybe longer, I don't know."

"How young?"

"Right out of college, early twenties. Medium height, maybe a little shorter. He wants to be an actor."

"Why should we be interested in him?"

"He's been hanging around a lot, especially where Nicoletti is. He's staying across the plaza from Nicoletti's office at Gateway Towers. And I'm pretty sure I noticed him in the crowd watching when Nicoletti was filming downtown."

"Doesn't sound like a killing matter to me."

"Yeah, but the last time I talked to him—actually it was the first time I talked to him—he was really upset, really bitter. I guess he tried to get an audition at Nicoletti's office but it didn't go well, he couldn't even get past Nicoletti's wife, he felt humiliated. And he was talking crazy about me working for you as an undercover or something. I guess he saw us talking together—"

"When was this?" Nathan said, suddenly more interested.

"When I talked to him? Sunday morning. I don't know when he saw us talking together—"

"Go on."

"That's it. But I got the impression talking to him that he's really capable of doing something crazy."

"Why are you telling me this?" Nathan said, studying him carefully. "What's up, Sam? I don't believe you've suddenly become civic-minded."

"No," Sam laughed a little. "Anything but that. No, I want some information. About a girl, her name is Carla Brunnel."

"Carla Brunnel. She was a friend of Sandy Love, you're the one who told us about her. We started to look for her but then got sidetracked. What about her?"

"She's disappeared. I was helping her at her apartment, she had a run-in with one or more of Ianni's goons, but now she's gone. I want to know what happened to her, is she in a hospital somewhere? Did Ianni come and take her away? Did they do to her what they did to Sandy—"

"And why are you so concerned about her? Are you involved with her?"

"Yeah. You could say that."

Nathan thought a moment. "Yes, if she's missing we definitely need to find out what happened to her and where she is." He got up off the stool, smoothed the wrinkles from his suit coat—until he realized what he was doing. Sam gave him a wry smile.

"But you still haven't told me anything about Jeff Berner that would make me think he's especially dangerous or a suspect. A disappointed actor. You and I are disappointed musicians but it didn't turn us into killers—at least I don't think it did. Or should I be taking a closer look at you?"

Sam ignored what seemed Nathan's feeble attempt at humor. "Berner is wearing a red anorak, you know, one of those shiny pullover jobs with a large zippered kangaroo pocket across the front. Whenever he stretches a certain way you can see the outline of what he's got in it."

"What's he got? A baby kangaroo?"

"A gun."

Forty-Three

There were headlights behind him. Half a block behind him. Following him, Nathan was sure. He noticed them when he was on the Boulevard of the Allies, after leaving the Public Safety Building for the day, along the bluffs past Duquesne University and Mercy Hospital, following him as he took the turnoff to Oakland and up Forbes into the University District, past the O where he talked to Sam earlier. Which reminded him: he still hadn't looked into what had happened to Sam's friend Carla, as he said he would. It was something that needed to be done, both for her own protection and safety, and because there might, just might, be some tie-in with Sandy Love's murder, but he simply hadn't gotten to it yet, the Nicoletti murder was taking precedence. For that matter, he hadn't had time to do anything but make preliminary inquiries into the guy Sam said was acting suspicious, Jeff Berner, found that the guy had no police record, nothing showed up on any database. When would this Berner have seen him talking to Sam, and why would he think Sam might be an undercover? You don't suppose, the other night, he saw me leaving Nicoletti's office, Fran—No. He shook his head, he couldn't start thinking such things.

He turned off Forbes, made a half circle around the deserted parking lot beside the Carnegie and crossed the bridge over Panther Hollow on Schenley Drive, past Phipps Conservatory glowing like a glass palace in the night and into Schenley Park. Now he was certain the headlights were following him. He watched them in the rearview mirror along the winding roads, they slowed when he slowed, sped up when he sped up, always half a city block behind. The Big Hand on his back was pressing, pressing. Who would be following him? Somebody from the papers? A reporter? A TV crew? Or maybe MacCarron, checking up on me, I've noticed him looking at me funny the last day or so. What does he know? What does he suspect? The ache between his shoulders was becoming unbearable. As he neared the exit of the park into Squirrel Hill he stopped abruptly and slammed the car into Park and got out, his suitcoat open to show his badge, so he could get at his gun quickly if he needed to, walking back along the lane toward the headlights, his hand up shielding his eyes trying to get a look at the driver.

"Who are you?" he shouted, continuing toward the car. Thinking *If whoever it is has a gun I'm a dead man.* "Why are you following me?" The car had stopped as well, for a long moment just sitting there as Nathan approached, then it jumped backwards twenty feet or so, spun around in the center of the road, and sped back down the slight hill into the park again. Nathan stood in the middle of the road watching the car disappear into the night. *I've just scared an innocent citizen half to death. Some guy coming home late from the office. Some mother returning from a night class at Pitt. I'm cracking up. I've got to get my shit together.* He walked back to his car as the ache returned between his shoulder blades. At this point he almost welcomed it, like an old friend he could rely on, something whose presence gripped him to the real world.

As he drove out of the park into Squirrel Hill, the headlights were behind him again.

Forty-Four

Fran's red Alfa was in the driveway, evidently she had been out since Nathan and MacCarron were here earlier. When he rang the bell, she opened the door with a flourish, though she seemed surprised to see who it was.

"Lieutenant."

"You sound like you were expecting someone else. I hope I'm not interrupting you."

"No, I don't think I was expecting anyone at all. Come in."

Nathan was disappointed; he didn't know what kind of welcome he expected, much less what he wanted from her, but whatever it was, this wasn't it. There had been no opportunity to speak to her privately since her husband was murdered, and there were a number of things he felt they needed to talk about. Among other things, he needed to retrieve the tie he left here Sunday night, he wondered if it was still hanging from her bedstead where she had him bind her wrists. Now she was dressed in a puffy white peasant-style blouse and a long peasant skirt, a full skirt in a dark red and blue and black pattern, extending almost to her ankles, over a pair of black boots. She led the way—she was businesslike, though with a decided swing to her step—into the living room and sat across from him on the other twin leather sofa.

"You don't have your gorilla with you this time." She smiled sweetly but with a decided edge as she spread out her skirt around her on the couch, making a display of it or herself or both as she got settled.

"Sergeant MacCarron tends to leave an impression with people," Nathan tried to smile.

"That he does, that he does."

"I'm sorry I couldn't come by myself earlier today but—"

"I understand." She bowed her head once, a kind of acknowledgment. "It was probably better that way anyway. There's been a steady stream of people wanting one thing or another since it happened. Talking to you and your Sergeant MacCarron was far from the worst thing I've had to go through today."

"And I'm sorry we had to ask you all those questions. But until we have something more to go on with this, we have to pursue every possibility. . . ." He let the sentence trail away. The ache in his neck and shoulders had evolved into a clamp, an iron brace, so that it was difficult for him to raise his head. He felt as if he were talking to her from under a table.

"I hope what I told you was some help."

He deferred comment in favor of a noncommittal shrug. "Who all has contacted you since it happened?"

"Oh, reporters wanting stories, photographers wanting pictures, people calling up and asking if I'm Mrs. Nicoletti and then hanging up. People from Nickolodeon and the film he was making wanting to know if they still have jobs. That's why I opened the door as I did, I was afraid it was going to be some kind of crank."

"Has there been a lot of that—someone calling and then hanging up right away?"

"A few times," she shrugged it off. "It's to be expected, I suppose. Nicko's earlier movies attracted, shall we say, a strange kind of audience. You should have seen some of the things they sent us after *A House Turned Red* and *The Killing Kind*—bloody hammers and mangled dogs, things like that. People are sick, but they have money to spend."

He looked around at the decorations in the rented house: carved wooden sculptures from the Spanish Inquisition of saints writhing in pain, medieval pikes and battle-axes hanging on the walls, the spiked mace sitting on the white carpet near her feet.

Apparently she didn't get the irony.

"Do you know of anyone who was hanging around lately where your husband was filming? Did he speak of anyone to you?"

"What kind of anyone? There are always people hanging around when you shoot on location."

"Let's say one of your cranks."

She thought a moment. "No, not that I know of. I've had one or two come up to the office lately, but I didn't hear about anyone in particular at the locations."

"Who came up to the office?"

"Oh, you know, kids, college kids, wanting to be stars."

"What kind of college kids?"

"*A* college kid, if you're so interested, a young man."

"Can you describe him?"

Fran sighed, exasperated. "Blond-haired, just a boy really, medium height, in an atrocious corduroy disco outfit. I ended up calling him Corduroy Boy, at least in my mind. Why do you want to know?"

Nathan shook his head, carefully, slowly, against the pain. For a moment it sounded like the guy Sam had told him about, but Berner was dressed much differently according to Sam, he didn't sound like a guy who would wear such an outfit. It didn't sound like the guy Nathan was interested in either. "Are you familiar with someone named Paul?"

"Paul who? Is he an actor, technician, what?"

"I'm afraid we don't know. We just have the name Paul. Apparently he was seen around the filming lately."

Fran shook her head. "It doesn't ring any bells. But a lot of names pass through my office."

"He's tall, thin, strong jaw and cheekbones, in his early forties, dark hair—"

"Lieutenant, that could be just about anyone."

It's Lieutenant. Not Nathan. But I guess it's better this way, given the circumstances. Keep it on an official level. All business. As if nothing ever happened. . . . This was getting him nowhere. There were other things he wanted to talk to her about, wanted to ask her, but this was a different Fran from the one he had known before. A different Fran from the woman who had made her bedroom into the site of a candlelit celebration. He rubbed the back of his neck, his arm wrapped across himself as if it were a boa.

"What will you do?"

"About all the cranks?"

"No, about the company. Nickolodeon. And the movie Nicko was working on."

"We'll go on." She didn't say "of course," but her tone of voice implied it. The look she gave him.

"I thought—"

"I'm taking over the company. I always did run the financial end of things, and all the important papers have my name on them. So now I think it's time for me to get involved in the creative end of things too. I'm not dumb, you know, Lieutenant."

No, he never thought she was. Funny that she would even think he might. Probably the only dumb thing she's done in a long time was sleep with me. But there were other things he was beginning to think about her.

"I'm going to start right away," she went on, giving a quick little lift of her head. "Going over the rushes to find out what Nicko was trying to do, see what I can salvage of it and finish it off. There should be quite a lot of interest in it now, regardless how good it is. Ironic, I won't have any trouble finding the financing to finish it, now that he's dead. And then I have some ideas for projects of my own."

"You don't sound very enthusiastic about what your husband was doing."

"Did I give that impression?" she said smiling innocently, as if to say Sweet li'l ol' me? Then she laughed silently, opening her mouth too wide, showing her unfortunate teeth. "Nicko could never find the handle on this project. He knew he wanted to do something different from what he'd done before, he knew he wanted to stretch himself. He even wanted to show, quote, goodness, unquote, whatever that is, instead of the violence he always showed before. But I think what he was finding out about himself was that he simply didn't have very much to say about anything except violence. Deep down inside violence was the only thing he was really interested in—that and sex, and they were pretty much the same to Nicko, ha ha. He could barely decide on a name for the movie, much less what the story was about. I've thought in some ways maybe it was better that he died when he did—not the way he did, of course. But at least this way he doesn't have to face the reality that he couldn't do what he was trying to do. That he wasn't the genius he liked to think he was."

Harsh words. Harsh lady. And to think I . . . a couple of times. . . . The weight on his shoulders burned, the hump he imagined on his back felt like a sack of hot coals. He worked his shoulders inside his suit coat, trying to find a position that was comfortable.

"So in some ways, you actually gain by Nicko's death."

Her gaze leveled at him as if she looked at him in a different light. "What are you getting at, Nathan?"

Oh, now it's Nathan. Now. He was glad for the chance to look away from her as he took his notebook from his inside coat pocket and found the notation. "You said you were here alone after I left on Sunday night. I need to ask if you thought of any way to verify that, such as maybe you called someone, or someone stopped by. . . ."

When he looked at her again, she was smiling at him, her mocking smile, full of derision. "If I didn't know you better, I'd think you were wondering if I was seeing somebody else, trying to find out who else visits me in my bedroom."

"This isn't about you and me. This is about—"

"This is about who killed Nicko. And you want to know if I can verify that I was here—alone—when he was killed because you're wondering if I was the one who killed him. My, my, my. Suddenly your Sergeant MacCarron doesn't seem so bad after all; at least you know where you stand with him. No, Lieutenant White, I have no alibi for Sunday night—after you left, that is. I was here by myself with only a bottle of Tanqueray for company. Not a very effective lover, I might add, but one I can always count on. And no, I did not kill my husband. Nor did I have him killed. There were certainly times I wanted to kill the man, but I never would have given him the satisfaction."

"I'm sorry to have to ask that, Fran." He hated himself for calling her Fran.

"You don't need to apologize, you're only doing your job. And that's what I am to you now, part of the job. In the same way that you're. . . ." She waved away whatever it was she was about to say and recomposed herself. "Funny, isn't it? The different paths the world puts you on at different times. And you're right in a way to suspect me. I wish I didn't feel this way, but I'm glad Nicko's dead. Not because it ended his life—no, I didn't want that. But because now I can start mine. I loved the man, or at least I always said I did. I even fucked another man for him, to keep Nickolodeon in money. But the more I think about it, I wonder if I didn't really love the other man more, but stayed with Nicko because I knew that was the only way I could guarantee seeing the man I really wanted. I don't know. I guess none of it matters now. I do know this though: from now on I do everything for this little girl, no one else. And now I think it's time that you left. Lieutenant."

. . . and Nathan gets in his unmarked police car, turns around in

her driveway, his headlights washing over the front of the hacienda-inspired house, and heads back down the late-night streets, the upscale houses on their manicured lawns mostly dark at this hour, only an occasional light on, thinking So that's that. Better this way. Should never have happened in the first place, but no harm done. Just an interesting interlude. One for the books. Nothing was going to come of it regardless, as he realizes the headlights are behind him again, keeping pace with him half a block behind as he makes his way through Squirrel Hill, turns into the lighted business district along Murray Avenue where he thinks he'll finally get a look at the car but it turns off before he can, disappears down a side street and doesn't appear again as he continues into Oakland, heading downtown . . . as back in the rented house in Squirrel Hill, Fran is in the kitchen standing at the island draining the last of her glass of wine when the doorbell rings and she heads back through the downstairs, thinking Oh good, Nathan came back, I didn't mean to be so hard on him, there's no reason why we can't still be friends, and more than that, right, little girl? opens the door with a flourish and finds a young man standing there who seems vaguely familiar though she can't quite place him, wearing a red anorak with the hood pulled up, his tousled blond hair poking out the front, so he looks like a preppie monk, a nice clean-cut young man except that his eyes are wild, desperate, he looks like he's about to cry or scream, and he has a gun in his hand. . . .

Tuesday, May 6, 1975

boat teams, distribution of equipment
and supplies, methods of debarkation,
and means of navigation to the landing
beach are carefully planned. In addition,
consideration is given to methods of
recognizing the reception committee and
disposing of the landing craft.

b. Water infiltration operations normally ter-
minate in a land movement phase.

c. Infiltration by means of a sea plane landing
on large lakes, rivers, or coastal waters may be
possible. In such a case, infiltration planning by
the detachment considers the ship-to-shore and
subsequent land movement characteristics of
water infiltration operations.

29. Land

Land infiltration is conducted similar to that
of a long-range patrol into enemy territory.
Generally, guides are required. If guides are not
available, the detachment must have detailed in-
telligence of the route, particularly if borders are
to be crossed. Routes are selected to take maxi-
mum advantage of cover and concealment and to
avoid enemy outposts, patrols, and installations.
The location and means of contacting selected
individuals who will furnish assistance are provided to the detachment. These individuals may
be used as local guides and sources of information, food, and shelter. Equipment and supplies
to be carried will necessarily be restricted to
individual arms and equipment and communications equipment.

Forty-Five

Paul thought it must be some kind of flu, a bug going around, whatever it was that laid him out the following day. It came on him as he was driving back from Seven Springs on Sunday night, he suddenly broke out in a cold sweat, his body wracked with feverish chills, he was so weak by the time he got home that he could barely climb out of his truck and stagger into the house. He had sweated through his clothes, he was soaking wet; he dragged himself into the shower and stood braced against the wall with the scalding water pounding on him until he used up all the hot water in the tank and the spray turned icy cold. Then he wrapped himself in a blanket, teeth chattering, trembling all over, and lay on the bed in the spare bedroom—he didn't want to disturb Sharon but she got up when she heard him and stayed with him, sitting in a chair across the room, paging through old copies of *Better Homes and Gardens* to keep herself company. Through the night and all the next day he lay there, getting up periodically for another scalding-to-icy shower, before lying down again—Sharon in the meantime having exchanged his sweaty blanket for a dry one, running the damp one through the washer and dryer—curled in a ball with the blanket pulled up to his ears, dreaming fitfully, whimpering at times, until his shaking, his head snapping back and forth as if it might come off, woke him and he dragged himself into the bathroom again to take another shower.

And then it was over, as quickly as it began. He woke late Tuesday morning feeling cleansed, purged, the same as he had when he lived with the Montagnards and woke after a night of drinking rice wine in the community house, still weak, drained, something of a convalescent, but better now, stronger in some way than before. And anxious to set things right. When Sharon came into the bedroom after his shower, she found him without his shirt standing in front of the mirror, looking at himself in the same way he would examine his truck or a piece of turned metal, looking for flaws, imperfections.

"You must be feeling better."

He looked at her in the mirror and nodded. "I am. Much."

He patted his stomach, still at his age without an ounce of flab to him, to show he was sound, but it was a feeble gesture, it only called attention to how weak he still was. He pulled on an under-shirt and took a shirt from the dresser. A good sport shirt.

"Are you going out?"

"There are some things I need to take care of."

"I already called the shop and told them you weren't coming in."

"That's okay. I wasn't going there anyway. I'll go in tomor-row."

He was aware that Sharon was watching him as he finished buttoning up his shirt, put on his socks and shoes. Gathered his wallet. Handkerchief. Pocket change. She stood in the doorway, wearing one of Stephen's Grateful Dead T-shirts and shorts, her arms folded under her breasts, cradling herself, her long brown hair in tangles down to her shoulders, leaning against the door-frame, the toes of one bare foot resting on the arch of the other. She finally worked up the courage to say what she had to.

"When I called, they asked me if you were seriously ill. They said you'd missed a lot of time lately. I didn't know a thing about it."

Paul looked at her again in the mirror. Watched her. Waiting for what else she had to say.

"I felt like a fool," she said, tearing up though fighting hard not to.

What could he say to her? That he had lost his head over a little taste of glamour and excitement in Pittsburgh? That he had made a total fool of himself over a younger woman? *I've been unfair to her, I've hurt her badly. . . .* How could he tell her what had been going through his mind the last few days when he barely understood it himself? That without fully realizing what he was up to, he had almost killed a man over this younger woman—or at least it seemed that's what almost happened. He could hardly believe it of himself, that he would do such a thing, but there seemed no other explanation for his behavior on Sunday, for watching the apartment all night, following Suzy and Nicoletti to Seven Springs, and then sneaking inside . . . he must have wanted to kill him. But I didn't kill him, that's the important thing, I could have and I didn't, I'm not that kind of person after all, I'm not a bad person. . . . He wouldn't know where to begin to tell Sharon.

And how could he tell her what he felt he had to do to set things right, right with himself? He had never run from anything in his life, it was his nature to stand and fight, and he wanted to fight now whatever it was that had drawn him to the city. Drawn him away from himself and the things he knew were right. You're a big tease, that's what you are, a big tease. He wanted to show the part of him that was attracted to all the phony glamour and excitement that it had no hold on him. Held no attraction for him. That he could take it or leave it. You know, Paul, you're really a very nice man. Now, good-bye, I've got other things to do. . . . He needed to prove to himself that he was neither beaten by it nor afraid of it. Then life could get back to normal.

He knew Sharon had been worried about him, he had put her through a lot lately, all the secretiveness, his acting strange. After he took care of this business he would find some way to make it up to her. He loved her more at this moment, appreciated her for the unique and loving person she was, than he ever had before in his life. But Paul, being who he was, couldn't say any of that to her. He could only walk past her and out of the room, out of the house. As it so happened, forever.

Forty-Six

When he got into Pittsburgh, he parked as he usually did in Market Square—he took his .45 from its holster under the seat and stuck it in his jacket pocket, he wasn't sure why, a sense of security perhaps, he was still weak from his sudden illness and it made him feel more like himself, something familiar, something sure, something that was his—and headed down Forbes to Stanwix. He looked in the windows of the McDonald's at the corner but Sam wasn't there; he didn't particularly want to see the hippie, but he didn't want to avoid seeing him either. For an hour or more he took a walk along the places where he had walked before, through Gateway Center past Gateway Towers and the Hilton, across Commonwealth and into Point State Park, around the fountain at the Point and back again—he looked up across the river at the buildings along the ridgeline of Mount Washington overlooking the city, the white apartment building where Suzy was at Nicoletti's party; he shook his head at himself, turned away—back uptown to the shopping district along Smithfield Street, past Kaufmann's and Gimbels and the park at Mellon Square, then back down Fifth and over to Market Square again, unable to understand why he thought these places so fascinating. Whatever it was that had compelled his interest before was gone, there was nothing for him here.

In a way, he wished Nicoletti were filming nearby so he could see Suzy again, to prove to himself that his attraction to her was over as well. But it didn't seem necessary; and there were a number of reasons why it wouldn't be such a good idea. He didn't want to have to explain to her what he was doing when she saw him at Nicoletti's cabin at Seven Springs on Sunday night. And he didn't want to have to listen to any more of her phony ideas or rationalizations. Francis and I have an open relationship, he does his thing and I do mine. Better to forget her completely. What was done was done. For that matter, after what he had witnessed that night, he couldn't imagine that she would want to see him. *You're such a wonderful man, Paul. I never have to worry about things getting out of hand when I'm with you.* To hell with her. He was ready to go home and take a nap, relieved of a great burden, get rested up to go to work tomorrow. Resume his old way of life. But when he got back to his truck, he found Sam standing beside it, digging in his shoulder bag for something. The guy looked genuinely surprised to see him.

"The man of the hour," Sam said, a curious smile on his face.

"What's the matter, did my meter run out?" Without thinking that he was about to leave anyway, he put in another quarter. "Don't tell me you were going to put some money in it for me."

"Okay, I won't tell you that," Sam said, closing up his shoulder bag again. "But while you're at it, there's probably chalk marks on the tires too."

Paul walked out in the street, around to the other side of the truck; sure enough, there was a blue chalk mark across the tread of the front wheel. As he got a rag from the utility box to wipe it off, he thought he shouldn't be too hard on the guy. After all, he had sort of enjoyed some of their talks, and Sam had genuinely tried to be helpful at times. The guy was a weirdo, but he meant well.

"Look, I've got to get something to eat before I keel over," Paul said, coming back to the curb. "How about if I treat you to a burger?"

Sam studied him a moment, a bewildered look on his face, then shrugged, hitched up his shoulder bag and followed him across the square.

Forty-Seven

When Nathan finally got to Squirrel Hill through the heavy early afternoon traffic around the universities, the street was filled with emergency vehicles, police cars, and the truck from the lab and the coroner's van. A small crowd had gathered, and the television trucks were busy setting up, sections of the house and lawn and the neighborhood taken over as the reporters prepared for their remotes. Nathan parked where he could among the patrol cars, acknowledged the acknowledgments of the uniform officers, and walked across the dew-damp lawn to the open front door of the house.

Technicians were dusting for fingerprints in the living room; from somewhere upstairs someone said, "Boy, this is sure one hell of a house. Did you see this?" Nathan looked at the sofa where he sat a few hours earlier; across from it was the other sofa where she sat across from him. On the far side of the room, away from the front door and the windows, was a small pile of clothes—the expensive peasant-style skirt, the puffy white blouse, her slip and bra—as if here was where she was first told to undress; closer to the kitchen were her boots and underwear, though her panties and pantyhose were torn and thrown about, as if ripped from her body, as if the intruder had become impatient. A smudge of blood was on the wall near the door, perhaps where he hit her, perhaps because she was too slow or because she finally realized what was going to happen to her and tried to refuse, tried to fight him off. Inside the kitchen, Simon, the photographer, was finishing up his pictures.

"You want one with you in it, Sarge?" Simon said.

"No," MacCarron said.

"I thought you liked to keep these for your scrapbook."

"Not this time."

Nathan stood in the doorway for a moment, taking in the scene in front of him. The thing tied to the straight chair that had once been a woman. Fran. The mass of blood and pulp that had once been her head, her face. Getting himself adjusted. Getting himself used to the fact that the world would never be the same again.

Simon was the first to notice him. "Oh hi, Lieutenant. Just like in the movies, huh?"

"If you're through in here," Mac said, "why don't you go get the other shots you need?"

The sergeant patted him on the shoulder and artfully moved him out of the room. When Mac returned, Nathan was still standing in front of the body.

"You okay?" Mac said.

"Yeah. Yeah. I'm okay."

"I tried to get hold of you when the call came in but they said—"

"Yeah. I know. That's okay. I disappeared for a while, had some things to think through. . . ."

"There's bloody fingerprints and other physical evidence all over the place, we won't have any trouble getting the samples of who did this."

"That's good. Good."

"There's no sign of forced entry. She must have opened the door for him. Which probably means she knew him or recognized him. When he left, he left the front door standing open, as if hoping someone would notice and get suspicious. And sure enough, someone in the neighborhood did."

Nathan nodded. "You've got people. . . ."

"I've got people going through the house inch by inch. And there's a team going around the neighborhood. Everything's covered. There are some similarities to the girl in the park, but there are some important differences. The main thing is whoever tied her up didn't know knots like the first one. I'm thinking it's a different guy."

It wasn't that he was in a daze; in a way, he was never clearer. But it was as if his mind had pulled back from him momentarily while it sorted through everything he was thinking and feeling. So he would have no questions for himself later, no hesitations, when it was time for him to act.

Stan from the coroner's office came in, ready to remove the body. Mac nodded for Nathan to follow him out of the kitchen, into the solarium. The two men stood side by side in front of the windows glaring with light. When he was sure no one was nearby, Mac spoke in an undertone.

"The neighbor who found the body said he noticed a guy going into the house last evening but didn't see him leave again. Said it looked like a slim, well-dressed black man."

"That was me."

"I figured it was. When the neighbor saw the door standing open all morning, he came over to investigate."

Nathan looked at him questioningly. Mac moved closer to him, inches from the side of his face, his voice barely audible but as intense as he'd ever heard it. "Upstairs in her bedroom. I found a necktie tied to her brass bedstead. It looks like one of yours."

"Yes. It's mine."

"I snatched it up and stuck it in my pocket before anyone else saw it, just in case."

"My fingerprints are undoubtedly all over the house too."

"There are a lot of candlesticks up there in the bedroom, lots of candles. All of them burned down pretty far. You ready to tell me what's going on? I need to know what we're dealing with here."

"Yes. I know."

Nathan told him the whole story with Fran, including the first time in her office at Gateway Towers when he talked to Sam afterward, his visit to the house on Sunday night, and his talk with Fran Monday evening when she told him it was over between them. He also told him that he thought he was followed last evening—he omitted the part about getting out of his car and challenging the driver. The sergeant listened, his hands in the pockets of his baggy suit, head at an angle, taking it all in. If he had any feelings about what Nathan was telling him, nothing crossed his face.

"You said Mrs. Nicoletti told you that the only suspicious person hanging around that she knew of was some blond-haired college kid who came to her office. Corduroy Boy. That's something we could ask your friend Sam about, we're not doing any good here. Maybe the kid was hanging around town before he went to see her and the hippie knows something about him. We need to check in with the Captain, make an appearance at headquarters as if nothing's out of the ordinary, maybe by that time some of the lab reports will be in. Then we'll go for a drive and look for the hippie."

Mac turned to leave but Nathan touched his arm. "Wait, I want to explain—"

Mac held up his hand to stop him. "Whatever it is, I don't want to hear it. I've heard enough. Whatever happened is your business, and that's the end of it as far as I'm concerned. But now that I know about your little necktie party, we've got an added incentive to find the guy who did this before your fun and games hang us all."

Forty-Eight

After they ordered and collected their Big Macs and fries and coffees, Paul led Sam to the table where they sat before, beside the window looking out at the small triangular plaza at the corner of Stanwix and Liberty. Sam got himself settled, his shoulder bag dumped on the chair beside him so the fringe wouldn't drag on the floor, watching Paul unwrap his burger as if he were discovering a treasure, rubbing his hands together in anticipation. What is it with this guy? He's acting like he's discovering the hamburger for the first time. Some kind of innocent act? A put-on to throw me off the track? Or maybe he really is this far gone. Shellshocked. PTSD or whatever it's called. Careful, it could be a trap.

Maybe he knows that I know. . . .

"You seem very pleased with yourself," Sam said finally.

"I am. I've taken care of something that needed taken care of. Wrapped up a couple of loose ends."

"I suppose you could call it that."

"What?"

Sam shook his head. Bemused. "How's Suzy?"

"I haven't seen her."

"No, I don't suppose you would. For a while."

"I don't plan to see her at all. I want—"

"I'll bet you do," Sam interrupted him. He lowered his head and gazed around the restaurant—there were half a dozen black men sitting at adjacent tables drinking coffee, discussing the prospects of the Steelers this year; a woman in layers of sweaters going through the contents of her dozen plastic bags; a couple of secretaries from nearby offices waiting for their orders—then studied Paul again, wagging a limp French fry at him. "You want. I want, everybody wants. It's the human condition. It's what makes the world go round. The only question is, what one is willing to do to get it, isn't it? And it seems like you've already done quite a lot."

"I don't think we're talking about the same thing."

Sam tilted his head from side to side, as if to say Maybe so, maybe not.

"Well, life goes on," Paul said, before taking another bite of his burger. Wiping special sauce from the corners of his mouth with a crumpled napkin.

Sam looked at him over the tops of his sunglasses. "Not always, dude." Thinking Coolest-headed guy I've ever seen, but then they're trained that way, aren't they? Become like robots of death, ice water in their veins.

"No, you're right, not always," Paul was saying between bites of burger. "But what surprises me is that it goes on at all. Life, living, can drive you crazy, all the things you go through. Sometimes you wonder how people hold it together. I guess the real surprise, all things considered, is that more people don't go off the deep end and start killing each other."

"Interesting," Sam said, holding a French fry between his fingers like it was a cigarette. "That you think that's what would happen. If people were given the chance."

"You're acting a little strange today."

"Most people think I act strange every day."

"No, something's different. What's up?"

Sam hunched over the table, studying him over the remains of his fries for a long minute. Then straightened up. "Dude, I may have done you a serious injustice. I'm getting the idea you really don't know, do you? Either that, or you genuinely missed your calling as an actor."

"Know what?"

"Where have you been the last day or so? Don't you read the papers, or watch television or anything?"

"I was home sick yesterday, if it's any of your business."

"And you didn't hear any news."

Paul laughed. "The way I was feeling, I wasn't looking or listening to anything. Why, what did I miss?"

Sam settled back in his chair, legs stretched under the table, hands folded on his lap. "Francis Nicoletti, the guy you were so interested in lately, was murdered late Sunday night or early yesterday morning. He was shot in the Stanwix Street parking garage. The police think somebody must have followed him while he was going to his car."

"I didn't know a thing about it," Paul murmured.

"Oh, and it gets better. Or worse, as the case may be. His wife, Fran Nicoletti, was killed at their home in Squirrel Hill last night. Pretty gruesome, according to the reports. Her head was bashed in, like in a scene from one of Nicoletti's movies. And

Nicoletti was supposedly shot like in a scene from another of his films. Ironic, huh? Do you want the rest of your fries? I have trouble eating beef raised by machines but so far I can justify devouring the hapless potato."

"You think I had something to do with it?"

Sam waggled his head, his mouth full.

"But why?"

After he swallowed again, Sam hung his head regretfully. "Well, you have to admit you were following him around the last few days before it happened. And there's that whole business with Suzy."

"I wasn't following him," Paul said without conviction.

"Okay, have it your way. Let's just say that you had the incredible luck to be a number of places where Nicoletti also happened to be. Incidentally, I'm not the only who is aware of that."

"The police know?"

Sam nodded. "And you have been walking around with that gun in your pocket. The police are interested in that too."

On reflex Paul touched the .45 through the fabric of his windbreaker.

Sam pretended to duck. "Don't shoot, Hornet."

"That's crazy."

Sam was busy digging out a few remaining French fries from inside their container. "I can see why you'd kill Nicoletti, for screwing the girl you're interested in, get him out of the way, but why the missus.? What did Mrs. Nicoletti ever do to you? Only thing I can figure is to make it a complete set. Can't fault you on that—kill 'em all if they get in your way. Can't even call that the American way. It's the way of the world."

"And you think the police know about me?"

"I'm sure of it. You weren't exactly invisible, you know, following Nicoletti around. Hundreds of people can say they saw you."

"What about Suzy?"

"I certainly think she'd have something to say about you, if the police asked. And I'm pretty sure they'll ask. You might not have been stalking Nicoletti, but you were certainly stalking the girl."

"I've got to tell her I didn't have anything to do with this," Paul said standing up. "Oh my God. And she saw me at Nicoletti's cabin at Seven Springs."

"You went all the way to Seven Springs? Wow, you were doing some serious stalking."

"What must she think of me?"

"If I was her, I'd be thinking that you are one dangerous dude. And I'd be wondering if I was the next one on your list."

Paul stood there a moment looking down at him. What's he thinking? Did I push him too far this time? He could kill me in a second. . . . Finally Paul said, "I've got to go see her. Tell her I never meant to hurt her."

"Yeah. Good luck with that. I'm sure she'll welcome you with open arms." Sam stood up, collected his fringed bag from the chair and slung it over his shoulder. "And now you're probably wondering if I'm going to turn you in. Well, don't worry, I'm a panhandler, not a bastard. Call it part of the Brotherhood of Men Who Have Been Done In by Women. . . ." But Paul was already headed toward the door. Sam picked up the fries container and turned it on end to get the last little stubs, but mainly what he got was a palm full of salt.

Forty-Nine

It was rush hour before White and MacCarron could get loose from the paperwork at headquarters; they began their search for Sam downtown where they'd encountered him previously, Market Square, around the Point, the shopping district along Smithfield, then headed out to the known places in Oakland but with no success. On a hunch they headed back downtown to the Cultural District.

"There he is," Nathan said and pulled over to the curb in front of Heinz Hall. "I wondered if he'd be someplace around the theaters at this time of evening."

Nathan put the car in Park and started to get out but MacCarron said, "You stay put. This is my party."

Under the marquee the theater lights in the gloom of evening snaked along in their progression, creating a strobe-like stop-action effect on the patrons filing in the doors and the passers-by. Sam stood off to one side, his back to the street, as he watched a well-dressed elderly couple coming along the sidewalk toward the theater. Mac slipped his hand up into Sam's armpit, nearly lifting him off his feet as he turned him around and started him toward the car.

"Why, Sergeant MacCarron, I didn't know you cared," Sam said, walking on tippy-toe.

"I'll show you how much I care if you give me any shit. Get in the car."

Mac opened the door and more or less tossed Sam across the backseat. As he righted himself, Sam looked up at Nathan watching him over his shoulder.

"You okay with this, Lieutenant?" Sam said.

"Sorry, Sam, but we need information and we need it fast."

They both watched MacCarron go over to mollify the elderly couple, show them his badge, tell them it was a police matter; they heard him explain that Sam was a dangerous character and that the sergeant appreciated their cooperation. Without looking at Nathan, Sam said, "You didn't do anything to trace that girl Carla, did you?"

"I checked the hospitals, but with these murders and all—"

"I was going to tell you to forget it. She's gone and that's that."

"Change of heart?"

Sam laughed a little. "You might call it that. I figure if she had a reason to stay, she would have stayed. I guess she didn't. That was then, this is now."

Mac came back and settled himself in the front seat. He turned and looked at Sam as if regarding a lower form of life.

"All set to deal with your dangerous character, Sergeant Mac-Carron?" Sam said.

"I'm the dangerous character as far as you're concerned, Sammy-boy. This time you're talking to me, not your friend the lieutenant. And if you try any of your well-known games, I will personally break your ass and make sure it's not safe for you on any street in the 'Burgh. We clear on that?"

"What if I try some of my games that aren't so well known?"

MacCarron started to reach over the seat at him but Nathan put his hand on his arm. "Sam's going to cooperate, aren't you, Sam? This is important, people's lives might depend on it."

"Seems like my life is one of them," Sam said. He held up his hands in front of him, waved them a little. "No, no, I can see it must be important, if the good sergeant is at the controls rather than his lieutenant. Must be a case of one partner helping out the other, and never let it be said that—"

"Shut up, weirdo," Mac said.

For a moment the three of them sat in silence before Mac continued. "Just tell us what you know about this kid in the red anorak."

"The kid you told me about the other night," Nathan interjected. "The one you thought had a gun in his pocket."

"Jeff Berner. And I don't think it was a gun. I know it was a gun. I could see it through the material."

"We need to know as much we can about him. Is he still around?"

"I'm not sure. I haven't seen him since Sunday morning. I had a rather long talk with him then, but he didn't say all that much about himself. And yes, he still had the gun."

"Any idea where we can find him?" Mac said. "Do you know where he was staying?"

"He was at the Gateway Hilton, of all places. That's got to cost him a bit. But listen, there's another guy—"

"Was he there Saturday night when I saw you outside Gateway Towers? Maybe he saw us together and that's how he got the idea you were an undercover."

"You guys now holding conferences in the middle of the night?" Mac said.

"I told you," Nathan said. "After I saw Fran at her office."

Mac winced, a look on his face as if he tasted something sour. Evening had turned to night, the only illumination in the car coming from the lights under the marquee, the three men little more than shadows.

"Will you listen a minute?" Sam said. "I'm trying to tell you, there's another guy you should be checking up on, and I think he's a whole lot more dangerous than Berner. His name is Paul and—"

Nathan and Mac looked at each other. "The guy Suzy-girl told us about," Mac said.

"So Suzy knows about him?" Sam said. "That's cool, because I told the guy Suzy was probably telling the police all about him. I wasn't sure they had actually talked or if he was only stalking her."

"So he was stalking her? How do you know?"

"Saturday night he looked me up and asked me to show him where Nicoletti was having a party that she was going to. The place was up on Mount Washington, so I took him down to Point Park to show him where it was."

"Which is where you were coming from when you saw me going into Gateway Towers," Nathan said.

MacCarron frowned again. "Tell me more about this guy."

"Scary. Really scary. Ex–Green Beret or maybe CIA executioner. Wears a Montagnard bracelet, must have spent a lot of time on his own over there. He's all the scarier because when you first look at him he looks normal. Then you realize he's kind of supernormal. Too normal. There's all kinds of stuff going on that you can't see and he doesn't want you to see."

"Is he staying in town too?"

"Pretty sure he isn't. He drives a black pickup truck that he usually parks in Market Square. Matter of fact it was there earlier today, I know because I talked to him, he even bought me breakfast. The really strange thing is that he claimed he didn't know either Nicoletti or his wife had been murdered. How could you miss that, it's all over the news. Claimed he was sick or something. And, oh yes, he's carrying a gun too."

"Christ," Mac said, turning around in his seat and looking out the windshield at the traffic passing in the street. "First we don't have any suspects, now we've got two of them."

"He said he was going to talk with Suzy," Sam said. "Something about her seeing him at a cabin at Seven Springs this weekend."

"Which is where Suzy was with Nicoletti on Sunday," Nathan said.

"If he did kill one or both the Nicolettis," Mac said, "it's possible he'll be after the girl next. Clean up anyone who could finger him."

"I wouldn't put it past him," Sam said. "Spooky dude."

Sam gave a shiver that Nathan didn't believe for a second. Thinking *Why would he fake a thing like that? What's he getting at? Why's he volunteering all this information? Is he playing us? One of the unfamiliar games he mentioned? We've got to be careful. . . .*

"We need to make sure Suzy is safe," Nathan said to Mac.

"Look, I'll call for backup to meet you at the Hilton, then I'll drop you off there and you pick up Berner. Take Sam with you—he can make sure of the identification. I'm heading back to Suzy's."

Fifty

Paul was about to get out of his truck when a police car swung around the corner at the end of the block and came toward him. He ducked down across the seat and waited. The headlights swept through the cab over his head; he expected them to stop, but he heard the car go past, the radio crackling, garbled voices he couldn't understand, on down South Highland, past Suzy's apartment. He waited another couple minutes before rising up again.

What are they doing here? Coincidence? Or looking for me? Maybe she sicced them on me. Guessed I might come here. . . .

He looked at his watch; it was almost nine. He had been watching the apartment for hours, waiting to see if there were lights in Suzy's windows to indicate that she was home, but the windows were dark, there were no signs of life. Waiting to see if she had gone somewhere and would come back. He didn't see her car, but that didn't mean anything, maybe she had a garage for it or parked it on another street. Maybe she was in the apartment hiding, keeping the lights off, afraid he was coming after her. Maybe somebody else got to her already, whoever was doing these killings. He waited a few minutes more, to make sure the police car didn't come back, then took a screwdriver and a flashlight from the glove compartment and got out of his truck.

When he was sure the street was clear, he crossed and slipped through the gate beside the building, down the walk between the buildings to the backyard, up the outside stairs she led him down that magical afternoon when she twirled for him, and then to her apartment. Thinking, on some level of his mind, A raid is one of the basic operational techniques employed by Special Forces

in both unconventional warfare and counterinsurgency operations
. . . A raid is a surprise attack against an enemy force or installation. Such attacks are characterized by secret movement to the objective area: brief, violent combat; rapid disengagement from action; and swift, deceptive withdrawal. . . .

With the screwdriver, he pried the door away from the frame far enough to pop the latch bolt free of the strike plate; through the partially open door, he stuck the screwdriver through a link of the safety chain and twisted the chain on its axis until it broke. He waited a few moments to make sure no one inside her apartment or the apartment across the landing had heard him and was coming to investigate, then eased the door open farther, took the gun from the pocket of his windbreaker, pulled back the slide to throw the first round home in the chamber, and stepped inside the pantry. Waiting. Listening.

The apartment was dark, nothing stirred. After several moments, he crossed the kitchen, gun at the ready, and moved down the hall, carefully checking each door, each room, making quick sweeps with the flashlight before turning it off again, returned to the darkness, making his way to the bedroom—he saw her dead in the tangle of sheets on the bed, he saw her battered body crumpled amid the pile of clothes on the floor; in the bathroom he pulled back the shower curtain slowly, terrified of the blond, bloodied horror in the tub—then back into the living room. But Suzy wasn't here.

He relaxed a little, but not much. He swept the flashlight around the room. The place was in shambles, as if she had left, or had been taken away, in a hurry. He worked his way back through the apartment looking for anything that would give him an indication what happened to her or where she went. On the nightstand next to the bed was a tape recorder; he ran the tape back a few seconds and punched the button marked play, hoping it would tell him something. In the darkness her voice said,

Rain, rain, gentle rain,
Where do you go out of sight?
Rain, rain, gentle rain,
When the day turns warm and bright?

There was the sound of her moving around and coughing to clear her throat. The sound of restless children, a child's voice saying, "Miss Konecki, can we—" and then only the hiss of the tape. He punched the off button.

He wandered back through the dark apartment, wondering what to do next. He didn't know any of her friends, didn't know anyplace where she might go. Maybe she was so frightened of him that she thought it safer to run out into the night. Maybe she was right. In the living room, he went to the front windows, looking out carefully between the slats of the shutters to make sure no one was watching the apartment. To make sure the police car hadn't returned. He was ready to give up when he remembered the guy on the second floor who kept his door open— Brandon, he thought his name was. Paul looked around the apartment one last time, to make sure he hadn't missed anything or left any trace that he had been there, then unlocked the front door and went downstairs.

The apartment door was open; Brandon was tilted back in a shabby recliner watching a quiz show as if he were ready to launch, dressed in an old football practice jersey, shorts, and shower sandals. When he noticed Paul in the doorway, he said, "Hey, Uncle Dudley. You looking for Suzy?"

Paul looked at him quizzically. Is he making a joke? Is he making fun of me?

"She went out this afternoon. Said she needed to take a drive to clear her head. And there was something about stopping by her office, but I didn't catch it all. Did she know you were coming over?"

"No, it was supposed to be a surprise."

"Well, I'm sure she'll be sorry she missed you. Suzy told me all about you, I can see why you're her favorite uncle. You want to leave a message for her?"

He considered it, so she'd know that he knew she pawned him off as her uncle, nothing more, but decided no, it didn't matter now. He could almost understand it. "No, don't tell her, it'll just make her feel bad."

"Okay, Uncle Dudley. Whatever you say. Hey, how about putting in a good word for me with her? She seems to listen to you."

"Yeah. I'll do that."

"Groovy."

. . . as on the apron before a gate at Saint Louis Lambert International Airport, a motorized scissor-lift maneuvers into position beside the belly of a Boeing 737 recently landed from Pittsburgh until the lift is level with the open hatch of the cargo hold and the casket of Sandy Love is moved out of the hold on a portable conveyor belt and then lowered to the ground, the crew assigned to attend the unloading of the casket and deliver it to the waiting hearse from a local funeral home not disrespectful but not overly respectful either, simply doing their job to get a piece of freight to where it's going so they can move on to the next piece of freight that needs attending to, two of the men, the driver of the lift and one of the handlers, in fact, so engrossed in their conversation about the chances of the Cardinals this year that they momentarily forget to lock the rollers on the conveyor belt so that when the lift starts to move forward the casket rolls backwards and for a moment threatens to go shooting off the rear end of the cart onto the apron, it is only the shout of one of the other handlers and the frantic grabs of the driver and handlers that prevent the

catastrophe, the men looking around sheepishly to see if someone saw what just happened, all the crewmen super focused now on their charge as the lift moves slowly under the wing of the plane toward the gate . . . as several stories above the maintenance area, in the glassed-in observation deck, one person certainly did observe what almost happened: Brian Love, Sandy's father, a distinguished figure in a double-breasted suit, his raincoat folded over his arm, his gray felt fedora in his hand down at his side, looking like a character from a '40s film noir movie, stands vigil at the windows, watching the men unload his beloved daughter, his precious little girl, in her casket, his wife too distraught to accompany him and is already back at their house, his heart in his throat as he watches the casket almost roll off the lift when the crew doesn't lock the rollers, watching as the men look around guiltily afraid that someone saw what happened, thinking Yes, you fools, I saw that, let something happen to that casket and I will personally track you down and kill each one of you, aware even as he thinks it that now he's prepared to protect his daughter in death as he was never prepared to do while she was alive, moaning out loud as he realizes all over again that the girl is gone now, forever, thinking about what the black police lieutenant in Pittsburgh said about the possibility that they'll never find the man who did this to his little girl, quoting statistics to him about random killers and unknown perpetrators, the nerve of that black son-of-a-bitch, Love unwilling to accept that there might not be retribution in this world, that a terrible crime like this could go unpunished, that the universe might be determined by laws and principles beyond comprehension—or worse, that there is nothing at all determining actions and outcomes, that all is random, all happenstance and accident, aimless and arbitrary, without purpose or meaning—and as the small cortege below, the casket on its motorized platform escorted by several workmen in international orange Day-Glo safety vests, disappears under the edge of the building, Love turns away, thinking that he'll never forgive the police lieutenant for suggesting such a thing, never . . . as at the Gateway Hilton, Jeff sits in his room on his king-size bed, naked, his blood-stained blood-soaked clothes in a heap on the floor where he dumped them the night before, unable to move from where he is since he got back to the room, alternately crying and sleeping and waking again to start crying again, sitting there as two flak-jacketed police officers with a battering ram between them burst through the door followed by more flak-jacketed officers with their guns trained on him and a stocky plainclothes detective in an ill-fitting suit and his already flushed-red drinker's face all the more flushed from the exertion of keeping up with the uniformed officers, a tearful, almost grateful smile on Jeff's face, almost as if he were waiting for them, trying to explain to them as the officers grab him and throw him on the floor and pin him as they bend his arms behind him to put on the cuffs, "She laughed at me, don't you understand? She laughed at me" . . . as across the plaza at Gateway Towers, Suzy roams through the dark silent offices of Nickolodeon Productions, after hearing on the news this afternoon—on easy listening WSHH radio, Wonderful Wish as it's known, between Captain & Tennille's "Love Will Keep Us Together" and America's "Sister Golden Hair"—that Fran Nicoletti had been murdered, Suzy got dressed in the first thing she found among the piles of clothes on the floor, her tennis outfit from last Saturday, her trench coat over top, and spent the afternoon driving to places that had some meaning or significance to her, an act of freedom and independence in her mind, to her way of thinking an act of bravery and defiance in the face of fear, thinking back over the scary interview with those detectives who questioned her after Nicko's murder, aware now that if whoever killed Nicko was killing those involved with him that her own life might be in danger, ranging in her travels from the zoo in Highland Park to the cabin at Seven Springs where she spent Sunday with Nicko, from the apartment on Mount Washington where she attended the party with Nicko on Saturday night to the café at the Carnegie Museum where she liked to go after tennis at the PAA, getting out at each place and walking around a bit, for no particular purpose except to show that she could, to demonstrate to herself that wouldn't let the deaths of Nicko and Fran in any way deter her from living her life the way she wanted, to do the things she wanted, that she wasn't going to let anything or anyone keep her from being the person she wanted to be—Help Yourself Tootsie, and she meant it—makes her way past Fran's office and on down the corridor to Nicko's office at the end, pushes open the half-open door and enters as if it is the site of the Holy of Holies, which to her it kind of is, for it's the place where she first got to know Nicko, those evenings he worked late and she hung around in case he needed anything, and more often than not he did, a sandwich from a local restaurant or some copies made on the copier that totally stymied him, dear man, coming here at this time in the evening because it reminds her of times with Nicko and that she was fairly certain no one would be here, that now with both Nicko and Fran gone she was unsure whether she would have a reason to be in the offices ever again and she wants a keepsake of the man and of their time together, a memento, something to remind herself at a later date that it actually happened, that for however brief a time she was the man's lover, looks at his cluttered desk and credenza and finds nothing among the ashtrays and coasters from Hollywood restaurants and an obscene parody of an Oscar, then on a shelf across the room she sees the perfect thing: the camera that Nicko kept as a good luck charm from his childhood, a Keystone 8mm camera that his family had when he growing up and that Nicko made his first movies with—Suzy was in the office next door eavesdropping when Nicko was interviewed recently by Rolling Stone *about the film he was making here and Nicko walked over and took the camera from the shelf and said to the reporter, "This is where it all started, I used to make monster movies in my backyard with all the neighborhood kids as actors, and, I might add, then sold them tickets when it was done so they could see themselves on the screen"— and Suzy takes the camera from the shelf and cradles it briefly as if just for the moment she is cradling the man's head in her lap again when she becomes aware of the flashing blue and red lights coming from the windows in the direction of the Hilton across the plaza and goes to the window and sees the collection of police cars and emergency vehicles parked in all directions in the hotel's driveway and with the camera tucked protectively in the crook of her arm returns through the offices and locks the door behind her, takes the elevator down to the lobby and goes outside into the plaza, walking over to the hotel and joining the crowd of spectators gathering beside the drive, recognizes Sam standing beside one of the police cars and threads her way through the crowd and goes over to him, "Hi, Sam, what's going on?" and Sam looks at her as if he can't quite believe that she's standing there in front of him and says, "That's pretty funny, Nathan's out looking for you, and you're standing here; from what I've seen that's the story of Nathan's life," and Suzy says, "What are you talking about?" then laughs and swats at him, "Oh you, you're such a big tease. No, seriously, what's all this about?" and Sam looks around at the squad cars with their strobe-like red and blue lights flashing and the uniformed officers standing around and says, "They caught the guy who killed your boyfriend Nicoletti and his wife," and Suzy pouts, "I told the police that I was acquainted with Mr. Nicoletti because he was my employer but that was all there was to it," and Sam, obviously weary of the game, says, "Of course you did, and I'm sure they believed you too. What's with the camera? You going to start making your own movies?" and Suzy puts the camera to her eye and frames him in the viewfinder and says, "I should, shouldn't I? Action!" and Sam regards her again though this time with more than disbelief, now it's with real distaste, and Suzy lowers the camera, thinking Well, I certainly don't need this from some dirty hippie, but says out loud, "Well, it just goes to show, doesn't it?" "What do you think it shows, Suzy-girl?" and Suzy knows very well what it shows, it shows that bad things might happen in the world but that there are good people like policemen to put things right, that people say all those negatives about what a bad and dangerous place the world is but it's only that way if you let it be that way, that there's nothing to be afraid of unless you let yourself be afraid, but she doesn't say this, she lowers the camera and gives Sam a little smile, reaches in the pocket of her raincoat and pulls out some change, several quarters and dimes and a couple pennies and hands them to Sam who takes them from habit, "Here, you probably need this. Goodbye, Sam," and walks away, back through the crowd and then across the street and into Point State Park, heading across the grass, the lights of the Hilton and the streetlights and the skyline behind her, the darkness absorbing her as she leaves the circular path and wanders out into the grass, pointing her toes and swinging each foot back and forth through the blades of grass as she walks along, her canvas shoes darkening with dew as she progresses further into the darkness of the park, embraces herself in a wrap of arms and feels so lucky to be alive, thinking It's such a beautiful night, such a beautiful world, I don't know why people have to make such a fuss about everything, things always work out for the best just as long as you keep a good heart . . . and Sam watches her walk back through the crowd of onlookers who gathered to see what's going on with all the police cars, watches her cross the street, oblivious of oncoming traffic, watches her walk out in front of a black pickup truck that barely stops in time, Suzy never acknowledging that the vehicle is there at all, a black pickup truck that she doesn't recognize but Sam recognizes immediately, Sam and the driver, each from his own perspective, watching the girl head into the darkness of the park at the Point, disappear into the darkness, Sam continuing to watch with the fascination and dread of witnessing the impending doom of a fatal accident as the black pickup truck pulls into the first available parking space and Paul gets out and hurries after Suzy, melding into the darkness of the park as well, and Sam thinks Funny ol' world, sweet ol' world, serendipitous ol' world, we are drawn together by forces and ties of which we have no concept and no control, so why is Paul following her now, as protector or destroyer, devil or angel? Oh it's wonderful, wonderful, this I've got to see, and Sam starts to leave where he's been standing next to the squad car when Sergeant MacCarron comes out the door of the Hilton and says, "Hey, weirdo, where do you think you're going? Nobody told you you could leave," and Sam calls back, "Hey, guess what? Suzy was here the whole time and that guy Paul just followed her into the park, I'll go keep an eye on 'em for you," and before the sergeant can say anything else Sam is away, across the street and into the park, in the direction of the others . . . as ten miles down the Ohio River in the mill town of Furnass, in a seemingly different world, in what might as well be a parallel universe, Sharon Slater kneels in a pew at Holy Innocents along with a dozen other women, the members of her prayer group who meet once a week to say the rosary and make their novenas, in the pews before the side altar to Our Lady of Fatima, fingering the beads of her rosary as she works her way through the pattern of prayers, the same pattern of prayers and devotions that she said for Paul while he was in the army in Southeast Asia, before he even knew she was praying for him, the prayers she knows were responsible for bringing him back safely then, praying again for him now even though she has no idea where he is at the moment or what he's doing or why he felt he had to go take care of something, knowing only that after he left the house this morning she's more afraid for him than she ever was during the war, a feeling she can't deny or dismiss, Hail Mary, full of grace, the Lord is with thee, though afraid as she is, never doubting for an instant that the pattern of prayers and devotions will keep Paul safe again and bring him back to her in one piece, Blessed art thou among women and blessed is the fruit of thy womb Jesus, while beside her in the pew their seven-year-old daughter Mandy scribbles furiously on her pad of paper as she looks around at the white marble statue of the beautiful woman and the dozens of dancing red votive candles and the sweet smell of incense everywhere, pray for us sinners now and at the hour of our death, saying in time with the voices of the women around her, "Daddy Daddy, fly fly, Daddy gone?" . . .*

Fifty-One

He slowed as soon as he saw her, walking in the grass beyond the underpass under the freeway, in the field leading to the fountain at the Point, cradling something in one hand, occasionally lifting it to her eye and scanning things in the darkness, the lighted fountain at the Point in front of them, the white column of water lifting ten feet into the air, or the lights of the skyline behind them, the lights of Three Rivers Stadium across the dark waters of the Allegheny, the pulse against the night sky of the mills farther down the Ohio River, from his home in Furnass. She was in the midst of one of these pans—he could see now it was some kind of camera—when she turned slowly toward him and focused on him a moment, then lowered it from her eye. She said something as he approached but he couldn't hear her over the plashing of the fountain.

"I can't hear you," he called to her and moved closer.

"I said, 'Hello Paul,'" she said calmly when he was a few feet from her. "What are you doing here? Are you still following me?"

"Don't be afraid. I'm not going to hurt you."

She cocked her head and laughed.

"What's funny?"

"You. The expression on your face. You look so serious and worried. You don't have to worry about me, I'm fine." She brushed her tennis shoe back and forth a couple of times through the grass in front of her, then looked at him again and smiled.

He wondered which Suzy he was dealing with here, it was sometimes difficult to keep track of them. "I didn't know what happened to you. You weren't at your apartment. . . ."

"You were at my apartment? You really are following me, aren't you?"

She turned and walked on a little ways, pointing her toes, watching her shoes in the grass. She said coyly, "The way the police talk, I should be worried in case you're the one who killed Francis, and maybe Fran as well. Don't I look worried?"

"I was afraid they thought something of the sort. That's what I wanted to explain, about Sunday night and all—"

"They also wanted to know if I thought you had anything to do with that girl who was murdered in Schenley Park."

"What? Why would they think I had something to do with that?" How'd they ever get that idea? Maybe they found out I used to go to the clubs where they said she worked, but how? Somebody must have told them something. . . .

"You don't have to worry, I didn't believe them when they said it. And I don't believe you'd do anything to hurt me either. You're like my guardian angel, that's what you are." She laughed—he thought with a touch of sarcasm—then her eyes grew wide with a new idea. "As a matter of fact, I'm really glad you're here. Come on!"

"You are?"

She ran a few steps across the grass. When Paul just stood there, she came back and grabbed him by the hand. "Yes, I'm glad. You big silly, I said come on."

She pulled him by the arm, tugged at him to get him started—

Paul smiled in spite of himself at her efforts, let himself be towed along, though he felt himself getting more depressed by the minute—back toward a patch of smooth grass in front of the empty band shell. She dropped his hand, gave him the camera, and ran on ahead. Then she faced him, giggled, and ran toward him, arms raised above her head, trying to do a cartwheel except that her trench coat bound her up and she careened off to the side. In the darkness it appeared to Paul that she didn't have much on under the coat.

"Damn it," she said, brushing off her hands.

"Suzy, you shouldn't be out here dressed like that."

"It's okay. I love the night air, it feels good. And you're here to protect me."

Her face registered another idea. She undid the coat, took it off, and tossed it to him, kicking off her canvas shoes as well; the coat billowed and fell like spread wings away from him. He was too surprised to pick it up. She was wearing only the white tennis outfit she had on the other day, the tiny pleated skirt that barely covered her ass, her crotch. She raised her arms over her head again and posed for him, one leg cocked in front of the other: "Ta-da!" Then she laughed and ran a few steps and turned a perfect cartwheel on the grass. She laughed again, delighted with herself.

"Did you see that? I can still do it after all this time!"

He looked around in the darkness, the lighted plume of the fountain at the Point, the empty band shell at the edge of the field, gray and ghostlike, the skyline of the city behind them in the distance. There was no telling who was watching them, watching her, from the dark trees along the paths, the dark bushes on the hillock behind the shell. His mind raced with fragments of thoughts, he was embarrassed and didn't know what to do. *What the hell am I doing with this camera? Does she want me to take her picture or something? What's she playing at now?*

He shifted the camera to his left hand, fingered the gun in his pocket.

"Come on, Suzy, let's go back now."

She ignored him. Ran off and did another cartwheel, then a second one; her short white skirt belled down over her torso as she wheeled, exposing her white panties.

"Oh dear," she laughed when she was back on her feet. "Don't look."

She ran a finger along the leg opening of her panties to free the material from her crotch, then danced around in a small circle, doing the steps of some routine, smiling at him, the stagy, put-on smile of cheerleaders and majorettes and showgirls, humming the music to herself.

"Come on, Suzy." It wasn't funny anymore. It was never funny. . . .

"Paul, Paul, Paul. You worry too much. You're always so serious and glum."

She came over to him, shaking first one leg and then the other as she again pulled the elastic of her panties free from the tops of her thighs. He was embarrassed being this close to her, dressed the way she was, to him she might as well be naked.

"You never have any fun. You should learn from somebody like Francis. Francis had fun, he knew how to live."

"I'm not Nicoletti." I never could be, even if I wanted to. . . .

She laughed. "No, you certainly aren't."

She became a wild-eyed little girl then, a child, prancing around and trying to tickle him, poking at him, trying to grab his ass, pinch him, telling him he should have more fun, more fun, more fun. He swatted at her with his left hand holding the camera, he was having trouble keeping his hand on the gun in his pocket, he could have hit her, really hit her, he wanted to.

"Stop it now!" Please stop it now, you don't know. . . .

"See? You're no fun at all."

She stopped abruptly and he took the opportunity to give her back the camera, pushed it on her. She took it and walked away, flat-footed, pouty, wiggling her ass more than ever, then turned back to him, raised the camera to her eye and pointed it at him.

"You said you wanted to explain something to me. So go ahead. I'm listening."

"It isn't important," he said, more to himself than to her. It seemed useless to try to explain anything to her now, to her it was just another game, playing with the camera and all; he had been so wrong about her, the kind of girl she was, why did he ever think he was interested in her? Wrong. So very wrong, about so many things. . . .

"It was important enough for you to come out here tonight after me. So what is it? You said it had something to do with Sunday night."

He looked around at the bushes around the deserted stage and into the darkness. "It doesn't matter anymore." Nothing matters anymore . . . I must have been desperate, a desperate man, to let myself fall for a girl like her . . . I've been such a fool . . . but I knew that before, and here I am all over again. . . . He sighed, lowered his head; he noticed a blade of grass sticking up between her toes.

"I only wanted to tell you that I didn't mean any harm, I wasn't going to hurt Nicoletti when you saw me at the cabin."

"I don't know what you're talking about," she said, still talking to him behind the cyclops eye of the camera, pretending to shoot him. "I never saw you at the cabin. How do you even know about his cabin?"

"You saw me. You looked right at me."

She laughed. "You must have dreamt it. Where was I?"

Paul hesitated. Why am I doing this, why do I even care? She's not taking this seriously, she never took me seriously. "You were there with Nicoletti. You . . . were on the floor, in the living room. Everyone else was gone."

He expected her to deny it; he expected her to explode in his face. Instead she lowered the camera from her face, grinning, she seemed intrigued. "You were there? You saw us?"

He couldn't say anything.

"When we were making love?"

He nodded. No, when he was fucking you. When you were fucking him.

She laughed again. "I had my contacts out. I could hardly see Francis, if you want to know the truth, much less anything else." She turned away and giggled before turning back to him, coming closer. "If you saw us then, you must have gotten an eyeful." She gripped her bottom lip between her teeth for an instant. "How did we look?"

"I didn't like it."

She shrugged and turned away. "That's too bad. I guess some people get their kicks that way. I want to try another cartwheel." She put the camera down in the grass.

"The ground's damp, it'll hurt it."

"So what? There isn't any film it. I don't know why I thought I wanted it in the first place. It's just an old camera."

She ran off into the darkness, arms in the air, wheeling forward, but this time her arms didn't hold her and she tumbled sideways and fell; she plopped down heavily on her bottom, legs sprawled, propped up on her arms, a surprised look on her face.

"Oh look at me! I'm all dirty!" she moaned. She held up her hands to show him the grass and dirt stuck to her palms; there was something on her foot and she rubbed it back and forth in the grass. Then she lifted back her head and laughed as if it were the funniest thing in the world. Paul saw movement out of the corner of his eye in the direction of the empty stage. He spun to his left, crouched, ready.

"Whoa, dude! Jesus, don't point that thing at me!" Sam said

as he came from the bushes beside the band shell.

Suzy, still sitting on the ground, shook her head. "Looks like all the weirdos are out tonight."

Paul remained crouched in the regulation two-hand position, the gun aimed at Sam's chest.

Fifty-Two

Nathan left his car among the other police cars and vans parked under the hotel's marquee and hurried toward the entrance where MacCarron was talking to a couple of uniformed officers, laughing among themselves about something, the camaraderie of men after a dangerous situation. Just the way they were kidding around got under Nathan's skin. When Mac saw Nathan approaching, he broke away from the others to meet him.

"Was he here? Did you get him?"

Mac nodded, grinning broadly. "Yep, no problem. He was sitting on his bed, naked as a baby bird, crying his eyes out about what a bad boy he'd been. Confessed to killing both Nicoletti and his wife. Maybe he's on something, or maybe he's just a flake, I couldn't tell. He's on his way to Mercy for evaluation. And I guess you went on a wild goose chase."

"What do you mean by that?"

The sergeant looked at him surprised, a little taken aback. "Well, there you went chasing all the way across the city to talk to our Suzy-girl, and it turns out she was here the whole time— her and that guy Paul, right under your nose. Though I figured now that we got Berner here and he admitted the whole thing, Paul whoever-he-is isn't a suspect anymore—"

"They're here?" Nathan looked around the hotel driveway, inside the glass doors.

"Over in the park. Ironic, huh? Your friend Sam said he'd keep an eye on 'em for you." MacCarron chuckled.

What was Mac getting at? Nathan was in a rotten mood to

begin with; the sergeant was right, it was a wasted trip out to Suzy's, he didn't need to be reminded; there was nobody there, her apartment was dark as could be, the guy downstairs said Suzy had left hours earlier. Nathan felt stupid and useless, why did he think it was so important to check up on her in the first place? This Paul character didn't sound that dangerous, all things considered, a little quirky perhaps, mooning around after a younger woman, a stage-struck wannabe maybe, but no real threat compared to Berner with his murders of Nicoletti and Fran. Fran; poor Fran. No matter that he didn't know earlier that Berner was solely responsible for the murders, that this other guy Paul had nothing to do with them; he should have known better than to put so much credence in the information Sam gave them, the guy always was a freak, not to be trusted, MacCarron was right about that. By going to Suzy's, he missed out on Berner's arrest—he hated to think this way, but it *was* his case after all, he *was* the lead investigator, the media coverage would have been good for his image with the department, help get some of the pressure off him, set anyone straight who thought he was just a token, who thought he didn't belong in his position. It wouldn't have hurt either to remind the sergeant who was the lead in this working relationship, there were times MacCarron could be patronizing to him, like now when he seemed to suggest he needed Sam to do his work for him.

"So, you're saying you think I shouldn't have gone to check on Suzy?"

Mac turned sober, drew back and looked at him, squinty-eyed. "Where did that come from?"

"You've had something on your mind about me since we started this case. And its only gotten worse after I told you about me and Fran, like that only confirmed what—"

Mac had him under the right armpit and was propelling him away from the hotel entrance before Nathan knew what was happening. "What the fuck, what are you doing? Get your hand—"

When they got into the shadows close to the windows Mac dropped his hand, pushed Nathan away like he was flicking something away from him. "What I'm doing is getting you away from that door so nobody hears this crazy talk and it's splattered all over the papers."

"You've had a problem with me and white women since they put us together as partners. If you have a problem working with me you should just admit it."

Mac gave him a look that Nathan had only seen a few times in the couple of years they worked together, and the results were never pretty. "You dumb, jacking-off—. If you weren't my partner and I didn't give a shit about you, I'd put you through that plate-glass window."

Nathan turned away. What's he talking, give a shit about me? He never—but Mac grabbed his arm, spun him back again.

"You don't walk away from this, Nathan. You're the one who brought it up. Just for the record, I don't give a fuck who you fuck, you can fuck goats for all I care, as long as you don't hurt the goat. But to get yourself involved with a woman in one of our cases, the wife of a murder victim—"

"He wasn't a murder victim then, when it started—"

"Oh, excuse me, that makes it okay. No matter that we were already investigating the similarity between the murder of a girl in the park with one of Nicoletti's violent little masterpieces."

"Nothing happened with Fran when I went to see her Sunday night. . . ."

"It didn't have to. You had already used her bedstead as a tie rack. You don't seem to get it, that I not only risked my career by sticking that tie in my pocket, I risked jail time. Because that's what partners do, they watch the other guy's back. But I'm still waiting for you to start watching out for mine."

Mac was right. Nathan hadn't considered the risk MacCarron had taken for him with the necktie. Suppose he was wrong this whole time about Mac's problem working with him, suppose it wasn't Mac's problem at all, suppose it was his? Now he didn't know what to think. What had gotten into him lately?

"Mac, I—"

"Okay. Forget it. We said what needed to be said, now let's move on. There's things we still have to do to wrap this up." Mac turned and headed toward the entrance of the hotel; when he got to the revolving door, he looked back. "You coming?"

And there it was, Mac was giving him the opportunity to pick things up between them as they were before, to go on as partners, take his place in the investigation as if he hadn't missed a step, as if nothing had happened between them. But he couldn't do it, it wasn't in him, it wasn't what made himself to himself, he hadn't gotten as far as he had in the world by simply bowing down and following along. That wasn't Nathan. He'd do it his way or not at all. Besides, who said this Paul-character was so innocent? There was still the fact of him following Suzy around, that didn't sound normal to Nathan's way of thinking. The more he thought about it, it was MacCarron trying to tell him what to do all over again. Nathan didn't need that shit. From anybody.

"No, you go ahead. I'm going to see what's going on in the park."

Mac looked at him a moment. "Yeah. You do that," he said, before heading inside.

Fifty-Three

"Don't point that thing at me," Sam said, coming toward them across the grass, holding his shoulder bag in front of him as if it were a shield. "You going to shoot anyone, shoot her."

"Why would I want to shoot her?" Paul said, lowering the gun.

"Paul, is that a gun?" Suzy asked from where she was sitting.

"Awareness is a wonderful thing, isn't it?" Sam said. He looked at Suzy sitting on the ground and shook his head. "There's nothing so obvious they can't overlook or obscure."

"Well, if neither of you gentlemen is going to help me. . . ." Suzy got to her feet, bits of grass clinging to her bare legs.

"Why did you say I should want to shoot her?" Paul said, his voice sounding far away, even to himself.

"I didn't say 'want to,' actually," Sam said. "Interesting that you would think I did."

"Don't kid around, fella," Paul said.

"Me? Kid around? Who knows if I'm kidding or not? I'm not sure myself anymore."

Sam grinned without mirth. With a distant streetlight behind his head, his bushy hair seemed to glow.

"Why would you say something like that? Why would I want to hurt her?"

Sam laughed derisively. "Don't tell me it hasn't occurred to you. After the way she's treated you? She's made a fool out of you, you know that. Led you around like a little puppy dog. Here Paul, here Paul. Sit up, roll over. Beg. That's a good boy."

It was true, he was aware of it, she had treated him badly, but that wasn't it, that wasn't it at all.

Suzy came over to them, pulling her panties away from her skin. She looked at the gun curiously. "Why are you carrying that around for?"

Sam looked at Paul and rolled his eyes as if to say See what I mean? Suzy shivered from the breeze from the river and went over to retrieve her coat and the camera. The seat of her tennis skirt was dirty, speckled with bits of grass and leaves.

Sam clucked his tongue. "Amazing. No wonder Saint Paul thought they were the devil incarnate. They lie and steal your soul and they never let you know what they're thinking. The thing is, they don't know what they're thinking themselves most of the time. I don't blame you for wanting to blow her away."

"You keep saying that, and that isn't it at all. I was never trying to hurt them, either Nicoletti or her. I wanted to see what their life was like, how they were together. I wanted to see what it was like to live like that. A way I'll never be."

Sam didn't seem to hear him. "They're all the same when you come right down to it. They toy with you and parade themselves in front of you, then act hurt or surprised if you want to take them up on it—either that or they kick you right in the balls. There isn't a man alive who hasn't felt like you do in his heart of hearts at some time or other."

Across the grass, Suzy put on her trench coat again and picked up the camera. She held it to her eye again. "Smile pretty for the camera, boys. Come on, show me some action."

"She deserves it," Sam hissed. "They all deserve it. For what they do to us."

A man was coming from the underpass, hurrying across the grass toward them. Sam looked at him then back at Paul. "Go on, do it."

Suzy lowered the camera, looking at the two of them. "What's going on?"

The figure coming toward them was calling. "Police! Drop your weapon!"

Paul looked at the gun in his hand as if surprised to see it there. He was about to drop it when Sam lunged at Suzy, grabbed the camera from her, appeared as if he was going hit her with it.

Paul's shot dropped him like a stone. Then he felt the blow to his own chest that spun him around before he heard the report and caught a glimpse of Suzy running away—Thank God, she's safe, Sharon, I—and then he was on the ground, looking up at the tops of the distant black trees and the sky flickering orange and yellow from the mills—It hurts now, so this is it, I don't know what to do—and the well-dressed black man looking down at him kicking the gun from his hand, saying "No, No! Shit! Shit! Shit!" as the blades of grass reached for Paul, some caressing his cheek, some with their points pinpricking his face.

Images

Frontispiece...................... Flyleaf, *Modern Shop Practice* (Chicago: American Technical Society, 1931)

10..................................... *Modern Shop Practice*, page 2
11..................................... *Modern Shop Practice*, page 19
13..................................... *Modern Shop Practice*, page 20
15..................................... *Modern Shop Practice*, page 80
38..................................... *Modern Shop Practice*, page 33
134................................... *Modern Shop Practice*, page 177
198................................... *Special Forces Operational Techniques*, Department of the Army Field Manual 31–20 (1965), pages 192–193
222................................... *Modern Shop Practice*, page 96
242...................................*Special Forces Operational Techniques*, page 45

Acknowledgments

There are four people—friends, actually; dream catchers—without whom I could never have brought these books to publication:

Barbara Clark
Kim Francis
Dave Meek
Jack Ritchie

I also thank Eileen Chetti for struggling through my quirks of style and punctuation; Linnea Duly for writing a study guide; Aimee Downing for her patience with all my questions about self-publishing; and Bob Gelston, who is always around to answer questions and take on anything else that's needed. And then, of course, there's my wife Marty. . . .

Richard Snodgrass lives in Pittsburgh, PA with his wife Marty and two indomitable female tuxedo cats, raised from feral kittens, named Frankie and Becca.

To read more about the Furnass series, the town of Furnass, and special features for *The Pattern Maker*—including a Reader's Study Guide, author interviews, and omitted scenes—go to www.RichardSnodgrass.com.